Where We Belong

§

EMILY GIFFIN

An Orion paperback

First published in Great Britain in 2012
by Orion
This paperback edition published in 2013
by Orion Books,
an imprint of The Orion Publishing Group Ltd,
Orion House, 5 Upper St Martin's Lane,
London WC2H 9EA

An Hachette UK company

1 3 5 7 9 10 8 6 4 2

A CIP catalogue record for this book
is available from the British Library.

ISBN 978-1-4091-1835-0

Printed and bound in Great Britain
by Clays Ltd, St Ives plc

The Orion Publishing Group's policy is to use papers
that are natural, renewable and recyclable products and
made from wood grown in sustainable forests. The logging
and manufacturing processes are expected to conform to
the environmental regulations of the country of origin.

www.orionbooks.co.uk

For Nancy LeCroy Mohler, my BFF

Acknowledgements

First and foremost, I'd like to thank my loyal readers—from Atlanta to Rio to Warsaw and everywhere in between—for making my job both meaningful and fun. Talking to you on Facebook, Twitter, airplanes, and my book tours gets me through every painful bout of writer's block and reminds me why I continue to tell stories. Thank you for reading them.

My eternal thanks to Jennifer Enderlin, my editor since this ride began. Thank you for everything, especially your thoughtful edits that always elevate my books (these were your best notes ever!).

Thank you to Stephen Lee, my publicist and close friend. How far we've come, together, since that first signing at Borders when the manager pleaded for people to go listen to "Emily Griffin" on the second floor.

Thank you to so many others at St. Martin's Press, including Sally Richardson (could you *be* any more elegant?), Matthew Shear (with the best laugh ever), and my dear puppy John Murphy (meow). Thanks also to Jeff Dodes, Matt Baldacci, Jeanne-Marie Hudson, Paul Hochman, Nancy Trypuc, Anne Marie Tallberg, Sara Goodman, Katie Ginda, Bailey Usdin, Stephanie Davis, and the entire Broadway and Fifth Avenue sales forces. Big shout-out to Olga Grlic for her artistic talent. And in the UK, thank you to Lorella Belli and the team at Orion, especially Kate Mills, Susan Lamb, Juliet Ewers and Gaby Young.

I am so grateful to Theresa Park, my world-class agent, and her team, Emily Sweet, Abigail Koons, and Pete Knapp. There is nobody out there who does a better job for a client—and I really like you, too.

Thanks to all those who helped with this manuscript, especially Kevin A. Garnett for the insight into the world of television; Lisa Elgin Ponder, Doug Elgin, and McGraw Milhaven for your help with all things St. Louis; Allyson Wenig Jacoutot and Jennifer New for your New York-related edits (or else Kirby might still be on the Triborough); Adam Duritz and Yvonne Boyd for your four cents on drumming; and Alexandra Shelley for helping to shape this book in its nascent stages. And thank you, Mollie Smith and Maura Lubell, for my beautiful and well-functioning site. (Visit www.emilygiffin.com!)

I can't thank my family and friends enough—for your moral support and for listening to me complain about how I'd never make this deadline. (Word of advice to my fellow writers: checking into a hotel, ordering room service, and drinking wine while watching Jennifer Aniston movies generally doesn't get you to the finish line any faster.) With respect to the one edit I couldn't fix: Kirby was conceived in 1995 during the famous Chicago heat wave, yet is now eighteen. Just read the book again in two years, and we'll be straight.

Deepest appreciation to my assistant and confidante, Kate Brown McDavid, and to the amazing Martha Arias, for all that you do to keep my life in order and sanity in check. I love seeing you both every morning.

Very special thanks to Nancy LeCroy Mohler, Mary Ann Elgin, and Sarah Giffin for your tireless input on the many, *many* drafts of this manuscript (and every book before this one). A decade ago, you three were the first to meet Rachel and Darcy; I'm so grateful that you encouraged me to introduce them to the world.

And most of all, my enduring love and gratitude to my four favorite people—Buddy, Edward, George, and Harriet. Hip hip hooray for Team Blaha!

Where We Belong

1

Marian

I know what they say about secrets. I've heard it all. That they can haunt and govern you. That they can poison relationships and divide families. That in the end, only the truth will set you free. Maybe that's the case for some people and some secrets. But I truly believed I was the exception to such portents, and never once breathed the smallest mention of my nearly two-decade-long secret to anyone. Not to my closest friends in my most intoxicated moments or to my boyfriend, Peter, in our most intimate ones. My father knew nothing of it—and I didn't even discuss it with my mother, the only person who was there when it all happened, almost as if we took an unspoken vow of silence, willing ourselves to let go, move on. I never forgot, not for a single day, yet I was also convinced that sometimes, the past really was the past.

I should have known better. I should have taken those words to heart—the ones that started it all on that sweltering night so long ago: *You can run but you can't hide.*

But those words, that night, my secret, are the farthest things from my mind as Peter and I stroll down Bleecker Street following a lingering dinner at Lupa, one of our favorite restaurants in the city. After several stops and starts, winter seems over for good, and the balmy spring night is made warmer by the bottle of Barolo Peter ordered. It's one of the many things I admire about him—his fine taste coupled with his firm belief that life is too short for unexceptional wine. Unexceptional anything really. He is too kind and hardworking to be considered a snob, shunning his lazy trust fund acquaintances who accomplished "nothing on their own," but he's certainly an elitist, having always traveled in prep school, power circles. I'm not uncomfortable in that world—but had always existed on the fringe of it before Peter brought me into his vortex of jet shares, yachts, and vacation homes in Nantucket and St. Bart's.

"Ah! Finally. No slush on the sidewalks," I say, happy to be wearing heels and a light cardigan after months of unseemly rubber boots and puffy winter coats.

"I know ... *Quel soulagement,*" Peter murmurs, draping his arm around me. He is possibly the only guy I know who can get away with musing in French without sounding insufferably pretentious, perhaps because he spent much of his childhood in Paris, the son of a French runway model and an American diplomat. Even after he moved to the States when he was twelve, he was allowed to speak only French at home, his accent as flawless as his manners.

I smile and bury my cheek against his broad shoulder as he plants a kiss on the top of my head and says, "Where to now, Champ?"

He coined the nickname after I beat him in a contentious game of Scrabble on our third date, then doubled down and did it again, gloating all the while. I laughed and made the fatal mistake of telling him "Champ" was the ironic name of my childhood dog, a blind chocolate Lab with a bad limp, thus sealing the term of endearment. "Marian" was quickly relegated to mixed company, throes of passion, and our rare arguments.

2

"Dessert?" I suggest, as we turn the corner. We contemplate Magnolia's cupcakes or Rocco's cannolis, but decide we are too full for either, and instead walk in comfortable silence, wandering by cafés and bars and throngs of contented Villagers. Then, moved by the wine and the weather and a whiff of his spicy cologne, I find myself blurting out, "How about marriage?"

At thirty-six and after nearly two years of dating, I've had the question on my mind, the subject one of speculation among my friends. But this night marks the first time I've broached the topic with him directly, and I instantly regret my lapse of discipline and brace myself for an unsatisfying response. Sure enough, the mood of the night instantly shifts, and I feel his arm tense around me. I tell myself it isn't necessarily a bad sign; it could just be poor timing. It even occurs to me that he could already have the ring—and that his reaction has more to do with my stealing his thunder.

"Oh, forget it," I say with a high-pitched, forced laugh, which only makes things more awkward. It's like trying to retract an "I love you" or undo a one-night stand. Impossible.

"Champ," he says, then pauses for a few beats. "We're so good together."

The sentiment is sweet, even promising, but it's not even close to being an answer—and I can't resist telling him as much. "*Sooo* that means . . . what, exactly? Status quo forever? Let's hit City Hall tonight? Something in between?" My tone is playful, and Peter seizes the opportunity to make light of things.

"Maybe we should get those cupcakes after all," he says.

I don't smile, the vision of an emerald-cut diamond tucked into one of his Italian loafers beginning to fade.

3

"Kidding," he says, pulling me tighter against him. "Repeat the question?"

"Marriage. Us. What do you think?" I say. "Does it ever even . . . cross your mind?"

"Yes. Of course it does . . ."

I feel a "but" coming like you can feel rain on your face after a deafening clap of thunder. Sure enough, he finishes, "But my divorce was just finalized." Another noncommittal nonanswer.

"Right," I say, feeling defeated as he glances into a darkened storefront, seemingly enthralled by a display of letterpress stationery and Montblanc pens. I make a mental note to buy him one, having nearly exhausted gifts in the "what to buy someone who has everything" category, especially someone as meticulous as Peter. Cuff links, electronic gadgets, weekend stays at rustic New England B and Bs. Even a custom LEGO statue of a moose, the unofficial mascot of his beloved Dartmouth.

"But your marriage has been over for a long time. You haven't lived with Robin in over *four* years," I say.

It is a point I make often, but never in this context, rather when we are out with other couples, on the off chance that someone sees me as the culprit—the mistress who swooped in and stole someone else's husband. Unlike some of my friends who seem to specialize in married men, I have never entertained so much as a wink or a drink from a man with a ring on his left hand, just as I, in the dating years before Peter, had zero tolerance for shadiness, game playing, commitment phobias, or any other symptom of the Peter Pan syndrome, a seeming epidemic, at least in Manhattan. In part, it was about principle and self-respect. But it was also a matter of pragmatism, of thirty-something

4

life engineering. I knew exactly what I wanted—*who* I wanted—and believed I could get there through sheer effort and determination just as I had doggedly pursued my entire career in television.

That road hadn't been easy, either. Right after I graduated from film school at NYU, I moved to L.A. and worked as a lowly production assistant on a short-lived Nickelodeon teen sitcom. After eighteen months of trying to get lunch orders straight in my head and not writing a single word for the show, I got a job as a staff writer on a medical drama series. It was a great gig, as I learned a lot, made amazing contacts, and worked my way up to story editor, but I had no life, and didn't really care for the show. So at some point, I took a gamble, left the safety of a hit show, and moved back to New York into a cozy garden apartment in Park Slope. To pay the bills, I sold a couple specs and did freelance assignments for existing shows. My favorite spot to write became a little family-owned bar named Aggie's where there was constant drama between the four brothers, much of it inspired by the women they married and their Irish-immigrant mother. I found myself ditching my other projects and sketching out their backstories, until suddenly *South Second Street* was born (I moved the bar from modern-day Brooklyn to Philly in the seventies). It wasn't high concept like everything in television seemed to be becoming, but I was old-school, and believed I could create a compelling world with my writing and characters—rather than gimmicks. My agent believed in me, too, and after getting me in to pitch my pilot to all the major networks, a bidding war ensued. I took a deal with a little less money (but still enough for me to move to Manhattan) and more creative license. And voilà. My dream had come true. I was finally an executive producer. A showrunner.

Then, one intense year later, I met Peter. I knew his name long before I actually met him from the industry and snippets in *Variety*: Peter Standish, the esteemed television executive poached from another network, the would-be savior to turn around our overall struggling ratings and revamp our identity. As the new CEO, he was technically my boss, another one of my rules for whom not to date. However, the morning I ran into him at the Starbucks in our building lobby, I granted myself an exception, rationalizing that I wasn't one of his direct reports—the director of programming buffered us in the chain of command. Besides, I already had a name. My series was considered a modest hit, a tough feat for a mid-season show, so nobody could accuse me of using him to get ahead or jump-start a stalling career.

Of course at that point, as I stood behind him in line, eavesdropping as he ordered a "double tall cappuccino extra dry," the matter was completely theoretical. He wasn't wearing a ring (I noticed instantly), but he gave off an unavailable vibe as I tapped him on the shoulder, introduced myself, and issued a brisk, professional welcome. I knew how old he was by the press release still sitting in my in-box—forty-seven—but with a full head of dark hair, he looked younger than I expected. He was also taller and broader than I thought he'd be, everything on a larger scale, including his hand around his cup of extra dry cappuccino.

"It's nice to meet you, Marian," he said with a charming but still sincere tilt of his head, pausing as I ordered my own tall latte, even lingering as the barista made my drink, telling me I was doing a hell of a job on my show. "It's got a nice little following, doesn't it?"

I nodded modestly, trying not to focus on the elegant cut of his suit and the cleft in his clean-shaven, square jaw. "Yes. We've been lucky so far. But we can do more to expand our audience . . . Have you ever watched it?"

It was bold to put your boss's boss on the spot, and I knew the answer in his hesitation, saw that he was debating whether to admit he'd never seen my show.

He sheepishly told the truth, then added, "But I will tonight. And that's a promise." I had the gut feeling that he really *was* a man of his word—a reputation he had earned in a business full of lecherous, egomaniacal slicksters.

"Well, at least you know it's on Thursday nights," I say, feeling a wave of attraction and suddenly sensing that it wasn't completely one-sided. It had been a long time since I had felt anything close to chemistry with someone—at least not someone so eligible on paper.

The next morning, to my delight, we both showed up at Starbucks at 7:50 A.M., once again, and I couldn't help but wonder if he had done it on purpose, as I had.

"So, what did you think?" I asked with a hint of coyness—which wasn't my usual style, especially at work. "Did you watch it?"

"Yes. And I loved it," he announced, ordering his same drink but this time opting for whipped cream, proving he could be spontaneous. I felt myself beaming as I thanked him.

"Tight writing. And great acting. That Angela Rivers sure is a pistol, isn't she?" he asked, referring to our up-and-coming, quirky, redhead lead who often drew comparisons to Lucille Ball. During casting, I had gone out on a limb

7

and chosen her over a more established star, one of the best decisions I had ever made as a producer.

"Yes," I said. "I can see an Emmy in her future."

He nodded, duly noting. "Oh, and by the way," he said, an endearing smile behind his eyes. "I not only watched the show, but I went back and watched the pilot online. And the rest of the first season. So I have you to thank for less than four hours of sleep last night."

I laughed. "Afternoon espresso," I said as we strolled to the elevator bank. "Works like a charm."

He winked and said, "Sounds good. Around four-thirty?"

My heart pounded as I nodded, counting down the minutes to four-thirty that day, and for several weeks after that. It became our ritual, although for appearances, we always pretended that it was a coincidence.

Then one day, after I mentioned my love of hats, a package from Barneys appeared by messenger. Inside was a jaunty, black grosgrain beret with a card that read: *To Marian, the only girl I know who could pull this one off.*

I promptly called his direct dial from the network directory, delighted when he answered his own phone.

"Thank you," I said.

"You're welcome," he said—with what I could tell was a smile.

"I love it," I said, beaming back at him.

"How about the card? Was 'girl' okay? I debated 'girl' versus 'woman.'" His second-guessing confirmed that he cared—and that he could be vulnerable. I felt myself falling for him a little more.

"I like 'girl' from *you*," I said. "And I love the beret. Just glad that it wasn't raspberry."

"Or from a secondhand store," he deadpanned. "Although I would love to see you in it. And if it was warm . . ."

I laughed, feeling flushed, a churning in my stomach, wondering when—not if—he was going to ask me out on an official date.

Three days later, we flew to Los Angeles for the Emmys on the network jet. Although my show hadn't been nominated, we were getting a lot of great buzz and I had never felt better about my career. Meanwhile, Peter and I were getting some buzz of our own, a few rumors circulating, clearly due to our coffee break repartee. But we played it cool on the red carpet, and even more so at the after-parties, until neither of us could take it another second, and he sent me a text I still have saved on my iPhone: *That dress is stunning.*

I smiled, grateful that I had not only overspent on an Alberta Ferretti gown but had opted for emerald green instead of my usual black. Feeling myself blush, I turned to look in his direction as another text came in: *Although it would look better on the floor.*

I blushed and shook my head as he sent a final text: *I promise I won't try to find out if you meet me upstairs. Room 732.*

Less than ten minutes later we were in his room, finally alone, grinning at each other. I felt sure that he'd kiss me immediately, but he showed a restraint that I found irresistible, increasingly more so with every glass of champagne we poured. We grew tipsier by the hour as we talked about everything—the state of television, our network, my show, gossip about actors, and even more drama among the executives. He told me about his thirteen-year-old son Aidan and his ongoing divorce proceedings. Despite the fact that he jokingly referred to his ex as "the plaintiff," he didn't make her out to be the villain, which I found to be a refreshing change from the few other divorcés I had dated. We talked about places we had traveled, our favorite hotels and cities, and where we hoped to someday go, both literally and in our careers. We were different in some ways—I preferred the Caribbean or traditional urban trips to places like Rome and London, while he loved exotic adventure, once pedaling through the Golden Triangle in Thailand, another time trekking up the Pacaya volcano in Guatemala. He had also taken more risks in business, which of course had paid off, while I generally avoided conflict and preferred to stick with something if it was working, even a little. Yet at the core, we had a common sensibility—a belief in striving for excellence and never settling, a love of New York and all that came with it, a sense of conservatism with a core philosophy that we should all live and let live, whatever our political or religious beliefs. He was handsome, confident, intelligent, and thoughtful—the closest I'd ever come to perfection.

Then, as the California sky showed its first streaks of muted pink, he reached over and took my hand, pulled me onto his lap and kissed me in a way I hadn't been kissed for years. We said good night a few minutes later, then laughed, and said good morning.

Within a few weeks, we were an established couple, even having the conversation about no longer wanting to see others. One evening, we were photographed dining together, our picture appearing in a blurb on Page Six with the caption: "Powerful Love Connection: TV Exec Peter Standish with Producer Marian Caldwell." As the calls rolled in from friends and acquaintances who had seen the press, I pretended to be some combination of annoyed and amused, but I secretly loved it, saving the clipping for our future children. Things would have seemed too good to be true, if I hadn't always believed I could—and *would*—find someone like him.

But maybe they *were* too good to be true, I think now, squinting up at him as we turn the corner, hand in hand. Maybe we had stalled. Maybe this was as good as it was ever going to get. Maybe I was one of those girls, after all. Girls who wait or settle—or do some combination of both. Disappointment and muted anger well inside me. Anger at him, but more anger at myself for not facing the fact that when a person avoids a topic, it's generally for a reason.

"I think I'm going home," I say after a long stretch of silence, hoping that my statement doesn't come across as self-pitying or manipulative, the two cards that never work in relationships—especially with someone like Peter.

"C'mon. Really?" Peter asks, a trace of surrender in his voice where I'd hoped to hear urgency. He was always so controlled, so measured, and although I usually loved this quality, it irritated me now. He abruptly stops, turns, and gazes down at me, taking both of my hands in his.

"Yeah. I'm really tired," I lie, pulling my hands free.

"Marian. Don't do this," he meagerly protests.

"I'm not doing anything, Peter," I say. "I was just trying to have a conversation with you . . ."

"Fine," he says, exhaling, all but rolling his eyes. "Let's have a conversation."

I swallow my dwindling pride and, feeling very small, say, "Okay. Well . . . can you see yourself getting married again? Or having another child?"

He sighs, starts to speak, stops, and tries again. "Nothing is missing in my life if that's what you're asking. I have

11

Aidan. I have you. I have my work. Life is good. Really good. But I *do* love you, Marian. I *adore* you. You know that."

I wait for more, thinking how easy it would be for him to appease me with a nonspecific promise: *I don't know what I see exactly, but I see you in my life.* Or: *I want to make you happy.* Or even: *I wouldn't rule anything out.* Something. Anything.

Instead, he gives me a helpless look as two cabs materialize, one after the other, a coincidence to which I ascribe all sorts of meaning. I flag the first and force a tight-lipped smile. "Let's just talk tomorrow. Okay?" I say, trying to salvage what's left of my image as a strong, independent woman and wondering if it's only an image.

He nods as I accept a staccato kiss on the cheek. Then I slide in the cab and close my door, careful not to slam it, yet equally careful not to make eye contact with him as we pull away from the curb, headed toward my apartment on the Upper East Side.

Thirty minutes later, I'm changed into my oldest, coziest pair of flannel pajamas, feeling completely sorry for myself, when my apartment intercom buzzes.

Peter.

My heart leaps with shameful, giddy relief as I nearly run to my foyer. I take a deep breath and buzz him up, staring at the door like my namesake Champ waiting for the mailman. I imagine that Peter and I will make up, make love, maybe even make plans. I don't need a ring or a promise of a baby, I will say, as long as I know that he feels the way I do. That he sees us sharing a life together. That he can't imagine us apart. I tell myself it isn't settling—it's the opposite—it's what you do for love.

But a few seconds later, I round the corner to find not Peter at my door, but a young girl with angular features, a narrow face, and small, pointed chin. She is slight, pale, and almost pretty—at least I think she will be in a few years. She is dressed like a typical teenager down to her oversized backpack and peace sign necklace, but she has a composed air, something telling me that she is not a follower.

"Hello," I say, wondering if she is lost or has the wrong apartment or is peddling something. "Can I help you?"

She clears her throat, shifts her weight from side to side, and asks in a small, raspy voice, "Are you Marian Caldwell?"

"Yes," I say, waiting.

"My name is Kirby Rose," she finally says, tucking her long, dirty-blond hair behind her ears, which are a little on the big side or at least at an unfortunate angle to her head, a trait I understand too well, then glances down at her scuffed black boots. When her eyes meet mine again, I notice their distinctive color—bluish-gray and banded by black—and in that instant, I know *exactly* who she is and why she has come here.

"Are you? . . ." I try to finish my sentence, but can't inhale or exhale, let alone speak.

Her chin trembles as she nods the smallest of nods, then wipes her palms on her jeans, threadbare at the left knee.

I stand frozen, anticipating the words I have imagined and feared, dreaded and dreamt about, for the last eighteen years. Then, just as I think my racing heart will explode, I finally hear her say them: *"I think you're my mother."*

2

July 14, 1995

It was the hottest day ever recorded in Chicago history, the mercury hitting 106 and the heat index topping out at 120 degrees, a record that still stands today, nearly two decades later. The heat wave was all anyone could talk about, eventually killing seven hundred fifty people, making bigger headlines than the Iran Disarmament Crisis, the Bosnian war, and the Grateful Dead's final performance at Soldier Field—at least on B96, my sole source of news at eighteen.

That blistering morning, as I lounged by our pool in the white string bikini I had ordered from the Victoria's Secret catalogue, I tuned in to the Kevin and JoBo show, listening to their banter about how the heat makes people do crazy things: fall in love, commit crimes, run naked through the streets. They were obviously joking, the way DJs do, but looking back, I actually believe that the temperature was at least partly to blame for what happened later that night at my best friend Janie's house. That it would have been a different story during any other season or even on an ordinarily hot summer's day.

There were other factors, too, of course, such as alcohol, everyone's favorite culprit, specifically the four strawberry Boone's Farm coolers I downed on an empty stomach. Throw in the intensity of emotions that come with that bittersweet summer sandwiched between high school

14

graduation and the rest of your life, supreme hometown boredom, and a dash of bad luck—or good, depending on who you ask. And of course, the final ingredient: Conrad Knight himself.

Conrad wasn't my type up close and in reality, but he was pretty much everyone's type from afar and in fantasy, and I certainly wasn't immune to his seductive blue-gray eyes, just-long-enough dark hair, and cheekbones Janie called "epic" years before the word became overused. He seemed mysterious and a little dangerous, an image some kids tried to cultivate—but only Conrad seemed to achieve naturally. He had a tattoo on his forearm, rumored to be his mother's initials and the date of the car crash that killed her. He smoked hand-rolled cigarettes, drove an old, black Mustang, and sang in a garage band downtown. A few girls with fake IDs who had gone to see him compared his voice to Eddie Vedder's, swearing that he'd be famous someday. His father, who was actually a retired actor, having starred in a now-defunct soap opera and a still-running commercial for Tums, returned to L.A. intermittently for auditions, taking Conrad with him for long stretches of time. Despite his absences from school and spotty academic record, he seemed smart and somehow worldly—or at least profoundly indifferent to the social order of high school, which gave him an aura of sophistication. In short, he was nothing like the affable jocks I had dated throughout high school—nothing like I was, for that matter—but not in a dramatic, cliques-at-war way, just in a way where our paths never really crossed. We occasionally said hello in the halls, but hadn't really talked since elementary school.

"Marian Caldwell," Conrad declared when I ran into him in Janie's backyard. At least half of Glencoe had come to the party after word had spread that her parents were out of town. He was expressionless, yet something in his eyes told me that we were about to have a meaningful exchange.

"Hey Conrad," I said, self-consciously swaying to the swell of Sarah McLachlan's "I Will Remember You" coming from the boom box in Janie's upstairs bedroom window.

He gave me a half-smile, and then, as if continuing a long-running conversation, said those words I'd replay for years to come. "You can run, but you can't hide."

As he took a sip from a can of Dr Pepper, I surveyed the scruff on his face and inhaled the scent of his skin—a mix of cedar, salt, and Calvin Klein's Eternity cologne.

"Who's running?" I said. "And what are you doing at a party like this?"

I still cringe when I think of the question. I might as well have said a party with the "popular crowd," of which we both knew I was a sustaining benefactor.

"Lookin' for you," he said, his eyes smoldering as much as light eyes can. I glanced around, assuming he was joking, expecting his fellow bandmates or his girlfriend to be returning from the bathroom. I had never seen her—she went to another school—but Janie had spotted them at the mall together once and said she was a dead ringer for Kate Moss, right down to her gypsy top, long, floral skirt, and Birkenstocks.

"Well. Looks like you found me." I laughed, feeling bolder than usual as I touched his forearm, right on the black ink numbers, like Braille on his skin, determining that he was not only alone but completely sober.

"So how you been?" He glanced at his naked wrist where a watch would have been if he had worn one. "For the past six years?"

16

"Six years?" I asked, then reminded him that we had gone to school together since the fourth grade.

"Last time we talked," he said, running his hand through his hair, wavier than usual from the humidity that was so thick I felt like we were treading water. "I mean, *really* talked. We were on the bus coming back from that field trip."

"From the Shedd," I said, nodding, remembering the trip to the aquarium in the sixth grade—and especially the bus ride back to school.

Conrad smiled, and for one second relinquished his cool posture. He looked twelve again, and I told him so.

His smile grew wider as he said, "You gave me half of your Twix and told me you wanted to be a marine biologist."

I laughed and rolled my eyes. "Yeah . . . I don't want to be a marine biologist anymore."

"I know," he said. "You're going to Michigan, then film school, then L.A. or New York where you're going to do great things and become huge. The next Nora Ephron or . . . well, that's about the only girl director I know."

I gave him a look of surprise until he divulged his obvious source. "The yearbook. Remember? Plans for the future?" He made quotes in the air, clearly mocking the whole exercise.

"Right," I said, thinking that he must also be aware that I had been voted "most likely to succeed"—just as I was aware that he had won "best eyes."

"And what are your plans?" I asked, something telling me that he had left the yearbook questionnaire blank, until I remembered his three-word reply: *Color me gone.*

I asked him what he meant by this and he told me, "Just get the hell out of here. That's all."

"So nothing . . . more specific?" I asked, meaning of

course, college. Which in my mind, and among my circle of friends, was simply a given.

"Nope," he said, draining his Dr Pepper. He crushed the can with one hand and tossed it into a nearby wastebasket. "Except to kiss you tonight. And probably tomorrow night, too. And if you're not careful . . . maybe even the one after that."

I felt myself shiver, even as perspiration trickled down my back, and decided that I would let him. Or more accurately, I acknowledged to myself that I wouldn't be able to say no. But I pretended to be in complete control, reaching up to adjust my long, blond ponytail, the humidity having the reverse effect on my straight, now limp hair. "Now why would you do such a thing?" I asked, my heart pounding as I gave him a coy look.

"Because I *like* you."

The word was juvenile, but he made it sound otherwise.

"Since when?" I said, my voice stronger than my knees.

"Since always. Since day one." He said it matter-of-factly, as if he were telling me a trivial piece of information like the time of day or the temperature—which was likely still in triple digits, nightfall providing no relief from the stifling heat. He then rattled off a catalogue of memories, dispelling any lingering doubt about his sincerity, if not his motives: the location of my locker over the last four years; the scar on my left knee that he had studied whenever I wore skirts to school; the purple dress I wore to the homecoming dance, silk pumps dyed to match.

"I don't remember you ever going to a dance," I said, breathless.

"I didn't," he said, holding my gaze. "I saw the snapshot in what's his name's locker."

I stared back at him, remembering how I had taped it in my boyfriend's locker, right over an annoying photo of

18

Rebecca Romijn and Angie Everhart lounging on the beach in the *Sports Illustrated* swimsuit issue. "Todd," I said.

"Yeah. Him," he said, rolling his eyes.

"We broke up," I said.

"I know. About time."

"What about your girlfriend?"

"We broke up, too," he said. "What a coincidence."

He took another step toward me and we began to slow dance to Sade, his hand on my back, and his breath in my ear, the distinct smell of pot wafting toward us. A few minutes later, amid many stares, we made our way inside, nestling into the corner of the tweed sectional in Janie's family room, sweaty bodies gyrating all around us. For over an hour, we sat together, making light conversation that still felt heavy. There was an electricity between us, a sense of fresh discovery, but also a profound familiarity—the kind that comes when you grow up with someone, passing each other in the same halls, day after day. I found myself wondering why we had never talked like this before—and yet I knew exactly why.

"Let's find somewhere more quiet," he said at one point, after the first lull in our conversation.

I nodded, leading him to the foyer, then up the stairs, then down the hall to Janie's parents' bedroom, past the sign she had posted that said DO NOT ENTER!!! We no longer spoke, both of us nervous yet intent, as we locked the door, kissing, peeling off our clothes, then crawling under the covers of the four-poster king bed. At some point, he reached down on the floor, finding his jeans, pulling his wallet out of the back pocket. I knew what he was doing even before he produced the square, foil package, fumbling in the dark. I closed my eyes, letting it all unfold, waiting for him, wanting him.

What happened next is predictable, except that it is never entirely predictable when it is happening to you, for the first time, after you've said no a hundred times before. I thought of all the times I had come close with Todd, trying to pinpoint what the difference was now, deciding that it all came down to a desire I had never felt before. A desire so intense that it felt like need.

"Are you sure?" he asked, even though we were nearly past the point of no return. I looked into his eyes, then up toward the ceiling, dizzy from my feelings and the fan whirring above us, trying to make a final decision as Conrad held himself steadily over me, breathing, waiting.

My mind raced, my thoughts disjointed and blurry—yet remarkably clear, too. I told myself that there were risks, that I might regret it in the morning, if not sooner. I told myself he might only be pretending to like me—that he was really just using me to get laid, that surely I was only one of many. I told myself that it wasn't the kind of thing a girl like me did, especially with someone like him.

But the answer was still yes. With every beat of my heart, I heard yes. And then I said it aloud, holding his gaze, so there would be no mistake about my decision. Heat, lust, and alcohol aside, I knew exactly what I was doing—that I was making an indelible, irrevocable choice. I knew it as I felt him enter me slowly, lingering for a few seconds before he withdrew to put on the condom and begin again. I knew I was changed forever.

Yet in that still, salty aftermath, I never imagined what would follow. I never dreamed that it would be anything other than a moment in time. A story from my youth. A chapter from that summer. A heat wave with a beginning, middle, and definite end.

3

Kirby

My name is Kirby Rose, and I'm adopted.
I don't mean to make it sound like an AA confession, although sometimes that's how people take it, like it's something they should be supportive about. I just mean that they are two basic facts about me. Just as you can't pinpoint the moment you learn your name, I can't remember the first time I heard my parents tell the story of that out-of-the-blue phone call announcing my birth and the news that I would be theirs in seventy-two hours. All they had to do was drive to Chicago (a short trip from their neighborhood in South City, St. Louis, where they both grew up and still lived), sign some papers, and pick me up at the hospital. All they had to do was say yes.

It was April Fools' Day and for a second my mom thought it was a joke, until she reassured herself that nobody would be cruel enough to play such a trick on a couple who had been trying and wishing, waiting and praying for a baby for over ten years, from virtually the day they got married. My dad was an electrician, my mom an administrative assistant at a big law firm in town, so they made decent money, but they couldn't afford any fancy fertility clinics. Instead, they looked into adoption—first sticking with domestic Catholic agencies, then gradually registering with any organization in any country that might have a baby to give them. China.

Russia. Colombia. Shady lawyers. It didn't matter; they just wanted a baby.

So of course my mother shouted yes into the phone before she knew a single fact about me. Then, as my dad picked up the other extension, the lady on the phone calmly reported that I was a healthy six-pound-three-ounce baby girl. Nineteen inches long, with big, blue eyes and a head covered with peach fuzz. She said I had a big appetite and a sweet disposition. She called me "perfect"—and told them that they were the lucky ones chosen by the agency from hundreds of adoptive parents.

"Congratulations," she said. "We'll see you soon."

My parents hung up, wept, embraced, then laughed through more tears. Then they rushed out to Babies "R" Us the way people hit grocery stores before a blizzard. They bought tiny pink clothes and a crib and a car seat and more toys and dolls than I could ever hope to play with, then came home and transformed my mother's sewing room into a lavender and yellow nursery.

The next day, they drove to Chicago and checked into a hotel near Northwestern Memorial Hospital. They had to wait three more days to meet me, neither of them sleeping for more than a few minutes here and there, even though they knew it was the last good rest they'd have for a while. In the meantime, they discussed baby names, my mother lobbying hard for her maiden name, Kirby. We have to see her first, my dad insisted. I had to look like a Kirby— whatever *that* was.

My dad typically picks up the story from there, telling me how he cut himself shaving, his hands shaking so much that he almost let my mother drive to the hospital, something he never does because she sucks so badly at it.

Then he skips ahead to the papers they hurriedly signed, and the moment the lady from the agency returned with a baby—*me*—swaddled in a pink fleece blanket.

"Meet your daughter," the lady said as she handed me to my parents. "Dear one, meet Lynn and Art Rose. Your parents."

It has always been my favorite part of the story. The first time they held me, gazed down at my face, felt the warmth of my body against their chests.

"She has your nose," my dad joked, and then declared me a Kirby.

It was the moment, they said, when we became a family. They said it felt like an absolute miracle, not unlike the moment they met Charlotte, my little sister who was conceived by complete surprise shortly after they adopted me. The only difference, my mother was fond of saying, was that she wasn't in any pain when she met me. That came later.

Growing up, I heard the story a million times, along with all the sentimental quotes about adoption, like the one framed in my bedroom for years: "Not flesh of my flesh, nor bone of my bone, but somehow miraculously still my own. Never forget for a single minute, you didn't grow under my heart but in it." I knew which celebrities had adopted babies, and more important, who had been adopted themselves: Steve Jobs, two presidents, including Bill Clinton (who was in the White House when I was born), two first ladies, Faith Hill *and* Tim McGraw (who happened to also be married—how cool is *that*?), Darryl McDaniels from Run-DMC and, as my mother sometimes pointed out, Moses and Jesus.

Yet despite my full understanding of my adoption, I

didn't give much thought to my birth mother, and even less to my birth father. It was as if they were both bit players in the whole drama, completely beside the point but for their necessary contribution of a little DNA. And I *certainly* never felt rejected because they had given me up. My parents knew nothing about my birth mother, yet always explained with certainty that she didn't "give me up" or "give me away"—she made a *plan* for me, the best one she could make under her circumstances, whatever those were. Looking back, I think they were probably just following the advice of some adoption book, but at the time I bought it, hook, line, and sinker. If anything, I felt sorry for her, believing that I was *her* loss; she wasn't mine.

In fact, the first time I really wondered about her with anything more than a passing curiosity was in the fifth grade when we researched our family ancestry in social studies. I did my report on Ireland, like many of the kids in my class, explaining that my father's people came from Galway, my mother's from Cork. Of course, I understood that they weren't really *my* bloodlines or my ancestors— and I made no bones about that fact in my report. Most everyone knew I was adopted, as I'd been in the same school since kindergarten, and it was no big deal, simply one of those bits of trivia, like being double-jointed or having an identical twin.

So I matter-of-factly informed the class that I knew nothing about my birth mother except that she was from Chicago. I didn't know her name, and we had never seen a photo of her, but based on my blond hair and blue eyes, I guessed that she was Scandinavian—then narrowed it to Danish, maybe because I have a sweet tooth and liked the sound of it. My classmates seemed satisfied with this theory, except for annoying Gary Rusk who raised his hand, and without waiting to be called on, asked whether I was mad at my mother and if I ever planned on tracking her down. Envisioning a bounty hunter with a rifle and a couple of bloodhounds, I exchanged a look with my best friend, Belinda Greene. Then I cleared my throat and calmly replied, "I already have a mother. And no, I'm not mad at anyone."

The seed was planted. Maybe I *should* be mad; clearly others *would* be—at least Gary would. He pressed on with his nosy line of questioning. "Could you find her if you wanted to? Like with a private investigator?"

"No. I don't even, like, know her *name*. So how would I find her?" I said, thinking of all the many women who must have given birth at my hospital in Chicago on April Fools' Day 1996.

Finished with my report, I sat down, and we went on to hear about Debbie Talierco's Italian heritage. But for the rest of the class, and all that day in school, I couldn't shake the thought of my birth mother. I didn't yet *want* to find her, but I kept wondering if there was even a chance that I *could*.

So that night at the dinner table, during a tedious conversation about the Gallaghers' newly adopted Yorkie puppy and how he kept nipping their toddler, and that they really needed to show that dog who was boss, I silently rehearsed the question that Gary had posed to me, somehow anticipating that it wasn't something my parents, particularly my mother, wanted to discuss. It was one thing when they brought it up in the context of *their* prayers being answered; I knew it would be another thing altogether for me to focus on *her*.

"Why'd they get a Yorkie anyway? They should have *rescued* a dog," Charlotte said, a tenderhearted animal lover. "I mean, it *saves* a life."

I suddenly felt like a rescue dog myself, a total *mutt*, as I casually shook A.1. onto my pork chops, a habit I had picked up from my dad, who puts it on everything, including scrambled eggs.

"So I did this report today on my ancestors," I began. "And, umm . . . my adoption came up."

My mother stared at me, chewing, swallowing, waiting.

"And anyway, I was wondering . . . if there was any way I could find my birth mother? If I wanted to? I mean, do we even know her name?"

I could tell right away that asking the question was a mistake. The air felt thick with tension and my mother began to blink back tears. *Tears!* Over a stupid *question.* Meanwhile, Charlotte looked down at her plate with this guilty look on her face while my dad strapped on his most somber, preachy one, the same one he wore when he gave my sister and me the big "don't do drugs" speech. Rather than just answering the question, he said, "Well. This is a pretty serious subject."

"It's not *that* serious," I said.

"Well, sure it is," he said. "And it's important. Very, very important. I mean, if it's important to you, it's important to us. Right, Lynn?"

"I don't *want* to find her or anything," I backpedaled. "I just wanted to know if I *could. Geez.*"

"Don't take His name in vain," my mother said.

I told her I was spelling it with a *g,* not a *j,* fighting back the urge to ask if she thought I'd go to *heck* for it.

Charlotte laughed at this, and I flashed her a smile. No

matter how much she got on my nerves, I loved making my sister laugh.

Then I looked back at my mother and mumbled, "I mean, I don't care a single thing about her. I'd probably hate her."

My mother looked relieved, while my father said, "Don't say that. She did a brave thing. She did what was best for you."

"Whatever," I said, at my peril. It was one of my parents' least favorite words. "It's no biggie."

My father pressed on. "Do you want to find her, Kirbs?"

"I already said I didn't!"

He nodded, clearly not believing me, as he went on to carefully explain that Heartstrings, the agency that had arranged my adoption, had a provision in the documents which granted me access to my birth mother when I turned eighteen, should I want to meet her.

"Access?" I said, as casually as I could.

"If you want her contact information, the agency will provide it to you," my father said. "Assuming she has kept her records current. She agreed to this term, but understood that it was *your* decision, not hers. Currently, she has no information about you or us, nor will she ever be given it. And," he said, raising his eyebrows as if about to make an important point, "she was okay with this."

In other words, she didn't want to find me so why should I want to find her? I shrugged, as if the details of the legal arrangement bored me. To myself, I silently vowed never to bring the subject up again, at least not with my parents.

But from that day forward, I became intrigued by adoption in a way I hadn't been before, acutely aware of stories about adopted children finding their birth mothers and vice versa. I lived for talk shows that orchestrated reunions, riveted by the emotional tales. Sometimes there was guilt and regret, sometimes anger, usually a complex mix of emotions. Occasionally there was a dramatic health issue at stake—or in a few rare cases, a murder, mystery, or kidnapping. I gathered the anecdotes in my mind as I wondered about my own birth mother, her story. I never thought of her as a second mother, more like a distant relative, a long-lost aunt or cousin who was doing something far more interesting (I hoped) than anyone in my life. Perhaps she was a musician, or a CEO, or a surgeon, or a missionary in a third-world country. I had no feelings of bitterness or resentment or abandonment, just a growing curiosity and an occasional, fleeting, romanticized notion of who she might be—and what that might make me by association. Deep down, I had the feeling that she was the missing piece of me—and I wondered if the same was true for her. I still insisted to myself that I didn't want to find her, but I was starting to also believe that I could never really know myself until I did.

All these feelings only intensified by the time I entered Bishop DuBourg High School, and realized just how lost I felt. I had no real identity and didn't seem to belong anywhere—even places I had once felt comfortable. I quit the volleyball team, avoided mass and anything related to our parish, and completely blew off my schoolwork. I even felt myself drifting from Belinda. We were still best friends, but I couldn't stand the way she obsessed over every three-ounce weight gain, boys who had nothing going for them, and worst of all, the Jonas Brothers and other crappy Disney packaged bands. I could forgive a lot of things, but cheesy taste in music wasn't one of them.

For a short time, I started hanging out with a new group of kids who I thought shared my sensibilities or at least my taste in music. But they turned out to be even more fake than the popular crowd, spending hours cultivating their emo image, listening to obscure indie bands no one had ever heard of (and who they'd immediately disown as soon as someone outside the group "discovered" them, too), spending a fortune at Hot Topic and Urban Outfitters to look as if they went to a thrift shop, and in the worst example, drawing fake scars onto their wrists and lying about suicide attempts. I decided I'd much rather hang with Belinda than a bunch of posers—because at least she was authentic in her complete lack of good taste (and even I had to admit that it was fun belting out a Kelly Clarkson song now and then). Mostly, though, I just wanted to be alone with my thoughts and music. In fact, music—*good* music— was one of the few things guaranteed to make me happy. Much to my parents' frustration, who thought that fresh air was synonymous with *any* air, I spent hours in my room, listening to records, writing songs, singing (when no one was home to hear me), and playing the drums. I had picked them up in the sixth grade when my music teacher told me they were the hardest instrument to learn, and although I had long since quit the band, the drums were the only thing I didn't abandon altogether. In fact, I played them all the time, saving every dollar I made bagging groceries at Schnuck's, until I could afford to upgrade from my first Ludwig junior drum set to a sick Pearl Masters MCX kit with the coolest maple shells finished in a black sparkle glitter wrap. It was the sweetest thing I had ever seen, and for the first few nights after I bought it, I moved it next to my bed so I could sleep right beside it and then see it first thing in the morning. My parents humored me, pretending to get my fascination with drums. My dad even bought me a Sabian eighteen-inch HHX Evolution Crash cymbal that he researched on his own for my birthday, which was supercool of him. But I could tell they both wished I did something a little more normal and social. Or at the very least, found a quieter hobby.

The only person who seemed to respect and accept me was Mr. Tully, our school guidance counselor, who I was required to visit about my falling grades and the fact that I was, in everyone's words, not living up to my potential. I pretended to be annoyed when the pink counselor slips came, but I secretly loved spending time in his office, even though he constantly nagged me to sing in the school liturgical choir, join the symphonic or jazz band, or at least play the percussion in our high school musical. (*Not* gonna happen—any of it.) Mr. Tully was young and funny and handsome with light brown eyes and dimples that showed up even when he wasn't smiling. But more than his looks or fun personality, he was the only member of the faculty—the only adult, for that matter—who really seemed to get that being a teenager generally sucked and that it certainly wasn't the best time of your life the way my parents always said it should be and the way it seemed to be for Charlotte. When pressed, I could even get him to admit that some of our school rules were overkill, such as the requirement that every class start with a prayer (although he was an alum himself and promised that one day I'd be proud of it, and if I put my mind to it, this place could be a launching pad for greatness as it had been for the Twitter founder Jack Dorsey). But for all his coolness, I never opened up to him completely. I believed he liked me, but I was well aware

30

that he was getting *paid* to have empathy—so just in case, I wasn't about to admit to him just how shitty I felt on the inside.

To that point, during one counselor visit about my failing grade in chemistry, the subject of my sister came up, and Mr. Tully came right out and asked me the question nobody else had ever dared ask: Did it ever bother me that I was adopted and Charlotte wasn't? I thought hard about the answer, waited a beat longer than felt comfortable before I shook my head no. I wondered if it was the truth. I honestly didn't think that was the problem. Charlotte never lorded this over me, or mentioned it at all, and we had very little sibling rivalry, kind of weird given that we were only eleven months and one grade apart.

I still found myself resenting her for reasons I couldn't quite pinpoint. Yes, she had a great figure (or at least *a* figure while I was scrawny, flat-chested, and barely five feet two), more classic features, and the best, thick, curly hair. But I preferred my gray-blue eyes and blond hair to her muddy brown combination. She did better in school, but only because she worked twice as hard and cared three times more. She was a far superior athlete; I was a middling, retired-from-the-JV-squad volleyball player, while she was a star swimmer, breaking all kinds of school and even citywide records, routinely making headlines in the *St. Louis Post-Dispatch*. Our dining room table doubled as a scrapbook center, a newspaper-clipping shrine to Charlotte's prowess in the pool. But even that didn't faze me. I had no desire to train twenty hours a week at anything, even drumming, and jumping into a cold pool on dark winter mornings seemed like a sick form of torture.

So if it wasn't her miraculous conception, her looks,

her brains, or her athletic ability, I wondered why I was jealous, sometimes even wishing to be her. I wasn't sure, but had the feeling it had something to do with the way Charlotte felt on the inside. She genuinely seemed to like who she was—or at least had the luxury of giving it no thought whatsoever, all of which translated to massive popularity. Everyone knew her and loved her regardless of clique—the jocks, geeks, burnouts, and hoosiers—while I felt downright invisible most of the time.

On one particularly bad day during my junior year, the gulf between Charlotte and me was illustrated in dramatic fashion. First, I failed an American history pop quiz on the one day that week I had blown off my homework. Then, I got my period all over my khaki pants, which was called to my attention as I did a problem *wrong* on the whiteboard in trig. Third, I heard that Tricia Henry had started a rumor that I was a lesbian (which wouldn't matter if it was true, although she was too much of an ignoramus to realize that distinction) simply based on the fact that I play the drums.

Meanwhile, Charlotte made the homecoming court. As a *sophomore*—virtually unheard of at DuBourg. To her credit, she looked genuinely surprised, and completely humble as she elegantly made her way down from the bleachers to the center of the gym where Seth O'Malley, the most beautiful boy in the entire school, gave her a high five and threw his muscled arm around her neck. I didn't want to be on the homecoming court, nor did I want our entire class body watching me, in bloodstained pants or otherwise, but I ached with envy over how effortless it all was for her. How she could stand there with no trace of self-consciousness, even waving at a group of obnoxious freshmen boys bellowing, "Hottie Lottie!" It didn't help matters that Belinda shot me sympathetic stares during the pep rally and asked me no fewer than four times if I was jealous of my little sister, a more direct version of Mr. Tully's question. Clearly, I was *supposed* to feel that way, even in the eyes of my guidance counselor and best friend.

Later that day, I passed Charlotte in the hall in a pack of happy, pretty girls. She was still wearing her red sash from the assembly over her long-sleeved, button-down white blouse and red plaid kilt. (I could never understand how she could make a uniform look good when I looked like crap every day. Then again maybe it was because I typically went with the more comfortable but decidedly unstylish polo shirt and khaki pants option.) We made eye contact, and she eagerly smiled at me, pausing as if on the verge of breaking free of her posse. But I didn't give her the chance. I put my head down and kept walking. I glanced back just long enough to tell I had hurt her feelings, maybe even tarnished her big day. Instead of feeling guilty, I felt a dark, shameful satisfaction that I had managed to wipe that near-constant grin off her face.

It was short-lived, though, as she was back to her same old cheery self that evening, chatting with our mother in the kitchen like the best friends they were. The two had heart-to-hearts all the time, if you can call surface revelations such as "if only green beans tasted as good as chocolate cake" and "isn't Suri Cruise precious?!" heart-to-hearts, while she and my father bonded over her swimming. There were few things as sacred as sports to my dad, and I watched him brimming with pride whenever they returned from her meets, memorizing every boring race, then rehashing the details, over and over and over. So I guess it was inevitable that our parents would come to like her better, all but saying the words they were thinking: "Why can't you be more like your sister?"

Deep down, I knew they *loved* us both equally, and that any favoritism had to do with the fact that she brought them daily pleasure and was just plain easier to live with— not that she was their biological kid. Yet over time, that fact certainly didn't help matters in my head. Nor did the fact that they all looked alike. Even my parents could pass for siblings, with their athletic builds, curly brown hair, and perky Irish noses complete with a smattering of outdoorsy freckles. Their personalities were similar, too, all of them hardwired to be cheerful and outgoing, even with strangers. The three of them all talked nonstop about anything and everything and nothing. They could talk to a freakin' wall while I couldn't conceive of making small talk just for the heck of it, especially with a stranger (much to the annoyance of my boss at Schnuck's who seemed to think that chatting up the customer while I bagged their groceries was crucial to their shopping experience). It was just another example of me feeling like an outsider.

Things went downhill my senior year, the chilly standoff with my parents escalating to an outright war—and believe me, my parents didn't subscribe to the "choose your battles" strategy. *Everything* was a battle with them. We fought over the volume of my music (my iPod was going to make me go deaf; my drums disturbed the neighbors). We fought over my decision to be a vegetarian (unwise for a growing girl). We fought over my Facebook page (somehow they found the status update "my parents suck" offensive). We fought about my messy room (that they weren't supposed to go into in the first place). We fought about the cigarettes and bottle of vodka they "found" *in* my messy room (earning them another status update comparing them to the Gestapo). We fought over the Catholic church, my attendance at mass, the fact that I was agnostic (okay, maybe this was just to piss them off—I did *sorta* believe in Him). We fought over Belinda after she got busted at school with a dime bag (thank God they didn't find my dime bag during their unconstitutional search and seizure). We fought over my ten o'clock curfew that I broke more in protest of how stupidly early it was than because I had anything that interesting to do (translation: *nothing* interesting to do and certainly nothing that involved boys—only the lame ones liked me). We fought over my shitty grades (and shittier attitude). We even managed to fight over my shockingly high SAT score—because, in their words, it was further evidence that I wasn't living up to my potential. And most of all, we fought over the fact that I wasn't going to college—not even to the School of Music at the University of Missouri, Mr. Tully's grand plan for me (which I might have considered if I didn't have to study any other subject or see anyone else from my high school while I was there). We fought over *everything*.

Then one freezing January night (we fought over the thermostat, too—there was frost on the inside of my windows, for Christ's sake), I woke up to go the bathroom and overheard my parents talking in the kitchen. As I crept down the hall, I felt oddly soothed by the cadence of their voices and the sound of my mother's teaspoon clinking against her cup, just as I secretly loved the sound of Charlotte snoring on the nights she had a bad dream and asked to sleep in my room. For one second, I felt like my little-girl self again—and wondered why I couldn't just will myself to be happy.

That's when I overheard the word "adoption." Then: "her mother."

I froze, my cheeks burning despite the fact that I was shivering, then crept closer to the banister, craning to listen, hoping I had heard them wrong.

But no. My mother continued, "Who knows what *she* was like. Who knows what really happened."

"I know," my father said. "The agency could have lied."

My heart pounded as I kept listening. *Depression . . . mental illness . . . alcohol and drugs . . . teen pregnancy.*

Their words slashed through me, filling me with rage. I knew I was a difficult, moody disappointment, but in a lot of ways, it all seemed like typical teenager stuff—hardly a big enough crime for them to start casting stones at the woman who birthed me and had given them the "treasure" they always claimed I was. Yet the worst part was that suddenly, it all rang true to me. Their theories about my birth mother would certainly explain a few things, that's for sure. Maybe she was the root of my problem—she *and* my birth dad. And so now, along with the rage, I realized I was feeling shame, too. A lovely combination.

"Do you think we can talk her into going to college?" I heard my mother say.

"If she even gets in."

My mother said even if I did, it made no sense to pay all that money if I wasn't going to try. It was bad enough that they had to pull teeth to get me to fill out the application for Missouri. They weren't going to keep spoon-feeding me. I'd have to find out on my own what the world was like.

That's when they took it to a whole new level, saying you couldn't really make someone change. My dad said he would have killed to go to college. My mom said if only I tried half as hard as Charlotte. Then they circled right back to where they started, blaming my biology, coming right out and saying *it's the only thing that explains the difference between the girls.* In other words, nature over nurture. I wasn't *their* fault; I was *her* fault. I felt myself blaming her, too, while a sad irony washed over me. Even though she had given me away, this was the first time in my life that I had truly felt rejected, disowned, downright unloved. And it was my own parents' fault.

Devastated, I returned to bed, putting my face under the covers, clenching my fists, telling myself not to cry if only because it would make me look like shit in the morning. I couldn't afford to be one drop more ugly than I already was.

I squeezed my eyes shut, thinking of her as I often did at night, a rapid succession of faces flashing in my brain, until I settled where I usually did: on a cross between Meryl Streep and Laura Linney. But this time, she was a sickly, crackhead version of the two actresses, my fantasies of a glamorous, successful mother quickly fading.

In that moment, I decided I was going to find her. I was going to find out the truth about who she was and why she had given me away. I would turn eighteen in just a few months, and the day I did, the very *morning* I did, I would call the agency and get her name and address. Until then, I would save up for a ticket to wherever she was. I would show my parents, show *everyone*. Show them what, I wasn't exactly sure, but I would figure that out once I got there.

So on April Fools' Day (the biggest *joke* of a birthday), I called the agency, then, as directed, sent them a fax with my social security number and signature. Two minutes later, I had an answer in my in-box. My hands shaking, I read: *Marian Caldwell,* along with a New York City address. It took everything I had not to Google her, but I worried that if I did, I'd somehow find an excuse to chicken out, even if it was as simple as her looking mean in her picture. I didn't want anything to sway me from my plan. I didn't want to write her a letter and wait for months for it to be answered—or worse, *not* answered. I didn't want anything to be on her terms when everything had been on her terms in the beginning. It was my turn. And this was my way.

So right after my birthday, and before a long, four-day weekend, I put the genius plan that Belinda helped me orchestrate into action (genius because it was so easy). I simply asked my parents if I could join Belinda and her mother on a road trip to Mobile to visit Belinda's aunt (after planting a few offhand fibs about said aunt being a former Catholic missionary). I got permission after they called Belinda's mom to confirm the trip. Then I told Belinda's mom that I wasn't feeling well, banking on the only element of luck—that Mrs. Greene wouldn't phone my parents to discuss the cancellation. Sure enough, she did not, and the next day I went down to the bus station on Fifteenth Street and bought a two-hundred-seventy-five-dollar round-trip ticket to New York City, and boarded a foul-smelling Greyhound bus with what seemed to be a good many ex-cons, including a shady driver.

For the next twenty-four hours, I rode that bus halfway across the country, listening to my iPod and wondering about her and her story. Had she been too poor, too young, or too sick to keep me? Or did she just not want me? Had she ever regretted her decision? Had she pulled herself up by her bootstraps since then, changing her life completely?

Did she want me to find her? Had she ever looked for me? Was she married now? Did she have children who she kept who would be my half siblings? Who was my father (there was nothing on him in the file)? Did I get all my loser genes from her, him, or both of them? Were they still together, raising my full-blooded siblings? Would meeting her help me understand why I am the way I am? Or just make me feel worse? With every scenario, I made a list of pros and cons. If she was an awful loser, my parents would be right— and maybe I'd be destined to be that way, too. On the other hand, if my parents were wrong about her, then I disproved their theory, but would have to confront another problem: Why didn't she want me? And would my life have been so much better if she had? Would I still feel the way I do now inside—dark and frustrated and lonely? There seemed to be no winning—and a huge chance for losing. But then again, what else was new?

And then I finally arrive at the Port Authority terminal, a scary shit hole, smelling worse than the bus, which I didn't think was possible. I look around with no clue where to go. The three people I ask either don't speak English or have no desire to reply to me. I finally see a sign for taxis and follow the arrows to the street, emerging onto Eighth Avenue, which looks nothing like the New York I've seen on television and in the movies. Overwhelmed, I find a uniformed worker barking at everyone. She looks right through me, but I speak up, ask her if this is where I can get a taxi. She points to the back of a very long line. As I wait, I keep my eyes fixed on a homeless woman across the street. She is huddled under a gray quilt, a cardboard sign propped against her, a paper cup at her feet. I wonder if she's my mother—maybe she's just been evicted from the address the agency sent.

Twenty minutes later, I am climbing into a cab, which is surprisingly clean, a hopeful sign. I give the driver the address I've memorized as he lurches full speed ahead, stopping and starting every few blocks, the scenery quickly improving. We drive through a wooded area, that I assume is Central Park, and then emerge into a neighborhood that looks residential. A minute later, he stops, looks at me, points at the meter. It reads $9.60. I hand him eleven dollars—and remember advice my dad once gave me: When in doubt, tip. I give him another buck. Then I grab my backpack from the seat next to me, slide out of the car onto Eighty-eighth Street and Madison Avenue and look up at the residence of my birth mother.

Damn, I think. *I did it.*

I glance down at my black Swatch watch, nervously loosening the polyurethane strap one notch, then tightening it again. It is nearly eleven, probably too late to go knocking on her door, but I can't wait until the morning to find out the truth. I remind myself that this is the city that never sleeps, hoping she is up, then hoping nobody is home.

I pace in the shadows of the sidewalk, my stomach in knots. It's hard to say what I want more—for me to like her or for her to like me. After stalling a few more seconds, I finally force myself to walk to the open doorway of her building and peer around the lobby. It is fancy, with a gleaming, black-and-white marble floor and formal furniture. The crack den notion quickly vanishes, but I'm more intimidated than relieved. My heart pounding, a doorman suddenly materializes, asking if he can help me.

I jump, then say hello. He says hello back, friendly enough. He has shiny black hair, neatly gelled into a low side part, and wears a navy and gold uniform with a matching hat. His nametag reads JAVIER—but for a second, I think it says "Caviar"—which I picture her eating on a high floor above me.

"I'm here to see Marian Caldwell," I say, trying to sound more official than I must look in my jeans, T-shirt, and pilled sweater coat. I nervously pluck a few balls of fuzz from my sleeve, wishing I had Googled her, after all. Belinda was right—I should have been more prepared for this moment. I would have worn something nicer. Maybe I wouldn't have come at all.

"She expecting you?" Javier asks, giving me a curious once-over.

I panic, worried that he has been warned about the possible arrival of a troubled teenager. Then, as I hear Belinda telling me not to be paranoid, frequent advice from her, I reassure myself Javier doesn't know a thing about me—he's just doing his job. Just in case, though, I smile, so as to look, at the very least, untroubled. Then I clear my throat and say, "Yes . . . I mean, she very well *might* be."

Technically this is true. She *might* be waiting for me, expecting me, hoping for me. After all, she did sign the paper that said I could know her name on my eighteenth birthday—which she had to have remembered was a week ago. Surely she keeps track of my birthdays. It seems the very least a woman could do who, you know, gives *birth* to a child and then gives her away. She might even have a little annual ritual or ceremony she performs. Maybe she sips champagne with her closest friends or her own mother, my grandmother. Maybe she bakes a cake, adding a candle with every passing year. I wonder if she loves chocolate as much as I do. Or maybe she will tell me the sweet tooth came straight from my birth father. The answers might be seconds away.

As Javier turns and pushes a button on a large switchboard, I strongly consider bolting. But instead, I hold as still as the marble statues flanking the elevator, even holding my breath as I anticipate the sound of her voice, asking who is here to see her. But there is only a loud buzzing noise in response and Javier turns to me and says, "You can go ahead up!" with a grand gesture toward the elevator.

I take this as a good sign. She is, by nature, welcoming, granting permission to visit when she has no idea who is at her door. Then again, maybe she thinks I'm someone else. Maybe she has a real daughter who ran out to the store for some gum or milk—and frequently forgets her key.

In any event, there is no turning back now. "Um . . . what floor?"

"That'd be the penthouse!" Javier says, pointing skyward with great flair.

I nod, as if I'm told to go to the penthouse every day of the week, but inside, the word causes panic. I readjust my backpack, swallow, and take the few steps to the polished elevator doors. They suddenly open, exposing an old man in high-waisted pants walking a tidily groomed toy poodle in a pink sweater and purple rhinestone collar. The two don't go together at all, except for the fact that they both survey me with disapproval as I step past them. Once in the elevator alone, I take a deep breath, and push the PH button. When the doors close, I quickly practice my introduction, with slight variations:

42

Hello. I'm Kirby Rose. Your daughter.

Hello. I'm your daughter. Kirby Rose.

Hi. My name is Kirby Rose. I think I'm your daughter?

The word daughter seems too intimate, but there is really no other word to use (besides technical ones like "offspring" or "progeny"), and no adjective to clarify the relationship, as there is with *birth* mother. My thoughts jolt to a standstill as the elevator doors open directly into the foyer of an apartment. Beyond the foyer, I can see the living room with large windows covering one whole wall. Everything is neat, sleek, perfect, and there is no sign of children or babies. My relief over this fact makes me uneasy; I already care too much.

And then. There she is, walking gracefully toward me in cotton pajamas in a preppy pink and green print. They are a bit baggy, but I can tell she is slim, an average height. She looks younger than my parents, about thirty-five, although it's tough to guess the age of grown-ups. She has blond hair highlighted even blonder, pulled back in a messy but stylish ponytail. Her face is thin and longish, and for a second I see myself in her. Maybe our noses or chins? I decide that it's just wishful thinking; she is way prettier than I am.

I look down at her bare feet, dainty and narrow, her toes painted a deep plum—so unlike my mother's broad, callused feet and oddly shaped toes. I look back at her face, into her eyes, and decide she looks kind. At the very least she doesn't look bitchy, and she is probably smart and hardworking, too, because dumb, lazy people don't end up in the penthouse. Then again, maybe she has a really rich family, but she doesn't have that Paris Hilton-y, spoiled look.

"Hello," she says, her voice light and pleasant, her expression curious. "Can I help you?"

43

I clear my throat and ask, "Are you Marian Caldwell?"

"Yes," she says, and for one second, I have the feeling she knows. But then I see a flicker of impatience. The baby she had eighteen years ago is the farthest thing from her mind.

I look down at my shoes, take a deep breath, and try not to mumble. "My name is Kirby Rose."

No reaction, of course. She doesn't know my name. I tuck a piece of hair behind my ears and force myself to look into her eyes again. Something changes in them.

Sure enough, she says, "Are you? . . ."

My pulse quickens as I nod, trying to breathe, trying not to faint. Then I say the words I've said in my head a thousand times. "I think you're my mother."

Her smile fades, all the color draining from her already fair complexion, as she stares into my eyes. She looks more scared than I am, completely frozen. An eternity seems to go by before she reaches out and touches my arm and says, "Oh . . . Goodness. It *is* you."

I smile, but my throat feels so tight and dry that I can't speak and start to worry that I'm going to cry. I don't, though. It feels like a pretty major victory.

"Please. Come in," she says, backing up, motioning for me to step forward.

I take a few small steps and say, "I'm sorry to roll up on you like this. I can come back another time. . . ."

"No. Stay. *Please* stay," she says.

I nod, telling myself she means it. That she has to be at least a *little* bit happy to see me again.

4

Marian

It is the most surreal, disorienting, and downright dreamlike thing that has ever happened to me. Yet at the same time, I don't know why I'm so shocked. After all, I always knew that this moment could happen and was acutely aware that she turned eighteen on the first of this month: the golden birthday when all she had to do was call the agency and ask for the contact information that I updated every few years, as a matter of course. I was under no legal obligation to do so—I could have chosen to remain anonymous—so I'm not really sure what made me do it. Maybe it was strictly to alleviate guilt, because it seemed like the right thing to do. Maybe part of me was waiting for the assurance that she was okay—that I hadn't given her to a dysfunctional, ignorant, impoverished family. But maybe, on some deep-down level, I wanted her to return to me. Maybe I wanted to see and touch her again.

Regardless of why I did it or what I wanted, I truly didn't think she would try to contact me, at least not for years and years, until after she had children of her own. And I certainly didn't imagine that it would happen out of the complete blue at eleven o'clock at night in a city where drop-in visits simply don't occur, even among the closest of friends. After a fight with my boyfriend, no less. That is all beside the point now. Because she is right here, standing before me, waiting for me to say something.

In a haze of emotion, I insist that she come in, silently hanging her jacket in the hall closet and stowing her heavy backpack under a long ottoman in my foyer. I pause awkwardly, considering a venue for our first conversation. The living room feels too formal, while my small den, where I keep all my personal mementos, too intimate. I don't think I'm trying to hide anything from her; I just don't want to overwhelm her—or somehow give myself a home court advantage. So I settle on the kitchen, flipping on the lights, then dimming them, then turning them up again. I gesture toward two stools positioned at my marble-top island and we sit on opposite sides, nervously gazing at each other, our faces frozen in expectant smiles. I know that as uneasy as I am, she has to be more so, if only because she is half my age and in unfamiliar surroundings.

I frantically search for something to say, something weightier than idle small talk and something lighter than the cold, bare facts of how her life began. I come up empty-handed, which only makes me more anxious and flustered.

"Are you hungry?" I finally say, standing to open the refrigerator. I stare down at a row of Vitamin Waters, a bag of European lettuce, a container of egg whites, and a large container of Greek yogurt, cursing myself for not swinging by Dean & Deluca on the way home from work yesterday, my usual Friday routine.

"No, thank you," she says as I repeat her name in my head, a name that never once occurred to me in all of these years of wondering what it could be. *Kirby. Kirby. Kirby.* I can't decide whether I hate it or love it, but give her parents points for originality—and resist the sudden, overwhelming urge to ask about them. What do they do for a living? What are their politics and religion? Do they look anything like her? Like *us,* I think, still startled by our resemblance, one that is becoming increasingly clear to me despite the fact that I've never been good at seeing such likenesses. I suppress all questions about them, worried that my curiosity will come across as invasive or jealous, just as I realize that for the first time ever, I actually *am* a bit jealous that another woman had a hand in shaping the person sitting before me. The fact that I have absolutely no right to feel this way, that it was entirely my decision to give her to them, only makes the wistfulness grow and expand in my chest. I tell myself that I've endured none of the hardships of motherhood, that it's like watching a marathon and wishing you were crossing the finish line. I tell myself to stop being so self-centered. This night is about *her* needs, not mine, and although I am not her mother in the true sense of the word, I try to conjure something of a maternal instinct. I think of my own mother, and her solution to many problems: comfort food and a good night's sleep.

"Are you sure you're not hungry? We can order. There's a great deli nearby that will deliver a grilled cheese and tomato soup inside ten minutes. It's like they always have one ready, figuring someone in a ten-block radius has to be in the mood for a grilled cheese."

Realizing that I'm babbling, I stop talking, and she shakes her head, thanking me again.

Overcome with a fresh wave of emotion, I hide my face, turning back to the refrigerator. "Can I at least get you something to drink? Coffee? Tea? Vitamin Water?"

She hesitates, then, almost as if she's humoring me, says, "Sure. I'll take a Vitamin Water."

"What flavor?" I ask. "Orange or lemon?"

47

"It doesn't matter."

"No. I guess it really doesn't," I say more to myself than her. Then I steady my hands as I select an orange one, unscrew the cap, and pour it into a tall glass.

"How did you get here?" I ask, dying to know where her journey began, craving a visual of her neighborhood, her house, her bedroom. I have never been this greedy for information—not even at the start of a relationship when you're eager, even desperate, to know everything about someone. In fact, it occurs to me that staring at her face, waiting for her to speak, feels a little bit like falling in love. There is intrigue and affection, with a narcissistic, needy ingredient.

"I took a bus," she says, as I notice a complete lack of an accent. At least there is nothing in her voice that I can detect or trace to a particular geography. "Greyhound."

"Oh," I say, horrified, remembering the story of the man who decapitated his seatmate on a Greyhound bus.

"Yeah. It was sort of gross. But it got me here."

I nod and say, "And where do you live?"

"St. Louis."

"Is that where you're from? Originally?"

"Well. Originally I'm from Chicago," she says, flashing me a pointed look. "But yeah, I've lived my whole life in St. Louis. In the same house."

I digest this with the eerie memory of my first and only trip to St. Louis, about ten years ago, when Kirby would have been seven or eight. I went there for a friend's wedding, and after the ceremony, rather than heading straight to the reception, I went for a walk alone, meandering around the blocks surrounding the church. I distinctly remember the damp chill of the air, the steel-gray of the sky, and the thin, low-hanging clouds, all of which compounded the loneliness that comes with attending a wedding solo. I remember the sound of my heels crunching in the scattered remains of late fall leaves and the look of the modest brick bungalows with their gambrel roofs, stained-glass windows, and tidy, manicured yards. House after cozy house, many with American flags, window boxes filled with flowers, and metal screen doors adorned with initials. Most of all I remember turning the corner back toward the church parking lot and being filled with an intense pang, almost a longing for her, along with the chilling sense that she was nearby. Looking back, it seems an unlikely, eerie premonition—but then I realize that the feeling wasn't at all unusual. I got it almost any time I was in a new setting, with strangers, and sometimes even in my own neighborhood. Yet I still confide the story now, telling her of the coincidence.

She looks skeptical but humors me. "Where was the wedding, exactly? What part of town?"

"I don't recall," I tell her. "It was a big Catholic church. Huge. Stone. Stained glass. St. Joseph's? Or Mary's, maybe?"

She says, "That really doesn't narrow it down."

Her reply isn't impolite, but from it, I glean that she is not only smart but capable of being a smartass.

"No. I guess it doesn't," I say.

"But it *could* have been in my neighborhood," she says, softening slightly. "I live in South St. Louis. Near St. Gabriel the Archangel. That's our parish. Could the wedding have been there?"

"Maybe," I say, picturing her skipping along the sidewalk in a gaggle of girls, clad in navy and white Catholic-school girl uniforms. Crisp, pleated plaid skirts and woolen cable knee socks. On the way to a soda shop. One of them daring the others to smoke a cigarette that Kirby refuses.

She holds my gaze then hesitates, taking a deep breath. "Well, guess what?"

"What?" I ask.

"Even though you had me in Chicago . . . I had a feeling you lived in New York." She shrugs as if this admission embarrasses her as I wonder what she knows about me. Has she seen any of the few press photos of me at red-carpet events? Or maybe even the blurb with Peter from Page Six?

"Yes," I say. "I've lived here a few years. I work in television—so it's sort of here or L.A."

She looks surprised—which in turn surprises me. "Television? Are you an actress?"

"No. I'm a producer."

"Of movies?"

"No. Television. Have you heard of the show *South Second Street* . . . ?"

"Yes!" she says with a jolt of girly enthusiasm and a huge smile. I notice that her bottom teeth are slightly crooked, the middle two overlapping. She clearly hasn't had braces, and I wonder whether her parents can't afford them or simply decided she didn't need them badly enough, maybe even wanting to keep the character in her smile.

I smile back at her. "That's my show."

"I love that show. It's *so* good," she says. "I like that contractor guy. Shaba Derazi? Is that his name?"

I nod. "Yeah. He's a good guy. . . . He's actually filming a movie in Toronto right now. With Matt Damon."

She looks giddy with the inside information—although not as thrilled as I am that she knows and likes my work.

At the same time, I feel guilty that I know nothing about her fears or passions or dreams for the future. I don't know whether she is left or right brained, athletic or uncoordinated, introverted or extroverted. I don't know if she's ever been in love or had her heart broken. And although I understand that being in the dark about these things is part of the deal with adoptions, at least closed adoptions, I still feel a sense of shame for being so clueless about my own flesh and blood. I look away, as my mind races through the last eighteen years, filling her face and name in to all the generic scenes I've imagined, often against my absolute determination not to think about her. *Kirby swaddled in a bassinet. Kirby learning to crawl, walk, talk. Kirby climbing onto a big yellow school bus on her first day of kindergarten. Kirby losing her first tooth. Kirby waking up on Christmas morning and racing downstairs in a red flannel nightgown to find a Barbie Dream House.* At least I hoped these were the visions of her life, and nothing resembling the guilty nightmares I sometimes had. *Kirby, hungry, cold, lonely, abused.* I look at her, overwhelmed with the relief that she is okay. At least she appears to be okay.

"So. Tell me more. Tell me all about yourself," I say.

She crosses her arms, and says, "What do you want to know?"

"I'm sorry. I don't mean to sound like I'm interviewing you."

"It's okay," she says, but still offers no information.

"So. I know how old you are," I say. "Eighteen."

She nods, expressionless. "Yeah. I had to be eighteen to get your name."

I nod, remembering the contract I signed—as well as the lie I told on the signed, sworn affidavit. *I don't know the identity of the birth father.* I push him out of my brain, as I've done a thousand times before, and at least a dozen tonight.

"So you're a senior?" I say.

She nods.

"Are you going to college next year?"

"I don't know. I just got into Missouri . . . Last week." She shrugs, then glances out the window overlooking a darkened Madison Avenue. "But I really don't want to go to college."

Her answer disappoints me, but I pretend to be unfazed. "You can always take a year off to think about it," I say. "That's what I did."

My voice trails off. She gives me a look, and I can tell she suspects what I did during that year, but she doesn't ask. Instead she clears her throat and says, "So I'm sure you're wondering why I'm here . . ."

Without thinking or hesitating, I reach across the table and cover her hand with mine. Her fingers are cool, slender, delicate, her middle one dwarfed by a large turquoise ring that extends up to her knuckle. She tenses, but doesn't recoil, and I return my hand to my lap. "You don't need a reason," I say.

She gives me a look I can't read and says, "I just . . . needed to meet you . . . I felt like . . . something was missing . . . you know . . . not knowing . . . where I came from and stuff . . ."

I consider echoing the sentiment in a knee-jerk fashion, implying that something has been missing in my life, too, but know this isn't true. Earlier tonight the only thing I thought was missing was a proposal from Peter.

"Well, I'm glad you're here," I say instead, although

I'm fairly certain that this is an overstatement if not an outright lie.

She swallows and waits as we both stare at each other awkwardly then look away in unison.

"Okay. How about this," I say, focusing on a fleck of gold in the marble counter. "I ask you a question. Then you ask me one. We'll take turns. Anything goes."

She nods, as I realize that it is a dangerous game for me. What will I tell her when she asks about him? The truth, of course, but there are so many gradations and interpretations of the truth that such a thing, in its pure form, practically doesn't exist. At least it hasn't in my life—and maybe that is true for everyone.

"Okay. Let's see . . . Do you have any siblings?" I say.

"One sister," she says, and then tells me that her parents thought they couldn't have children but then got pregnant right after they adopted her. "Her name is Charlotte. She was a miracle," Kirby adds, expressionless.

"Are you close?"

She shrugs. "Yeah, Charlotte's cool. Really nice. And she's a crazy good swimmer with the best butterfly time in the city's history. She has Olympic potential—she's that good." She gives me a telltale eye roll and says, "Everyone loves her."

"Wow. Maybe a little too perfect?" I guess.

"You could say that."

I smile, but she remains stone-faced.

"Your turn," I say.

She bites her lip, then copies my question and asks if I have any siblings.

"No. I'm an only child. My parents love to travel and thought it was easier with one child," I say, the explanation

I've always accepted at face value suddenly sounding ridiculous.

She nods, then whispers. "Your turn."

I glance up at the pair of chrome pendant light fixtures above the island and remember watching Peter change the bulbs last week. It is the extent of his handiness. "Do you have a boyfriend?" I ask, hoping the answer is no.

She shakes her head and fires back, "No. Do you?"

I nod, thinking of my conversation with Peter, one that now feels as if it took place at least two weeks ago rather than less than two hours ago. "Yes. We've been together a few years." I stop there, deciding that anything else is too much information, at least for now. Then I swallow and ask her about her favorite subject in school.

"I don't have one," she says.

"Fair enough," I say, then wait for her turn.

"Okay. I know this is sort of a rude question," she finally says. "But how old are you?"

I smile and say, "It's not rude for another four years. I'm thirty-six."

I can see her doing the math in her head as I give her the answer. "I was eighteen when I had you. Your age."

She inhales sharply. "Oh," she says, glancing away again. I study her profile, deciding that while our chins are similar, hers is better, slightly stronger than mine but still feminine. Her cheekbones are more defined, too, and I know where she gets them. I think of him now, again, in a rush of visual memories, wondering how many more questions until we get to him. I feel myself start to yawn, try to stifle it and lose the fight. She yawns back, as I remember reading that the urge to sleep is a powerful biological response to stress and pain, both of which I'm feeling now.

54

"I should go," she says, as I notice dark, bluish circles under her eyes. "I know it's really late."

My heart sinks, yet a larger part of me is relieved that she won't be staying. That his name hasn't come up—and that maybe it never will. Maybe I'll never have to tell her the painful memories that I've spent eighteen years trying to bury.

She stands, making a slow move toward the doorway.

"Where are you going?" I ask, expecting her to tell me she has a friend or relative in the city.

She removes a wrinkled piece of paper from her back pocket and reads off the name of a youth hostel with an address near Chinatown. I feel an enormous rush of guilt and shake my head. "Absolutely not. You're staying here."

She opens her mouth, as if poised to protest, but then closes it, looking too exhausted to try.

"One more thing," I say, bracing myself.

She raises her eyebrows, as I clear my throat and ask if her parents know she's here.

She stares into her glass, a clear no.

"Do you still live with them?" I say.

She nods, looking slightly indignant, and says, "I didn't run away if that's what you're asking."

"I'm sorry," I say. "I just . . . wondered . . . ?"

"They think I'm in Alabama. With my friend and her mother."

"So they don't know that you planned to do . . . this?"

"Do this?" she says with the faintest trace of hostility, although she must know what I'm getting at.

"Meet me," I clarify.

Now downright defiant, she shakes her head. I wait

for her to meet my gaze, knowing that we're at a pivotal moment. I know what I should do—insist that she phone them—but I'm afraid to do it. What if she gets angry? What if she leaves and never comes back? Then again, she's a teenager, thousands of miles away from her parents. I ask why she lied to them, trying to understand her situation before I make a decision or pass judgment.

"This is none of their business," she says. "And frankly, they are none of yours."

"Okay . . . Listen . . . I'm not going to try to make you do anything, but—"

"But what?" she snaps, her eyes flashing, her jaw set in a stubborn line. Although I know I'm not her real mother, it is my first taste of what it's like to be one. It fills me with a sense of fear and inadequacy. "There's no reason to call and upset them. Besides, I'm eighteen. An adult. Technically. So it's cool."

I nod, afraid of pressing her and upsetting the fragile understanding that we've crafted in the last few moments. "Okay. We can talk about it tomorrow," I say. "I just—I just want you to be okay. Whatever is going on in your life. Whatever you're feeling . . . I just want to help you."

I mean what I'm saying—at least I think I do—but the words sound thin. Like an actor who has no emotional connection to a scene and has to use a menthol tear stick to cry.

"Thank you," she says as we yawn in unison again. Then we stand and face each other.

"You're welcome, Kirby," I say. It is the first time I've said her name aloud, and I wonder how I possibly could have ever not known it. That I ever could have thought of her as a Katherine, the name I had called her during those first three days—now seeming too formal, too traditional, too ordinary for the girl she seems to be.

I lead her back into the hall, collect her bag, and show her to the guest bedroom, next to mine. I point out the attached bathroom, the linen closet full of towels and extra blankets, and the drawer stocked with hotel toiletries in case she forgot anything. Then I wish her a good night and tell her to come get me if she needs anything. Anything at all.

An hour after I've taken an Ambien, I am still alert and wide-eyed, staring into the complete blackness of my bedroom—a tough thing to achieve in New York City, especially in a corner building. I think of the day I told my decorator that I didn't much care whether we went with cool colors or warm, an upholstered headboard or iron bed, as long as I had custom window treatments that blocked out all traces of light from the street below. Yet suddenly, for the first time in my adulthood, I am afraid of the dark—or at least afraid *in* the dark. It is an irrational feeling yet I roll over and quickly snap on the light the way I did as a child, my eyes darting about the corners of the room. It occurs to me that maybe I'm afraid for Kirby, but I resist the urge to go and check on her; it feels presumptuous on the heels of eighteen years of utter cluelessness.

So instead, I check my phone, wishing there was someone I could talk to about the biggest news I've had since she was born. Without a much longer conversation, there is only one option—my mother. But I know she is asleep next to my father and the only way to call her would be to awaken both of them. My father would assume the worst—that there is terrible news. Which he would probably deem this to be—one of the reasons my mother and I chose to keep this secret from him in the first place. Besides, I really don't want to talk to her about it, not yet anyway, remembering her advice to check a different box on that form. *It is for the best if you cut all ties, forever.* It was clear that's what she wanted, and although I never knew if it were for her sake, mine, or both, the memory has often kept me from discussing it with her.

I nervously scroll through my e-mail and texts, wondering if Peter is awake. I suddenly miss him, and desperately wish we hadn't ended our evening the way we did. More important, I wish he knew my secret. I wish I had told him, suddenly regretting my decision not to tell him. I think of all the logical times I could have—every time a friend had a baby; when he told me Aidan's birth story, how Robin's water broke during an opera and how she nearly delivered in a taxi on Third Avenue; or when he confessed *his* own deepest secrets—that he plagiarized a paper at Dartmouth and once slept with a stripper at a bachelor party in Vegas. I didn't judge him—and don't believe he would have judged me. And yet, he *might*. He might decide that any woman who could give up a child isn't fit to be a mother. At least not a mother of *his* child. He might have a problem, at the very least, with the fact that I kept the secret from my own father, from the *baby*'s father. There were just too many risks involved, too much downside. It was easier to leave it alone. Cleaner. Simpler. Safer. Or so I thought until now.

I switch off the light and close my eyes, but the desperate feeling of wanting to talk to him will not subside. So I send him a text, asking if he's up. Seconds later, my phone vibrates. I grab it, eager for his words, the way I always am when he writes, but much more so tonight. I text as fast as I can, reassured with every exchange.

PETER: Yup.
MARIAN: Can't sleep?
PETER: Nope. Feel bad about earlier.
MARIAN: It's okay.
PETER: No. It's not. I'm sorry.
MARIAN: I am too. Wish you were here.
PETER: Do you want me to come over?

Before I can reply no, the phone rings and I greedily answer it, still following my ingrained instinct to keep my secret, spinning fresh justifications, excuses.

"You okay, sweetie?" he says, his voice sexy and scratchy. I hear ice in a glass and know that he is sipping scotch, his version of Ambien.

I try to answer, but can't.

"Champ?" he says. "You there?"

"I'm here," I say, managing to make my voice sound even and normal.

He asks again if I'm okay, a tinge of guilt in his voice— which, in turn, makes me feel guilty for being upset with him. How can I expect a man to commit to me forever when I've omitted such an important detail about my life?

"Yes," I say. "I'm here."

"Do you want me to come over?" he asks gently.

I desperately want him to be beside me, but then think of Kirby in the next room and tell him no, it's late, I'll call him in the morning.

But he's already made his decision. "I'm coming over," he says, then hangs up before I can protest again.

*

Twenty minutes later he is in my room, undressing down to his white Brooks Brothers boxers, the only kind he ever wears. The smell of his skin comforts me, as does the heat of his body next to mine.

"Now," he says. "That's much better. Talk to me."

I glance toward the door, even though he's whispering, worried that she'll hear us.

I swallow hard, wondering what to say, how to begin.

"I'm sorry I upset you," he starts, holding me.

"No. It was my fault . . ." I say, trying to stop him right there, the guilt beginning to choke me.

But he continues, "No. You were trying to talk about our future—and I was . . . dismissive. Let's talk about it now."

"It's okay," I say.

"Why not? C'mon, Champ . . . I didn't mean to imply that I *never* want to marry again . . . I just meant that—"

The conversation I was so desperate to have suddenly feels trivial as I say, "Peter. This isn't what you think. I'm not upset about that . . . I mean, I was—but this is . . . something else."

"What? What is it?" he asks, his voice kind but with a tinge of frustration, impatience.

My mind races, knowing exactly how I *could* cut to the chase: *Peter, my eighteen-year-old daughter is asleep in the next room.*

But I'm unable to get those words out—or begin the story at all.

Instead I stammer, "It's something else—something I have to tell you. I—I've kept a secret from you." I feel relieved the second the words are out. At the same time, I regret my cryptic Lifetime television preamble.

"What kind of secret?" he asks.

"A pretty big one," I say.

"What? Did you kill someone?" he asks with a nervous laugh. And then—"Sorry. That wasn't funny. Even if you did, you could tell me. You can tell me anything."

"I didn't *kill* anyone, Peter," I say, thinking of that word, *abortion,* that haunted me that summer. Was it taking a life? I could not decide, then or now. All I knew was that I couldn't go through with it. I wonder if I had made another choice, whether I would have kept that a secret, too. I wonder how I would feel if I were making that confession to Peter. If the shame would have felt greater than it does now. I remind myself that I did the right thing—by having her, by giving her away. Then I bury my face in my pillow as he continues his questioning.

"Was it before me? I mean—it's not about us, is it? You didn't make out with Damien Brady, did you?" he asks, referring to the male star of my show. He is joking, but I wonder if he'd view that as a lesser or greater betrayal.

"No," I say, burying my face in my pillow. "It's not about you. It's about me. And something that happened to me eighteen years ago."

"What? What, Marian? Please just tell me. It's not going to change the way I feel about you."

"You can't promise that," I say.

He takes a deep breath, then reaches over and kisses me, a hard, openmouthed kiss that lasts more than a few seconds. His tongue is soft, warm, reassuring. When we separate, he says, "Rip off the Band-Aid, Marian. Just tell me."

And so I do, the words awkwardly tumbling out of me, the story unfolding in its bare-bones form, starting with that summer, ending with the knock on the door a few hours ago. I can't look at him until I have finished, afraid of what I might find. Disapproval, disappointment, judgment. And sure enough, when I do, it is all there, although he is doing his best to hide it.

"I never told anyone," I say, as if this makes it better that I didn't tell him. "Except for my mother."

"Well. Thank you for finally telling me," he says.

"Do you still love me?" I ask him.

"Of course," he says, and although he sounds convincing, I know there is a big difference between love and trust.

"Are you sure?" I ask.

"Yes," he says.

But what choice does he have? We both know he can't retrade on the grand promise he just made. At least not tonight, here in the dark. At least not before he hears the part of the story that I intentionally left out.

5

Kirby

I find the photograph of Marian and what must be her parents—my grandparents—the following morning as I tiptoe around her sleek living room, one eye on her closed bedroom door, careful not to get caught snooping. There are a lot of abstract paintings in the room, but it is the only photo—a black-and-white eight-by-ten in a sterling frame engraved with Marian's initials. In it, she and her mother are wearing party dresses, her mother's beaded, Marian's long and floral. Her father is in a tuxedo. They are standing in a vineyard, next to an olive tree with a dramatic background of a valley and blue mountains. Marian is in the middle, her arms around her parents, and they are all laughing. I have the feeling that Marian's father just cracked a joke as he has the sort of satisfied look that comes after you've said something funny. He is lean and tall with a long nose placed on a long face, and a neatly trimmed beard, all of which remind me of a bearded Atticus or a modern-day Abraham Lincoln. And although he is not that handsome, he has the sort of face you want to keep looking at. Her mother is the opposite—petite, elegant, and beautiful, but generic. Her hair is sprayed into a stylish bob, and she is dripping with diamonds. Marian looks about like she does now, only younger and thinner, her hair longer. She is barefoot, her strappy sandals kicked off in the grassy foreground, and she wears no jewelry other than a small gold pendant that appears to be a cursive *M*. I imagine that they are at a family wedding, at some fancy spot like Napa Valley (although I'm not even sure exactly where that is). In a few moments, some huge-ass cake will be cut, pink champagne poured, and a big brass band will play Sinatra while everyone dances, ballroom style, under the stars.

As I pick up the photo and stare at it more closely, I feel a sudden longing, although I can't describe exactly why. Would I rather be part of this family? Or is it a simple matter of wishing I had been at the party that night? I put the frame back down on the table, one fact crystallizing in my mind: Marian is rich. I think of the photos in my house—class pictures lining the stairwell and fuzzy snapshots cluttering up the mantel—and can't help but wonder how different my life would have been if she had kept me. It's not that we're poor, but still. Who doesn't want to be rich? Besides, she can no longer use money as an excuse to give me away. She could have easily afforded to keep me. It *could* have been done. She just didn't *want* to. The realization doesn't make me angry, but it does sting a little, and I can't help feeling a little bitter that here she was, living large, when, for all she knew, I could have been on food stamps. Somehow it makes it more of a rejection than if she *had* to give me up.

I make my way over to a boxy, white sofa and sit, trying to get comfortable on the rock-hard cushions as I examine the large, glossy books on the glass-topped coffee table, searching for clues about what she likes, who she is. I pick one up called *Hamptons Havens* and begin to flip through it. It is filled with more photos like the one I've just examined, and I wonder if Marian has a summer house there. I'm betting that she does—a huge one she still calls

64

a cottage. Or maybe she prefers Martha's Vineyard, Cape Cod, Nantucket, all the spots in New England that blur together and only ring a bell from my mother's obsession with the Kennedys.

A few seconds later, I hear her bedroom door open. I nervously close the book, doing my best to look as inconspicuous as possible, a difficult task on a white sofa in a sun-drenched room. I look toward the doorway as she emerges in gray velour sweats. Her hair is swept up in a bun, fixed with a comb, and she is wearing brown tortoiseshell glasses that explain my nearsightedness.

"Well, you're an early bird," she says when she spots me, her voice too high, too friendly, fake.

I force a smile back, but feel it fade as my gaze shifts to a male interloper, walking a few paces behind her. Wondering when he arrived, in the middle of the night or this morning, I self-consciously cross my arms in front of my Gap sweatshirt, resenting him for being here and Marian for feeling the need to call in reinforcements. As he comes closer, I can see that he is older than Marian— maybe as many as ten years older—but is handsome in that older-guy kind of way, and he looks important. I can tell by the way she glances back at him, and he gives her an encouraging nod, that she cares very much about his opinion of her—his opinion, period. I fleetingly wonder if he could be my birth father, having heard stories about couples giving their first child away, only to marry later. But I know the far more likely scenario is that my birth father is nothing like this man.

"Kirby, I'd like you to meet Peter. Peter, this is Kirby."

"Nice to meet you, Kirby," Peter says in the confident, deep voice of a news anchorman. He steps toward me, his posture as perfect as his smile, and extends his hand. Sunlight glints off his gold watch, as I stand and nervously shake his hand. His handshake, of course, is strong, borderline painful. I wonder if he is making a point. Regardless, I decide I don't like him—at least I don't like his type.

"It's nice to meet you, too," I mumble, glancing at Marian, waiting for her to fill the silence. But she says nothing, the three of us forming an awkward triangle. Peter finally asks a question that fills the room. "So? I heard you arrived last night?"

I nod, recross my arms, and say yes, my voice as small as his is large. I find myself wondering if he really knows who I am, and how she told the story of my arrival. Was she happy? Upset? Annoyed? Stunned? Was she worried that I'd try to move in, mess up her perfect life? Maybe he had warned her that although we were related, she knew nothing about this stranger in her home. I might be here to steal from her or sneak into her room at night and attack her. Had she called him last night, in a panic? Is that why he had come over? For protection?

If he is suspicious of my motives, he fakes it well (as I bet he always can), booming, "Great. Great." And then, "So what are you girls going to do today?"

Marian shrugs and says, "Oh, I don't know. I think we'll probably just do a little Upper East Side tour. Walk around. Show Kirby my neighborhood."

"The park? The Guggenheim? French toast at Caffe Grazie?" he says.

Marian says, "All of the above. And maybe a little shopping. If Kirby is up for it."

I nod and force a smile, but seriously can't believe that

she's suggesting shopping. Not only do I have zero desire to shop, but the thought also intimidates me, the retail equivalent of not knowing which fork to use at a restaurant.

"Ahh. Barneys. How could I forget?" Peter's tone is teasing. He winks and looks at me. "Be careful. Marian has been known to get trapped in that building, poor thing."

She rolls her eyes and tells him to hush, but he makes another quip about how he's had to rescue her from the jaws of that beast on Madison Avenue. The whole thing is very Hollywood, very Manhattan. Very strange.

A few beats of laughter later, he rubs his palms together and says, "All right. I'm out. Gotta go get Aidan from his mom's."

I process that he is divorced as he looks at me and explains, "My son. Maybe if you're here for a bit, you can meet him. He's about your age. Fifteen. Wait. How old are you, again?"

"Eighteen," I say. "I just look fifteen."

"You'll appreciate it one day," Marian says.

I watch as Peter leans over and kisses Marian on the lips, no other part of their bodies touching, before walking to the door. As I sit back down on the sofa, he turns and gives her a look I can't read. Perhaps it is moral support, maybe it is sympathy. But whatever it is, I glance at her, just in time to see her mouth, *Thank you.*

I look away, wondering what she is thanking him for, if it has anything to do with me.

Fifteen minutes later Marian and I are walking into Caffe Grazie, a bustling restaurant in a two-story town house near Marian's apartment. The hostess smiles at her in recognition, then leads us to a narrow booth in the back of the room where Marian pushes aside her menu and tells me there is only one way to go.

"The French toast?" I say, remembering Peter's words.

"You bet," she says, as our waitress arrives with two glasses of ice water and Marian's coffee.

"Would you like some, hon?" the waitress asks me, holding up the carafe.

I tell her no thank you, and after glancing at my menu and noticing that the orange juice is six dollars a glass, I mumble that I will stick with water.

"We'll both have the chocolate croissant French toast," Marian says.

The waitress nods, then briskly departs as Marian looks at me and says, "So? Is there something in particular that you wanted to do today?"

I shake my head, feeling tempted to make the point that I didn't exactly come here to see the Statue of Liberty or the Empire State Building. And if we *must* do the tourism thing to avoid real conversation, then I'd prefer to check out Carnegie Hall or the Brooklyn Philharmonic or the Jazz Museum in Harlem or one of the city's many music stores I found on the Internet. Like Drummers World that carries everything from Epstein castanets made of rosewood and black grenadillo, to Albright Milt Jackson jazz mallets, to a vintage Rogers kit from the seventies with a fourteen-inch dynasonic snare. I obviously can't afford to buy any of it, but I'd kill to see it up close and test it out. Rogers drums have a richer, more musical sound than most other drums, which are more about a big upfront attack. They are the best freaking drums on the planet—noticeably better sounding as well as being really beautiful. But I don't say any of this—mostly because I have the feeling that she really doesn't want to know.

Instead I shrug and say, "I don't care. Whatever you want to do is cool with me."

"Well . . . Let's see," she says as I stare at her huge diamond stud earrings. "When do you have to be back at school?"

I know what she is getting at—when will I be hitting the road?—so I say, "Wednesday. But . . . I can leave before then. I mean, whatever you want . . . I can go anytime. It's totally up to you."

"Let's play it by ear," Marian says with a little too much cheer. "Stay at least for the night, okay?"

In other words, *not two nights*, I think, and mumble thanks.

She starts to say something, but then stops and taps the newspaper that she toted along with her. "Do you read the Sunday *Times*?"

I tell her no, but in case she thinks I'm some apathetic, clueless teen, I add, "I do read the paper, though. We get the *St. Louis Post-Dispatch*."

I mean, I am apathetic, but only about *my* life, not the whole world, and I do follow current events, unlike most of the kids I know.

She smiles and says, "Well? Would you like a section?"

I tell her I'll take the front page unless she wants it, wondering why we're reading the paper when we've covered about one percent of what I think we need to cover. Including, like, oh, I don't know, who my father is and why they gave me away. Apparently she doesn't feel the same, though, because she hands me the front page as if we've been sharing Sunday newspapers for years. I take it from her, with a surge of frustration, bowing my head to read an article about a suicide bombing in Tel Aviv. I can't concentrate on anything other than the fact that she is across the table from me, which suddenly feels like the freakiest thing ever, our silence only making it more weird. I have the feeling that she is marveling over our reunion, too, because every couple minutes, I can feel her glancing at me up over the Styles section. But maybe that's just wishful thinking. Maybe she's really just moved by something in the newspaper. Something earth-shattering, like the fact that bell bottoms are back in again.

After breakfast, we stroll one block over to Fifth Avenue, where I see my first glimpse of the Metropolitan Museum of Art. The building is huge and important looking, spanning several long blocks—a quarter mile according to Marian—people covering the expanse of steps, some snapping photos, some sitting and reading guidebooks, some just standing there. There is even a group of skaters about my age in hoodies and cargo shorts lounging about as if it is their everyday hangout. A far cry from Francis Park where kids I know hang out—although the clothing is pretty much the same and they are all wearing the same bored expression.

She watches me taking it all in and says, "Impressive, isn't it?"

I say yes, and then drop my only real frame of literary reference, albeit a juvenile one. "I loved *From the Mixed-up Files of Mrs. Basil E. Frankweiler*," I say, trying to remember the details about the little girl who runs away and hides out in the museum. I think her name was Claudia.

Her face lights up as she tells me that she, too, loved that book as a child.

Then she says, "And have you read Edith Wharton's *The Age of Innocence*?"

70

Edith Wharton rings a faint bell, but I haven't read the book—I haven't read any books for pleasure in years except the *Twilight* series (which I liked but for the incessant description of Edward as hot—I mean, how many times and in how many ways can an author tell us that the dude is good-looking?).

"The two protagonists have a clandestine meeting here and one of them says, 'Some day, I suppose, it will be a great Museum' . . . She was actually pretty instrumental in establishing it."

I can't help hanging on her every cultured word, even though I have the feeling she's sort of showing off. Or worse, testing me. Like those college admissions interviews where they're pretending to chat, but really making mental notes about how smart you are. Or in my case, how dumb.

We walk north a block as Marian points across the street at a white limestone building with a green awning. "See that building?" she says. "Ten-forty? Jackie O moved there the year after JFK was killed. She lived there for thirty years. On the fifteenth floor."

She goes on to tell me that her apartment wasn't as grand as you would think; it didn't even have central air. "But it has a gorgeous view of the Central Park Reservoir and the thirty-four-hundred-year-old Temple of Dendur, which she helped bring to the Met from Egypt."

I nod, remembering the one thing my mom always said about Jackie—that she was a world-class mother to John and Caroline—which suddenly seems a lot more important than some temple. I glance at Marian, wondering when—or if—she's going to get real.

We keep walking, finally arriving at the Guggenheim, a large, modern building corkscrewed onto Fifth like a big white ribbon. As I gaze up at it, Marian lapses into tour guide mode again, telling me that it was Frank Lloyd Wright's last major work and that it was very controversial when it opened back in 1959. It took him fifteen years and seven hundred sketches to design, she says, and then laughs and adds, "He once said that it would make the Met look like a Protestant barn. What do you think?"

"I like it," I say, still feeling some weird combination of nervous and resentful, wondering whether I just gave her the right answer. "It's pretty cool looking."

"I *love* it," she says. "I mean, the Met is the Met, but this is one of my favorite spots in the city. Would you like to go in?"

I shrug and nod, then follow her into the cool, dark lobby. She heads to the ticket counter, as I drift toward the center of the room, gaping up at the open-floor spiral toward the ceiling. Like the outside, the interior is like nothing I've ever seen—which apparently is the consensus, as the ground floor is dotted with tourists craning their necks toward the ceiling, snapping photos. I take one with my phone and send it to Belinda with a text (about the fourth update since I arrived) that says: *At the Guggenheim. She's pretty badass. More later.*

It occurs to me that I'm putting a certain spin on the visit, a more positive one than I feel so far, and I find myself wondering what I'm trying to prove, especially when Belinda writes back: *OMG. Way kool! Take one of her!*

I put my phone back into my purse, thinking there's no chance that I'll do that, as we slowly ascend through the tiers of the museum, Marian continuing her soft, competent commentary. She tells me that along with the architectural critics, many artists protested the museum in the early days, too, saying that the curved walls and nooks didn't properly showcase their work. Just like with the newspaper, I realize that I can't fully focus on her words, or the works themselves, just the sound of her voice, the way her face lights up when she points out her favorite Chagalls and Picassos.

When we get to the dead end of the very top layer of the museum, she says, "You know what's crazy?"

"What?" I ask, hoping that she's finally going to say something of substance.

She looks at me, then returns her gaze to the lobby far below. "I've stood right here. Right in this very spot, and thought about you. Wondered where you were. If you were happy."

In spite of myself, a warm, tingly feeling fills my chest, but I don't let on that her words have affected me. Instead, I look down, memorizing the stark white view and say, "Well, now you know."

"Yes," she says. "Now I know."

The morning has warmed and the crowds have swelled when we emerge back onto the sidewalk. I take off my fleece and tie it around my waist as we stroll back down Fifth Avenue, lingering on the stairs of the Met, people-watching, and then making our way down the sidewalk to the shade of Central Park, until we hit the Plaza Hotel, home of Eloise. We cross the street in front of FAO Schwarz then continue over to Madison Avenue, ending up at Barneys, just as Peter predicted.

"Do you like to shop?" she says.

"Yeah," I say, even though I hate shopping. For one, nothing really looks good on me—or at least nothing looks any different on me than it would look on a ten-year-old girl. Or boy for that matter. For another, we don't really have money to shop—so it's always frustrating and winds up feeling like too much pressure. And finally, I'd so much rather spend my money on iTunes or sheet music or concert tickets than clothes. But I know this isn't the right answer, so I nod, and give her a smile that says, *What girl doesn't?*

Marian beams in response as we enter the front doors, pass the security guards, concierge, and a display of plasticy looking handbags marked with a logo I don't recognize, over to one of several, large glass-topped cases filled with jewelry. It is clear that Marian has the whole joint memorized because she beelines to one corner, then another, showing me her favorite designers: Jamie Wolf, Irene Neuwirth, Mark Davis. Blah blah blah.

I nod, wondering if the pieces are a few hundred dollars or a few thousand. Not that it makes much of a difference when you can't afford any of them. After we've made our rounds past all three cases, we continue toward the back of the room, wandering past handbags with exotic names and questionable pronunciations. Balenciaga, Nina Ricci, Givenchy. Marian lingers for a moment, sliding a large gray Givenchy off a hook. She throws it over her shoulder, inspecting her reflection in a mirrored column.

"Do you like this?" she asks me, gazing in the mirror again, this time with a frown. "Or do you think it's too large?"

I take her cue and say, "Um. Yeah. Maybe a little big?"

She agrees, replacing it on the hook and then leading me over to the escalators, up several flights to a floor of artfully arranged clothing with plenty of blank space between the racks. As we make our way around the perimeter of the room, Marian flips through dresses and pants and tops, rarely checking price tags, as if it doesn't matter. At one point, we run into a glamorously bohemian woman with long-layered hair who embraces Marian and says in an Eastern European accent, "I was just going to call you. I got in a fabulous Giambattista Valli dress you've got to try. Emerald green. Stunning. It was seriously made for you. And I have a L'Wren Scott cardigan in a more muted pink than that magenta one you tried. Do you have time to try? My one o'clock client just canceled so I'm free." She glances at me for the second time as Marian hesitates then tentatively introduces me. "Oh, I'm sorry. Agnes, this is Kirby." There is another long, awkward pause before she says, "Kirby is visiting from St. Louis."

Her vague description is not lost on me as she continues more fluidly, "Agnes gives me my style."

Agnes laughs and says, "Don't believe that for a second. Marian was born with style." She turns and gives me a nonjudgmental once-over, then says, "You have a darling figure. Do you wear skirts?"

"Just my school uniform," I say. "Otherwise, it's pretty much jeans."

Agnes tells me I've come to the right store for denim, and that she'd be happy to have her assistant go downstairs and pull some for me. "Would you like to try a few things?"

"She'd love to," Marian replies for me, and before I know it, I'm in a dressing room in Agnes's office, with a pile of jeans, and a dozen or more funky, bejeweled tops. At one point, when I'm standing alone in the dressing room, wearing a pair of killer J.Brand jeans and Prada wedge heels that would make me the envy of any girl at my school, I snap a photo of myself in the mirror and send it to Belinda: *At Barneys. Very Gossip Girl.* I take a separate close-up shot of my shoes and then another of the price on the box. Four hundred and fifty freaking dollars.

Within seconds, my phone buzzes back with Belinda's reply: *OMG. No fuckin' way!!!! You're sooo lucky!*

I start to reply, just as I hear Agnes ask Marian how she knows me.

I freeze, craning my neck toward the dressing room door to hear her answer, hoping that she not only tells Agnes the truth but that she says it with pride. Instead, I hear her muffled reply. "Oh. It's a long story."

My heart sinks as I glance back at my reflection and watch my smile fade. I tell myself that she doesn't owe her life's story to every Tom, Dick, and Agnes—and that I'm being oversensitive, probably because I'm trying on clothes and shoes that no one in my life could possibly afford.

Suddenly, I hear Marian ask, in a much louder voice, "Anything to show us yet?"

"Um, I guess so," I say, opening the door and standing awkwardly in a black tank, skinny jeans, and wedges that shoot me into the realm of "average" height. Agnes instructs me to turn around as they both praise the fit. "A-dorr-able! Those jeans look sooo good on you," Agnes says, handing me a cropped black cardigan. I put it on and she adjusts the zipper of the sweater, cuffs the sleeves twice, and examines me with a poker face before delivering her verdict. "Fantastic," she says, with a somber nod. "Soo cute."

"Wow. Yes. You're getting all of that," Marian says. "You look amazing."

"I can't," I say.

"You must," Marian says.

I start to protest again, for the same reason I turned down the six-dollar glass of orange juice, but Marian shakes her head. "I insist. My treat."

"It's too much," I mumble, looking down at the Prada shoe box splayed open on the floor.

"You're going to deprive me of the fun of shopping with . . ."

She hesitates, both of us knowing what she's thinking, but she finishes her sentence with "you."

"I guess not," I say. "Thanks so much. This is really nice of you."

"It's nothing," Marian says, as Agnes pulls a sequined cardigan off the rack and tells her it's her turn.

As I watch Marian slip it on over her white blouse, snapping the buttons with as much strategic care as Agnes zipped my cardigan, I think to myself that it's really not *that* long a story.

"Are those your parents?" I ask Marian, pointing at the framed photo in her living room and breaking a long spell of silence that seemed to descend upon us on the way out of Barneys. I consider this a warm-up to the question I really want to ask—and the topic she is clearly trying to avoid: *Who is my father?*

"Yes," she says, glancing in its direction, nodding, distracted.

"What are their names?" I ask, determined to make her talk.

"Pamela and James. Jim," she says, then looks away, as if I've just asked her a random question about two random people—rather than the identity of my blood relatives.

"What do they do for a living?" I demand.

"He's a trial lawyer. She's a homemaker."

I wait patiently, but she gives me nothing more. Frustration wells inside me as I clear my throat and say, "So what are they like?"

Marian shrugs then yawns. "Oh—I don't know. It's always hard to say what your own parents are like, isn't it? They're just—your parents."

I narrow my eyes and stare her down, hoping that my expression conveys what I'm thinking: that this is a totally lame and completely unacceptable answer. She seems to get the hint because she clears her throat and says, "My mom's very social and outgoing . . . She loves to throw parties and entertain. She has a ton of friends and lots of hobbies. She can never sit still." She smiles without showing her teeth, then continues. "My father is more quiet. Serious. He's a thinker. An introvert."

"Who are you more like?" I fire back at her.

"My dad. Definitely," she says. "I mean, I can do the party thing. I have to in the business I'm in. Just like my dad can turn on the charm for the jury and clients. But it's not really him. My mom has to drag him to all her parties and charity functions. He'd always rather stay home, read, play solitaire, watch old movies and television. He even bird-watches," she says, finally smiling a real smile. "He's nothing like the guy you see in the courtroom."

"Is he a criminal lawyer?" I ask.

She shakes her head. "No. He practices corporate litigation. He has big clients like GE, Abbott Labs, Dell. Even Oprah."

I don't want to be impressed but I am. "Oprah?"

"Yeah. He's pretty big-time."

"Is he . . . famous?" I say, thinking that it usually works the other way around—the adopted kids get to be famous, not the family who gives them up. I feel the bitterness starting to return as I wait for her answer.

"As famous as a lawyer can be, I guess. He was in politics for a while . . . when I was a kid . . . Mayor of Glencoe . . . And he was going to run for Congress, but decided not to . . ." Her voice trails off as I wonder when this happened, whether the end of his political career had anything to do with the scandal of his pregnant teenage daughter.

"Is he a Republican?" I ask.

She nods. "Both my parents are." She seems to anticipate my next question and says, "I'm an Independent."

"My parents are Democrats," I volunteer. "Even though they're very pro-life."

She doesn't take the hint. I feel my frustration growing, but tell myself to be patient. I've waited this long. What's another few hours? The answers will come—even if I have to pry them out of her. Besides, if we don't talk about anything serious, I can just sip Perrier and imagine what my life would have been like if she hadn't given me away. But then it occurs to me that even if she had kept me, I probably wouldn't fit in here any more than I do at home. And that maybe I'm doomed to never belong anywhere.

6

Marian

Kirby has been here nearly twenty-four hours, and she has yet to ask about him. But nearly every time I look in her eyes, I think of him and that night, especially the aftermath, in some ways more vivid than the act itself. I can see the two of us sprawled across the bed, naked and exposed, yet completely unself-conscious. There was no awkwardness or embarrassment, no trace of regret or panic or instinct to escape the room as we stared at the ceiling, and occasionally at each other, in perfect silence. There wasn't even much pain, just a dull, pleasant ache. We stayed that way for a long time, our sweat evaporating, our breathing returning to normal, until he finally leaned over, kissed my cheek, and said, "Beautiful."

"Hmm?" I asked, even though I had heard him. I wanted him to say it again. I wanted to be sure to remember this perfect word from his lips, red and raw.

"That. Was. Beautiful," he said, which I decided was even better than calling *me* beautiful.

"Yes," I said, because I agreed. It *was* beautiful. Although before he said it, I would have chosen a different word. "Thrilling," maybe. Or something far less meaningful, more juvenile—such as "hot." It was thrilling. It was hot. But it was more than that and he had just nailed it.

He exhaled, as if mustering the strength to get up, which he then did, slowly sitting up and peering around the room, before looking down at me with an expression of contentment. I covered myself with the sheets, not because of shyness, but because of a sudden chill that came over me.

Transfixed, I watched him stand, and walk naked through the shadows to the bathroom where he turned on the faucet and splashed water onto his face. His body was thin yet strong—more muscular than it looked in his baggy clothes—and I wondered how he could have a six-pack when he completely rejected the notion of sports, seldom even participated in PE. I watched him reach for a hand towel folded on a bar near the shower, drying his face with it, and then slowly and methodically running it under the water, wringing it into the sink. Seconds later, he was standing over me, holding the wet towel. He pressed the coolness against my forehead and cheek, then peeled back the sheets, and before I could protest, he wrung it harder over my bare stomach, a few drops falling onto my stomach, before he wiped the faint streaks of blood from the insides of my thighs.

I tensed, embarrassed by the evidence of my inexperience, and said, "Here. Let me do it."

But he pulled the cloth away and continued, with a look of concentration and care. Helpless, I reclined again, forced myself to relax and let him finish his diligent, careful work. I even shifted my weight for him, until I noticed a spot of red on the white fitted sheet beneath me.

"Shit. Look," I said, touching the mark with my finger.

He put his free hand on my stomach as if to hold me in place, his other still wiping my leg with long, slow strokes. Then he made a reassuring noise and said, "Don't worry. I'll throw it in the wash tonight, after everyone leaves. It'll come out . . . and I make a great bed. It'll be fine."

I felt the corners of my mouth rise in a smile, feeling both relieved and impressed, but too young to know how impressed I should have been. How unusual it was for a boy, or even a grown man, to wash me, offer to do laundry, remain stoic to the sight of blood, especially blood of this variety.

"So. This was your first time?" he deadpanned, with no hint of either pride or apology.

"Obviously," I whispered.

"It's not obvious. It could be . . . your time of the month."

Blushing, I made a face and said, "Eww. Gross. No."

"It's not gross," he said. "You couldn't be gross if you tried."

I smiled, accepting this compliment, looking at him sideways. "So I assume this . . . wasn't your . . . first?"

"Um, thank you?" he said, grinning back at me.

I opened my eyes, closed them again, completely sober. "Answer the question."

"Okay. No. Not my first. But not as many as you might think . . ."

"Not many girls or times?" My toes clenched to the beat of a rap song downstairs, the bass causing the overhead fan to wobble.

He laughed. "Fair distinction. Not many girls. You're only the second. But many times with the first."

"Triple digits?" I asked, trying to be playful, cool, as I thought about his Kate Moss ex in all her hippie, cool glory.

"Easily," he said.

I felt a surprising jolt of jealousy as I started to ask more questions about her. But I stopped myself. It didn't make a difference. This was a one-time thing, which sounded better than a one-night stand, but really meant the same. I felt sure of this despite the fact that I was already fantasizing about it happening again. The thought made me lean over to kiss his shoulder, just as Janie's voice suddenly cut through the darkness, her fist pounding on the door, bringing me back to reality.

"Hey! Who's in there?" she shouted. "That's my parents' room!"

I sat up and cleared my throat to shout a reply, but Conrad held up his hand, telling me not to panic, to slow down. Something in his eyes also told me what I was already beginning to feel—that I didn't owe her, or anyone, the details of what just happened. It belonged to us.

"It's just me, Janie. I'm . . . resting for a second," I called out to her.

Her voice came back, worried. "Marian? Are you okay?"

I could see her face, knew she was both concerned and intrigued, but likely not imagining that I had gone the whole way. Until tonight, we were both virgins together, sworn to wait for something truly special. Or at least college.

"I'll be right out," I said as Conrad nodded, coaching me with his eyes. "Everything's fine."

"Okay then," she said, her voice fading as she turned back to the party.

"We gotta go," I said, sitting up and reaching for my tank top, but Conrad stopped me, lowered me back to the bed and held me as if we had done this a hundred times before.

He asked if I had a curfew, and I told him yes, but that my parents were up at our house in Lake Geneva—and that I planned to sleep over at Janie's.

"Really?" he said, a half-smile on his face. "What a coincidence. So have I."

I smiled back at him, and we began another long, stream-of-consciousness conversation. We talked about school, the kids we both knew in common, his friends and mine. He told me about his music—his passion for the guitar and songwriting. We talked about our favorite movies and books. We even talked about God and religion and politics. Then he told me about the accident that took his mother's life, that he and his father were in the car, but that he had switched places with her on the ride home because he got carsick in the backseat. He told me he believed his father was mad at him for that—that he would have chosen to save his mother over him.

"Don't say that," I said.

"Why? It's the truth," he said.

I shook my head. "Impossible."

"It's not," he said. "They were crazy in love. He would have picked her over anyone. Anything."

"Not over his own child."

Conrad nodded. "Yeah. I really think he would have. And I'm okay with that. In fact, I kind of like it. It gives me something to believe in . . . Something to shoot for."

I folded my hand around his, thinking that there was nothing more beautiful than true love, hoping that I'd someday experience it, wondering if it would resemble anything about this moment.

Then we drifted in and out of sleep, my head on his chest, my ear right over his beating heart. In the predawn light, he awakened me, handing me my clothes, turning to give me privacy as he dressed himself. Then, as promised, he stripped the sheets, gathered them along with the towel he had used to clean me, and took them downstairs. I followed him, noticing a distinct drop in temperature. The heat had finally broken, or at least the air was finally in motion. A breeze ruffled the curtains in the kitchen window. Janie stood at the counter, looking out over her backyard, scattered with empty cans, bottles, and cigarette butts. She turned to face us, a questioning smile on her face.

"Well, hello there," she said, glancing at the sheets.

"I got a little sick," I said.

Conrad didn't miss a beat. "Beer before liquor. I warned her—"

"But I didn't listen," I said.

"It happens," he said with a shrug and then asked Janie to point him toward the laundry room.

As he turned and headed down the hall, she gave me an excited look, but I returned it with a blank stare, then a small shake of my head. *Nothing happened.* It was not only the first time I had ever lied to Janie but it was the first time I screened a single thought of any importance from her. It felt like a defining moment. I just didn't know how big the lie would become.

"You were up there for six hours. And ... *nothing*?" Janie crossed her arms across her tight Chicago Cubs T-shirt, looking more disappointed than incredulous.

I shrugged. "We made out a little."

"That's it? He didn't even go up your shirt?" she whispered, deflated, one eye in the direction of the laundry room.

I said no, as I imagined his hands covering my breasts, his lips on my neck and stomach and shoulders.

"Well? Was he a good kisser?"

"Yeah," I said. "He was."

"I knew it," she said. "He's *so* fine."

I smiled.

"Are you going to see him again?"

"I doubt it," I said, although I was pretty sure that I had just told her another lie—and wondered when, exactly, I had decided it wasn't going to be a one-time thing, after all.

While we waited for the sheets to wash, then dry, the three of us watched MTV in Janie's living room. Conrad and I sat side by side on the same couch we cozied up on earlier, but ironically, we now sat several strategic inches apart. Meanwhile Janie lay sprawled on the floor in front of us, intermittently groaning and asking if the room was spinning for us, too. I feigned a hangover of my own, to go along with the soiled-sheet yarn, when I actually felt surprisingly alert, bright-eyed, all my senses heightened as we watched video after video. I had seen them all before— hundreds of times, but every lyric, every image that flashed on the screen, seemed imbued with new meaning, even when there was really none to be found, from Green Day's "Basket Case" to PJ Harvey's "Down by the Water" to Annie Lennox's "No More I Love You's." Conrad kept a running commentary going, his opinions about music passionate and definite, as he heaped praise on some bands, and scorned others, often the more popular ones, which he deemed tired or overplayed. He had a particular problem with Hootie & the Blowfish, one of my favorites, but as Hootie began crooning the first refrain of "Hold My Hand," Conrad finally reached over and did just that, mocking himself with raised eyebrows. At this point, Janie was passed out and snoring, and it was like Conrad and I were alone in the world again. I closed my eyes, wondering why I had never had this dizzy, light-headed sensation with any other boy.

A short time later, the dryer buzzer sounded like an alarm clock. Conrad promptly got up, collected the warm sheets, led me upstairs, and began making the bed, remembering exactly how the Wattenbergs folded their duvet cover, as well as the precise position of their tasseled, brocade throw pillows. I asked if he had a photographic memory, or did he know all along that he would be here until morning? He smiled, continuing to smooth and straighten. When the bed was made and the hand towel hung back on the bar next to the sink, there was no more stalling to be done. So we walked downstairs, out the garage door, into the humid early morning. Steam rose over Janie's brown lawn, her mother's flowers wilted from the drought and ban on watering. Conrad reached out to take my hand on the last few steps to his car. I hadn't yet heard the expression "walk of shame," only learning it later when I got to Michigan, but felt a trace of it then, hoping Janie's neighbors weren't out getting the morning paper.

When we reached his car door, he said, "I'd kiss you good-bye, but I'm pretty sure my breath isn't too nice."

I laughed and said I was sure mine was in a similar state, although I had secretly gargled with Listerine when I last went to the bathroom. I tilted my chin up toward him, hoping he'd kiss me anyway. He took the bait, our tongues meeting for a lingering few seconds, as I discovered he'd also found the mouthwash.

"And I'd ask for your number," he continued shyly. "But . . ."

I looked in his serious face, nodding somberly, expecting him to say "But we both know this can't go anywhere."

Instead, he finished, "But I already have it."

"Oh, you do, do you?" I replied, sliding my arm around his waist.

"Yeah," he said, turning his head to whisper in my ear. "I even memorized it. Just in case."

"In case what?" I said, certain that he was joking until he smirked and rattled it off.

"In case I finally got this chance. To, um . . . make a bed with you."

I felt a grin spread over my face as I lightly asked, "Talk to you later, then?"

He opened his door, ducking to get in the car, grinning up at me. "Yeah. You sure will," he said.

I opened my mouth to answer, but the door was already shut, his engine turning, our conversation clearly to be continued.

Over the next three and half weeks, we talked every day. It became a given, yet it was something we didn't discuss or analyze. Nor did we speak of my impending departure for Ann Arbor, or anything about college or the future, mine or his. We lived in the moment, literally, sometimes not making a plan until I was in the front seat of his car. We went to the movies or to his house—where we watched television or he played the guitar, taking requests. Often we just drove aimlessly around town, talking, playing the radio. But we never spent time with my friends or his, nor did I introduce him to my parents. I even kept Janie in the dark, and although she suspected that we were spending time together, her curiosity dampened as she prepared for her own countdown to the University of Illinois—spending more time with our circle of friends who were also going there, particularly Ty Huggins, her summer fling.

In some ways, the drift felt natural, expected. We were all preparing to go our separate ways, mentally gearing up for a new chapter in our lives—a chapter we had been anticipating and planning for and dreaming about for at least four years. And in some cases like mine, much longer, since my father, a Michigan grad, took me to my first football game in Ann Arbor when I was ten. My friends and I were excited and nostalgic, melancholy and nervous. We bickered with our parents, growing increasingly resentful of their rules and control, craving independence. But we were also terrified to leave them. We were happy for one another, but had the sad sense that these golden years would soon recede and fade, as they seemed to do with all grown-ups. College would usurp these memories—and our experiences there would change us, starting us down permanent paths toward adulthood. We would decide who we were, what we were going to become. We were hurtling toward something bigger and better. We could feel it in that thick summer air, waiting for us.

In a funny way, Conrad was part of this transition. Even though I knew he wouldn't be part of my future, he also wasn't about the tired past, the childhood from which I so wanted to break free. We shared almost no memories, so there was no reminiscing to be done, except for some detailed analysis of our sporadic interactions. "What could have been" was a game we sometimes played—what if he had called me rather than just looking up my phone number? What if Janie and I had been brave enough to use our fake IDs and go see him play last year, the same night he met his ex-girlfriend. Deep down, I didn't really think we could have been much more than friends, when my high school experience was about all the things he scorned—football games and cheerleading and student government and report cards—but that was all moot now. We had a clean slate, ready for new experiences—and Conrad was my first. He was a symbol of independence and possibility. The ultimate fantasy.

There were moments, though, when I let my guard down and thought of him as something more, imagined that we could somehow endure in the months and years ahead. Realistically, I knew it couldn't happen, but one night, as we ate Raisinets in a dark, cold theater, watching *Braveheart* for the second time, I wondered if things would be different if he were going to college, too. *Any* college. Maybe then I could have conceived of a long-distance relationship like my friends Emily and Kevin who were going to Wake Forest and Stanford but had plans to stay together. I told myself that it wasn't so much that I'd be ashamed to have a boyfriend who wasn't college-bound (although I knew that was part of it), it was more that we'd share no frame of reference. Our worlds would be even more different than they were in high school. It simply wasn't possible.

So there the two of us were. Frozen in time, living in the moment, focused only on our immediate desires. Which of course included sex. Lots and lots of it. "Fucking" he sometimes called it, which I always pretended to hate, but gave me a secret thrill. "Making love," he once slipped and said. "Or something like it," he quickly added. Whatever the name, we would do it nine more times, for a grand total of ten, and I memorized virtually every second, sometimes even recording the details in my journal.

The second time was eight days after the first. We were in my bedroom. It was the middle of the day, and my dad was working, my mother at a charity luncheon. We were lying diagonal across my rainbow-striped comforter, the late afternoon sun streaming in through my window.

Dave Matthews garbled his way through "Satellite," on repeat, as I helped Conrad unroll the condom, ribbed "for her pleasure." Our eyes were open and we never stopped looking at each other.

The third time was at his house—a small ranch on the other side of town. I met his father that night, a silver-haired, thicker, tanned version of Conrad. Mr. Knight and I spoke only briefly, as he was occupied with his own lady friend, the two of them playing cards and drinking blush wine out of a large carton, which my mother had called tacky just the week before. After the introduction, Conrad openly took two Coors Lights out of the refrigerator and led me down the hall. His bedroom was surprisingly tidy (although I shouldn't have been surprised after seeing the way he made a bed); the only decoration on the wall was a poster of Jimi Hendrix. He immediately locked the door and started roughly kissing me, stopping only to undress me and crank up his music. I didn't know the band, had never heard the song, and later forgot to ask. Afterward, we drank our beers and shared a joint. My first.

I had another "first" during our fourth time together, which I shyly confessed.

"You've never had the big O?" he asked, mocking me with his expressive gray eyes. "Even by yourself?"

I put my head in his lap and looked up at him, my endorphins still firing. "No . . . And I finally get what all the commotion is about. Goodness."

Number five came a few minutes later, yielding the same result.

We went to a Super 8 for our sixth time, an impromptu stop after I couldn't keep my hands off him on the way to a pizza joint in Evanston. He made me laugh in the middle of it—I forget the deprecating one-liner—but in that moment, I decided that I liked him as much as I desired him. I could tell he felt the same as there was a lot of talking and cuddling and laughing afterward. We even spooned, something Conrad told me he had once vowed never to do. As we dressed later, dangerously close to my curfew, he told me he could "really get used to this." I told him he'd better not, but I smiled when I said it.

He talked dirty to me during our seventh time; I talked dirty back during our eighth. I was starting to feel experienced, like I might, someday, even be considered good in bed.

We went on our only proper date before the ninth, to a nice Italian restaurant in the city. I wore new, black lingerie for the occasion, flashing him my lacy bra during dinner. Later that night, we both smelled like garlic when he removed the ensemble and made love to me in the backseat of his Mustang, parked in an empty church parking lot. The smell of garlic still conjures that memory. As do all muscle cars and occasional church parking lots.

"Look at us," he said that night as I straddled him, checking for cops out the back window of his car. "It's the first time I've ever been happy to be a cliché."

"A sacrilegious cliché, no less," I said, trying to be clever.

"Yep. We're going . . . straight . . . to . . . hell," he said with each thrust, his eyes closed, his head back, his hands tight on my hips.

The tenth, and what would be our final time, was my favorite. We were in a forest clearing—even those two words sound romantic—with a picnic lunch that I made. Gouda and ham sandwiches with slices of mango, chocolate chip cookies, and a bottle of Chardonnay, all tucked into an old-fashioned wicker basket, complete with a red-checkered tablecloth. We hiked far into the woods, with the basket and his guitar, stopping on the embankment of the Fox River, mottled with sunlight. We got tipsy and naked—I'm not sure of the order. Afterward, he played his guitar for me, taking requests. He played Pearl Jam's "Daughter" and "Small Town," two of my favorites—and then he made up his own songs, first with serious lyrics, then funny ones, then serious ones again.

As I watched him play, shirtless, his muscles straining as he strummed, the L word escaped my lips, but I amended it to "I love your body."

"What about my mind?" he asked. He was smiling but wasn't kidding.

"That too," I said.

"Even though I'm not going to college?"

"That has nothing to do with anything," I said, and for a second, I really believed what I was saying.

"I love your body and mind, too," he said. "And your eyes. And that smile. And those cute Dumbo ears of yours that stick out."

Blushing, I shook my hair to hide them, covering the tops of my breasts with it as well, although I was no longer shy about showing him anything he wanted to see. The answer was always yes.

We were lovers, but we had also become the unlikeliest of best friends. He was all I could think about—and I knew he felt the same. Yet we stubbornly refused to name it, refused to talk about the impending end—of the summer, of our relationship. There was a tinge of sadness, but in truth, I think the sadness made it better. It all felt impossibly passionate and romantic because we *hadn't* named it, because no one knew about us, because it would all soon come to an end.

And then, the unthinkable happened. Or more accurately— *didn't* happen. My period didn't come on the twenty-ninth day of my like-clockwork twenty-nine-day schedule. Nor did it arrive the next day. Or the day after that.

"It's not possible," he kept saying into the phone. "We used a condom every time."

"Condoms aren't one hundred percent," I said, remembering the chart in health class, indicating that the only foolproof "method" was abstinence.

"That's because of user error," he said.

"Well?"

"I didn't *err.*"

I wasn't convinced, carefully retracing the specifics of our ten times together. We had always been so careful, except for the first time at Janie's house, when he found his way inside me for several long moments before he stopped, reached down for his wallet and began again.

"It had to have happened then," I said. "That was the only time you didn't have a condom on. And the timing works out . . ."

"You're not pregnant," he said, resolute.

"Some must have, you know, leaked out," I said. "A few drops."

It was another thing they had warned us about in health—preejaculatory fluid, a term that sounded as foreboding as it was.

"Zero chance."

"It's higher than zero," I said, pacing, panic rising in my throat.

"Okay. Higher than zero. But less than one percent. Less than a half of one percent."

"Well, that means it happens to someone! Someone has to be the less than half of one percent!"

"Yeah. But it's not us, baby."

"Don't say that word."

"What word?"

"*Baby.*"

"Okay. You're not pregnant, *honey.*"

"How can you be so sure?"

"I'm psychic," he said in a spooky voice.

"It's not funny."

"I'm sorry," he said, and I could tell he was. "Do you want to come over? I could reassure you in person?"

"Define 'reassure,' " I said. "Because that's how we got into this mess."

"We're not in a mess. And that's not what I meant. We don't have to have sex every time we see each other."

"Apparently, we do," I said. It came out an accusation, the first seeds of regret and resentment planted even though I initiated sex more than he did.

"Come over. Please," he said more gently.

At that moment, I desperately wanted to be in his arms, but as I reached up and felt my breasts, detecting a phantom tenderness in the left one, I said, "I can't. I have stuff to do. To, you know, get ready for college." My voice was cool, a way I had never spoken to him before.

He heard it, too, of course. "Right," he said. "Got it."

The next morning—a Saturday—I threw off my covers, pulled up my nightgown and held my breath, praying as I checked my underwear. Nothing. The liner I had hopefully

95

inserted was still bright white. I called Conrad, with the teary report.

"Shit," he said. "I'm coming over. Now. I need to see you."

"No. My parents are here," I said. I was still unsure why I was hiding him from them, why I continued to lie to Janie about what I was doing every night. There was the obvious explanation, at least when it came to my parents: that they would think Conrad wasn't "good enough" for me. But until now, I swore to myself that that wasn't the reason, at least not entirely. That it was more complicated than that—or conversely, quite simple: that there was no point in divulging details of something so temporary. But now, of course, I had a new reason to hide him.

"I don't care if they're there. I'm coming over to pick you up and we're going to go get a test. And then you're going to take it. Okay? . . . Marian?"

"Yes," I whispered, feeling one drop better that, at least for the moment, I had no decision to make. All I had to do was follow instructions.

"So be ready in ten minutes," he said. "I'm serious."

As threatened, he stood in my kitchen ten minutes later, in a faded Rolling Stones T-shirt, Levi's, and blue Adidas flip-flops, shaking my father's hand for the first time. A collared shirt would have gone a long way, I thought to myself, as my mother took off her reading glasses and put the *Chicago Tribune* down next to a plate of thinly sliced pineapple, complete with a raspberry garnish and dollop of yogurt.

"So how do you know each other?" my mother asked, her head cocked to the side, as she does whenever she meets a newcomer, trying to determine how the person fits into her world. Or in this case, doesn't.

"From school," I said, twisting my hair into a ponytail, unable to make eye contact with my parents, both of whom I loved and respected—and had never lied to in any significant way before Conrad.

They nodded, smiling, asking a few more questions, until the inevitable one from my father, the Michigan grad with a law degree from Yale. "So, Conrad, where are you headed next year?"

Conrad crossed his arms, then uncrossed them, leaning on the kitchen counter, as if to steady himself. Then he cleared his throat and said, "I'm not sure yet."

I thought of his words in the yearbook—*Color me gone*— and that night in Janie's yard. It seemed like a lifetime ago. Maybe it was.

Conrad glanced down at his feet as my father translated the answer and came up with the best possible spin. "Ahh. A gap year? To discover yourself?"

"Something like that. Yes, sir," Conrad said, his eyes darting over to mine as if to ask for help.

"So anyway," I said. "We're going out for a little while."

"Oh. Where are you headed?" my mother asked, attempting to sound breezy when I knew she was consumed with curiosity, likely planning a course of due diligence on the phone with her friends.

"Green to Tee," I said, regretting my choice of lies as soon as I saw my father's face light up.

"Oh! You play golf?" my father said to Conrad. "We should play sometime. What's your handicap?"

Conrad gave him a blank stare; it was like asking my father what he liked best about The Smashing Pumpkins.

"Let them go, honey," my mother said, looking momentarily pleased that, at the very least, Conrad played golf.

Maybe his family even belonged to Skokie Country Club where we had been members for years. She would find out soon enough.

Conrad and I silently drove across town, straight to the Jewel-Osco near his house, parking near the pharmacy end of the sprawling parking lot, already bustling with shoppers, mostly young mothers juggling shopping bags, carts, and small children.

"I'll be right back," Conrad said, leaving the radio and air-conditioning on.

Relieved that I didn't have to buy the test myself, I slouched down in my seat, switching the stations, wondering what last song I'd hear before I got the bad news confirmed. TLC was singing "Waterfalls" when he returned with a plastic bag and a somber expression. I turned the radio off as he ducked into the car and handed me the bag filled with a jumbo pack of Juicy Fruit, a bottle of Dr Pepper, and a *Rolling Stone* magazine with Courtney Love on the cover. I pulled the magazine out of the bag, silently reading the headlines: "Live from Lollapalooza"; "Hole Is a Band; Courtney Love Is a Soap Opera"; and "How to Stay Cool This Summer." Flipping through the pages, I did my best to ignore the last item in the bag.

"Do you like her?" I said, pointing to Courtney.

"I like her music. And I think she's interesting—the subversive feminism and slut-diva image stuff. And her music is legit. *Live Through This* will stand the test of time. I mean, 'Doll Parts'? 'Violet'? Pretty brilliant stuff. But she's a mess," Conrad said, backing out of the lot. "I feel sorry for her . . ."

"Because she's a single parent?" I asked, singularly focused.

"Because the man she loved blew his brains out . . ."

I nodded, then glanced out my window as he accelerated onto the main road toward his house. At some point, Conrad put his hand on my knee and kept it there, even as he took hard, sharp turns through his neighborhood, moving it only to shift gears as needed. When he pulled into his driveway, he took my chin and made me look in his eyes. "It's going to be okay," he said. "I got your back."

I nodded, only vaguely hearing him, and said, "Is your dad home?"

"No. We're good."

He opened the door, swung himself out of the car, and when I didn't move, he jogged around to the passenger side, opened my door, and took my arm. "Come on now."

When we walked in his house, he handed me the pink box and pointed toward the bathroom door. "Go. Now. Just do it," he said.

"But I don't have to pee."

He exhaled patiently, reached into the bag once again, grabbed his Dr Pepper, opened it, and handed it to me. I took a few swallows, then handed it back to him.

"I still don't," I said.

"Come here," he said, leading me over to his couch, making me sit, putting his arm around me and giving me a kiss on the forehead.

I bit my lip, my whole body filled with sick, numbing dread. "I don't know why I'm taking this test. I already know I'm pregnant."

"You don't know," he said.

"I'm four days late. My boobs are sore. And I'm about to puke."

"You're nauseated because you're scared. Your boobs

hurt because you're about to get your period. And—couldn't your cycle be off because you're all worked up?"

"My cycle's off because I'm *knocked* up," I said, biting my nails, a habit I had broken in junior high.

"Look," he said. "You're going to go take that test—and either one of two things is going to happen."

I stare at him, waiting.

"It's either going to be negative. And you're going to be relieved beyond belief and we can celebrate . . ." He smiled, then leaned over to kiss my neck, lingering when he got to my ear.

I pushed him away and said, "Or?"

"Or you're pregnant," he said. "Which would suck. But we would deal with it."

"How?"

"How would you want to deal with it?" he said. "I'd do whatever you wanted to do."

"I can't have a baby. I'm going to college."

"Right," he said. "So we'd find a clinic, somewhere out of town—way out in the burbs or in Indianapolis. Somewhere where we're not gonna know anyone. And . . . and I have plenty of money saved from working—so we're covered there . . . And I'll be with you the whole time, holding your hand." He put his arms around me and said, "And then I'd take you back here. To my bed. And feed you chicken soup and sing to you."

Staring at a spot on his wall, I heard him say my name twice, then three times. I finally looked at him.

"I'd do anything for you, Marian. You know that, right?"

"Yeah," I said, even though I wasn't so sure.

"*Any*thing," he said again as I stood, pink box in hand, and headed toward the bathroom, gripped with fear.

Once alone, I sat on the closed toilet seat and read every word on the box twice, including the words "unsurpassed accuracy." Then I followed the directions as precisely as I could, wondering how I could have ever thought that the SAT would be the most important test of my life. All the while, I prayed as hard as I've ever prayed, especially during that torturous, brutal, heart-pounding, ear-ringing three-minute waiting period, my eyes moving rapidly between the stick and the second hand of my watch. *Please, God, do not let a pink line appear,* I repeated, over and over and over.

But it did. So gradually that at first I could almost convince myself that it was an optical illusion. Then brighter and more vivid, until finally, it was darker than the control line, capillary action making a lighter pink halo around it. I had my answer; there was no wondering or praying or hoping left to be done.

Staring at my reflection in the mirror, I knew that no matter what I did from here, I would never be my old self again. Nothing would ever be the same again. I slipped the stick into my purse and opened the door to face Conrad and the rest of my life.

"Well?" he said, his skin and lips colorless.

At that second, something came over me that I will never fully understand. Maybe it was denial. Maybe I was protecting him. Maybe I was beginning the painful process of pulling away from him. Whatever it was, I forced a small smile and said, "Guess what?"

"What?" he said.

"False alarm."

All the air in Conrad's body seemed to escape as he knelt to the ground, his hands clasped. Then he stood and made a whooping sound of a cowboy in an open plain full of buffalo. He followed that up with a high five that made my palm sting and a slap just as hard on my ass. "I told you, girl!" he shouted. "Man! I told you!"

"You were right," I said, as he wrapped his arms around me.

Then we separated and he looked at me, deep into my eyes, as he said those words for the first time, clear and unmistakable as the second pink line. "I love you, Marian."

I opened my mouth, but he stopped me, putting his finger to my lips. "Shh. Don't say anything. I just—I wanted to say it. Whether we had good news or bad. I *really* love you."

7

Kirby

The following morning, I cave and call my parents. It is a little before seven Central time, and because they are the most predictable people on the face of the planet, I can picture exactly what they are doing. I know my mother is sitting at her dressing table, getting ready for morning mass, and my father is puttering around the kitchen, listening to *The McGraw Show* on AM radio. On the third ring, they answer the line together, one hello echoing the other. For one weak moment, as I hear McGraw's gleeful chortle in the background and can nearly smell my dad's Jimmy Dean sausage cooking up in the griddle, I am overcome with inexplicable homesickness. But the feeling passes almost instantly, replaced by the familiar blanket of animosity. I suddenly can't wait to tell them where I am.

"Turbo Kirbo!" my dad bellows. His voice is relaxed —probably because I'm not around. "How's the Yellow-hammer State?"

My mother chimes in with her first accusation. "Why haven't you answered our calls?"

"I e-mailed *and* texted you guys," I say, rolling my eyes.

"Well, you should have called, too," she says.

"Sorry," I say, pleased that I don't sound the slightest bit sorry.

"Are you having fun?" my dad asks. "I saw that it was eighty in Mobile yesterday."

"Oh, yeah?" I say. *And about sixty in New York.*

"Are you remembering to put on sunscreen?" my mother says. "And reapply every few hours? You're so fair, honey. You don't want to get burned."

I think of Marian's complexion, now knowing where I get it, and therefore hating it a little less. It looks good on her—so maybe it will on me one day, too. Wondering what I'm waiting for, I walk to the window and push the blinds open a few inches, just enough to get a view of the street below, already buzzing with morning activity, traffic, people—which couldn't be more different than my quiet street.

"How's Charlotte?" I ask. It is a red flag—I never ask about my sister—and my father seems suddenly on to me.

"She's fine. She's sleeping. What's going on, Kirbs?"

I turn and cross the room, sitting on the bed, relishing what's to come. "Um, guys. I'm actually not in Mobile with Belinda and her mother," I say, listening to the satisfying sound of stunned silence.

"Where are you?" they finally ask in unison.

"New York City," I say, holding up my middle finger and pointing it toward my phone. If this isn't payback for what I overheard, I don't know what is.

"New York City!" my mother shouts as if I've just said the front line in Afghanistan.

"What are you doing in New York?" my dad asks, trying to counteract her hysteria.

"Is Belinda with you?" my mom demands. "Is her mother?"

"No. I'm alone . . . Well . . . Not exactly alone . . . I'm at my birth mother's apartment," I say, closing my eyes and wondering how it's possible to both cringe and gloat.

"What in the world?" My mother's voice trails off and I can see her staring into her dressing table mirror, her hair still wrapped up in large pink and medium purple Velcro curlers, always removing them right before she leaves the house, sometimes even waiting until she's in the car, much to the disapproval of my sister and me. "Why?"

"Why, what?" I snap, thinking that it has to be the dumbest question ever posed.

"Why are you . . . there?" she says.

"Why do you think, Mom?"

"Honey," my dad says, although I'm not sure if he's talking to me or my mom. And then, "We understand why you went. Why you might want to meet her. But you should have told us. We could have helped you."

"I didn't need your help," I say. Which obviously is the truth.

"I know. But we would have liked to . . . at least . . . *support* you."

"Yeah, *right*," I mumble.

I can hear my mother breathing—and I would bet my iPod that she has begun to cry.

"How did you get there?" my dad asks.

"I took the Greyhound," I say, thinking of the lyrics to "America," the classic Simon and Garfunkel song about the couple boarding the Greyhound in Pittsburgh; my favorite line—which seems appropriate now: *I'm empty and aching and I don't know why.*

"Well," my mother says, her voice cracking just as I predicted. "Do you like her? Or . . . not?"

There it is, I think. What this journey is all about to my mother. Not my need to understand who I am and where I came from, but rather *her* need to be the one who saved

105

me from a selfish woman. The kind of woman who gives away her baby.

"She's awesome," I say. I can't help myself.

"Well, that's . . . wonderful," she says with a sniff. "I'm happy to hear that."

"Are you sure you're happy to hear that?" I ask. "Or were you kinda hoping she'd be awful?"

"Kirby!" my dad says. "That's not fair."

"Sorry," I say again, perfecting the art of not sounding sorry.

"When are you coming home?" my mother asks.

I tell them I don't know, probably in a day or two.

"You have school on Wednesday," my mother says.

"I know."

"So you'll be home by tomorrow night?" my dad asks, as I note with satisfaction that it is a question—not a demand. They can't *make* me come home and they know it.

"Yeah," I say. "But I gotta go now."

"Where are you going?" my mother asks.

"She invited me to go to work with her today," I say. "She's a famous television producer."

"Of what program?" my mother asks suspiciously.

"You wouldn't know it," I say, her shows limited to soap operas, crime dramas, and, ironically, feel-good reality television.

"Can we talk to her?" my dad asks.

"Nope," I say. "She's in the shower."

"When she gets out?"

"I doubt it," I say. "She's, like, really busy. Anyway. I gotta go."

"Okay, sweetie. Have a great day," my dad says. "Be careful. Keep your wits about you in that big city."

"Yeah," I say, wondering why I feel one drop guilty. "I will."

"We love you," my mom says, but I'm already hanging up, envisioning the scene at my house, knowing there will be more tears followed by melodramatic prayers at morning mass. For my safe return. For my misguided soul. For me to forget all about the woman who selfishly gave me away.

8

Marian

"So I called my parents this morning," Kirby says as we ride the subway to my office. I'm taking her to work in part because I don't know what else to do with her—in part because I can't afford a day off.

"Did you tell them where you were?" I ask as we screech to a halt at the Seventy-seventh Street station, more bodies pressing toward us as I hold our tiny patch of real estate with squared shoulders and firmly planted feet. The air is thick and steamy the way it always is underground on a rainy day, no matter what the season.

Kirby nods, her gold chandelier earrings swinging along her jawline. She has pulled her hair back in a bun and is wearing makeup, her charcoal liner applied a little too heavily. Combined with my black trench coat I insisted she borrow, she could practically pass for an intern in the office—which I'm frankly hoping people will assume she is.

"And? What did they say?" I prod, the reality of our situation kicking in the way it has every few hours, sometimes every few minutes, since she knocked on my door. She is my *daughter*. It is still so hard to believe.

Kirby loses her balance as the train lurches forward and it takes her a few seconds to regain her footing under her slight, unpracticed frame. "My dad was pretty calm, but my mom was upset."

I ask her why, hoping that it has everything to do with

her lie to them, and nothing to do with me, but I can tell by the look she gives me that I played a role in her mom's reaction.

"I think she's a little jealous of you," Kirby says, peering past me at a deceivingly normal-looking man preaching Jesus and veganism, in no particular order.

"We need to add a commandment," I say to deflect the statement about her mother. "'Thou shalt not proselytize on the subway, at least not on rainy Monday mornings.'"

Kirby smiles, watching him out of the corner of her eye, fascinated, as he gives elaborate instructions about drinking prune juice in anticipation of the imminent Second Coming.

"Your mother has no reason to be jealous," I say, wanting it on the record, out of respect and gratitude to the woman who raised her—but also to put Kirby at ease.

She appears thoughtful, as our preacher shouts, "Lemme hear you say *praaaaaise* Jesus!"

Nobody plays along so he bellows a big "praise Jesus" to his own call to action.

"I don't know. Maybe it's not jealousy . . . Maybe 'threatened' is more accurate," Kirby says.

I feel myself cringe inside and say, "I think the whole thing probably just took her by surprise. Maybe if you had told her up front, she'd be fine with it . . ."

Kirby shakes her head, adjusting her hold on our pole. "No. She would have been upset regardless. I think she views my coming here as an act of disloyalty."

"But she's your *mother*," I say. "I'm just . . . some woman in New York."

The insensitivity of my remark is unclear until I see the look of hurt cross Kirby's face. I replay my words, realizing

109

that they sound more like a disclaimer than how I intended them—as humility and deference to her mother.

"I mean, obviously it's much more than that," I say, scrambling to backtrack. "I carried you for forty weeks . . . well, thirty-nine. You came a week early. Thank you for that small act of kindness." I smile.

She smiles back at me and says that might be the first and only time she's been early.

Seconds later, we arrive at our stop on Fifty-first Street. "This is us," I say, leading her off the subway, up the stairs, through the station onto Lexington Avenue where we dodge traffic, commuters, and pools of rain dotting the sidewalks and crosswalks. As we pass through the glass revolving doors of my building, we are windblown and damp despite our large black golf umbrellas that we both shake and close in unison. I catch my breath and mumble that I'm dying for coffee and ask if she wants anything at Starbucks. "A hot chocolate?"

She gives me a dry look. "I'm eighteen, not ten."

"Right," I say with a nervous laugh just as I catch a glimpse of Peter in line for coffee, scrolling through his BlackBerry. I get a nervous jolt for reasons that aren't entirely clear to me as I walk toward him, Kirby trailing a few steps behind. When he glances in our direction, I give him a little wave.

"Champ," he says, flashing me a stiff smile that only heightens my uneasiness. Then he turns to Kirby and says hello. "A network field trip?" he asks her.

She nods, looking flustered.

I save her. "Yes, Kirby's going to help out a little bit. We can always use a little extra help in the writers' room."

"Sure," he says, and then flashes her one of his high-wattage, press-conference smiles that has sometimes earned him the reputation of slick, even ruthless to the few who have dared to cross him. "To referee and break up fights? Good luck with that."

"They are healthy debates, not fights," I say, as I migrate to the back of the line, a few half-awake customers sandwiched between us.

"Did Marian tell you the rule for the first time you enter that hallowed room?" Peter asks Kirby over his shoulder.

She shakes her head as I reply, "It's not a rule; it's a tradition."

"It's a *rule,*" Peter says.

"What rule?" Kirby asks.

"The first time anyone enters the writers' room, they have to perform," he says, rolling his eyes. "Or they can't leave. Someone watches the door."

She instantly tenses, then looks as if she might puke—or run. "Perform how?"

Feeling protective but knowing that it will be virtually impossible to shield her from the ironclad custom that I, myself, instituted, I say, "Oh, whatever you're in the mood for. You can tell a knock-knock joke. Speak in pig Latin. Juggle. Recite the state capitals. Touch your tongue to your nose. One writer did the ganda-bherundasana yoga pose—which was bizarre—and rather vulgar given that he had to strip down to his boxers for maximum mobility . . . Anything goes but you have to do something . . . We even made our CEO perform when he dared to enter our domain."

Peter makes a clucking sound. "I wasn't prepared. I haven't been hazed since college rugby."

"It's not hazing," I insist. "It's just a little . . . rite of passage."

"What did you do?" Kirby asks him—and I can see in

her face that she is putting the pieces of the puzzle together. *Peter* is the CEO. The head honcho. *My* boss.

"I sang the preposition song," he says, "to the tune of 'Yankee Doodle Dandy.'"

Kirby smiles, as do the two women in line in front of me who likely recognize him.

"So you better come up with something in the next five minutes. No pressure or anything," Peter says.

Then, upon hearing his name called out by the barista, he turns, grabs his drink from the counter, picks up his briefcase with his other hand, and tells us to have a good one.

"You, too," I say, as if we are nothing more than colleagues bantering in line for morning coffee.

"I don't know what to do," Kirby says, looking nervous, on the way up in the elevator with her orange juice and bagel. She shoves both in her purse as I note that the shoulder strap is frayed. Perhaps I can get her a new one for high school graduation—maybe a classic Chanel—although her mother might not like the idea of that. Maybe a Coach bag would be okay. Maybe I already went too far with the clothes I bought her.

"What's your favorite subject in school?" I ask, trying to brainstorm an idea.

She gives me a blank look.

"Um. Can you whistle?"

She shakes her head.

"Can you carry a tune?"

She nods modestly, and I translate this to mean she has a beautiful voice. I think of Conrad, my heart racing, remembering.

112

"So sing something," I say. "Hum a few lines of the national anthem or your favorite song. Whatever. Trust me, this really isn't a big deal—don't stress about it."

She nods, her eyes wide and darting, as we step off the elevator and head up the hall, buzzing with Monday morning activity. When we arrive at my small, corner office, I tell Kirby to have a seat on one of the leather chairs opposite my desk as I take a few minutes to get organized, powering up my computer, reviewing a few messages from my assistant, and checking my voice mail and e-mails.

"It's going to be a long day," I say, more to myself than her.

She nods seriously. "Let me know if I can help. I'm good at filing and stuff," she says.

I look at her, wondering if she has any real ambition—and if there's anything I can do to help get her on the right path. Or at least get her to go to college so she can do something more than file. "Well, right now we're gearing up for preproduction and preparing for upfronts," I say. "Last year we were on Thursdays, but we still need to see who we're up against."

"So you're not shooting and stuff yet?" she asks, looking disappointed.

I shake my head. "No. We're just going through story lines, coming up with outlines and drafts of scripts for the studio and network so they can give us their notes. Then there's the business of guest casting, managing the cast and crew, approval of blueprints of new sets, dealing with the lighting and camera departments, hair and makeup, grip and electric, and sound. Plus staying on top of how the show is being marketed by the network."

"Wow," she says. "That's a lot."

"Yeah. You could say that," I say, grabbing a few very sharpened yellow pencils, a spiral notebook, and my iPad from my desk. "But it's worth it when you see your show come to life . . . You ready?"

She nods, and I stand and lead her down the hall to the long, narrow, windowless conference room otherwise known as the writers' room or, sometimes, the torture chamber. Inside sits our core team of six writers (more will join next month once we really start rolling and shooting episodes), bantering about their weekends, topics from the tabloids, possible story ideas. We've already turned in extensive outlines for the first three episodes, and I've assigned scripts for the first two episodes so we're just picking up where we left off last week, brainstorming more story lines and working on various characters' arcs.

"Hey there! Sorry I'm late," I say as half the room quiets down and gives Kirby a once-over, while the other continues their sardonic, irreverent chatter.

"All right, everyone. This is Kirby," I say as she stands frozen in the doorway. "She's here from St. Louis and is going to be helping me out today."

I glance around the room, hoping that everyone will forget about my rule, but right away Kate McQuillan, straight from film school with no prior show experience, and apparently no prior experience on the hula hoop, her trick of choice, demands, "What's she going to do for us?"

"I think we're putting a moratorium on that today," I say as I glance at Kirby, who looks positively pale and petrified.

"Hell, nah," says Alexandre José, my go-to guy for male humor. Alexandre got his start in improv, coming to television from a long stint doing Boom Chicago in

Amsterdam, and although he has less tenure than other writers, I consider him my copilot on the show. I can also count on him to bridge bruised egos and keep the mood light when occasional arguments break out, invaluable traits in any writers' room. He stares Kirby down, then says to me, "I didn't river dance for nothin'. Let's see what she's got."

Kirby glances at me, and I raise my hands in surrender, knowing I'm not going to be able to budge Alexandre. *Sorry, kid. Showtime.*

After a painful thirty seconds, Kirby takes a few small steps into the room and says, "Um. I'm gonna sing."

"All right! A vocalist!" says Emily Grace Fuller, a young Southern writer with a debutante background. You'd never know it to look at her, but she's a real workhorse, nothing fragile about her, and has delivered some of the more clever lines of the show. She's especially good with Elsa, our naïve character who moved from Mississippi to Philly to follow her boyfriend, a law student at Temple.

"It's about time we had one of those," Emily Grace says, glancing at another junior writer who sang an off-note *Brady Bunch* theme song her first time in the room.

I take my usual seat at the head of the table, as Kirby takes a few more baby steps forward, right to the edge of the opposite head, then clears her throat and begins the unlikeliest rap complete with elaborate drumming on the table, using both her hands. Her voice is very quiet but pretty, her rhythm shockingly good, both hands working separate beats. *I said a hip hop a hippie to the hippie to the hip hip hop, a you don't stop a rock it to the bang bang boogie say up jumped the boogie to the rhythm of the boogie . . .*

115

To the rapt amusement of everyone in the room, she continues through the next few verses, not missing a beat or syllable, the drumming becoming more rapid and complex, until she gets to the end and takes a little bow. It is the most understated performance I've seen in a long time, yet one of the best. I grin with relief and satisfaction as Jeanelle Chambers, an edgy writer from Queens, leads a round of applause and says, "Damn. Way to go, white girl."

"Thanks," Kirby mumbles, still standing but now looking down at her feet.

"Aren't you about twenty years too young to know the Sugarhill Gang?" Alexandre asks. "Even the Def Squad version had to be before you were born?"

" 'Rapper's Delight' is a classic," Kirby says to her toes. "The granddaddy of hip hop."

Alexandre nods, impressed and intrigued. "Right on."

I feel a burst of pride, wondering how a real parent must feel when their child overcomes an obstacle or achieves something big, as I point to the empty chair beside me. She shuffles over and sits, without looking at me or smiling, and I notice that her hands are shaking, her breathing irregular.

She's just a little girl, I think. *My age when I had her.* For a moment, I lose my train of thought, Conrad materializing again. I force him from my mind. Again.

"Okay," I say, putting on my game face as I point to the whiteboard story wall covered with a diagram of ideas, characters, and plot lines. "We only have two hours for this notes meeting—so let's make it count. Let's pick up with Damien and Carrie. Sorry. Roger and Evvie," I say, switching to their character names. "End of our first episode—Roger's finally confessed his feelings to Evvie."

116

"Heard he did that in real life, too," Jeanelle says, the only writer on staff who has any sort of rapport with the cast. She takes a sip of her coffee, looking out over her cup for a reaction.

"No shit?" Alexandre says, drawing a big "Roger + Evvie" on our board with a red dry-erase marker. "I thought Damien was scoobin' Angela?"

"He *was*," Jeanelle says. "No longer."

I glance at Kirby—her eyes huge, relishing every second—and, for her sake, allow the room to indulge in a few minutes of idle gossip, specifically how pissed Angela will be if she finds out.

"Tell them what else you heard," Emily Grace says to Jeanelle, laughing.

"Oh, yeah. I heard he's well endowed."

Alexandre shakes his head and feigns a very homosexual accent. "You know what? This is making me uncomfortable," he says, grinning at the mostly female staff. "I think I'm gonna sue the showrunner and the network for fostering an uncomfortable environment."

"And that offends me," Benjie Carr, the only other man in the room, who happens to actually be gay. He's kidding, of course, as nothing offends Benjie. He then points to a box of pastries on the table and says to Alexandre, "See those? Don't let me near them. I'm on a cleanse."

"Okay, okay!" I say, glancing at my watch. "Let's go. Off your phones. No more surfing. Let's go! Ideas, people!"

Alexandre resumes his job as stenographer as the brainstorming commences, Kirby's eyes darting around the room, taking everything in. For the most part, there is minimal conflict—other than a rather extensive debate about a character named Max, a buttoned-up Penn grad student who spends a lot of time in the bar, drinking Jameson, criticizing everyone's jukebox selections, and generally pontificating while doing a poor job of hitting on our girl from Mississippi.

"He's getting way too much face time. He's a total Wesley," Jeanelle says, referring to the phenomenon coined after the hated Wesley Crusher in *Star Trek: The Next Generation*. In other words, the fans hate him—and we, the writers, don't realize they hate him. In fact, they hate him for the very transparent fact that we're trying to *make* them like the character. Force him down their throats. Sure enough, she says, "He's annoying and boring—and the fact that he keeps telling us how smart and interesting he is . . . is annoying and boring."

"I totally disagree," Emily Grace says.

"Um. Would that have anything to do with the fact that you created him?" Jeanelle asks. "Or wrote the script where he won't shut up about how swell he is?"

Alexandre makes a sizzling sound, touches the table, and pulls his finger away. "Damn. That burned."

I smile and say, "I think he's interesting. And very well drawn."

"Thanks," Emily Grace says, shooting me a small, injured smile.

"Still. Dude's a tool," Alexandre says, doodling a large rifle. "Let's kill him. I'm thinking a racially motivated mugging. Or maybe a murder suicide so we can take out that little slimy attorney while we're at it."

"Or at least we can put him on a bus," Jeanelle says, employing another expression, this one used for temporarily writing off a character whom we might want to resurrect at a later date. "A Greyhound to nowhere, perhaps?"

Kirby and I exchange a knowing glance as she raises her eyebrows and sips orange juice through her straw, making a gurgling sound.

Or he can get on a Greyhound to go find his birth mother and then find out that she never told his birth father the truth about him. Yeah, that's a good one.

9

Kirby

Where did you learn to sing . . . rap like that? And play the drums? That was amazing," Marian asks me later that night as we sit in her office eating Chinese delivery. It has been a completely crazy day—I had no idea that people worked so hard or so long—and this has been the first real chance we've had to talk alone.

"Thanks," I say. Then I tell her the story about how my elementary school music teacher said that the drums and the French horn were the two hardest instruments to play, and my dad said it was cheaper to bang on the table than buy a horn so I went with that.

Marian pushes aside her plate of shrimp fried rice that she's barely touched (I've begun to notice she barely eats much of anything) and says, "Well, you were incredible. Very impressive."

I thank her again, then stare her down for a long beat before I say, "So I guess I'm leaving tomorrow."

"Oh. Yeah. Right," Marian says, pretending to be disappointed. "Are you sure you can't stay longer?"

"I guess I could," I say, wanting her to want me to stay—or at least actually *talk* to me. "I have school on Wednesday, but I could blow it off . . . But I should probably get back."

She nods, and says she understands, folding easily. My heart drops but I tell myself not to be so soft and give a little shrug.

She continues, talking nervously. "This week is pretty hectic anyway. We're back in the writers' room tomorrow—and then I have a bunch of meetings with marketing and finance and interviews with new DPs . . . I wouldn't want you to be bored. So tell me more about the drums?"

I stare at her a beat, then shake my head and tell her there's not much more to say. I mean—how ridiculous is it to start talking about drumming when she's yet to say a single word about my birth father? I don't know if she's trying to hide stuff from me—or if she just doesn't want to talk about him—but after nearly forty-eight hours, it is clear that she's not going to bring him up on her own.

So later that night, after we're back in her apartment and she starts yawning and talking about bed, I tell myself it's now or never. My heart is pounding in my ears as I hear myself say, "So. Can you please tell me about my father?"

She looks at me, confused, then surprised, as if it never occurred to her that I would ask such a question, then takes a deep breath and looks so stone-faced and anxious that I'm sure a long story is forthcoming. Instead, she simply says, "His name is Conrad. Conrad Knight."

"Night?" I ask. "As in day and night?"

"As in the Round Table."

For one second, I am stupidly enchanted by the romantic image of the Round Table, until I catch her frowning, and instantly start to worry about all the things I've always worried about. That there will be a story that I don't want to hear, one of the scenarios I overheard my parents discussing: date rape, jail, drugs. Or simply what I always assumed, a notion that never bothered me until now: a loveless one-night stand that meant absolutely nothing to

121

either of them. I mean, it seems pretty clear that I was an accident, but it would be nice, at least, to be an accident that came from genuine feelings as opposed to lust of the Belinda variety.

"How did you meet him?" I ask, my heart starting to race.

"We went to school together," she says. Then she tells me she had known him since the fourth grade but that she didn't *really* know him until the summer after they graduated. "I was exactly your age," she says. "We both were. We ran into each other at a party . . ."

Marian draws a long breath. I can see in her frozen expression that her mind is racing, and I am determined to wait for her to speak. But when several more seconds of silence elapse, I lose my resolve and fire off another question. "So . . . what was he like?"

She takes a deep breath, then continues, carefully calibrating her words. "He was smart. Street-smart—although he could have done well in school if he had cared."

I nod, feeling connected to my birth father for the first time, ever, in my life.

She continues, lost in thought. "He wasn't exactly a rebel, but he did his own thing. He didn't care what other people thought—and it wasn't just an act. He really and *truly* didn't care. Which wasn't something I could relate to, but boy, did I admire it. We all did."

"Was he a loner?" I ask.

"Yeah. Kind of. At least at school. He didn't really have much use for anyone there. But he had friends outside of school—in his band. So I wouldn't say he was a total loner . . . More just . . . independent."

"He was in a band?" I say, both thrilled by this revelation

122

and relieved that he wasn't some dumb jock. Somehow, a football player looking to get laid seems more offensive than a musician doing the same.

"Yes," she says. "He was a talented musician. He could play the guitar, the piano, and a little saxophone. He had a beautiful voice. Like yours."

I can't help giving her the smallest of smiles. "What did he look like?" I ask her.

She doesn't hesitate. "He was gorgeous. Dark hair. Beautiful eyes. You have his eyes."

"I do?" I say, my heart pounding even harder.

"Yes. The same exact blue-gray color, the same darker rim. The same shape and size." She stares at the wall behind me as if trying to remember more details.

"Do you have any pictures of him?" I say, feeling dizzy.

"I have one," she says, then stands and tells me she'll be right back. Several minutes later, she returns with a dingy, once-white envelope. Inside there is a sheet of notebook paper, folded in thirds, covered with wild script. As she unfolds it, I crane to make out some of the words, burning with curiosity. She reads a few lines silently to herself, then refolds it, and returns it to the envelope before pulling out the photo. Biting her lower lip, she examines it, breathing fast. She finally hands it to me. "That's him," she says, looking as nervous as I feel, "and me."

I look down at the photo of my biological parents, feeling stunned, although I'm not sure why. It is a close-up shot, off center, more of him than her—the kind that you snap with an outstretched arm. They are on their backs on a blanket, both of them wincing as if the sun is too bright. I can't see the sky but I imagine that it is cobalt and cloudless, almost as if I can see it reflected in their eyes—

at least his. Their cheeks are pressed together, and hers are flushed. His arm is around her, his fingers buried in a swirl of her long hair, bleached by the sun. The photo is grainy, a shadow across his face, but I can see clearly that he *is* dreamy in an artist-musician sort of way. Dark hair, fair skin, full lips, and large, domed eyelids, half closed over his eyes, *exactly* my shade, just as she said. Although he looks relaxed in this shot, there is an intensity in his eyes and face, something that tells me that he feels things deeply, loves completely. Or maybe I just want to see this. Maybe I just want to believe I have that in me, too, and so far I don't really see it in Marian. I start to hand the photo back to her, but can't stop looking at it, hoping she will give it to me.

"Were you in love?" I ask, feeling all my muscles tense, wanting her to say yes, although I have no idea why this is so important to me, what real difference it makes at this point.

She hesitates, and then says, "I don't know. It feels like a million years ago . . . And it was a strange summer, Kirby. A really strange, complicated time."

"Why? What made it strange?" I press, thinking of how often Belinda will deem a ridiculous romantic situation "complicated." She and some idiot are going out, they're not going out. They're seeing other people. They're on a break. They're just hanging out. Is this the sort of crap Marian dubs *complicated*—or is it something more substantive?

"Our relationship happened suddenly," she says as I focus on the word "relationship." "Very suddenly. It was like—I didn't know him at all—and then he became my whole world . . ."

I consider my next question, feeling that each one is

critical, as if perhaps there is a limit and I might run out. What I really want is the full story, the *long* story about how they decided to have me—then give me away. So I finally blurt out, "Did he want you to have me? Or get an abortion?"

She flinches then takes several deep breaths before she finally meets my eyes. Then she takes my hands in hers and says my name as if ready to make a confession. And then she does.

"I never told him," she says.

I know there is only one interpretation of her reply, but I still search for another as I look back down at the boy and girl in the photo. "You never told him you had me?"

She glances at me, then shakes her head, her cheeks turning as pink as they are in the picture but clearly from a very different emotion.

"So . . . did he even know you were pregnant?" I ask, the facts beginning to crystallize.

She shakes her head again, this time unable to meet my eyes.

"Why? Did he . . . leave?" I ask, imagining him standing her up, breaking up with her in a Dear Jane letter, perhaps the one she is holding, skipping town, never to be heard from again.

But she shakes her head again, her voice barely audible as she says, "No. *I* left."

"*You* left *him*?" I say.

She nods and says, "Yes. When I found out I was pregnant with you. I broke up with him."

"So . . . he doesn't know about me at *all*?" I ask, still thinking that there is a possibility that she told him years later. That he now knows the truth, that he has a child out

125

there, somewhere. Perhaps he is even dying to meet me. Maybe she contacted him in the past forty-eight hours and gave him the news.

But she shakes her head. "*Nobody* knew I had you," she says. "Nobody even knew I was pregnant—except for my mother."

I try to comprehend a secret of this magnitude, how she could have possibly pulled off such a thing. "What about your father? Or your best friend?" I say, thinking of Belinda, how she would be the first person I'd call if such a thing happened to me. Although I can't even begin to imagine it, my sexual encounters limited to three pitiful kisses, all under the influence, awkward, forgettable.

She shakes her head again. "Just my mom."

"So how did you hide it from everyone?" I ask.

"I deferred college for a year. Told the admissions people at Michigan I had a health issue. Told everyone else I was burned out from high school and needed time to just think. My father thought I was writing a script. He knew how obsessed I was with writing so . . . he believed me. And so . . . I went away for a while . . ."

"Where did you go?"

"To our lake house in Wisconsin. My mom went back and forth. She took me to all my appointments and to the adoption agency. Otherwise, I stayed in hiding until it was time to have the baby. Have *you*."

I am speechless, spellbound by the story that is as much a part of me as the one my parents have told me a hundred times. "And then you went to Chicago to have me?"

She nods. "Yes. I went into labor on March thirty-first— it lasted all day and night. Then I had you on April first. Well, you know that." She smiles a stiff, small smile. "Then

126

I spent three days with you. Three of the hardest, saddest days of my life."

"Did we . . . *bond*?" I ask, my eyes burning, my stomach churning.

"Oh, Kirby. God, yes," she says. "I spent every minute— every second—with you."

I ask her if she had a name for me. Did she call me anything for those three days?

She nods and whispers yes. Katherine, with a *K*.

"That's my middle name," I say. "After my aunt."

"Wow. That's crazy, isn't it?"

I shrug. "It's a pretty common name. Go on."

She hesitates, then says, "So I named you, even though the social worker said not to. And I nursed you even though they said it was a really bad idea, that it would only make our separation more difficult. But I wanted to . . . I *had* to. At one point, a nurse tried to take you from me so that I could get some sleep but I refused. I knew I'd have to hand you over at some point—I couldn't do it twice."

She takes a couple shallow breaths and then continues, "Then the time came. The lady from the agency arrived in my hospital room with a nurse and two people from the Department of Supportive Services. There were four or five people in my room, all of them formal, official, with their folders and explanations. They handed me the papers, including a document called a Final and Irrevocable Consent to Adoption, and my mother held you on a rocking chair in a corner while I read and listened and then signed the papers."

I feel myself start to well up, just as she asks me if I'm okay. I nod. She stares into my eyes and I stare right back, waiting.

"You had been fussy all morning, but stopped crying while they were all in the room," she says. "It's like you knew something really big was about to happen and wanted to pay attention. You had that quality. This intelligent, alert look on your face—this way of making eye contact with people. With me." She swallows. "So then I asked for a minute alone with you. I asked my mother to leave, too."

"Did you . . . almost change your mind?" I ask, hopeful, wanting to believe that it wasn't easy for her to give me away.

"Oh, *yes*," she says convincingly. "Many, many times in those seventy-two hours. Of *course* I did. There is no way that anyone could look down at your face—those big, wide eyes that never seemed to blink and your tiny, expressive, fuzzy brows, and those little curly lips—and not want to hold you forever . . . But I was sure that it was the best thing for you. To have a mother and father who were married and fully prepared to have you, take care of you, give you a family."

"What about Conrad?" I ask, the emotion from her story giving way to a wave of indignation. "Did you think of telling him? Maybe you could have figured it out with him?"

She shakes her head and says, "There was already too much water under the bridge for that."

"What do you mean?"

"I hadn't spoken to him in nine months. It felt too late at that point. Besides, that would have been no life for you. Two teenagers pretending to be adults. And I knew there was a couple inside the walls of the hospital, waiting for you. I knew how desperately they wanted you."

"So . . . you just . . . said good-bye to me?" I ask, my voice quivering, wishing that newborns could have memories, that I could have a recollection of that time we spent together.

"Yes," she says. "First I nursed you one last time. Then I changed your diaper and dressed you in a little pink gown. It had a drawstring at the bottom to keep your feet warm, although I put little booties on your feet, too. And a tiny knit cap that matched the gown—pink with white stitching. My mother bought it for you . . ."

I nod, tell her that I remember the gown from a photo, obviously the first my parents ever took of me, but then remember I had another outfit on in a photo of the car ride home, which means they changed my clothes before leaving the hospital. I wonder why—whether I had spit up on it or whether they simply wanted me in an outfit they had chosen, as a symbolic fresh start, just as they gave me a new name.

"And then?" I say.

"And then . . . I sang you a lullaby, the only one I knew. 'All the Pretty Horses.'"

"How does it go?" I say.

She tells me she can't sing but then clears her throat and recites the lyrics. *Hush-a-bye, don't you cry. Go to sleep my little baby. When you wake you shall have all the pretty little horses.*

I breathe, waiting in suspense for the rest of the story, as if I don't already know exactly how things end.

"You finally fell asleep. And I kissed you good-bye. Both your cheeks and your nose and your chin." Her voice cracks. "And I forced myself to open the door and walk out into the hall where I found the counselor from the hospital talking to my mother. Without saying a word, I handed you over to her and went back in my room so I didn't have to watch her walk away."

I look at her, feeling suddenly very sorry for the girl in the story, trying to imagine how she must have felt as she packed up her room and changed back into her clothes and left the hospital without flowers or balloons or a baby in her arms. Then I think of Conrad again. Conrad, who is completely in the dark about my existence.

"So do you know where he is now?" I ask.

She shakes her head and looks guilty, but not guilty enough as far as I'm concerned.

"You've *never* tried to find him?"

She sighs, then admits she drove by his house once, but the Knights had moved; there was a new last name on the mailbox.

"And what about on Facebook? The Internet? Through friends? You've never once looked for him?"

"Oh. I've searched a few times over the years," she says. "But I never found him. And I don't really talk to anyone from high school anymore—not that he was the type to go back to reunions or keep in touch, either."

"So that's it? Nothing? It's just like he's . . . disappeared?"

She nods as we stare at each other, in silence. After a long time like this, she finally slides off her stool and pulls me into an embrace, the first since the day she gave me away. I let her do it, but refuse to hug her back, thinking only one thing: *How could you?*

10

Marian

I owe her an apology. For so many things. For being able to give her away. For pretending that it didn't happen, that she didn't exist outside of that room and those three days. For not having a baby picture of her in my apartment. For not writing her long letters over the years, if only to keep in a drawer in anticipation of this day.

But most of all I'm sorry for not telling Conrad, her *father,* the truth. It is the part of the story that I repress the most, the part I kept from Peter, telling myself that it was a small detail even though I know, deep down inside, that it is *way* more than a small detail. It is huge, and I feel it all bubbling to the surface now. Kirby didn't mention wanting to find her birth father, but I feel sure that she will. And what then?

I go to bed, remembering that day. The moment I lied to Conrad. Right before he told me he loved me and I said nothing in return. The beginning of my attempt to deny my feelings, erase him altogether. I remember the panic in my throat as I sat on the couch next to him, holding his hand as we watched *The Simpsons,* his relief over our "negative" test and occasional laughter over Bart's one-liners only sinking me into a deeper abyss.

"What's wrong, babe?" he asked at one point, when he determined that I was finding no humor in a show I usually enjoyed.

That's when I blurted it out. "I don't know if we should keep seeing each other."

"You mean you want to break up?" he said. His face reflected the panic and sadness I felt over the idea of losing him.

But I still said yes.

"Why?" he said, looking more grief-stricken by the second.

"Because the summer's almost over," I said, staring at my lap.

"But it's not over yet," he said, seeming to imply that our breakup was a given—it was just a question of when.

"But it will be soon. And . . . I think it might be easier now."

I looked back over at him, but he glanced away as if considering this. When he turned toward me again, his face was stoic. "If that's what you want . . ."

"I just think it's for the best," I said, unsure if I wanted him to acquiesce or fight for me. I wanted both. I wanted neither. I wanted that pink line to disappear.

"For the best?" he echoed.

"Yes."

He nodded. Then he shut off the TV and put the remote on the coffee table, staring at the blank screen, blinking, until suddenly, his long, dark lashes were damp. I looked away, horrified, fighting the urge to throw my arms around his neck, take it back, make love to him, and above all, tell him the truth.

The impulse only grew when I hear him whisper, "I don't want to lose you yet."

It was the "yet" that killed me the most, the desperation and resignation in that word. I held his gaze, both of us perfectly still, as I allowed myself to imagine another way, a different path. I could see the two of us having the baby, living together in Ann Arbor in off-campus housing, eventually marrying. Things would be really hard, but I knew my parents would help, and we could work it out. He could watch the baby during the day while I went to class—and he could pursue his music at night and on the weekends. It wouldn't be a traditional college experience. There would be no frat parties and drunken kisses. No football games or sorority dances. But it could be done. And in the end, it could still turn out fine. I could still go to film school. I could still become a real writer and a producer. Conrad, too, could become a musician or do whatever else he wanted to do. We could be a team. Forever. The two of us—then the three of us. Maybe this happened because we were meant to be.

For one second, I felt myself caving, but then another vision overcame me. A life of late-night fights, doors slamming, a screaming baby, a failing grade that came from utter exhaustion—a grade that would ultimately keep me out of graduate school, steering me into a nine-to-five, dead-end job. I could almost taste the shame and resentment and bitterness and anger. I could feel the hatred and self-loathing. I could hear the endless what ifs.

"I really have to go," I said, standing abruptly. "Can you take me home?"

He followed me to the door, then out to his car, looking frantic, devastated. But he didn't say anything, nor did we speak most of the way back to my house.

As he pulled into my driveway, he asked if I could please call him later, to talk about this more.

I nodded, but I could see in his eyes that he knew I wasn't going to call. Tonight or ever. That this was good-bye.

*

The next day, while sitting by the pool with my mother and going over a checklist of things I needed for my dorm room, I broke down in tears. By then, she had figured out the basics on Conrad: He was in a band, playing music with rated-R lyrics. He had an alcoholic father and no ambition, at least not the kind that she recognized. So of course, she assumed that he was the culprit, in some way.

"Did you and Conrad break up?" she guessed—which only made me cry harder.

I told her yes, but something else, too. Much worse than that. "Much, much worse," I said. "The worst thing that could ever happen."

"Are you pregnant?" she whispered.

I nodded, filled with shame—but also relief that she knew. My mother was smart—and always good in a crisis. One of our most oft-shared family tales was the time my dad choked on a bite of rib eye at Gene & Georgetti and she leaped to her feet and ran around the table, knocking over both of their wineglasses, and with swift textbook form, performed the Heimlich maneuver until the meat was dislodged from his throat. If she could save lives, she could fix this.

"I'm sorry, Mom," I said as I curled into a fetal position on my lawn chair, crumbling under the weight of so much guilt and shame and embarrassment. My parents had given me so much—*everything*—and this was the thanks I gave them.

But my mother remained strong. "Honey, it's going to be okay. We will take care of this," she said, running her fingers through my hair. "We will get through this . . . What did Conrad say?"

"I didn't tell him," I said.

"Good," she quickly replied. And then added some disparaging footnote, blaming him for my predicament.

I felt terrible for not defending him, but decided there was no point. We were in problem-solving mode now. And Conrad, good guy or bad, my type or not, was not part of the solution.

The next day, my mother took me to her ob-gyn, and my news was confirmed with a blood test. According to Dr. Kale, who looked disturbingly like my grandfather, I was six weeks along—which meant that I was right about my theory: I lost my virginity and got pregnant on the same night. The ultimate curse. It was downright cruel and unusual, especially given that Conrad and I had used protection. I stared numbly at Dr. Kale as he took my full health history and discussed my prenatal care "should I choose to have the baby."

Meanwhile, my mother took copious notes and asked occasional questions until there was nothing more to be said. Then the doctor put down his clipboard, took a seat on a stool, and slid over to the table next to me. I knew what was coming—and sure enough, he gave me a supportive smile, cleared his throat, and said given my age and circumstances, he wanted me to talk to a counselor. He looked at my mother for permission, and she nodded her consent.

Minutes later, after I had changed out of my paper gown back into my jeans and T-shirt, my mother and I were ushered down the hall to a small, cheerful office adorned with a child's crayon drawings and a collage of photographs of towheaded boy-girl twins. Behind the pristine desk sat a petite, blond counselor named Megan, presumably the mother of the twins, who smiled at us, made insipid small talk, then calmly explained my "options," all of which were perfectly obvious. I could terminate the pregnancy. I could continue the pregnancy and become a single parent. I could parent the child with the father's involvement and support. We could parent as a couple. We could parent with help from our parents or other relatives. I could have the baby and place it for adoption—which came with another menu of options that she was available to discuss at any time. "You have a lot to think about, honey," Megan said.

My mother thanked her for me.

"Is there anything you want to ask me?" she said.

I shook my head, although part of me wanted to make an announcement, for the record, for my file. I wanted to tell her that I was way smarter than other girls she had counseled in this predicament. That I wasn't "that kind of girl." That I'm sure everyone lied about it, but I actually *had* used birth control, and that I never, for a second, thought of abortion as a backstop. That I understood my options, yet I couldn't fathom having a child, any more than I could fathom aborting a baby, any more than I could fathom giving one away.

But of course I said none of this as Megan handed me her card and a pamphlet of the medical facility they recommended should I choose to terminate the pregnancy. My mother took it from my hands, slipped it into her own purse, and said we'd be in touch.

"What should I do?" I asked my mom on the way home.

She kept her eyes on the road and said it was my decision.

"Mom, tell me," I said.

She took a deep breath and then told me I was beautiful, talented, special. The light of her life. And that any child that came from me would be just as brilliant and special. She said she would help me raise the baby—she would do it herself if that's what it took, if that's what I wanted. Then she mentioned adoption. She called it noble, the ultimate in generosity and selflessness. She said she had always had such respect for girls and women who made that choice. She said it would be hard—in some ways the hardest—to go through with everything and then give the baby away, but for my whole life, I would know that I had given someone the most precious gift imaginable.

"But if I had the baby . . . what about college?" I asked.

"We could explain to admissions . . ."

I shook my head, adamant. The conversation was still so theoretical, but I was sure that I didn't want anyone at Michigan to know. Or anywhere for that matter. I told her this.

"Marian. It's nothing to be ashamed of," my mother said, but I could tell, for the first time in our conversation, she wasn't being sincere. Even she could not argue away the stigma of teen pregnancy.

"No. I don't want to tell anyone. Ever. Especially not Daddy," I said, thinking that it was one thing to disappoint my mother, another to disappoint my dad who was, deep down, my favorite parent. I worshipped him, and wanted to be like him, and wanted to make him proud, more than just about anything in the world at that time. But most of all, I simply *adored* him.

I stared out my window at the familiar landmarks of my hometown, as I was bombarded with childhood memories of my father. The crisp, cold fall football Saturdays in

Ann Arbor, the two of us yelling so hard for our beloved Wolverines that we were hoarse on the car ride home to Chicago. The smell of fresh lumber at Ace Hardware as I stood by his side, watching two-by-fours measured and sliced with a chain saw for his latest backyard project. All the nights doing math homework, the look of concentration on his face, his reading glasses perched on the end of his nose, as he showed me the right way to solve the problem, his figures so neat that they looked typed. Watching our favorite television shows together—from *Murphy Brown* to *Mad About You* to *Wonder Years*—while my mother could never sit still long enough to join us. The endless summer hours we spent on the back porch of our lake house reading books on our white rocking chairs, mine a smaller version of his.

I think of all his little sayings: "You never get a second chance to make a first impression" and "The purpose of life is a life of purpose" and "He who fails to plan, plans to fail." I think of the careful way he does everything—from stringing Christmas tree lights, to carving jack-o'-lanterns, to shoveling the driveway, to making sandwiches. I picture him arguing cases before the Seventh Circuit Court of Appeals, watching him with so much pride I thought my heart would burst, thinking I'd never be able to grow up and find a man as wise or handsome or good. Maybe all little girls think this about their dads—but the difference is: I was actually right about mine.

"Promise me you won't tell him," I say. "No matter what we decide."

My mother nodded, then reached across the seat and offered me her pinky, a practice we had abandoned years ago. Our little fingers intertwined, our secrecy officially sworn.

*

138

For the following two weeks, I remained paralyzed with indecision and filled with anger, fear, and guilt. I was also intensely lonely, feeling completely alienated from Janie and my other friends, who had begun to write me off after ignoring them for so many weeks. I knew the isolation would only be the beginning if I chose to have the baby. Then there was the heartache I felt over Conrad. I missed him desperately—more than I thought possible to miss anyone. He phoned a few times, and my mother always gave me his messages, but I did not return his calls, hoping that going cold turkey would break my addiction to him faster—and his to me. Part of me felt as if this were the punishment we both deserved for carrying on like lovesick puppies—*rabbits*—while the life inside me was growing, the cells multiplying again and again, a heart and its chambers beginning to form. Besides, I really couldn't call him when I wasn't willing to include him in this decision. And no matter what he had to say or how he said it, I was sure that the discussion would only make the pain that much worse.

If all of this wasn't bad enough, I was also struck with a severe onslaught of morning, afternoon, and evening sickness—which felt a little bit like riding a roller coaster with a hangover. I spent most of my time alone in my room, a trash can next to my bed in case I couldn't make it to the bathroom. I listened to music, flipping through my yearbook, wishing I could go back to the beginning of the school year, or even the summer, a simpler, happier, virginal time of my life that seemed like a million years ago. My mother knocked on the door a few times a day, bringing me crackers, sitting on the edge of my bed, smoothing my hair. Occasionally we'd talk about my choice, but mostly my mind was too cloudy to think, my heart filled with the strangling panic that no matter what I chose, I would regret it forever.

Then one morning, after puking three times, I made my decision. I found my parents in the kitchen, my father about to leave for his morning run, my mother drinking coffee in the pink cashmere robe I had given her for Mother's Day.

"Morning, kiddo," my dad said, stretching his long legs, fleetingly resembling the college tennis star he once was. His hair was still dark then, gray only at the temples, and I remember thinking it would all turn white if he knew.

"Morning," I mumbled, realizing that I hadn't made eye contact with him in days.

"I just got a letter from a history professor I had at Michigan. Name is Barfield. Thomas Barfield. Brilliant guy. And he's still at it."

"He must be ancient," I said, forcing a smile.

My dad laughed. "Yeah. Like your old man." He took a bite of an energy bar on the counter, the sight of which made me sick to my stomach. "I called and told him you were coming—to look out for you. He would be a great mentor for you. You might even be able to get a job as his research assistant. Would be a great experience. Be sure to swing by and introduce yourself."

"Okay. I will," I said, trying not to puke again.

Seconds later, as my dad headed out the door for his run, I looked at my mother and said, "I want it gone."

"Okay, honey," she said, looking relieved.

"Out of me. As soon as possible."

"I'll call today," my mother said. "We'll get an appointment right away."

"Am I doing the right thing?" I said.

"I think you are," she said, standing and giving me a tight hug. "I really think you are."

I had to wait three more excruciating days for that Tuesday to come, two weeks to the day before I was leaving for school. Unfortunately, it was also the rare day my father took off from work, and I was dismayed to find him puttering around downstairs in jeans and a polo shirt, working on a home improvement to-do list. Meanwhile, my mother and I had to carry on a charade about going shopping in the city for clothes to take to college, my dad cracking jokes about how he'd better get to work to cover the cost of the damage we were sure to do at Saks, somehow oblivious to my telltale loose sweats, no makeup, and ponytail pulled back in a scrunchie. I kept my eyes lowered until it was time to leave, feeling mostly numb with occasional bursts of terror.

It was a relief to finally get in the car and be on our way to the medical facility on North Elton. I kept envisioning the photos on the pamphlet, featuring the wholesome, doe-eyed young girl with a crisp, shiny bob and a staff of doctors and nurses with concerned, competent smiles.

My mother and I drove in silence, until at one point, she asked if I wanted to listen to music, holding up her ABBA CD. It was our nostalgic favorite, and I nodded, thinking that a little "Dancing Queen" and "Voulez-vous" might take my mind off things. For a few songs, it did the trick, the familiar lyrics and clean, clear soprano vocals almost hypnotizing me, but when the bittersweet notes

141

of "Chiquitita" filled the car, I had to fight back tears, remembering how I used to think the song was about bananas, how my mother had laughed when I told her this, explaining that it meant "little girl" in Spanish, that I was her chiquitita and always would be. The music washed over me, both soothing me and filling me with grief.

I looked at my mother gripping the steering wheel, and even though her oversized sunglasses hid her eyes and half of her face, I could tell the song was affecting her, too. I looked out my window as the sights of the city appeared, and told myself that this would all be over soon. I'd go to college in a few weeks where I'd learn from books and life and people, and turn into a real adult with a real career. Someday I'd fall in love again and marry. My husband and I would enjoy a few years alone, just the two of us, then plan for our first child. We would do everything the right way. The perfect way. I would call my parents with the news—or maybe tell them face-to-face if I still lived in Chicago. They would tell me it was the happiest news of their lives. By then, Conrad and that night at Janie's, this whole summer, and especially this morning, would have long since faded, maybe even disappeared altogether. After today, I would get a do-over. A clean slate. A fresh start.

I closed my eyes, leaned my head against the cool window, and moved my lips to the words I'd heard a thousand times before . . . *You'll be dancing once again and the pain will end, You will have no time for grievin'.*

But in the end, no matter how much I believed in my choice—and my right to make that choice—I just couldn't go through with it. Couldn't think of it as anything other than taking a life. And believe me, I tried. I really, *really*

142

tried. I tried as I filled out my forms and got my blood drawn. I tried as I changed into a gown and had my vital signs taken. I tried during my physical exam and the administering of local anesthesia. I tried when I was lying on that cold, steel table in the surgical suite with my mother holding my hand in much the same way I imagined she would in a few months if I had made another decision. I tried when I put my feet in those stirrups and the doctor turned on the little vacuum apparatus and said he was going to be "gently removing the contents of my uterus" and everyone in the room nodded encouragingly and braced themselves for what was billed and promised to be a very quick, painless procedure.

But it didn't feel like a procedure. And it didn't feel like the "contents of my uterus." It felt like a baby, and as I closed my eyes, I was filled with an intense need to know whether it was a boy or girl. In those few seconds, I knew I was done—and what I wanted or believed I wanted was immaterial. It was almost as if my head and heart were in a war, and my heart won. I jerked my feet out of the stirrups and sat upright on that table, the stiff white paper under me making a loud, crinkling sound as all those people, including my mother, watched with surprise and concern, and even, I think, disappointment.

"I can't," I said aloud to them, but mostly to myself. "I can't do this."

And that was that. I got dressed, and my mother and I reentered the bright, August morning and drove back home.

11

Kirby

The following morning, Marian knocks on my door just as the sun is coming up. I'm already awake. In fact, I probably only slept two hours the whole night, the rest of the time spent thinking about what she told me, trying to process it all, and even doing a few searches on my phone for Conrad Knights.

"Sorry to get you up so early. But I have to get to work," she says through the door, sounding all bright-eyed and cheerful—probably because she knows I'll soon be out of her hair. "I made you an oatmeal-whey-protein smoothie!"

"Okay. Be out in a second," I shout back at her.

Minutes later, after I've brushed my teeth and hair, I find her in the kitchen. She is fully dressed in a plain navy dress, high heels, and lots of gold jewelry.

"Good morning," she says, handing me a glass.

"Good morning," I say, taking the smoothie from her. It is an unappetizing gray color, but I take a sip, and it's not too bad.

We sit at the island, in our hundredth spell of awkward silence, before she acts as if she suddenly thought of something.

"Oh. Here. I got you this," she says, sliding a boarding pass across the counter. "An upgrade from the bus."

"I was going to take Amtrak," I say, thinking of the last

e-mail exchange I had with my parents—and my promise that I would take the train.

"Oh. That will take you forever . . . Travel by train is only nice in theory. Unless you're on the Orient Express."

"Right," I say. *'Cause that happens all the time in my family.*

"So I got you a direct flight back to St. Louis. It leaves at ten."

"You didn't have to do that," I say.

"Oh. It's okay. I have so many frequent-flyer miles . . ."

"Thank you," I say.

"You're welcome," she says, then glances at her watch. "So we have about an hour before you need to leave for the airport. Is that enough time for you to get ready?"

"Yeah," I say. "Plenty." I look down at the ticket and thank her again.

"It's nothing," she says.

I stare into her eyes, resisting the strong urge to agree with that sentiment.

An hour later, Marian and I are standing on the corner of Madison and Eighty-seventh. She has just handed me fifty bucks for cab fare which I reluctantly take, feeling guilty on the heels of the clothes and shoes and flight, but worried that I don't have enough to cover it. I watch her, staring intently down the block for a taxi, then pointing to a woman across the street and telling me she is our competition, we have to beat her to the punch. "You snooze, you lose in this town," she jokes. Seconds later, she steps out in the street, boldly flagging one, and in another deft, fluid motion, she is behind the car, stowing my bag in the trunk, then opening the side door and instructing my driver to deliver me to the Delta terminal at LaGuardia. The whole thing happens as fast as one of Charlotte's underwater flip turns.

When the logistics are handled, we stare at each other for a few painful seconds before she crosses her arms and says, "As you probably gathered from my story last night, I'm not the best with good-byes."

"Yeah. I kinda got that," I say.

She gives me a hug, slightly longer than the one last night. Her hair is silky on my cheek and smells like vanilla.

"Will you let me know when you're home safe and sound?" she asks, as I wonder if she feels that she has to say this—if it's just standard fare when a guest leaves your home. Or at least something you need to say to the child you gave up for adoption.

I nod, a knot in my stomach.

"You have my number," she says. "Call or text me if you need me."

And what if I don't need you? What if I just want to talk?

I thank her and she says, "No. Thank *you* for coming. For finding me."

I try to respond, but can't find the right words, and decide that saying nothing is better than saying the wrong thing. So I just nod and slip into the backseat, watching as she closes the door and waves. I wave back until she is gone from view. Then I sit back in my seat, wondering when or if I'll ever see her again. Something tells me I won't—that this is the way she wants it. That she met her birth daughter, gave her some nice shoes and a plane ticket, and now she can cross that off her list and get on with her life.

A few short minutes later, we are crossing a large bridge. Signs tell me it is the RFK. I look out my window at the sun rising in a pink sky, a backdrop to smokestacks and

146

buildings and billboards, feeling unsatisfied and sad, like I've just been given away, again.

Five and a half hours later, I walk in the front door of my house. I've only been gone for three days, but everything looks and smells different, sort of the way I feel on the inside. I hear laughter coming from the kitchen and turn the corner to find my sister with Noah Smith, one of the cutest boys in school, also a star swimmer, her male counterpart. They are drinking root beer floats and making eyes at each other, like it's nineteen-*freaking*-fifty-five and they're about to head out to a sock hop.

Charlotte leaps up from the table when she sees me and throws her arms around me so sincerely and pure-heartedly that I hug her back, something I haven't done in ages. In fact, this makes three hugs in twenty-four hours, which has to be a record for me since I was about eight.

"Dad told me where you were," she breathlessly whispers. Her eyes are shining the same way they do after she wins a first-place ribbon in a swim meet and I feel fleetingly guilty for not being happier for her at such moments. For not sharing in them at all.

I glance at Noah, noticing the stubble on his jawline, impressive for a teenager, as Charlotte says, "Do you know each other?"

We both shake our heads, even though I know exactly who he is, as she introduces us. He does a chivalrous half stand that makes Charlotte beam with pride while I mumble hello.

"'Scuse me one sec," she says to Noah, then pulls me around the corner into the dining room. "Omigod! So how was it? How was she? Dad said she's a producer!"

"Yeah. And the head writer on the show."

"Wow. That's *crrrazy!* So did you, like, meet anyone famous?"

I tell her I didn't meet any actors, explaining that the show is in preproduction, but that I saw the television studio where she works and met all the writers for the show. "They were all so smart and funny . . . It was really cool."

"Wow," she says. "You're *so* lucky."

It is the word that Belinda kept texting this weekend—but it carries more weight coming from my charmed sister. I consider the cute boy in the next room with his sexy five o'clock shadow and varsity letter jacket thrown over the back of his chair, and try to convince myself that she is right. That even though the weekend wasn't exactly what I'd hoped it'd be, maybe I am the lucky one for a change. After all, I'm related to someone kind of important. Which might make me a little bit important, too, at least in the eyes of my friends and sister.

"So?" she says. "More details!"

I take a deep breath, knowing that I can't possibly explain the complexity of my feelings about meeting my birth mother, but wishing I could at least convey the feeling I had as we sat in the writers' room watching the storyboard slowly fill with ideas, or stood at the top of the Guggenheim gazing down at tiers of masterpieces. "New York—her world—is so glamorous and interesting," I say.

"And she's cool?"

"Very," I say. "So sophisticated. Like . . . nobody else I know . . ."

"Wow. That's so great, Kirby! . . . And what about your father?" she asks.

For a second, I feel the familiar tinge of resentment,

thinking that my father is *her* father, but I know what she means and decide to cut her a break.

"He's a musician," I tell her.

"Omigod, that is so freakin' badass," she squeals. "You're like, the daughter of two artists. A writer and a singer. This explains a lot."

I smile, a warm feeling spreading inside me.

"Is he famous, too?" she asks.

I shake my head and say, "I don't think so. His name is Conrad Knight. Doesn't ring a bell."

"But maybe he changed it. Like a stage name?"

"Maybe. I guess it's possible," I say, not wanting to tell her the truth—that Marian has no idea where he is. That he doesn't even know I *exist*.

"*Anything* is possible," she says. "This proves that."

"Yeah. I guess so," I say, then return the attention to her, where it has belonged for so long. "So Noah Smith, huh?" I say, pointing toward the kitchen.

She grins and raises her eyebrows. "I know, right?! Isn't he freakin' *hottt*?"

"Yeah. He's really cute," I say. "Are you dating?"

"Not yet," she says, raising her crossed fingers in the air. Her nails are long and painted lavender. Last week I would have thought they looked pretty, but now I think of Marian saying she only likes neutral colors on her hands, and think I agree with her. "But give me a week."

I smile, admiring her confidence, but for once, not begrudging her for it. If anything, her quest to date Noah seems simple and dull in comparison to what I've just experienced.

"So how upset is Mom?" I say.

She winces and says, "Um. Yeah. Very."

149

"She told you that?" I say, thinking that it would be par for the course if my mom had confided in her about me.

But Charlotte shakes her head and says, "Nope. Dad did, though. He sat me down and got all serious and told me everything that was going on . . . Said Mom's feelings were hurt that you hadn't talked to her about it." She shrugs and says, "I told him that's just the way you are. You do things *your* way. I mean, I'm not pissed that you didn't tell me—and I'm your sister."

I nod, wishing I had.

"You're independent and strong and you know exactly who you are and what you want."

"Thanks," I say, thinking that it is probably the nicest thing anyone has ever said to me. And it'd be even nicer if it were actually true.

"I want to start by saying we're glad you're home safe," my father says later that evening in what is clearly scripted dialogue. We are seated in the family room, my mother and I on the couch, my father in his La-Z-Boy recliner.

"Yeah. Thanks," I mumble.

"And we understand why you wanted to meet your birth mother," he continues. "We even understand why you'd want to do it alone. *But,* we don't appreciate being lied to."

"Not at all," my mother chimes in. "Lying is the one thing in this house that we do not—*cannot*—tolerate."

"The *one* thing?" I say, giving in to a smirk that I know will infuriate her.

Sure enough, she looks chafed as she says, "It's a *big* one."

"We've always tried to keep the lines of communication open," my dad says.

"Uh-huh," I say.

"So why didn't you come to us?" he says, still calm, although I notice his clothing is even more wrinkled and disheveled than usual, as if he's been pacing and sleepless for days. Then again, maybe it's just how he seems in contrast to Marian and Peter, all pressed and perfect.

"Um. I guess because I didn't *want* to?" I say.

He ignores my flippant reply and says, "Why not?"

"Well. For starters, I heard what you guys said about me," I say, staring them both down as they pretend to be confused, and I prepare to drop my bomb. "I overheard you talking in the kitchen that night. About my birth mom and stuff."

My mother asks what in the world I'm talking about so I keep going. "About how you don't really know the true story of where I came from. Or who I am. And that my birth parents might be to blame for my problems. The root of all evil."

My parents exchange a guilty look and my mom says, "Nobody *ever* used the word 'evil,' Kirby."

"Whatever. I got the gist of it. So I thought I'd go find her. See if you were right about your little theories."

"Kirby. You misunderstood us," my dad says, running his hands along his bald spot.

"No. I think you were pretty clear, Dad. You basically accused them of being junkies and criminals."

"We said nothing of the sort!" my dad says, now officially shouting.

I win, I think, feeling smug. "And instead of her being the loser you think I take after, I meet this amazing, successful, smart producer," I say, knowing that I'm twisting the knife. "So I guess we can scratch that theory off the list. Gotta come up with another reason I'm such a screwup."

"Kirby!" my dad says. "Nobody thinks you're a screwup."

"Oh, no?"

"We just think you're an underachiever."

"Compared to who? You and Mom? Charlotte? Or my amazingly successful producer birth mother?" I say, my voice dripping with sarcasm. I know that I'm being mean but can't stop myself. After all, they compare me to their biological child every day; what's the difference?

"Hey! I don't appreciate your tone, young lady!" my dad says.

I stare at him. "Well, Dad. I don't appreciate the way I always feel like an outsider around here."

"You try to *make* yourself an outsider," my dad says, pointing his finger at me.

"How so?" I ask with a calculated smile.

"By not joining the family more," my mom says.

"At swim meets?" I say, glaring at her. "No offense to Charlotte, but I hate them. They're long and tedious and . . . And I don't like sports, period. I like other stuff. Like films and art and music. I'm not like the rest of you."

"See? The 'rest of you,'" my dad says. "Do you hear yourself?"

"I like movies and music," my mom chimes in, looking wounded.

"Okay—first, I said *films,* not lame blockbuster action movies and stupid, cheesy chick flicks," I say. "And two, Barry Manilow doesn't count as music."

"Hey!" my dad bellows, wagging his finger at me. I've obviously crossed a line bashing Barry.

"You used to love Barry Manilow," my mother says mournfully.

"When I was five. And you could still brainwash me," I

say. "Look. I'm sorry I went to New York without telling you. I just needed to meet her. On my own. And I did. And that's that."

"Is it?" my dad asks, adjusting the back of his recliner. "Do you feel better now?"

"Yes," I say. "I do." I close my mouth and cross my arms, uncertain why I'm not more willing to simply wave the white flag when they are obviously trying to be nice. And at the very least, they haven't threatened to ground me, a sign of a subtle and surprising shift of power.

"So. Are you going to stay in touch with her?" my mother asks.

I shrug as if it makes little difference to me when I've already checked my phone twenty times since I've been home, hoping for a reply to my "Made it back safely!" text.

"Well," my dad says. "On that note, we had an idea."

"What kind of idea?" I say, worried.

"We'd like to meet her," my mother says, looking like she's just eaten something sour.

My dad nods. "What do you think about inviting her out here? Maybe for graduation?"

"Yeah. Um . . . I don't think so," I say.

My mother looks shamelessly elated.

"Why not?" my dad says.

"She's really busy."

"Well, then she can decline," my dad says. "But we'd like to extend the invitation. If it's okay with you?"

"We'd like to at least talk to her," my mother says.

"You have nothing in common," I say.

"We have *you* in common," my dad says.

"And I bet we *all* think you should go to college," my mother chimes in, tipping her hand too early.

"Oh. So *that's* what this is about," I say, snapping my fingers as if a lightbulb just went off. "Get her on your side. Three against one?"

My mother shakes her head too quickly and vigorously, further blowing their cover.

"Okay. Look. I'll think about it," I say, wondering if I'm more agitated because they're so transparent about their intentions or because I know that Marian wouldn't want to come.

"Thank you," my dad says. "We appreciate it."

"Can I go now?"

"Yes," my dad says reluctantly.

I stand and head to my room so I can continue my search for Conrad Knight. I have no idea if he went to college, but I'd bet all the tuition in the world that he's not down with Barry Manilow.

12

Marian

A few days after Kirby leaves, I'm at Peter's loft in TriBeCa where he has lived since Robin kicked him out of their Upper East Side brownstone. We are on his couch, watching television, talking about work and Aidan, who will be coming over soon. Everything appears perfectly normal, but I can tell something is slightly off with us, and I have the strong feeling that it has something to do with Kirby. As much as I tried to turn the page when she left, I feel different now. Maybe I miss her. Or maybe I'm worried that Peter feels differently about me now, even less likely to want to marry me. Or maybe it's that I know I haven't yet told him the full story.

I wait for him to bring her up, but when he doesn't, I start to worry more, until I finally blurt it out. "For what it's worth," I say, resting my hand on his. "I'm sorry I didn't tell you about her sooner . . . I really wish I had."

"I wish you had, too," Peter says. "For *your* sake. Not mine."

"Are you sure this doesn't change . . . things?" I ask, looking in his eyes.

"Because you had a baby and put her up for adoption when you were eighteen years old?" Peter asks. "Do you really think I'm that shallow?"

"I don't think that would make you shallow," I say, knowing I'm avoiding the real issue. "Necessarily."

"Marian. What you did took courage. I admire it. I admire *you*." He shakes his head, as if he's still digesting the magnitude of the story. "But I guess I just don't fully understand . . . why you wouldn't tell me?"

"I didn't tell anyone."

"But I'm not just *anyone*." He puts his feet up on the coffee table, crossing them at his ankles. "Look. I understand that this is a very personal and private matter. I get why you wouldn't bring it up at *cocktail* parties . . . But we've been together for *two* years. We've discussed marriage."

I hesitate and then say, "*I've* discussed marriage."

He sighs, as if this is a technicality, and says, "So if she hadn't come, and we got engaged, would you have told me then?"

I feel myself start to squirm as I tell him I don't know.

"Yes, you do."

"Okay. Maybe not," I say. "Probably not."

"And you think that's okay?" he asks. "To keep a secret this big from the person you want to share your life with?"

"I don't know," I say, pulling my knees up under my chin. "I thought so . . . But now that I've met Kirby . . . It feels like a betrayal."

"You didn't betray me. You just didn't trust me," Peter says, as I realize that the people I really betrayed were Conrad and Kirby.

As if he senses this, he stares into my eyes and says, "So is that everything? Do I know the whole story now?"

"Well . . . There is a little more to it," I say, wiping my palms on my jeans.

He gives me a look that says he knew it, then gestures for me to continue.

"Kirby's birth father doesn't know about her," I say, my voice quivering.

He remains stone-faced as I tell him about the pregnancy test—that first lie to Conrad. And how I walked out the door, never to return, never to speak to him again.

Peter's expression finally changes, his face covered with judgment. "So this guy doesn't know he has a child?" he says.

I shake my head, my face burning, shame welling in my chest.

"Why?" Before I can answer, he continues, animated. "Why didn't you just tell him the truth? Why didn't you just say, 'Oh, shit. We have ourselves a little problem here.'"

He makes it sound so easy, and yet I have no answer.

"Were you in . . . denial?" Peter presses. "Is that why you lied? Is that why you kept the secret?"

I cringe, catching the way he has just used the words "secret" and "lie" interchangeably. "Maybe. I really don't know. I just—I just didn't think there was a point."

"You didn't think there was a *point*?" he says. "In telling a man he's conceived a child?"

I try another angle. "I felt as if I were sparing him."

"How so?" Peter fires back. He squares his shoulders to me and holds my gaze.

"What teenager wants to hear that they got a girl pregnant? It's the ultimate nightmare, Peter. Remember—we were eighteen. Kids."

"Well, don't you think he deserved to know? Don't you think that was *his* choice to make? Not yours?"

"Obviously not. I obviously thought it was *my* choice. You know . . . pro-*choice*," I say, even though I know I'm obfuscating his main point.

Peter's way too smart for this. "Right. I know it's your body—your choice . . . But we're not talking about whether

157

to *have* the baby. We're talking about *knowing* about the baby."

"Well, if you think I had the right to *abort* the pregnancy . . . Why couldn't I give her away? What's the difference to Conrad?"

"I'll tell you the difference," he says crisply. "One makes him a father. The other does not. Doesn't this guy have a right to know about his own child? As a father . . . God . . . I can't imagine . . ."

"But it wasn't like we were going to get married and start a family and a life together. I was going to college. He wasn't."

"Right. I got that," Peter says. "He was a loser in a band. Going nowhere. I got that part."

"He wasn't a *loser*," I say, feeling oddly defensive of Conrad, although it occurs to me that nobody could have treated him worse than I did. "We were just different. We wanted different things. But neither of us wanted a baby." I bite my lip. There is nothing I can say to defend myself, but I try anyway. "Giving Kirby two stable, loving parents was better for her than anything he could have given her alone. His father was an alcoholic. He was broke. And yes, he wasn't going anywhere. What if, for some reason, he wanted to keep her? What would I do then?"

"I don't know," Peter says, shaking his head. "I guess you would have had to make a choice."

"I did make a choice. And it was the right one for everyone involved," I say. But for the first time ever, I wonder whether this is true.

A few seconds later, in the worst possible timing, par for the course for Robin, I hear the sound of her voice in the hallway. Whether to irritate Peter, spend more time with

158

him, or simply catch me off guard, showing up early—or completely unexpectedly—is one of her signature moves, and I should have prepared for this possibility.

"Shit. They're forty-five minutes early," Peter says to himself. And then, because he knows this annoys me, "I'm sorry."

I nod and consider hiding in Peter's bedroom, but instead I gather myself as Robin saunters in without knocking, Aidan trailing behind. Peter stands, smiles, gives his son a high five, then musses up his swooping boy-band bangs that don't seem to go with his somber personality.

He turns to Robin and says, "When is he getting a haircut?"

"This is the look now, Peter," Robin says. "You're in television. You should know that."

"Hi, Aidan," I say.

"Hi, Marian," Aidan says back politely, shaking his hair from his left eye. He's a sweet, well-mannered kid, but we sadly have little rapport, perhaps because I really don't see that much of him. Sometimes it doesn't seem as if Peter sees that much of him, which you'd certainly think was the case if you listen to Robin complain about her ex's schedule.

Robin deposits her purse and two shopping bags on the floor, taking a seat across from me, sighing with exhaustion. Her chocolate-brown suede skirt is short, showing off a long expanse of tanned, toned thigh. Robin manages to ooze sex appeal in a barely tasteful way, and I smile remembering what Peter's sister once said about Robin: that if she had to take one thing to a desert island, it'd be lube. The comment should have bothered me, conjuring Peter's steamy days gone by, but for some reason, Robin has never made me jealous in that way, not even the few

159

times I've seen her in a bikini. The only time she bothers me is when she seems to still be in love with Peter, like the time we came to pick up Aidan at her place and she showed me their wedding album, prominently displayed on her coffee table. What made it worse is that Peter just shook it off with a laugh, saying what he always says, "That's Robin."

It's not that I don't want Peter to get along with her, and I actually like her pretty well myself—she can be incredibly funny and fun to be around—but I do resent it when they act as if they're still a couple.

"How are you, Robin?" I ask her now.

She sighs, then launches into a diatribe about how busy and stressed she is. She is the busiest, most stressed nonworking person I've ever met in my life. In mid-sentence about a charity ball she's chairing, she glances at my big toe, the polish chipping as of this morning.

"Oh, honey. What'd you do to that big toe? Stub it?" she says in a Southern accent. She grew up in Connecticut, but went to Auburn and turns the accent on and off when it suits her.

I shrug, glancing at Peter, engrossed in conversation with Aidan, and barb her back. "Who knows? Maybe playing tennis with Peter?"

This is a purposeful statement as Peter told me that it was a bone of contention during their marriage. It wasn't that he wanted her to run marathons or scale mountains, but she refused to so much as get her head wet on trips to the beach. He said it was a symbol for so much else wrong with them, namely that they had little in common, that she was materialistic and obsessed with her appearance (summed up by her face-lift at age forty-four).

But the biggest problem in their marriage—and ultimately the deal-breaker—was her chronic dishonesty. She never had an affair—at least none that Peter knew of—or told a huge lie, but there were enough little lies and half-truths to build a compelling case against her. The Devi Kroell alligator hobo she bought wasn't "that expensive" (it was *four thousand* dollars—a problem in and of itself). She only had one drink, not six. Her college boyfriend friended *her* on Facebook, not the other way around. In fact, Robin seemed to fit the definition of a pathological liar, telling lies when there seemed to be no reason to do so—about completely insignificant things—like not telling the truth about what she had for breakfast. Peter said when he could no longer trust her, he no longer liked her. My stomach churns with worry that he will feel the same about me now.

Robin chitchats (mostly to herself) for a few more minutes, then abruptly stands and prances to the door. "I gotta go. Have a hot date!" she says, passing Peter and Aidan on her way to the door.

To her obvious disappointment, Peter looks bored with her routine, showing no interest in her love life. Or her legs, for that matter.

"Don't you want to know who I'm seeing?" she asks him, raising her voice an octave, cocking her head to the side as Aidan migrates toward the couch, pulling an Ursula Le Guin novel out of his messenger bag. I have never seen a boy read as much as he does, which he obviously doesn't get from his mother who once, unabashedly, announced to me that she "hates to read." Who admits to something like that?

"Not particularly," Peter says, with an amused look. It's almost as if he's still fond of her—in the way you'd be fond of a dog with a few charming tricks. "But you're welcome to tell me if you'd like."

"I'll tell you. I wouldn't want to keep it a secret," she says, then looks at me for a long beat.

My heart starts to pound. Did he *tell* her? Surely he wouldn't do that to me. But what else could she mean by such a statement, such a lingering gaze my way? I give him the benefit of the doubt, waiting for her comedy routine to continue, wondering what I could borrow from her repertoire to put in a script. I've done it before.

"Nathan Bilet," she says.

Peter stares at her blankly.

"God, Peter. He's a world-*renowned* sculptor," she says. "You remember, you sat next to him at the Joyful Heart Gala a few years ago? He was just written up in the Arts section?"

She turns to me and says, "Nathan does kinetic sculpture. Art with moving parts."

"Yeah. I got that," I deadpan as I stand and join Peter, slipping my arm around his waist, half on purpose, half because I feel the sudden urge to touch him.

"And he does sound sculpture, too. He's so avant-garde," she says with a dreamy expression.

I wonder if she might define "avant-garde" for me, or perhaps "sound," but when she doesn't, I say, "Well. I bet he's a fascinating fellow."

"Yes, he is. And he is *French*," she says, fanning herself. "A little young for me, but I think I can keep up!"

"I'm sure you can, Rob," Peter says, reaching out to pat her shoulder and gently guiding her along. "You have yourself a great time."

"Are you pushing me out the door?" she says.

162

Peter smiles. "No. I wouldn't want you to be late for your date. It might be Nathan's pet peeve."

She beams, then shouts over to Aidan, "Love you, honey! See you tomorrow night!"

"Love you, too, Mom," he says, without looking up from his book.

"Well. Okay. I'll be on my way," she says, stalling. "I know you two have lots to discuss." She looks at me again, and this time it's unmistakable. She *definitely* knows. "Just do me a favor?"

"What's that?" I say, trying to control my hurt and anger that he would confide in her about me.

She drops her voice to a whisper. "Don't give Aidan *all* the details. It's just . . . not a topic I want to introduce to him. At his age," she says, relishing the chance to be the responsible parent—not her usual role.

"Oh, I understand, Robin," I say as sarcastically as possible.

"He knows about the birds and the bees," she says. "But still . . ."

Out of the corner of my eye, I see Aidan glance over at his parents, as if he knows exactly what's going on, then stand and make his way to his bedroom where he will likely spend most of the night.

"Sorry. I didn't mean anything bad by that," Robin says, turning to look at me with confusion, as if she doesn't know exactly what she did wrong. Crazily enough, I think she might not. She's not manipulative or mean, she's just *dumb*.

But Peter knows *exactly* what's going on. So as she gives us a wave with her pinky and waltzes out the door, I stare at the floor, unable to make eye contact with him. "How could you?" I say.

"How could I what?" he says.

"Tell her."

"I didn't tell her," he says, putting his arm around me.

I shake free. "Oh, puh-lease, Peter."

"I told Aidan," Peter says, lowering his voice. "He must have told his mother."

"You told *Aidan*?"

"Yes. Is that a problem?"

I recognize a trick question when I hear one; if I say yes, I'm implying that I don't see Aidan as an extension of him. A *big* problem when you want to marry someone. Still, I believe he should have asked me first. I believe we should have talked about it before he told his son, *anyone* for that matter, *especially* knowing that Aidan could tell Robin. I make these points to Peter, trying to remain calm and leave Robin out of the discussion. This isn't about her.

"He's my *son*, Marian. And I saw him that morning. Right after I met Kirby... Besides, we had talked about going to dinner, the four of us. So I assumed it was okay to talk to him. And wasn't that sort of a desired by-product of Kirby's visit? That you were going to face this story and come clean with everything?"

"Come *clean*?" I say. "See? Even *you* think it's shameful."

"Okay. Poor choice of words," Peter says. "I thought you were going to ... make it ... no longer a big secret. Of course—that was before I knew it was a big secret even from the father."

"God, Peter," I say. "It happened *eighteen* years ago. Why is this so important to you?"

"Because it is," Peter says. "It's the most important thing in the world, actually. Having a child. And the fact that you don't seem to see it that way—"

I cut him off. "Gives you another reason not to marry me?"

He looks at me, his silence telling.

"I have to go," I say, feeling numb, then scared by how numb I am.

I wait for Peter to stop me, but he just watches me. As I walk out of his apartment, the door closing behind me, a feeling of déjà vu washes over me. The feeling of leaving, even when you don't want to. The feeling that sometimes things just can't be fixed.

13

Kirby

Want one?" Mr. Tully asks me, motioning to an open box of doughnuts as he finishes one and starts another. I'm in his office on a get-out-of-gym free pass, purportedly to discuss my college plans although we have yet to touch on them. "They're from Ray's. Dy-na-*mite*."

I shake my head and tell him that powdered doughnuts are too messy, especially when you're wearing red. And why are there always so many baked goods here, anyway, I ask, then speculate: grateful parents? Bribes from students? Secretaries with a crush? He laughs, looking hotter than usual, then throws his head back and takes a large bite, powdered sugar flying everywhere. He licks his thumb, and as I stare at his lips, a vision of Mr. Tully making out pops into my head. Not with me—I've never gone there—but a giggly, big-breasted, sorority-girl type. Hoping that he had better taste than that in college, or at least now, I change my image to a slim, intellectual brunette, then squint over at the time on his computer monitor. Only twenty minutes left in the period.

"So," I say, reaching over to his desk to swat at a grinning, slightly maniacal-looking Nebraska Cornhusker baseball bobblehead doll. "I have some news for you."

"You finally memorized the quadratic formula?" he asks with a wink. " 'Cause that'd be huge."

"Ha. No. And it's not nice to mock someone's academic

166

shortcomings," I say. "I mean—that's the stuff that could put me in serious therapy later in life. My own guidance counselor calling me stupid."

"Stupid? No," he says. "Stubbornly refusing to learn, hmmm . . . yes." He points at me dramatically, grinning.

"Anyway," I say, dismissing the topic with a wave of my hand. "This has nothing to do with math. It has to do with where I went last week."

He glances up at the ceiling, still smiling, as if trying to come up with something funny, as Scooter Banks appears in the glass window, then opens the door, pokes his head in and bellows, "Yo! Mr. T! You like updog?"

"Is this the part where I'm supposed to say, 'What's updog?' "

Scooter bursts into laughter and shouts, "What up with you, dawwwg?!"

"Get back to class, Scooter," Mr. Tully says, shooing him.

Still cackling, Scooter saunters down the hall as I roll my eyes and mutter, "What a dullard."

"Impressive vocabulary," Mr. Tully says. "See? You are most definitely not stupid."

I smile, thinking the SAT class I took came in handy after all, and then come out with it. "So I met my birth mother. Over our long weekend. I found her in New York City. I went there. Alone."

Mr. Tully whistles, then gives me a look that I want to can and save forever. It is one of true respect. He is impressed and intrigued, and although I know he likes me, this is a first with him. With anyone for that matter. He motions for me to continue, and I tell him the whole story from the call to the agency six weeks ago to the bus ride to New York City to my late-evening knock at her door.

"Wow," he says. Then repeats the word twice more.

I grin, continuing, telling him all about Marian and her life. He listens more intently than Belinda or my sister, as I knew he would, and his first question is a quiet, thoughtful one. "Do you think you're alike?" he asks.

"Physically?" I say.

He nods, says we can start there, and I tell him yes, you can most definitely tell we are related. "Our coloring is the same. We have the same basic build. And the same big ears." I smile, blushing.

Mr. Tully taps his fist to his chest and says, "What about here? Are you alike here?"

It is the sort of thing that would sound cheesy coming from anyone else, especially coupled with the gesture to the heart, but he is cool and cute enough to get away with it.

"Not really, no . . . Maybe a tiny bit," I say.

"How so?"

I shrug and say, "It's hard to explain. She's smarter than I am. More of a go-getter." I laugh and continue, "Well. That's kind of the understatement of the century . . ."

"I don't know—she might be more of a go-getter but I doubt that she's smarter. You're her daughter after all. And you're very smart."

"Yeah. Says you."

"Says your test scores. Tell me more."

"I don't know. She's sort of quiet. Like me. But she's really good with people, too," I say, picturing her in the writers' room. "Like she always knows exactly what to say and do . . . And is always sort of . . . put together."

"Is that a good thing?"

"Well, yeah," I say. "Better than fumbling around like I do."

"You don't fumble."

168

"Yeah, I do."

"You just feel that way. For a teenager, you're very . . . self-possessed."

"Whatever that means."

"It means you sound like you have something else in common with your birth mother."

I shake my head. "No. She's perfect. Her hair and skin and clothes. And her apartment. It's all perfect and stylish. Everything."

"Sounds like a lot of work."

"Not for her."

"Well, then it sounds kind of . . . boring?" Mr. Tully says.

I shrug. "Well, it's not me. That's for sure," I say, thinking of the clothes she bought me—that I still have yet to wear. I nearly tell him, but don't want to put the feeling I have into words—that she tried to buy me off for the lie she told, like, *Hey, sorry your dad doesn't know you exist. But check out these Prada shoes!*

"What is it?" Mr. Tully says. It's uncanny how he does that—asks me what I'm thinking right at the moment I'm having a pretty major thought.

I swallow, stare at my hands, and decide to give him some of the dirt. "So. As it turns out . . . She never told anyone about me."

He cocks his head to the side. "No one?"

"Nope. Not a soul but her mother."

If he is shocked, he pretends not to be, and instead cuts right to the chase and asks, "How did that make you feel?"

"I don't know. I guess it surprised me."

"Did it hurt your feelings?"

"A little," I admit, then quickly add, "But whatever. No biggie."

"So your birth father doesn't know about you?" Mr. Tully says.

"No," I say, feeling my cheeks burn, as if this says something about me—instead of her. "She never told him she was pregnant."

When he doesn't respond, I say, "I know. Shocking, right?"

"I'm a guidance counselor," Mr. Tully says, cracking his knuckles. "Nothing shocks me."

"Well, I wish she'd had you to talk to," I say. "Back in the nineties."

"Why's that?" Mr. Tully probes. "Do you wish she had made another decision?"

"No," I quickly reply. "I'm not saying that. I just wish . . . she had told him about me."

"Of course you do," he says.

"And you know what? I think she does, too. And I think maybe someone like you could have convinced her of that."

"Well, then," Mr. Tully says. "What are you two waiting for?"

"What?" I say.

"Why don't you go find him? Like you did with her?"

"It's too late," I say, even though I spent two more hours last night looking for him on the computer. "At least it's too late to do it with her. Her life is all perfect and stuff."

"It's not perfect, Kirby," Mr. Tully says just as the bell rings over the intercom. "And it's *definitely* not too late."

14

Marian

On Tuesday morning, Peter knocks at my office door, virtually unprecedented without a scheduled meeting (which always take place in *his* office) and asks if I have a second.

"Sure," I say, my palms starting to feel clammy. We have not spoken in three days—since I left his apartment—and although I'm not sure what I want him to say, I'm hoping that this visit is personal in nature. But within seconds, I realize he is here for work-related reasons as he opens a file folder and slides the outline of episodes I gave him onto my desk. I notice right away that it is in track-changes mode and the margins are littered with comments.

"You didn't like it?" I say.

"Of course I liked it. Vicky and I both liked it," he says, referring to the director of programming, my immediate boss, who would probably be here if Peter and I weren't dating.

"But there are some things we need to discuss," he says. My heart sinks. I know this look from last season—and the season before. And the one before that. It's the look right before he tells me to change everything we've written.

I flip through the document, noticing a note in the margin that says "too much drinking." I point at it and say, "The show takes place in a bar, Peter. Did Norm drink too much on *Cheers*?"

"Look. Don't get defensive," he says.

"I'm not," I fire back, glancing down to read other notes, many of which have to do with the "tone" of a particular scene or dialogue.

"What are these tonal notes about?" I say. "What's wrong with our tone?"

"Nothing. It just needs to be toned down," he says, crossing his legs, man-style, and chuckling to himself.

I don't crack a smile.

"Sorry," he says, uncrossing his legs. "No time for jokes."

"No. It's really not," I say. "Just give it to me straight."

"All right. It's too gritty. Too much sex, drinking, language, violence . . ."

"This isn't ABC Family. You do know that, right?"

"Yes, I'm aware—"

"And it's the same tone we've always had."

"Not exactly. It's a slippery slope, and you're getting too . . . out there."

"But it's what people like about us. We're not generic and vanilla."

"Look, Marian," he says, all of his hard edges beginning to emerge. "You need to be aware of some facts. Being on Thursdays at nine carries a heavy burden. You're up against the big boys, and we expect to draw more eyeballs to justify what we're charging."

"So we're not a cash cow—"

He makes a snorting noise, then reaches into his file and tosses me another document. "Far from it."

I glance at the paper of figures and demographics then look back at him, shaking my head. "You're not giving us a chance to succeed. And with these notes—we'll never make it. You can't water us down like this."

"Look, Marian. You know what Vicky wants to do?" he asks. "She wants to put you in the Friday-night death slot. I saved your ass."

"Why?" I shout back at him, deciding I will skip the part about thinking Vicky is an insipid fool. He already knows my opinion of her.

"What do you mean 'why'?"

"Why'd you save my ass? Because we're having sex?" I say, intentionally mischaracterizing our relationship. "Or because you believe in the show that I created?"

"Honestly?" he says. "Both."

"Well, do me a favor—forget about the former when you're in your little meetings. I don't need that leg up," I say, my voice shaking, realizing I can't win. If the show does well as is, it's because he did me favors. If he waters us down, we lose our following and get canceled. I reach over and angrily clean out a few messages from my in-box, just to have something to do with my hands.

He sighs and says, "Look, Marian. I'm doing my best to keep you on Thursday, but we have to change you to eight o'clock. You don't have the numbers to compete in the nine slot, and the advertisers are complaining about your content in the eight. So you gotta tone some of it down. I'm sorry. I know it's not what you want to hear, but that's the way it is. We have to be profitable."

"This is bullshit," I say under my breath, skimming over the notes.

"It doesn't matter if millions watch your show if the content is scaring all the advertisers off and getting parents into a tizzy."

I glare at him. "Thank you for that lesson in television."

He ignores me and says, "The last thing I want is for

you to get canceled because you didn't want to tweak your content, and we had to put you in a time slot where your audience couldn't find you."

I ignore his condescending question and tell him I'm fully aware that it all comes down to money. "But you can't ask me not to balk when you take away all my creative integrity."

"We didn't take it all away. We just took *some* of it away," he says with another small smile that would be charming if he were talking about someone else's project. "Just do a little retooling. Make it a little more . . . *wholesome*. A little less gritty."

"So basically, change the whole show," I mutter. "God. Why do we have to cater to the schlubs out there? Smart people watch TV, too. Isn't that why you came to this network?"

"Marian. Calm down and read the notes. Your show will still be smart—just not quite as . . . edgy . . . We'll talk tomorrow," he says with infuriating control. "Okay?"

"Fine," I say, knowing that I will make all his changes—as I always do—that I don't have any other choice.

He starts to get up, then sits back down and looks at me.

"What?" I say.

"Is there anything else you want to talk about?"

"Not really," I say, desperate for him to stay a little longer although I know a sarcastic, counterproductive comment is about to escape my lips. "Except that I'm terribly sorry you don't agree with the choices I made when I was eighteen."

He crosses his arms and nods, then lowers his voice and says, "Well. To be fair—they are choices you've continued to make—every day, every year since then . . . but it's your life."

"And it's your network," I say before he shakes his head, stands up, and takes his turn to walk out the door.

We don't talk the next day, or the one after that, our Friday-night plans with friends looming on the calendar. He calls about thirty minutes before our reservation when I'm home, changing out of my work clothes.

"Let me guess. You're canceling?" I say.

"I just wanted to get the ground rules for tonight," he says, speaking in his best passive-aggressive voice.

"What's that supposed to mean?"

"It means do your friends know about Kirby?"

"So now they're only *my* friends?"

"Okay. *Our* friends."

"No," I say, hurriedly glancing around my dressing table for the right jewelry and accessories. "They don't. I've been a little busy rewriting my show."

"Are you going to tell them?" he asks.

"I don't know," I say. "If it comes up."

"Well, I don't think it's going to just come up on its own."

"Well, I guess you have your answer then," I say.

"So you're just going to pretend?"

"Pretend what, exactly?" I say, thinking, *Pretend that we are happy?*

He clears his throat. "Pretend that we aren't in the middle of a major happening in our lives."

Although I like that he said "we" and "our," and used "happening" rather than "crisis," I still feel a knot of resentment in my chest that he won't just let me move on with *my* life. Even Kirby has granted me that much. Other than a few texts back and forth, I haven't heard from her, and to my relief, there has been no further mention of

175

Conrad. My feelings about this remain ambivalent, but I've decided that the path we're on is the best for both of us. She has a family, and I want my own. With someone who understands why I did what I did.

"Okay. Look. You want me to tell them? I'll tell them. Over dessert maybe. 'Oh, by the way, guys . . . I had a baby eighteen years ago. Have I mentioned that?'"

"Don't be glib, Marian," he says.

"*Glib?* Is that what you call giving a baby up for adoption?" I say, freezing, staring down my reflection in the mirror. I look old, or at least tired—and glance away quickly. "Is that the vibe you've gotten from me these days? A *glib* vibe?"

He is silent.

"Actually, you can't be getting any kind of vibe," I say. "We've spent almost no time together since I met Kirby."

"I know," he says. "That's the point. I've given you space—and you used that space to keep your usual distance."

"This coming from a man who won't talk about marriage," I say, mentally tallying the number of times I've brought it up. Undoubtedly crossing the line from wondering about our future to pressuring him about it.

"We are in no position to talk about marriage," he says.

"How convenient for you," I say. "How tidy."

"You want to talk about tidy? Let's talk about your decision, Marian. The *perfect* decision. Have the baby, give it up for adoption, don't tell a soul. Bam. Neat and tidy."

I feel my cheeks burn, my hands beginning to shake. "There is nothing about childbirth that is neat and tidy. *Abortion* is neat and tidy. You have no *idea* what I went through. How hard that was."

"Okay. You're right. I'm sorry. I know that sounded

176

harsh. I just think . . ." He sighs and finishes his sentence. "I think you haven't dealt with this."

"I *have* dealt with this."

"You haven't. Just because you had a little 'bring your daughter to work' day? A field trip to a museum?"

"And *I'm* glib?" I say, even though I know, in some ways, he's right. "Wow, Peter. What did you want me to do with her?"

"Bond, maybe?"

"She wasn't here to get a new mother. She has one."

"Well, I'm quite sure that she came here for more than sightseeing and shopping. She obviously needs you."

"So what should I have done? Cry a river about how sad I am that I didn't keep her?" As soon as the words are out, I realize what I've said, and more important, that maybe, despite years of trying to convince myself otherwise, I do have remorse for my choices. I could have kept her. I could have opted for an open adoption. At the very least, I could have told the truth about her.

Peter hears it, too, of course, and makes a sound to say that I've just proven his point.

"Okay," I say. "You win."

His voice softens like a therapist who just got the breakthrough he's been probing for. "I'm not saying you did the wrong thing by giving her up for adoption. You've had a wonderful life. I'm sure she has, too."

Tears sting at my eyes as I grab my coat and keys, "I'm thirty-six years old, Peter. I want to be a mother. My boyfriend doesn't want another child . . ."

"I never said that."

"Well? Do you? Or don't you?"

Silence.

"So that's a no?"

"It's an 'I don't know.'"

"Okay. Well, my boyfriend of two years doesn't *know* if he wants another child," I say. "So therefore, assuming I stay with my boyfriend, I don't *know* if I will have a child. And assuming I break up with my boyfriend, it's anyone's guess whether I will find someone else in the quickly shrinking window of my fertility."

"I'm assuming you're staying with your boyfriend," Peter says.

"Well, that makes one of us . . . So maybe you should just skip dinner tonight," I say.

"Yeah. Maybe so," he says, finally as riled as I am.

"Fine. Later," I say, then hang up the phone before he can do it first.

Fifteen minutes later, I arrive at Campagnola, a classic Upper East Side Italian restaurant with a rustic décor and a well-heeled clientele. It is one of Peter's favorites. As I walk inside, I immediately spot Claudia and Jess, two of my closest friends in the city, sitting at the bar. Jess is holding court with three men, typical for her.

"Hello!" I say over the cheerful din and Sinatra tunes being played by the house pianist. My heart is heavy, but I'm breezy, smiling, and I find myself wondering if my whole life really is a façade.

"Hey, girl! Want a T.L.C.?" Jess asks, raising her glass.

"What's in a T.L.C.?" I say.

"Whiskey, Cointreau, pastis, vermouth, bitters. Even Claudia likes it," she proclaims, turning to signal our bartender that we'll have another.

"*Even* Claudia?" Claudia says. She knows she's the most

conservative in our trio—uptight, according to Jess—but she still resists the label.

Jess flashes a smug smile and turns back to her audience of suits. "Proves what I've always contended. Everyone likes whiskey; it's just a matter of how, when, and where."

The men laugh a little too heartily, clearly titillated by a whiskey-loving woman, especially one who looks like a model. What makes Jess even more appealing is that she's a hard-core investment banker who survived the Lehman Brothers bankruptcy and landed on her feet to become the head of health care banking at Goldman. I have often joked to Peter that the two of them would make a perfect couple, that she is a funnier, prettier, smarter version of me. And they both have commitment issues.

As we catch up with surface updates about work and life, Claudia and I do our best to exclude the random men from our conversation—which is easier to do once we are joined by Ben, Claudia's husband.

"Where's Petey boy?" Ben asks after we exchange another round of hellos and hugs.

"Working. He can't make it tonight," I say, which everyone takes at face value because it's hardly unusual. But as Jess leads us over to the hostess stand, and we are promptly ushered to a large round table in the center of the oil-painting-adorned dining room, I confess to Claudia that we're in a fight.

"Do you want to talk about it?" she asks as we're seated.

"Talk about what?" Jess demands.

"Nothing, really. I was just saying that Peter and I are in a little spat," I say, grateful for the whiskey that I'm now gulping. "Actually, I think we might be on the verge of breaking up."

"Shut up!" Jess says. "What happened? Oh, shit—did he cheat on you? Tell me he didn't cheat on you."

"No," I say, thinking of all the salacious married-men stories from her past and that I'm not surprised that this is her first theory of a split. "It's nothing like that. It's . . . a much longer story."

"Spill it," Jess says. "You'll feel better."

I smile, marveling at how different we are, the idea of a secret among friends inconceivable to her. "Is it that bitch ex-wife of his?" she guesses. "Causing trouble again?"

"Not exactly," I say.

"A problem with Aidan?" she speculates.

"Are you going to keep guessing or let her speak?" Claudia says.

"We've . . . just had some issues come up," I say, thinking of Kirby, a dull ache in my chest. "And I think he's using those discussions to justify his inability to take the next step."

"Christ. Wait. Back up and stop speaking in code," Jess says. "What's going on?"

"I don't think he wants to have another child," I say.

"But you're not sure he *doesn't,* right?" Claudia asks, an expert on the topic, having nearly broken up with Ben years ago, before they reunited months later. Ironically, their split was the reverse of my situation—he wanted a baby and she did not. It was a deal-breaker until they realized it wasn't. They now have a three-year-old daughter named Frances and I have never seen such a doting mother.

"You'll work it out," Ben says. I study his face, feeling comforted. He has that effect. He is the sort of husband and father you imagine marrying when you're eight years old and believe in happily ever after. All-American and

180

handsome but not too handsome. Funny but not full of himself. Smart and ambitious but with strong family values. In fact, when Frances was born, he took a two-year leave of absence from his architectural firm to care for her full-time. "Look at Claudia and me. Sometimes it just takes time."

"Maybe," I say. "But I'm sort of running out of that."

Claudia rolls her eyes and tells me not to be ridiculous, but I shut her down with a reminder that she was pregnant at my age.

"I'm two years older than you," Jess says, motioning around the table. "And I'm not at all panicked."

I carefully avoid the sore subject of Michael, her most recent ex, their breakup still raw, and simply remind her that she has a stash of frozen eggs and plans to use a surrogate anyway.

Claudia looks thoughtful and then says, "So that's why he's not here tonight? Because you want a baby and he's not sure?" It is clear by her tone that she knows I've left an important part of the story out—and it is one of the reasons I like her so much. She's astute, hearing what you're *not* saying as much as what you *are*.

I hesitate, feeling my defenses crumble as I think of Kirby. Her teenage-girl, cheap-perfume scent and unskilled eye-shadow application. Her big ears and her sweet, shy smile. Her surprising rap performance in the writers' room and wide-eyed wonder in the Guggenheim. I think of our final hug before I put her in the cab and how much I suddenly miss her and, most of all, what I missed out on by not being her mother. Aware that my friends are watching me, waiting for me to reply, I put my glass down and say, "Okay. In part, this disagreement with

Peter . . . is about marriage. I want to have a baby. I want to be a mother . . ."

Claudia reaches out and touches my hand as I take a breath and find a way to continue, wondering if I'm doing this more for myself or to make a point to Peter. "And I want that especially because . . . well . . . I had a baby once. A long time ago."

"What? When?" Jess shouts.

I stare down at the table, but stay the course. "I was eighteen. Before college. I had the baby, and then . . . and then gave her away."

"For adoption?" Jess asks.

I smile and say, "Well, I didn't put her in a basket on a church doorstep."

"God, Marian," Claudia says, as I think of her own sister, who adopted a baby in an open agreement, while Ben just stares at me, his face full of compassion.

"Damn," Jess says, reaching across the empty seat for my hand.

"Heavy stuff, huh?" I say, trying to smile and lighten the mood just as the waitress arrives to give her spiel. We listen and then Jess orders two bottles of a Tuscan red and a sampling of our usual, favorite appetizers.

A few seconds later, Jess resumes the questioning. "Why didn't you tell us?" she asks, mystified, unable to grasp holding back a juicy bit of information from so much as her cabdriver.

"I never told anyone," I say. "I kept the secret for eighteen years. From everyone but my mother. I didn't tell my own father. I didn't tell the baby's father. Nobody knew. Until last Saturday . . . when she knocked on my door. When she found me."

I wait for someone to speak, but when no one does—not even Jess—I keep talking, telling them about Kirby, realizing, with some panic, that I don't know all that much about her. I think of Peter's remarks about sightseeing and feel a wave of prickly shame.

"So wait. You didn't tell the baby daddy?" Jess says, honing in on the most salacious part of the story. "That's insane. And I always thought you were as square as Claudia."

Claudia and I both ignore her. "So that's pretty much why Peter didn't come. He thinks I haven't dealt with this," I say.

The table falls silent again. "Are you upset I didn't tell you?"

They all claim not to be, which I believe, the waitress once again giving us a break as she arrives to pour our wine.

Jess is the first to raise her glass. "To secret adoptions!"

We all laugh and shake our heads.

"There were times when I *wanted* to tell you," I say, looking at Claudia first. "When you told me about your sister adopting Luke ... when you were pregnant with Frances." Then I look at Jess. "And every time you confided one of your gems." I smile. "But I just decided long ago that I wasn't going to tell anyone. I just wanted to put it in the past and move on."

Ben asks, "So what do you think Peter's main issue with this is?"

I shake my head. "I really don't know. He seems to be implying that it's an honesty issue. That I was keeping something big from him."

Claudia turns to Ben and says, "Honey, would you feel that way?"

"It's really hard for me to imagine that . . . Given your resistance to having a baby in the first place," Ben says.

"Well, pretend that it's another secret," I say. "Anything that she kept from you."

"Like a three-way lesbian tryst?" Ben says.

"Don't pretend to be a pig," Claudia says. "You can't pull it off."

Ben smiles, takes a sip of wine, and then grows serious. "I want to say that I'd understand . . . I feel like understanding, no strings attached, is the right, bigger-person thing to do . . . But honestly, I think I'd be upset. Not so much angry—but hurt."

"You would?" I ask, a nervous pit returning to my stomach. If Ben would have a problem with it, anybody would.

He nods, then frowns and says, "And I might be a little worried, too. It sort of feels like a trust issue. I mean, don't you want to believe that he's told you everything? At least everything big that's happened to him? What if he held something back like this? Something of this magnitude?"

I try to imagine that Robin is actually his second wife, rather than his first. Or even, more on point, that he has another kid out there. "Yeah. Maybe it would give me pause, too," I say.

"But," Ben says. "I also think that if he can't get over this, then he doesn't love you the way he should love you."

I look at him, waiting for him to continue.

"This is not an unforgivable offense. Really—nothing is unforgivable if you truly love someone," he says, glancing at Claudia.

"And what about Kirby?" Claudia asks. "Are you glad she found you?"

184

"Yes," I say. "For the most part. I'm relieved that she's okay. She seems to have a good family . . . and a good head on her shoulders."

"But . . . ?" Jess says.

"But it definitely complicates my life. Not only with Peter. But with everything . . . Before she showed up, it felt like my decision whether to tell anyone about her. Now I have to think about her. Does she want to know her grandfather? Then I need to tell my dad. Does she want to be part of my life? I have to show her that she is welcome in it. And." I stop in my tracks, wondering if this part of the story will ever get easier. "And in Jess's eloquent words, I might have to confess to the baby daddy," I say, my stomach dropping. "I know she wants to find him. She didn't come right out and say it—but I can feel it."

"Do you want to find him?" Ben asks.

I try to sugarcoat it but don't have the energy. "No," I say. "I've spent my whole life trying to distance myself from this mistake. From him. From that time. The last thing I want to do is go back and unearth it all."

"Unearth what?" Jess asks, looking jubilant. "Your *feelings* for him?"

"This isn't a television show, Jess," I say.

"It could be."

"Shut up," I say, thinking that if were a show, Peter would change the story line and Conrad, Kirby, and I would be a happy little trio.

"*You* shut up," she snaps back at me. "Shut up and find him. You and your daughter need to go find him, *Thelma and Louise* style!" She grins and makes a ridiculous lassoing motion over her head.

185

15

Kirby

We *have* to go," Belinda says as we jog around the track during our timed mile in PE. She is referring to prom—the only topic I find more tedious than college. It is also the only topic I feel more decisive about than college. For the gazillionth time, I tell her I'm not going, my mind drifting back to Marian and Conrad. It's been a few days since I talked to Mr. Tully, and pretty much all I've been doing is obsessing over finding my other parent.

"C'mon, Kirby," she continues. "I refuse to be *that* girl—sitting home watching some rom-com and shoving my face full of popcorn."

"So don't watch movies or eat popcorn," I say as Justine Lewis laps us for the second time, her long blond ponytail dancing like a kite string, her neon-pink Nikes kicking up dust in a cloud that reminds me of Pig Pen on Charlie Brown. As ridiculous as I think it is to overachieve in PE, I'm kind of jealous of stupid ol' Justine, wishing I went out and played the drums like she runs track—proudly and for all the world to see.

"If we don't go," Belinda says, "we'll regret it for the rest of our lives."

"God, I sincerely hope we aren't thinking about prom for the rest of our lives, Belinda. Or anything about high school, for that matter," I say.

Short of a teenage pregnancy, I think. *And maybe not even then.*

"Shit. Cramp," she says, slowing to a walk as she limps and kneads her side.

Mrs. Tropper, our gym teacher, shakes her head in disgust as we pass her along a straightaway.

Belinda says, "It's a rite of passage."

"Says you."

"Says everyone."

"Except me."

"Kirby. Seriously. People will ask forever, 'Who did you go to prom with?'" she says. "And we'll be like, 'Uh, no one. We were total losers.'"

I tell her I've never heard the question posed to anyone over the age of twenty. That I have no idea if my parents went to theirs, although I seem to remember some weird story about my mother swapping dates with her best friend at the last minute.

"I bet Marian went," Belinda says. "I bet she was prom queen."

"It didn't come up. Shock, surprise," I say, although I wouldn't be surprised if Belinda was right. I mean, buying crazy-expensive designer clothes for your newly discovered daughter seems like something a former prom queen might do. Which is another reason I can't stomach wearing them—or even showing them to Belinda or my sister.

"Come on, Kirby. *Please.* Do it for me," she says, pausing to tie her shoelace and catch her breath. "For once, can we just not be the two *losers*?"

I watch as she double-knots both laces. "I think we'll be *bigger* losers if we go with each other than if we don't go at all."

She shakes her head. "No way. We'll look like sexy, liberated *women*. Like we don't need a man."

I let out a snort of laughter and tell her I've never seen anyone need a man as much as she does.

Proving my point, she says, "Although I actually might have a date. I'm really feelin' it with Jake Mahoney."

"Who?"

"The guy I met at the mall."

I groan.

"What?"

"The *mall*? Belinda, mall pickups are for *hoosiers*," I say, St. Louis slang for white trash. "With femullets."

"For your information, we were at the Galleria, shopping for sunglasses," she says. "Hoosiers don't shop at the Galleria."

"Until you and Jake went there," I say, smiling.

"Okay. Say what you will about your best friend in the world. But Jake's *no* hoosier. He lives in Clayton. He goes to Chaminade. He plays lacrosse. He's going to Wash U next year."

"Please, Belinda. You know a Chaminade guy is never going to go for a DuBourg girl," I say, referring to 101 in St. Louis high school snobbery.

"C'mon, Kirb. He really seems to like me. For real."

"Fine. So ask him to prom. Go for it," I say, finally breaking a sweat as we begin our fourth and final lap.

"Only if you go with us. He has this friend, Philip—"

"Philip? His name is *Philip*?"

"What's wrong with the name Philip?"

"Nothing. If you're a queen or duchess or something," I say.

"It's not like you to judge a book by its cover," she says, skillfully hitting a hot button.

"Look, Belinda. I'm not going to prom. And I'm certainly not going on a *blind* date to prom. With a Philip."

"He's cute, I swear. You can check him out on Facebook."

"Right. 'Cause people never misrepresent on Facebook. You, of all people, know that's not the case," I say, thinking of her many bogus status updates about all the fun she's having at fictional parties.

"I don't lie. I just stretch the truth. And do a lot of Photoshopping." She laughs and says, "Why don't you meet him? And if it goes well—"

"No, thanks," I say, as Mrs. Tropper blows her whistle and singles us out among a half-dozen other stragglers. "Belinda! Kirby! Zip it, ladies! C'mon! C'mon! Move it!"

I flip her off as she turns to heckle someone else, but we pick up the pace ever so slightly, falling silent as I think about prom. Way deep down, maybe I am just the tiniest bit disappointed not to be going, especially after Charlotte gave me the giddy update last night that Noah invited her, followed by her half-dozen visits back to my room to show me earmarked pages of evening wear in the Macy's mailer. Maybe, once upon a time, I, too, had a few girly visions of prom. Picking out the beautiful dress. Having a cute boy arrive at my house to pick me up. Taking a million photos with friends in the backyard. Sneaking a flask into the limo. Slow dancing at the end of the night. Kissing under a sky full of stars. All that shit.

But that just isn't my reality. And slapping together some version of prom with Belinda, whether just the two of us or with a couple of stuck-up idiots from another school probably only looking to get laid, isn't going to change the underlying facts about my high school experience. It isn't going to make me any cooler or happier—nor will it fool

189

anyone into thinking I'm cooler or happier. If anything, it's going to make me feel worse, especially because there is a high likelihood of Belinda getting sloppy drunk and hooking up in some hotel room while I stand in the corner, with a push-up bra, a streaky orange spray tan, and some dweeb named Philip. No, thanks.

As we cross the finish line, Mrs. Tropper bellows out our time, shaking her head. "Thirteen minutes, forty-two seconds. A sorry effort, ladies! My grandmother can run a faster mile."

I shrug and give her a blank stare, showing her how very little I care. The one thing I'm *really*, consistently good at.

16

Marian

First thing Monday morning, Angela Rivers makes an entrance into my office that is as dramatic as any scene she has performed to date, including the one in which she discovers that her boyfriend is having an affair with his ex. I realize, within seconds, that this is no coincidence.

"He's *fucking* her," she says, showing her range as an actress as she vacillates between pitiful sobs and manic rage. Her eyes are red, her skin is broken out, and I quickly notice that she has done something drastic to her gorgeous, long red hair. Her trademark. Not only is the color off—verging toward Cyndi Lauper orange—but as she drops her head to her hands, I notice that there is a whole chunk missing in the back where she (or a very mean-spirited hairdresser) whacked it good. I find myself silently brainstorming styles to fix it, and more important, how we could work the change into a story line.

She repeats her announcement, as I wonder why I can't take her pain more seriously. Am I being selfish, concerned only about how this turn of events (and bad hair) will impact my show? Or am I unconvinced that she is doing anything other than acting? I notice that in her impressive display of grief, there are no actual tears.

"Who is fucking whom?" I ask a little too loudly. I glance toward the hallway hoping that no one heard me, just as I can tell Angela hopes *everyone* hears us. After two assistants peek in and Angela has yet to reply to my question, I stand, walk past her, and push my door closed.

"Damien," she says. "I should have known not to trust someone whose name is synonymous with *Satan*!"

"What?" I say, confused.

"Damien Thorn? In *The Omen*?" she says, as if I'm stupid for not instantly making the connection between an actor's name and a horror film franchise from the seventies. "I can't work with him."

I stare at her, and process the possible magnitude of the situation. After Angela, Damien is our most important asset, dubbed "the next big thing" by the Hollywood hype machine and recently chosen as one of *People*'s "50 Most Beautiful." In other words, she *better* work with him. And then I remember Jeanelle's remarks in the writers' room and say a prayer that the rumors aren't true—and that he isn't fucking the *third* most important asset, Carrie England.

Sure enough, she says, "I just can't believe he cheated on *me*," she says. "And with *her*. He knows how much I *loathe* Carrie!"

Indeed, we *all* know how much she hates Carrie, even before this, although no one is quite sure why, as Carrie is one of the most gracious, humble, easygoing actresses I've ever worked with, practically an oxymoron. Maybe that's the very thing that chafes Angela—the fact that everyone constantly remarks on how lovely Carrie is, both outside and *in*. Maybe, deep down, Angela knows she only has half of that equation covered. And maybe she's starting to figure out that it's the part that matters the least. Though I doubt it.

Before I can get down to the nitty-gritty of the life-imitating-art situation, Angela shakes her head, clasps her hands in her lap, and strikes an Oscar-winning, injured pose for the ages.

"I'm sorry, Marian. But I quit."

"No. Just calm down," I say, although I'm now in a panic.

This advice only serves to rile her more, as she stands, tosses her massacred hair to one side, and says, "I won't work with them. Either of them. I quit. Unless—" She looks up at me, her timing as impeccable as it is on set. "Unless you fire them."

"Fire Damien and Carrie?" I say.

"Yes. Both of them." She thinks for a second and then says, "Or at least her."

She stares me down, a dare to do what she wants, as I realize the real purpose of her visit is revenge.

"They have contracts," I say, shaking my head, but mentally doing the figures and calculating the cost of buying out Carrie's contract and replacing her.

It's doable, of course, but there's *principle* involved. It would be egregious to let one series regular force another out—and a terrible precedent to set, an indication that Angela is the true showrunner. I would lose all control and respect. "I just can't do that," I say.

"Well, then I quit," she says, turning to leave.

"Wait. Wait! Let's call Standish," I say, as everyone refers to Peter. "Let's be rational here."

"I am rational," she says. "What about my reaction to infidelity is irrational? Have you ever been cheated on?"

For one second I feel sorry for her. "Not that I know of," I say.

"Well, then you can't possibly know how it feels."

"But this show is making your career," I say, appealing to the best thing I have in my arsenal: her ego. "You're becoming a star. You were nominated for a People's Choice Award. All that goodwill you built up will be gone if you pull a stunt like this."

"It's not a stunt," she retorts. "It's the way I *feel*. I'm being true to myself. Putting my heart over fame."

"But it won't be perceived that way. It will be perceived as a diva move."

Because it is.

"Diva? I'm not the diva. *She* is."

I sigh, thinking that maybe I should start writing novels so the characters wouldn't have to come to life when she blurts out, "You know, this is *your* fault!"

"*My* fault?" I say.

"You writers," she says, pointing at me. "You put them in bed together. I told you it was a bad idea."

"You told me it was inconsistent with Damien's character. Not that you were worried about this outcome," I say.

"Still," she says. "I warned you."

"Okay. Look. Let me call Standish," I say, swiveling in my chair, hitting speed dial, and lowering my voice into the phone. When he answers, I say, "Um. It's me. Hey. Can you come down here, please?"

"Right now?" he says.

"Um, yeah," I say. "It's sort of an emergency."

"I'd say it's an emergency!" she shouts over my shoulder.

"Shit. Is that Angela Rivers?" Peter asks. "I heard she was in the building."

"Uh-huh," I say.

"Tell me we don't have a Charlie Sheen on our hands?"

"Um, yeah. Can you just come down here, please?"

"Yep. Be right there," he says, with the same mix of irritation and urgency that I feel. We are both acutely aware

194

that this is how shows implode, especially one already put on the ropes.

I hang up the phone and stare Angela down. "He's coming," I say.

"How are things with you two, anyway?" she says.

"Great," I lie, wondering if anyone knows *we're* on the ropes, too.

A beat later, Peter arrives with a sexy air of calm competence. He takes a seat next to Angela and humors her, murmuring his concern as she repeats much of the same tirade about Carrie, along with her demands that she be fired from the show.

When she is finished ranting, he offers his condolences. "Be the bigger person," he says. "Show them what a pro you are."

She sniffs and says, "I *am* a pro."

"I know." He nods encouragingly but then glances at his watch. "Sorry, ladies. But I have a marketing meeting to get to."

"I have to go, too," Angela says. "But thank you, Mr. Standish. Thank you very, *very* much. For your perspective."

"Peter," he says with a condescending smile that, based on her sensual stare in return, she reads as something else.

"Thank you, *Peter* . . . You've given me a lot to think about."

"Super," he says. "We'll be in touch, okay?"

She smiles, shaking her chopped hair from her face and offering a final, coy, "I look forward to that."

When the door is closed behind her, I roll my eyes and say, "Unbelievable."

"Oh, it's believable," Peter says. "She's a nutball, delusional actress. They all are. And what's with the Pippi Longstocking look? What happened there?"

"I don't know. We didn't get into that."

He shakes his head and says, "She'll calm down."

"And what if she doesn't?" I ask. "Do we meet her demands and fire Carrie?"

"Are you serious?" Peter asks, aghast. "You want to lose clout with everyone on your show? Including the other writers, actors, and crew?"

"I know, I know," I say, wondering whether I've already lost all clout with him. "I was just asking."

"Hell, no. Let's just keep our eye on her. Closely monitor the situation. It could work to our advantage. Let's be sure to fill in Anita in publicity so we can be ready to spin this thing. Also, call her agent at CAA and get them to rein her in before she goes rogue with this story."

"Yeah. My girl Jennifer Peros at *Us Weekly* just e-mailed," I say, glancing in my in-box.

He shakes his head and cracks his knuckles. "What a complete train wreck."

"Yeah," I say. "It sure is."

Peter gazes at me across my desk. "I miss you," he says. "But maybe this is for the best. A little time apart."

I nod and pretend to agree with him when all I want to do is go give him a huge hug and bury my face in his neck.

"We both have a lot to straighten out," he continues. "In our heads."

I want to ask him what he has to straighten out, exactly. His feelings for me, my past, or our future? But I'm afraid of the answer I might get. I'm afraid to hear him say they are all inextricably, impossibly linked. Or, that he might just try to humor me as much as he just humored the star of my show.

*

When I get home that night, I find a package waiting for me. It is from Kirby, her St. Louis address written neatly in the upper left corner. I can't imagine what could be inside, but my heart sinks as I slice it open, and see that it is filled with all the clothes I bought her, the tags still on. The wedges, too, are unworn, tucked neatly into the sturdy navy Prada box. I find the note last, written in cursive so tiny that I need to get out my reading glasses.

Dear Marian,

Thank you again for letting me stay at your place when I came to New York and for buying my plane ticket home. That was very nice of you. It was also nice of you to take me to your work. I enjoyed it and look forward to watching your show this season. (Especially Shaba. Ha.) As you can see, I'm sending back the clothes you bought for me. I really appreciate it and everything, but don't feel right about keeping them. They are just too expensive of a gift, and besides, they aren't really me anyway. I hope you understand. Thanks again for everything.

Sincerely,
Kirby K. Rose

I read it again, as it registers that there is no mention of Conrad. No mention of being glad to have met me. No indication that we are anything more than acquaintances. I fold it and put it in the top drawer in my closet, along with the picture of Conrad, realizing that this is all I have of hers. My heart fills with shame that I know so little about her. That I never took a single photo of her while she was here. That I actually thought it was a good idea to buy her gifts like these—even before I told her the truth. That Peter is right—secrets and lies are really the same thing, and so in many ways, my life has just been one big, giant lie.

Then, before I can talk myself out of it, I pick up the phone and call her, actually hoping that she will answer. She does, sounding surprised, which only affirms my guilt.

"Hi, Kirby," I say. "It's Marian."

"I know," she says. "Hi."

"I got your box," I say.

"Yeah. I hope you didn't think that was rude. I really appreciate it and all . . . I just . . ."

I shake my head, on the verge of tears. "Kirby. No. I get it. And I'm sorry."

"Sorry? For what?" she says, but I can tell it's more of a test than a question.

"For taking you shopping like that. When we had so many more important things to do. To talk about. I honestly don't know what I was thinking. I was just . . . trying to find my comfort zone," I say, wondering what it says about me that Barneys is my comfort zone. "It was a really bad idea."

"Yeah," she says—and I can tell I just said the right thing. Finally.

"I was just so . . . terrified," I confess.

"I know," she says. "I was, too."

"I still am," I say as I'm hit with a wave of relief that I've not only told her the truth about what happened—but I've also told her the truth about how I feel. In some ways, it is an even bigger step. In some ways, it feels like our first truly honest moment.

We are both silent for a few seconds and then she clears her throat and says, "So . . . where do we go from here?"

"I don't know," I say. "But I hope we can figure it out together."

"Yeah," she says. "Me, too."

17

Kirby

So. Confession," Belinda trills as she fixes her bangs and lipstick in the rearview mirror. We've just pulled into the parking lot at the Tivoli, my favorite theater in town. "Don't hate me."

I raise my eyebrows as she continues her grooming, spritzing perfume in the crook of her arm and on the back of her neck. "Want some?" she says, holding up her small bottle of Vera Wang Glam Princess that she keeps in the car. She has one in her locker, and one in her room, as well.

"No, thanks," I say. "I'm good . . . What's up, Bel?"

"We-*ell*. I kinda sorta invited Jake and Philip to join us. And *there* they are!" she squeals, pointing excitedly toward two boys just getting out of their car.

"Oh. No. You didn't," I say, realizing now why she insisted on doing my makeup and tried, unsuccessfully, to talk me into wearing one of her low-cut sundresses.

"Come on! Look at them, Kirby. They're *hot*! Total lacrosse bods!"

I narrow my eyes and take a closer look. Only one of them looks like a jock with his broad shoulders and cocky walk. The other is shorter, skinny, and Asian. But regardless of their type, I don't want to talk to either of them. I fold my arms, shake my head, and tell her to take me home.

Belinda gives me a fierce look, jabs her finger into my

shoulder, and says, "Get out of the car, Kirby. Now. You're going on this date whether you like it or not."

I sit motionless for at least thirty seconds as the guys disappear toward the theater entrance, making her sweat, then whine, then beg. I glare at her, slam my way out of the car and trail behind her, mumbling that she is going to be sorry, and that I can promise her that the night is going to be a complete disaster.

"Please have an open mind and a positive attitude," she chirps, checking her reflection in her compact mirror, one final time, before we reach the ticket booth.

"Ja-aake!" Belinda calls out as he and his sidekick turn toward us. She waltzes over to him, then stands on her tiptoes and kisses his cheek. I gotta hand it to her—it's a pretty strong move. But still.

"Hey, Belinda," he says as I give him a once-over. He is tall, muscled, blond, and good-looking in a way that nobody can miss. It seems pretty clear that he knows it, too, as he is wearing a very fitted T-shirt, along with a CHAMINADE LACROSSE cap and Ray-Bans, the mirrored lenses making me trust him even less than I already did.

Sure enough, when he finally removes the glasses after a purposeful boob-brushing hug from Belinda, I catch a fleeting cocky look that she often elicits from boys she's teased, then satisfied. The "I've just been blown in the Taco Bell parking lot" look that Richie Hayworth flashed me last summer after the two finally emerged from the backseat of his mom's Audi. I suddenly don't believe that this is the first time Belinda's seen him since the mall—it also isn't the first time that Belinda has told me a white lie about the boys she's "dated." It's weird. Sometimes I have the feeling she is exaggerating her sexual prowess, the next minute I

201

think she's hiding something from me. Which leads me to believe that she isn't quite sure whether to be proud or ashamed of her escapades.

At least this Jake does have *some* manners, though, which is an upgrade from most of the others, as he promptly introduces me to his friend, shockingly remembering my name with no help from Belinda.

Philip nods and flashes me a knowing smile. I have the sudden sense that he's mocking the whole arrangement and that he, too, was dragged out tonight, but is more annoyed than pissed. In that second, I decide that he is actually pretty cute with his toast-colored skin and longish, shiny black hair.

"I hear you don't like blood or guts in your movies," he says with another wry smile.

"Yeah. Gratuitous violence doesn't do it for me," I say, catching the slight attitude still in my voice.

"Well, I vetoed gratuitous sex," Philip says, turning to look at the now canoodling Jake and Belinda. "But I guess they didn't get that memo."

I bust out laughing, and decide to give him a chance, or at least give the night a chance. We fall behind Jake and Belinda, the four of us sauntering inside. After our tickets are inspected and torn in half, Belinda takes the stubs from Jake and wedges them into the back pocket of her tight, white jeans. She glances over her shoulder and winks as if to say, "We're one prom date away from these things becoming mementos."

"So what are we seeing?" Belinda asks, turning to look at Philip.

"A Brazilian film," he replies.

"Hope you ladies took Spanish!" Jake bellows.

"Dude. Portuguese," Philip says. "And it has subtitles, moron."

I smile, scoring another one for Philip.

Belinda makes a face. "Subtitles?"

Jake shakes his head, turns and slaps Philip on the shoulder so hard that he takes a stutter step to keep his balance, then says to me, "Yo, Kirby. My boy's trying to look smart and impress you."

"I *am* smart," Philip retorts, grinning. "I'm tryin' to make *you* look smart. But you're sort of fuckin' that up, aren't you?"

"Whatever, dude," Jake says. "Anyone want popcorn?"

I tell him no, thanks, but Belinda says she'd love some, which I know she only wants so she can get the touchy-feely stuff started early. I know all her tricks. As she and Jake get in line at the concession stand, Philip gives me another pointed look, then smiles and says, "You sure you don't want anything?"

I shake my head. "Thanks, though." I search for something else to say, landing on, "So did they trick you into coming, too?"

He laughs and says, "No, I guess I was sort of in on it. Jake showed me your picture . . . So I was game."

I feel myself blush, actually believing the compliment as it sounds too matter-of-fact to be a line.

"But I'm sorry if you're not here by choice," he says.

"No. I didn't mean that," I say, remembering something Belinda once read to me from her magazine—"boys have feelings, too."

"So what year are you?" I ask, fumbling to make acceptable date small talk.

"A senior. You are, too, right?"

I nod as he asks the next unavoidable question about college and where I'm going.

"I haven't decided," I say.

He laughs. "You're cuttin' it kind of close, aren't you? What are your choices?"

"Mizzou," I say. "Or nothing. I think I'm going with nothing."

Rather than instantly dismissing me as a life loser, he surveys me with curiosity. "Why's that?"

I shrug and say, "I don't know. The idea of going to college with half my high school doesn't seem that appealing."

"I feel you on that," he says, and then asks why I didn't apply anywhere out of state.

"Money," I answer truthfully. "My parents can't afford it. And I'm not exactly in the running for a scholarship of any kind."

He nods without judging and I ask where he's going. "Ivy League?"

"I'm only half Korean," he says with a laugh. "My math scores were shit. And I don't play the cello or chess."

"I didn't mean it *that* way," I say sheepishly, realizing that I probably *was* stereotyping a little, although it honestly had more to do with the fact that he goes to Chaminade and picks foreign films.

"Just kidding," he says, giving me a look that says he is not at all offended. "I'm going to Colorado."

"Cool," I say.

"Yeah. I'm from Denver originally. We moved here six years ago when my dad got transferred. He's an engineer for Boeing."

"So you like it better out there?"

"Yeah. It's awesome. I love the water and mountains and just being outdoors."

"What about this summer?" I say, wondering if he's found a job or if he's one of those spoiled Clayton boys who spends his summer lounging at the country club or partying at his parents' fancy house at the Lake of the Ozarks.

"I'm going to Alaska," he says as his face lights up even more. "I got an internship working as a student field assistant for UNAVCO. At the Plate Boundary Observatory."

I ask him what that is and he tells me it's an organization that installs GPS stations to track the deformation of the Pacific and North American plate boundary.

"Cool," I say, too confused by his answer to ask any follow-up questions.

"Yeah. I'm super stoked. My buddy did it last year and said it's pretty intense labor. They use power tools, ride around in helicopters, and haul around heavy-ass gear." He flexes a nonexistent bicep and says, "Gotta get buff for the college chicks, right?"

"Why don't you just work for a moving company? Wouldn't that be easier?"

He laughs.

"Kidding. That sounds really amazing."

"Yeah. Even though there's a lot of grunt work, I also get to travel to remote parts of Alaska and learn about geology and geophysics." He gives me a shy smile and says, "I hear it's crazy beautiful."

I nod, getting the feeling in my chest that I got as I walked up Fifth Avenue and around the Guggenheim and into the writers' room. A feeling that I know so little about the world. And maybe the tiniest bit of excitement that there are real possibilities in life, too.

A second later, we are rejoined by Jake and Belinda carrying an enormous box of popcorn, a bag of strawberry

Twizzlers, and Cokes so large they could drown a squirrel. To her credit, Belinda also follows the advice: Boys don't like girls who only eat salads.

We all make our way into the mostly empty theater, Philip taking the lead up the stairs and selecting the first row on the balcony. I sit beside him, Belinda next to me, Jake on the other end. As we continue to talk about his trip to Alaska, I overhear an inane snippet of conversation from Belinda and Jake about the merits of various movie theater candy, and realize that so far, our unofficial date is off to a better start than their planned one.

"So what about you?" Philip asks. "Do you have any summer plans lined up?"

"Stuck in the Lou. Working at Schnuck's," I say, wishing I had something more interesting in my arsenal, then realizing that I do. "I just got back from New York City, though, and that was really fun."

"Cool. What'd you do there?" he asks, staring at me so intently that it makes my stomach feel funny.

"I was visiting my birth mother," I say.

"Your *birth* mother?"

"Yeah. I'm adopted," I say, aware that I'm using her to make myself sound more interesting.

"Oh. Right on," he says, nodding and smiling.

"Yeah. I just found her. I called the agency. Got her address and went to New York City. Manhattan," I say. I feel a tiny bit hypocritical bragging about my glamorous birth mother after I returned the glamorous clothes she bought me with something of a chip on my shoulder. But still. The fact remains she *is* my birth mother. And I did find her on my own. And that part, alone, does make me pretty damn cool.

Sure enough, Philip gives me an openmouthed, frozen smile, clearly impressed. It is the way Mr. Tully looked at me, but it is different coming from someone my own age, in a darkened theater on a date, real, pretend, blind, or otherwise. "That's wild," he says.

"Yeah," I say. "She's a television producer."

Belinda, eavesdropping on our conversation, leans over me, spilling popcorn onto my lap. "Her mom's totally famous," she informs Philip. "You know the show *South Second Street*?"

Philip nods. "I've heard of it."

"That's her mom's show!" Belinda shouts. I feel a wave of affection for Belinda's unwavering loyalty and enthusiasm. And maybe even for making me come tonight.

A moment later, when the lights are further dimmed, the commercials end and the real previews begin, Philip pulls a pair of dark-rimmed glasses out of his front pocket. "I can't see for shit," he says, putting them on and giving me a sideways smile. I decide he looks good in them.

"So?" he whispers. "How do you think it's going so far?"

"The movie?" I ask.

"No. The date?" he deadpans.

"So far," I say, the fluttery feeling returning to my stomach, "I think it's going pretty good."

18

Marian

"Well, well, well! She's alive!" my mother exclaims, her version of a humorous guilt trip, when she finally tracks me down at work. "I was about to have my people call your people . . ."

"Very funny," I say, putting her on speaker so I can stretch my stiff back and shoulders.

"But that wouldn't work. Because I don't have people," she says, laughing.

"Ha. You do *too* have people," I say, referring to her gardener, handyman, pool guy, dog sitter, and longtime housekeeper Martha.

"So how are you, honey? I've been worried about you," my mom says.

"I'm fine," I say, taking her off speaker. I catch her up to speed on work and the drama surrounding Angela. Namely, that she announced a "Zen-like indefinite time-out" in Uruguay to "clear her mind and get over a betrayal" two days before tabloid photos surfaced, suggesting anything other than a soul-searching getaway. In one series of shots taken at a beach bonfire at the chic resort Estancia Vik, Angela is topless, getting her groove on with a bronzed Brazilian soccer star known throughout South America and much of the world for his womanizing, boozing, and prolific yellow cards.

"Is that all?" she says. "Anything else going on with you?"

I feel myself tense, thinking of Kirby, my relationship with Peter, and most of all, Conrad. "I don't know, Mom," I say. "Things aren't so good, actually."

"What's going on?" she asks.

When I can't speak, she says, "Marian? Do you want me to fly out and come for dinner? I'm due for a little shopping. Maybe a show," she says. "Your father could use a little break, too."

"No. Don't bring Dad," I say so quickly that I give myself away.

Sure enough, she asks, "Honey. Is this about . . . what happened?"

It is the way we talk about Kirby on the rare occasions we bring her up at all, making veiled, wistful references, as if each of us wants to protect the other from more pain. I think of Peter's accusations—that I want things to be perfect and tidy—and suddenly see the truth in his charge, realizing exactly where I get it.

"Yes," I whisper, ashamed that it has taken me three weeks to tell my own mother that my daughter came back.

She asks no follow-up questions, just says, "I'll check on flights right this minute and be there tonight."

"Thanks, Mom," I say, hanging up the phone, feeling that we've just come full circle, back to that one, hot summer. And that once again, I *really* need my mother.

Later that evening, shortly after my mom has landed at LaGuardia, I run into Peter on the street outside of our building, ducking into a black Town Car. He catches me out of the corner of his eye and does a double take, before leaning out of the car and giving me a small, noncommittal wave.

I bite my lip and wave back, then turn in the other direction.

When I hear him yell my name, I turn and survey him as coolly as possible, then take the few steps over to him.

"Hi," he says.

"Hey," I say.

He glances up at the ominously dark sky. "It's about to storm."

"Yeah. Maybe it will cool things off a little," I say, thinking that this is what we've come to—chitchat about the weather.

"You headed home?" he asks.

"No. I'm going to dinner," I say.

He raises his eyebrows. "A date? Already?"

"Yeah. With my mom."

A big fan of my mother's, his face brightens. "Well, tell her I said hello."

"Will do," I say, staring at his green tie and matching pocket square. I can feel myself stalling as I ask, "So where're you off to?"

"JFK," he says. "I'm on the nine o'clock to L.A."

"Business or pleasure?" I ask with a careful measure of sarcasm.

"C'mon. What do you think?" he asks.

I shrug as if to say I have no idea what's going on in his life. He could be headed to the West Coast to go on a date with some moronic actress for all I know. Perhaps he's decided that if he's going to have to deal with all of my drama, he might as well be with a really hot twenty-five-year-old who doesn't want to have a baby. Who hasn't *had* a baby. I feel a wave of irrational jealousy commingled with sadness and anger and bitter disappointment.

"No. No pleasure these days. I'm just headed out to screen pilots and work on the final lineup," he says.

"So? Are we safe?" I ask.

He looks confused and then says, "Oh, right. I thought you meant *us*. You mean your show?"

"Yeah. Is it safe?"

I ask the question even though I'm not really worried about making the lineup, but he shrugs helplessly, as if he works in the mailroom rather than running the entire network, and says, "Do we know the status on Rivers?"

"No," I say, resisting the urge to tell him that I don't know the status of much of anything these days. "Why? Does the show hinge on *her*?"

He grimaces and I feel a jolt of panic that, in addition to my relationship, my show and career could be in peril, too. That we could be talking about more than just a changed time slot with dumbed-down story lines.

"Are you serious?" I say.

"The advertisers aren't happy about the development."

Desperation wells in my throat but I try to calm myself down, plead my best case to my boss. "We're an ensemble cast. We still have Damian and Carrie . . . and they have half a million Twitter followers between them. They've doubled their followers since this story broke. Tripled it, I bet."

"Marian. Relax."

"No, Peter. I can't relax. Not until you tell me we're safe. I mean, you have to have faith here . . . We'll be fine. Even without her. I mean, if *The Office* can stay on the air without Carell, then we can stay afloat without some C-list psycho."

"You're not exactly making your case by calling your leading lady—"

211

"It's not about the actors, though, Peter. That's the thing. It's about the writing."

He smiles, and for a second I think he's mocking me, but then I realize it's a look of fondness—the way he used to look at me. That he admires my tenacity. I realize he hasn't called me "Champ" in a long time.

"Keep us on the schedule, Peter. Convince your staff that we will hold our audience. I know we will. You know that, right?"

Before he can answer, the skies suddenly open and a downpour begins to pound the sidewalks. Fortunately the overhang on the building keeps me mostly dry, but I still curse under my breath, realizing that I don't have an umbrella and that it will be virtually impossible to get a cab. Especially at this hour. Peter gives me a sympathetic look, slides over, and pats the seat next to him.

"C'mon. Get in. I'll give you a lift."

I hesitate, doing my best to resist him. "You'll miss your flight," I say.

"Where's your dinner?"

"The Modern. It's out of the way."

"It's only *four* blocks out of the way," he says. "Come on. Don't be stubborn. Get in."

I climb in and close the door, then cross my legs and angle my body toward the window, away from him.

"Let's drop the lady off on Fifty-third between Fifth and Sixth," he tells his driver as rain pelts our car, the swish of the windshield wipers punctuating our silence. He finally clears his throat and reaches out to touch my hand, more in the way of a brother or close friend than a boyfriend or even an *ex*-boyfriend. "I'm going to do everything I can," he says.

"Well, then. I guess I shouldn't worry," I say pointedly. "You are the head of the network, after all. And as the head of the network, I know you'll look at the big picture."

"Of course," he says, as we fall silent again. Despite heavy traffic, we arrive at the restaurant a moment later—none too soon as far as I'm concerned.

"Thanks for the ride," I say curtly. "And the talk. I appreciate your honesty."

"C'mon," he pleads.

"What?" I snap.

I wait for him to speak but instead he shakes his head, and looks away, as if he knows he's going to cancel my show or our relationship. Maybe both.

"Bye for now," he finally says. "I'll call you the second I know anything."

"Fine," I say. Then I get out of the car, slam the door, and run through the rain toward my mother.

When I reach the end of the runwaylike tunnel entrance to the restaurant, I spot my mom in a red, double-breasted trench, her Goyard roller bag, which she recently boasted about "stealing" on eBay, at her feet.

"Perfect timing," she says, rushing toward me. We hug one beat longer than our usual hug hello before she kisses me on the cheek, then stares intently into my eyes. "It's *so* good to see you, honey."

"You, too," I say, now positive that she knows what this is about.

She shows her usual restraint, though, and says, "You look good. Really good. Did you change your hair?"

"I went a little lighter," I say, reaching up to flip a section of my hair. "You know—for summer."

She smiles and says she needs to do something to hers, maybe while she's here.

"When's your return flight?" I ask.

"Oh—I don't know. I just clicked something on the computer. I think I leave Friday afternoon . . . I'll have to check."

"I can try to make you an appointment with Dana," I say, referring to my longtime stylist at Louis Licari.

"That would be great," she says as we move into the restaurant, checking our coats and my mother's bag with an auburn-haired maître d' who would make a fine Angela Rivers replacement.

Then, without the ado characterized by lesser restaurants, we are instantly and silently ushered into the narrow, vaulted, gleaming white dining room to Peter's usual two-top overlooking the sculpture garden. It occurs to me that this would be another casualty of my life without him—I won't be able to get the best table at the best restaurants at a moment's notice.

After we are seated, my mother glances around the room, then out the window into the garden, gasping her approval. "What a gorgeous space. Just stunning . . . Now is this the same fellow who did Union Square Café and Gramercy Tavern?" she asks, always in the know about any of the best hotels or restaurants in Manhattan (along with Paris, London, and L.A., for that matter).

I nod and say, "Yes. Danny Meyer. He also did Eleven Madison . . . And the Shake Shack."

"And the chef?" she says, eyeing the enormous, exquisite, and very exotic pink and purple floral arrangements in the center of the room.

"Gabriel Kreuther. Classically trained. From Alsace

originally. Most recently from the Ritz on Central Park South. Marc Aumont is his pastry chef," I spew, realizing that my mother and Peter have culinary snobbishness in common—that I probably wouldn't have all of this memorized if not for him.

We turn our attention to the menus, silently reviewing the four-course, prix fixe menu, the selection itself a near religious experience for my mom. After some deliberation, we order a Sonoma sauvignon blanc and almost identical meals, both of us going with the asparagus soup, the scallops, and the cod until she switches at the last second to the lobster. For dessert, we go with the strawberry-rhubarb vacherin.

While we wait for our wine, I stall, avoiding the woolly mammoth in the room, and instead catch her up to speed with Angela and my most recent conversation with Peter. As always, she is fiercely and satisfyingly loyal, saying all the right things about the show, how strong the writing is, how little we need Angela, and that the network would be crazily shortsighted to cancel us. "You're just *too* good," she says.

"Thanks, Mom," I say. "Unfortunately, great shows get canceled all the time."

"Isn't that the truth," she says, rattling off a few of her favorites, some of them from over a decade ago. "And the horrid ones just chug right along. Goodness, I wish more people had *taste.*"

I smile, thinking this could sum up her major complaint in life, as our waiter brings our wine, uncorks it, and gives me the assignment that is usually Peter's. I swirl, taste, smile and nod, before staring, mesmerized by the waiter's expert pouring, both glasses filled to the exact millimeter.

When we are alone again, my mother picks up her glass, raises it and says, "To mothers and daughters."

I steady my hands and clink my glass against hers. Then we sip from our glasses and lower them in unison.

"So," I say, when I know I can't put it off another moment. "I think you know what's going on, don't you?"

"I have an idea, yes."

"She found me," I confirm.

"Oh, dear," she says, looking tragic. "Tell me everything."

And so I do, interweaving all the parts about Peter, beginning with the night I asked about marriage and she knocked on the door, and ending with my ride over to the restaurant this evening. "She is a wonderful girl," I say, thinking about her letter and the clothes and how *real* she is. "And I think we might actually develop a real relationship. I'm not sure what that will look like, exactly, but we've been talking . . . and it feels good."

I wait for her to say something—*anything*—about her flesh and blood, but instead she says, "Just be careful."

"Be careful?" I say, bristling that this is her first reaction. Yet deep down, I can't really blame her when I know I felt much the same way during Kirby's entire visit.

"Be careful about opening doors you really don't want opened. Peter may be supportive in theory . . . but does he really want a complication like this? You've worked hard for this life. *Really* hard."

I know she is talking more about Conrad than Kirby, and I can't disagree that finding him might complicate things. Yet I also find myself wondering what she means by "this life." And whether hard work brought me to this point—or just a whole lot of smoke and mirrors.

*

Later that night, I am sitting on the guest room bed where Kirby slept, watching my mother unpack her suitcase. She packed lightly for her, likely only because she didn't have time to throw more into her bag. After hanging her usual St. John knit ensembles in the closet, she pulls out a long floral dress that could only be described as a muumuu.

"What do you think of this?" she asks, holding it up in front of her.

I make a face and say, "It's okay . . . But it doesn't look like you. At all."

She laughs. "Believe it or not, I kind of like it. Your father bought it for me."

"Since when does Dad buy clothes for you?" I say. "*I* wouldn't even dare that one."

"Since lately. He's trying to be romantic, giving me gifts for no reason. Just to be sweet."

I smile, remembering the beret from Peter, then ask her why Dad's trying so hard.

"We had a rough patch," she says.

"When?" I say. This is news to me. My parents have always seemed to get along well, and I have very few childhood memories of them arguing.

"Oh, I don't know. Here and there. Little bumps. Bigger ones . . . But that's how relationships are. They go in cycles. They require so much effort and patience and, God, vigilance. Maybe you and Peter should go to counseling. Maybe it will help build back the trust. It's all about vigilance . . . and communication."

"So . . . you agree we need to tell Dad? About Kirby?"

A funny look crosses her face before she busies herself with the remaining contents of her suitcase.

I wait for her reply, but get only nervous humming as she turns to take her toiletries to the bathroom. "Mom? Did you hear the question?" I say, sensing an unmistakable change of mood when she returns to my room.

"Honey . . ." she begins, a slight tremor in her voice making me suddenly worry that he has cancer or some other serious illness. "Your father . . ." she begins, then stops, takes a deep breath and slowly exhales before continuing. "Your father already knows."

"You mean—you called him? Tonight?" I say, thinking that she might have phoned him between our entrée and dessert when she went to the ladies' room.

"No," she says with a grimace.

"Since *when*?" I demand, trying to control my emotions—a mix of shock, embarrassment, and betrayal.

"Since . . . pretty much the beginning," she says.

I stare at her, then walk out of the room.

Minutes later, she finds me in the darkened kitchen, sits on the stool next to mine, and launches into her explanation. She says that it was just too hard. That she could have kept the abortion a secret but not a pregnancy and birth. Beyond that, and more important, she believed telling him was the right thing to do. I was technically an adult, but still very much his little girl, and he had the right to know what was happening with his daughter. His *only* child.

I reluctantly accept this. After all, it is a thought that has crossed my mind since Kirby's visit. The part I can't accept, I tell her, is that she never *told* me he knew. That they didn't just come clean. That *they* were the ones with the secret—and that *I* was the one in the dark. For all these years. It occurs to me that I don't even know what he

218

thinks about everything, how he felt about my decision to give her away. I ask my mother now as I look down at her hands, wondering when they changed into the hands of an older woman.

She takes a deep breath and then says, "Well, for starters, your father was angry that I would take you to have an abortion without talking to him first. He very much wanted you to have the baby."

"He did?" I say, my throat tightening. I am relieved to hear this, but also saddened, thinking that he never got to hold Kirby or tell her good-bye. If my mother had only told me the truth, he could have been there with us.

"You know he's against abortion. And he thinks you would have lived to regret that choice."

I nod, wondering if that knowledge about his views played into my decision not to go through with it. I suddenly recall several pro-life comments he made during the '96 presidential election, at the time believing that it was an offhand philosophical remark in the context of a political discussion. Now I see that he could have been sending me a message. Now I have to rethink everything, all of our conversations over the years. I can feel the entire framework of our relationship shifting. Nothing is what it once seemed to be—and it occurs to me that this is the nature of keeping secrets. In this moment, I begin to understand how I've made Peter feel, but still can't fathom how Conrad would feel if he ever finds out.

"Do you agree with him?" I ask. "Do you think I would have regretted that . . . choice?"

"Honestly . . . I don't know," she says, finally getting choked up. "That day at the clinic . . . I very much wanted you to have it all done and over with . . . so that you could move on with your life. As quickly as possible. But I respected your decision. Just as I respected your decision to give her away."

"And what about Dad? How did he feel about the adoption?"

She sighs and says, "Your father wanted to keep her. He thought you should go to Northwestern or another nearby school or that we should move to Ann Arbor for a few years and help you raise her. He even suggested that we do it for you. Raise her as our child. Your sister."

"Talk about secrets," I say.

"I know." She nods. "But that's how he felt. It caused a problem in our marriage for a long time. The decision itself and the fact that I wouldn't let him talk to you about it. He resented me . . . And I think it changed his relationship with you, too."

"How so?" I ask, even though I've always had the same sense.

"You two used to be so close. It was always Daddy's little girl. . . . But ever since then . . . there's a distance between the two of you. You're so . . . formal with one another . . . Something."

I nod, thinking back to those pre-Kirby days when we were as tight as a father and daughter could be. "As thick as thieves," my grandmother used to say.

But after that summer, things were never really the same. At the time, I told myself it was just part of growing up, going off to college, getting my own life. I told myself that we were still close, just not in the same way. But now I can clearly see that he was another casualty of my lie. I was not only avoiding him, but he was doing the same with me. Even when we were alone, we never really talked about big, important things like marriage and babies, life and death. We stayed on the surface of things, the great gulf of our secrets between us.

I look at my mother, wondering if it would have been different had she kept my secret. Wondering if my father meeting Kirby might somehow fix things between us. Wondering if you can ever really go back to the way things once were.

19

Kirby

It is Sunday morning, my favorite time of the week since my mom gave up trying to make me go to mass, and I'm in my zone, playing my drums as hard as I can, knowing that our neighbors on either side of us are at church, too. I scroll through my "classic drum solo" play list, going from Led Zeppelin's "Moby Dick" (John Bonham's solo is one of the best of all time) to "One World" by the Police (can't get much better than Stewart Copeland) and then mixing in Gina Schock (I have a vintage poster of the Go-Go's over my bed), Sheila E. (who, even if she didn't kick ass in her own right, has played with all the greats, including Prince, Ringo, *and* Marvin), and even a little Karen Carpenter (probably the only artist on my iPod who my parents know a thing about).

Meanwhile, I find myself replaying my date the night before, putting the best moments to music like a little video in my head. After the movie, there was only time to grab a quick burger at Blueberry Hill before my curfew, but it was enough time to determine that Philip liked me. At least as a friend, but maybe more. It wasn't so much what he said, but the way he looked at me—with "that big goofy smile"—in Belinda's words when we convened in the ladies' room. I objected to the word "goofy," but agreed that it was a full-on, genuine smile.

Thinking of him now, I take off my headphones, put my sticks down, and reach over for my phone to find a

Facebook icon in my in-box—a friend request from Philip. I can feel my pulse as I click my acceptance, and seconds later there is a post on my wall: *Still trying to figure out the end of that film. Had a great time. Let's do it again soon, okay?*

I let the words sink in, feeling light-headed with the realization that I not only went on my first real date with a cute boy, but that he had a good enough time to ask me out again *and* post the invitation on my wall for all the world to see. Or at least for my 114 friends to see. It's sort of pathetic—but I've never felt so cool, not even rapping in the writers' room—and I post a comment back on his wall (for his 316 friends to see): *I did, too. As for round two, sounds great. Just let me know.*

As I greedily scroll through his four albums of photos, mostly consisting of outdoorsy camping and skiing shots, my phone rings. It's Belinda. I pick up, grinning. "Yesss?" I say. "May I help you?"

"OMG! Holy Facebook exchange!" she says, and then squeals so loudly that I pull the phone away from my ear.

"And what's with 'round *two*'?" she continues. "Did he sneak in your bedroom last night for round *one*?"

"God, Belinda. Would you *chill*," I say, wondering if the comment I posted actually sounded the way Belinda took it—or if her mind is just perpetually in the gutter, apparently even on Sunday mornings when she, too, should be in church. "I was referring to the movie. Jesus."

"Admit it. You love him," she says. "You *totally* love him."

"He's cool," I say, refusing to admit, even to my best friend, that I have a small crush—my first on someone other than a famous person or Mr. Tully.

"You wanna do him."

223

I sigh loudly but say nothing, as if the comment isn't worth one syllable in return.

"Do you think he's cute?" she asks.

"I answered that last night," I say. "Yes. I think he's cute. He has nice eyes."

"OMG! Prom here we come! You have to ask him."

"Whatever," I say. "Let's not jump the gun here."

"It's two weeks away," she says. "You have to jump the gun. C'mon!"

"Did you ask Jake?" I say, thinking of how handsy they got during the movie, likely the reason that neither of them had a single opinion about the very bizarre ending that Philip and I couldn't stop analyzing over our burgers.

"Yesss. I was just getting to that."

"And?"

"And he said yes." She squeals again and then bursts into an off-key rendition of Drake's "Best I Ever Had."

"So what did you do last night?" I ask, knowing that her curfew means nothing—and that her mother is a ridiculously sound sleeper.

"Topless make-out session in my basement followed by a BJ," she says. "*With* results. I'm still batting a thousand."

I make a face. "Ewww. That's disgusting, Belinda."

"BJs aren't disgusting," she says, and launches into further nauseating details about Jake's impressive anatomy. "It was hard to get it all in. But I managed. That practice with the cucumber really helped with my gag reflex."

"Stop!" I yell, cracking up.

"Okay," she says, laughing. "But only if you promise to ask Philip to prom."

"We'll see," I say, that strange feeling in my stomach returning.

"Yay!" she says. "Philip's gettin' a BJ of his own soon!"

I shake my head and unwittingly picture Philip in the front seat of his car, his jeans slid down to mid-thigh, the back of my head bumping against the steering wheel, his eyes rolled back with pleasure. I have no plans to make that happen soon, if *ever*, but am shocked to realize that the vision isn't altogether disgusting.

Later that week, after Philip has sent me several private messages on Facebook, including one asking for my number, my cell phone vibrates with an incoming call. I am in the family room with Charlotte who I've fully debriefed, telling her everything other than the way I'm starting to feel inside. I think she can tell, though, and is so excited for me, mentioning prom several times herself. She mutes the TV, raises her eyebrows and says, "Well? Is that him?"

I pick up my phone from the coffee table to see Philip's name, already programmed in my address book, lighting up my phone. I nod and smile, then scurry out of the room, answering once I'm halfway up the stairs.

"Hey. Whatcha doin?" he asks casually, as if we've spoken on the phone lots of times.

"Not much," I say, trying to catch my breath as I close my bedroom door and collapse onto my bed. "Just watching TV. Putting off homework. Avoiding my parents. The usual."

"Yeah. I hear ya," he says, right before he tells me, once again, that he had a good time going out with me. A warm, tingly feeling washes over me, like a giant wave, followed by another intimate vision of us, this one more PG-13 and romantic than my amateur, front-seat blow job. In it, Philip is wearing a tux; I'm in a beautiful organza gown, and the two of us are slow dancing.

225

"I did, too," I say, overcome with this feeling of "what the hell." So with clammy hands, a dry mouth, and a galloping heart, I say, "Hey. Philip. I have a question for you?"

"Shoot."

I take a deep breath but feel myself start to falter. "I don't know. It's probably sort of a dumb idea . . . Sort of cheesy . . . And I really am not this type of person . . . But it might be fun . . . And Belinda and Jake are going . . . So I just wondered if maybe—"

"Kirby," Philip says, throwing me a lifeline. "Are you trying to ask me to prom?"

"Um, yeah," I say, with a nervous laugh. "I guess I was trying to do that."

"So just ask me," he says, laughing back at me. "No more disclaimers."

"Would you like to go to my prom? With me?" I tack on the last question, just to make one hundred percent certain that there's no confusion about what he's getting.

"I'd *love* to," he says, his big, bright smile coming right through the phone.

"Good," I say, smiling back at him. "It's a date."

The very next day, my mother takes Charlotte, Belinda, and me to Robin's Bridal Mart to shop for prom dresses. It's *crunch time,* as Belinda keeps saying, prom only nine days away. As we pull dresses off the racks, it is clear that Belinda and Charlotte are leaning toward long gowns in bright, spring colors, while I find myself favoring shorter, black ones, perhaps because that is much of what I saw in Marian's closet. "LBDs" she called them, for "little black dresses"—and said that every girl needs at least one, really more like two or three.

My mother, of course, makes it clear that she thinks black dresses are inappropriate for teenagers and wrinkles her nose whenever I pull one off the rack. At one point, as I select a flapper-style black dress with fringe, my mom comes right out and says, "That dress is way too mature for you."

"Too mature?" I say. "I thought you wanted me to be mature?"

"You know what I mean," my mom says.

Charlotte springs to my defense. "Mom, that rule about black is from back in *your* day. Everyone wears it now. They even make baby clothes in black. Have you seen Angie and Brad's kids?"

My mom rolls her eyes and says she does not think we should aspire to be like "those weirdos."

"Regardless. You promised you wouldn't judge if we let you come along," I say.

"No offense, Mrs. Rose, but that's why I'd never shop with my mother," Belinda says. "Really nobody does."

"That's not true," my mom says, looking annoyed at Belinda—which is not unusual. "I saw Mary Margaret with her mother at Dillard's last week. They had just found a very pretty tea-length dress . . ."

"*Tea* length?" Belinda repeats as if she's just smelled something foul. "Talk about out of date. Short or long is the only way to go. What, is she going to a *tea*?"

"Well, the point is, I'm not the *only* mother—"

I interrupt her with an important distinction. "Mary Margaret sucks. She's only shopping with her mom because she has no friends."

"Her mother told me she's the prom *chair*," my mom says, doing her best to ignore the word sucks. "Surely the prom chair has friends."

"You'd think," Charlotte says. "But not in this case. No one can stand her."

"She doesn't even have a *date,*" Belinda says as we exchange smug smiles. In just a matter of days, we have transformed ourselves into the girls she's always wanted us to be—and that maybe, secretly, I've wanted to be as well. I even find myself feeling different in school where no one even knows—or cares—about my updated status. But *I* know it, and it feels pretty good.

"Okay. Okay. I get the hint. I'll zip it," my mom says, trying to be the fun mom, although it goes against her every grain. "I am eternally grateful for the invitation to join you in this momentous shopping spree and promise to keep my old-fashioned opinions to myself."

I nod my acceptance of her promise while the four of us, with the help of a young sales clerk named Shelly, continue to scour all the racks. About thirty minutes later, we are in three separate dressing rooms, frantically trying on dress after dress, casting most aside, asking Shelly for different sizes, mostly exclaiming how bad they make us look, and only occasionally emerging when one is either comically hideous or pretty enough to consider.

After much analyzing, vetoing, encouraging, and admiring, we each come down to our top choice, and stand before my mom and Shelly in the huge, three-way mirror for a final decision.

"Oh, girls! You look gorgeous! I could *cry,*" my mother says.

"You *are* crying," I say.

"Mom!" Charlotte says with uncharacteristic scorn. She casts her eyes around the store, then whispers, "Stop that. It's so embarrassing! I mean, *really,* it's not our wedding gowns!"

228

Then Charlotte turns to me, her posture perfect, and adds under her breath, "Although I'm *so* going to marry Noah one day."

"I can't help it. My little girls are all grown-up. I remember when the three of you were in diapers, running around at the pool with your little orange water wings. And now look at you," my mom says, so nostalgic that she seems to forget all her gripes with Belinda. And me for that matter.

"Okay, let's start with Lottie," Belinda says, examining my sister in her long chiffon gown.

"Turn around," I say.

She spins as Belinda and I murmur our approval. Unlike Belinda and me, Charlotte has looked good in just about everything, but this one is the clear winner, from the salmon color that complements her hair and tanned skin to the strapless style that showcases her cut swimmer's arms, shoulders, and back. The dress looks trendy, but still fairy-tale sweet, pleasing both generations in the room, and Belinda and I tell her that she is done, this is the *one*, there is no need to try on anything else. It is clear that Charlotte agrees because she sashays around the dressing area on tiptoes, admiring herself from every angle, even making sultry, come-hither stares into the mirror that my mom should find more disconcerting than the color black.

"How much is it?" my mom whispers to Shelly, although she knows we can all hear. She looks worried even after Shelly chirps that it's very reasonable.

"How reasonable?" my mom asks.

"It's three hundred—"

My mother gasps until Shelly finishes her sentence: "—but you're in luck, it's fifty percent off!" She leans over her large solar calculator, punching the numbers as Charlotte and I exchange an amused glance; even *I* can do that math in my head.

"One hundred fifty plus tax," Shelly says.

"Perfect," my mom says as we shift our attention to Belinda's top choice—a long turquoise gown made of raw silk with one shoulder and a fishtail, rhinestone-encrusted train that makes her look like a sexy mermaid. Belinda calls it a miracle gown because it hides her hips and belly while flattering her perfect, round butt (which she proudly calls her "ghetto booty") and big boobs.

"I love it," I say.

"Me, too," Charlotte says.

"Is it too racy?" my mom says.

"No, Mom," I say, as Charlotte points out that it doesn't even show much cleavage. Of course Belinda takes this as a cue to hoist up her "girls," as she calls them, but my mother doesn't say another word, probably figuring that Belinda's a lost cause.

"Now, I must tell you, my dear," Shelly says after a bit more raving, "this is one of our most expensive dresses."

"I know," Belinda says. "I saw the price tag."

"How much?" I ask.

"It's four hundred," Shelly says with a grimace.

"Is it on sale?" Belinda asks.

"I'm afraid not," Shelly says. "But you get what you pay for. That train is exquisite."

"Call your mom. Or your dad," I say. "Maybe they'll each pay half and let you splurge."

"Not a chance," Belinda says, but still steps inside her dressing room to make the call and begin the negotiating. I can hear her ask her mom if her dad has sent them any checks lately, and I can tell by Belinda's reply that the answer is no, as usual.

She emerges seconds later, changed back into her faded red polo and tight khaki skirt, looking gloomy. "Your turn, Kirb," she says.

Feeling sorry for her, I nod and gaze down at my black flapper dress, deciding that I definitely love it. It is flattering *enough*, sophisticated not just for the color, but the overall style, with extra points for originality. Nobody will have a dress like this one. And it shimmies when I walk in the most satisfying way; I can't even imagine how cool it would look if I were dancing.

"It's so *you*," Belinda says, sitting cross-legged on the floor. "Very cool."

My mom and Charlotte agree that it looks great on me, and I ask my sister to take a photo with her phone. I strike a pose with my hand on my hip, one leg forward, the way celebrities stand in magazines. I must be doing something wrong because I feel awkward—and look totally stupid in the picture. So I ask Charlotte to retake it, standing normally the second time.

"Are you sending Marian the photo?" my mom guesses. She tries to sound casual, but I can tell the idea makes her sad—which makes me feel simultaneously sorry for her and annoyed with her.

"No. Mom," I say. Although maybe, deep down somewhere, it had crossed my mind to show Marian my prom dress. Sort of as my way of telling her, once again, that there are no hard feelings about the clothes I sent back. And also because I just *know* she'd like it.

"Yeah! You totally should!" Charlotte says. "You can get her advice on shoes and bags and jewelry."

"Who-ah! Shoes and bags and jewelry?" my mother says. "I'm not so sure that's in the budget. You can borrow something of mine."

231

"Or better yet," Charlotte says, "maybe Marian will let you borrow some of her stuff! I bet she has some *sick* jewelry and shoes . . . What size does she wear?"

"My size," I say. "Seven."

My mother, who wears a nine, purses her lips, then says, "Well, I'm sure Marian will love your dress. And she'll probably approve of black, too."

I nod, positive that she will like it, and hoping that Philip will, too.

We determine the cost, just slightly more than Charlotte's but also on sale, and I look to my mother who nods her permission.

"I'll take it," I tell Shelly as I undo the side zipper, step out of the dress, and give my mother a grateful smile. "Thank you," I mouth, handing it to her.

"You're welcome," she whispers back, then takes both dresses to the front of the store to pay.

As I change back into my uniform, Belinda follows me into my dressing room, looking dejected.

I give her a sympathetic look and say, "Was there *nothing* else you liked?"

"Not compared to that one," she says.

"Okay. Well. How much do you have saved?" I ask, knowing the answer before she holds up her hand in a big goose egg.

"Well. I'd loan you some," I say. "But I spent it all going to New York. And besides—*four hundred* dollars! Belinda, that's just stupid money for a dress you'll wear once."

"Unless you're Marian," she says. "I bet it's chump change for her. You're so lucky to have a rich relative."

It is the first time anyone has referred to Marian as a "relative," rich or otherwise, and although I like the way it sounds, I think of the clothes I sent back and remind Belinda that it's not my money.

Belinda sighs, then heads to her dressing room to retrieve her big, fake Gucci tote.

Moments later, we are back in my mother's car, Charlotte in the front seat, Belinda and I in the back. I check my phone and see a new text from Philip, my third thrilling one of the day: *Any luck?*

He is referring to my dress, of course, so I type back: *Yep. Found a good one.*

He replies almost instantaneously: *Your dress or your date? LOL.*

Both, I write, feeling so flirty and bold that I then type a semicolon and a closed parenthesis, forming my first *ever* winking emoticon, something I always vowed never to do.

"Are you talkin' to Philip?" Belinda asks.

I smile and nod. "Have you heard from Jake today?" I ask.

"Lemme check," she says, reaching down into her tote to retrieve her iPhone, along with a pack of cinnamon Dentyne gum. She takes a piece for herself, then offers me one. I take the pack, punch out two red squares, then lean down to toss it back in her bag.

And that's when something catches my eye: a swatch of unmistakably bright turquoise silk buried deep in the bottom of her bag. I glance at Belinda, my eyebrows raised, as she looks up from her phone with an expression of guilt and embarrassment and defiance, a combination I haven't seen on her face since the fourth grade when I caught her in a lie about a sleepover with Amy Bunce. The two had invited me, then at the last second uninvited me with some story about Amy's mother having a migraine. I never confronted her about it, even to this day, but it hurt my feelings for ages, and I still don't understand how she could do that to me.

I have the same feeling of betrayal and confusion now, although I'm not sure why. Belinda has stolen things, right in front of me, like a pack of cigarettes or cheap costume jewelry. Once she even lifted a pair of leggings that she put on under her jeans. And although I never came right out and condoned it, and often mentioned that the goods weren't worth the risk of getting caught, I always sort of laughed it off. But this time feels different. For one, she didn't tell me what she was doing. For another, the dress is four hundred dollars. Shit—it could be a felony for all we know. I try to make eye contact with her, but she refuses to look back at me, and instead buries herself in her phone, texting like crazy. I think of what my parents would do if they knew—I'd *never* be allowed to spend time with her again. But for some reason, I find myself thinking of Marian, too. What her reaction would be. What she would think of Belinda. And what she would think of me for looking out the window and pretending there isn't a four-hundred-dollar stolen prom gown at my feet.

20

Marian

A few nights after my mom returns to Chicago, I'm watching *Mad Men* and wondering how much the execs at my network would screw up that show if they could, when the phone rings. I glance down at it, my heart speeding up when I see Kirby's name.

"Hey!" I say, answering quickly.

"Hi. Did I interrupt anything?" she says, sounding sad. I wonder if she's still upset about the clothing—or if her voice just has this innate quality—the way some girls always sound bubbly and others perpetually sarcastic.

"No. I was just watching television . . . What's up?" I ask, hoping that everything is all right in her world, and suddenly craving a conversation with her. About *anything*. Even Conrad.

"Well . . . I'm going to prom." She delivers the news shyly but proudly, as if this is something of a coup for her.

"That's great. Very exciting!" I say. "Who's the lucky guy?"

"His name's Philip Chang," she says. "He goes to another school but my friend Belinda introduced us. She's going with his best friend. The four of us."

"Do you like him?" I say. "Or are you going just as friends?"

She hesitates and then says, "I don't know. He's nice and really smart. And we have a lot in common. He's just . . .

different than the boys at my school. So yeah—I guess I kinda like him."

There is an excited, eager lilt in her voice that makes my heart ache with nostalgia and memories of Conrad, how connected I felt to him during our brief relationship, how much I loved that he wasn't like anyone else I knew. I wonder if he still has this quality or if the years have changed him into something more ordinary; somehow, I just can't picture him as a suburban dad with a couple of kids, a minivan, and an office job he hates. I push him out of my mind and tell Kirby I'm happy for her.

"Yeah. Thanks. It's no big deal, really . . . But I did find a dress," she says.

I ask her to describe it, and she says it is black in a flapper style. "I'll send you a picture," she says.

"Yeah, I want to see it . . . I want to see *all* your prom pictures. Take lots."

"For sure," she says, and then asks whether I went to my prom.

I tell her I missed it my junior year due to a raging case of mono, but went my senior year.

"With Conrad?" she asks.

"No," I say, tensing. "I went with my boyfriend at the time. Todd Peterson."

"Was it fun?" she asks.

"Yeah," I say halfheartedly, then laugh. "Well, no, not really, actually. We spent most of the night in a fight."

"About what?"

I tuck my phone between my ear and shoulder and tighten the tie of my terry-cloth robe. "He was very immature. And his friends were worse—just awful. I couldn't stand most of them and resented how they turned the whole night into a booze fest."

"And you wanted a little . . . romance?" Kirby asks.

"I wanted to at least *dance.* Heck, I would have settled for some face time *at* the actual dance. Instead I spent the whole night watching him booze it up in a dark, smoke-filled room at the DoubleTree. It was depressing."

"That sucks," she says.

"I'm not saying prom has to be the most important night of your life. But try to make it a *little* special, you know? At least try to stay sober enough so that you can *remember* it. Instead of passing out before nine o'clock."

"Is that why you broke up with him?" she asks, as I find myself wondering what would have happened if Todd *hadn't* been so immature. What if we had continued to date that summer? Would I have eventually had sex with him? What if he had gotten me pregnant? Would I have told him? Would I have kept the baby?

"Yeah. Pretty much, I guess. Although I don't think I ever really liked him very much. In any event, we broke up the next day at Great America in line to ride the Iron Wolf. He was showing off, bragging about how hungover he was—as if that is some kind of badge of honor. I just couldn't stand him another *second* . . . so I got out of line and went to get cotton candy alone." I laugh and say, "He ended up puking on some kid on the second loop, so it was a good decision."

She laughs, then grows silent again before saying, "So I wanted to ask you a question? Get your opinion on something? It's about Belinda. My best friend."

"Okay?" I say, waiting.

I can hear her take a deep breath before slowly continuing. "So we were shopping for prom dresses. Me, my sister, and her. With my mom. Charlotte and I found our dresses that were only, like, one-fifty. They were on sale—half price."

"That's a great deal," I nervously interject.

"Yeah. That part was good . . . But Belinda . . . She fell in love with this really fancy one with rhinestones and stuff. It was crazy expensive. Four hundred dollars. I know that's not a lot to you, but it's a lot to us. And Belinda definitely can't afford that."

I cringe at the word "us," and feel a fresh wave of shame over the Barneys trip as Kirby continues, "She has a single mom and kind of a deadbeat dad and she never saves her money. So it might as well have been a million dollars, ya know?"

"Yeah," I say, trying to follow the point of her story. "So did she get another one?"

"No," Kirby says. "She . . . got that one."

"How? Did she put it on a credit card?"

"*Noo*," she says as if I'm being obtuse.

When I don't instantly reply, she sighs and says, "She *stole* it, Marian. She put it right in her bag and walked out with it. Right into broad daylight."

I sit on my bed and shake my head, feeling oddly naïve, as if we've just reversed roles, and wonder how I didn't see this one coming. I think of my fast-girl acquaintances in high school who shoplifted for sport. Most of them could afford anything yet they got off on the adrenaline rush.

"Did you see her do it?" I ask, hoping she wasn't an accomplice or otherwise involved.

"No. Not in the act. I just saw the dress in the car. In her bag. After the fact."

"Did you ask her about it?"

"No. I just pretended I didn't see it. We both sort of pretended . . . Do you think I should, like, confront her about it?" Kirby says, as if prompting me to give her advice.

"Definitely," I say. It feels like my first truly decisive parenting decision and something of a defining moment.

"What should I say?"

"Tell her you know she took the dress and that you think it's wrong. Tell her she should take it back. She can even drop it off at the store anonymously. In a bag. There's no need to turn herself in. Just get the dress back to the store. Surely there are other dresses she can afford . . ."

Kirby is silent, as if looking for potential pitfalls with my advice. Sure enough, she says, "That's never gonna happen. Belinda wants what she wants. I saw the look on her face in the car. She's only going to be pissed at me if I say something . . ." Her voice trails off.

I hesitate, then ask if she talked to her parents about the situation.

"Hell, no," she says, as I feel simultaneously flattered and overwhelmed by the responsibility. "I didn't tell anyone. Could I get in trouble? Did I do anything against the law?"

"I don't think so," I say. "Not if you didn't help her take it . . . But I still think you should encourage her to return it. For her sake."

"Shit," she says.

"I know this sucks, Kirb. It's hard."

I can hear her breathing on the phone, as if digesting everything.

"Just talk to her . . . Tell her how you feel. Be as open and honest as you can."

As I say the words, I realize that this has been my shortcoming—and that I want better for Kirby.

"I also think maybe you should talk to your parents," I say.

"Hell, no. I can't. They already have an issue with Belinda.

Plus, they'd probably turn her in. They're totally black-and-white about everything," she says.

"Yeah. Some people are like that," I say, thinking of Peter's approach: Do the right thing and tell the truth at any cost, even when it's not convenient, even if it means hurting others. Then again, maybe there's more to be said for loyalty to a friend, to protecting those you love. Is that what I did, in part, when I lied to Conrad? And kept a secret from my dad? From Peter? Or was I only trying to protect myself? I am beginning to realize how few answers I have, and just how difficult it is to be a parent. To be in any *real* relationship.

"Just try to follow your heart," I say, knowing how simplistic, even trite it sounds, but that it guided one of the most difficult decisions I ever made—to have her. "Whenever I've followed my heart, I haven't been sorry. And when I haven't . . ."

I don't finish my sentence, but I feel the weight of it on the phone, both of us silently filling in the blanks. Filling in the past eighteen years of my life. All the secrets and lies. I had my reasons, of course. My rationalizations and justifications. But deep down, I think I always knew that what I was doing was wrong. And now I know that it might finally be time to fix things.

"Does that help at all?" I ask, hopeful that I'm giving the right advice.

"Yes," she says. "It does help. Thank you, Marian."

"You're welcome, Kirby," I say, wishing I had something more to tell her. Wishing that things were as easy as I was making them sound.

21

Kirby

After school, I find Belinda in her kitchen, making strawberry Jell-O as she watches *Days of Our Lives*. She barely looks up, she is so used to me walking into her house without knocking.

"Hey!" I say, masking my queasiness with a big smile.

She shushes me, pointing to the ancient television set on the counter while she stirs the thin liquid with a wooden spoon. I glance at the screen and ask her what's happening on the show.

Without removing her eyes from the set, she replies in rapid-fire monotone. "Taylor just confronted EJ. Asked if he's responsible for Arianna's death."

I nod, momentarily taken in by the drama I only cursorily follow—until I remember that we are living our own little soap opera. A second later, a commercial for carpet cleaner breaks her trance.

"What's up?" she says.

"Nothing much," I lie, picking up the empty box of Jell-O and reading the nutritional facts. "Holy shit. Only ten calories per serving?"

"I know, right?" she says. "I've lost four pounds since last week. Straight Jell-O diet."

"Huh," I say, searching for a lead-in. "Why are you dieting? You look great."

"Just want a flatter tummy," she says, patting her midsection.

"So that when Jake sees me without my Spanx—"

"So you found a dress?" I interrupt, the question sounding as awkward as I feel.

She picks up the remote, aims it at the television and aggressively mutes it before resuming her stirring. "Come off it, Kirb," she says.

"What?" I say, wide-eyed, as if *I'm* the guilty party who needs to feign innocence.

"You *know* I found a dress," she says, making air quotes around the word "found."

I stare at her as blankly as I can, waiting for her full confession. When it doesn't come, I fire off a lame retort. "*You* come off it."

She rolls her eyes.

"You stole the dress," I say.

"So?" she says.

"*So?*" I say. "What do you mean *so*?"

"So I stole the dress." She shrugs, licks the spoon, and nods her approval, as if she's just cooked an amazing sauce rather than added water to a powder mix.

"Well, it's . . . *wrong*," I say, cringing at how self-righteous I sound, but unsure how else to say it.

"No shit it's *wrong*," she says. "But it's, like, one dress. Do you know how much that place marks shit up? I bet they got that thing from China for forty bucks."

I stare at her. I've always known that it's impossible to argue with Belinda, not because she's particularly good at it, but because she's so *bad* at it—that there is no common ground to work from. She simply sees the world the way she wants to see it and no amount of logic can change her mind. Yet I still flounder about, looking for another angle. "C'mon, Belinda," I say. "It's not worth it. What if you get

242

busted this close to graduation? Look what happened to Louie for putting Alka-Seltzer in the pool. He's not going to graduate now—"

She shakes her head and says, "There's nothing the school can do to me. Even if I got arrested—they can't do shit because it happened outside of school."

"You can get kicked out of school for a felony," I say.

Belinda shakes her head. "It's not a felony. It's a misdemeanor."

"What, did you do research or something?" I ask. "Was it premeditated?"

"No—it wasn't premeditated," she says. "I would have paid for it if they weren't asking such a stupid price."

I say her name again, but she unmutes the television before her show even resumes, as if to make a point about just how boring she finds the conversation. More tedious than the long list of possible side effects being rattled off in a Zoloft commercial.

I can feel frustration verging on anger as I speak as loudly as I can without yelling. "Belinda," I sputter. "C'mon. Please just return the dress. Please."

She gives me an amused look, then imitates me in the same prim voice she uses to mock Sister Viola, the least respected teacher in our school. "Do you hear yourself? Since when did you get so high-and-mighty?"

Before I can reply, she offers a theory. "Is that snob Marian rubbing off on you?"

The statement doesn't even make sense, yet it still enrages me enough to throw out an ultimatum—my first *ever* in our friendship. "Return it or I'm not going to prom with you." As soon as the words are out, I want to take them back. But it's too late.

She shrugs. "That's fine, Kirby. I don't need you. I have a hot date. And a four-hundred-dollar dress that I got for *free . . .*"

"Wow. Okay, then," I say. "I'm out."

"Bye," Belinda says with utter, cold indifference. I've watched her turn on the meanness many times over the years, but she has never treated me this way.

I start to leave, but then stop and say, "And FYI . . . Marian isn't a snob. She's one of the coolest people I know."

"Well, it's too bad you didn't get any of her cool genes," she says.

I pretend not to hear her, but can't help repeating her words in my head the whole four blocks home. And even worse, I can't help believing them just a little.

Later that afternoon, I call Marian and give her the report. She answers right away, city noises in the background.

"What're you doing?" I say.

She says she's on the way to get a quick bite, then headed back to the office. "Did you talk to Belinda?" she asks.

I say yes and give her the update, minus the final closing insults. "So looks like I'm not going to prom."

"Well. I'm sorry it didn't go better," she says. "Maybe she'll come around."

"I don't think so," I say, the seriousness of what happened starting to sink in. It's not really that I'll be missing prom, that dream was too short-lived to mean much, but the fact that I really could have lost my best friend. "Did you ever get in a fight this big with a friend?" I ask Marian.

She tells me no, but that she has lost any meaningful touch with her best friend from high school. "We never had a fight, but we just grew apart."

"Why?"

"Oh, I don't know. A lot of reasons . . . But mostly because I wasn't truthful with her . . ."

"About me?" I guess.

She hesitates, then says yes. "I think it's so much better to handle things the way you did. You were straight with her."

"Yeah. Except now she hates me."

"She doesn't hate you. Just give it some time . . . Maybe you could write her a little note that says although you disagree with what she's doing, you still love her and hope she has a wonderful time at prom."

"What should I tell Philip?"

"Most boys don't care that much about prom," she says. "You can make it up to him."

"Yeah," I say, and then suddenly, I can't stand it another second. I have to tell her. "So I looked for him," I announce, cringing as I await her reply.

"Looked for who?" she says, predictably.

"For Conrad," I say. "Ever since I left. I've searched everywhere. On Facebook, LinkedIn, Google, even high school reunion Web sites."

"And?" she asks, sounding worried.

"And nothing. I thought I was close with the only Conrad Knight on Facebook—the profile photo was blank—but I waited a week for him to respond to my friend request and it wasn't him."

I pause, then continue in a rush, "I was just wondering how you would feel about helping me . . . you know . . . find him. Maybe giving me some leads at least? The names of some of his old friends?"

"Kirby," she starts, but I interrupt her.

"It's totally fine if you don't want to. I get it completely. And I'm totally cool—"

"Kirby," she says again more forcefully.

"What?" I ask, holding my breath, waiting, mentally regrouping about what my next step will be, without her.

"I already found him," she says.

I freeze in the shadows of my room. "You did? When?" I ask, my heart racing.

"Last night actually."

"Where is he?" I say.

"He's still in Chicago. In the city. About thirty minutes from where we grew up. I have his address and phone number right here," she says.

"How did you find him?" I say.

"He was listed in the white pages. He lives in Lincoln Park," she says.

I shake my head, wondering how I forgot to do the easiest, most straightforward search of them all: look in the freakin' phone book.

"Are you sure it's the right Conrad Knight?" I ask, now pacing again, my feet cold on the hardwood floor.

"Yes," she says.

"How?"

"Well. I . . . I called the number. From my office. And his voice is the same."

"Did you talk to him?" I ask excitedly.

"No," she says. "I got his voice mail. But I didn't leave a message."

"Oh," I say, part of me relieved. The last thing I want is for her to somehow screw this up for me. Have him decide that he wants nothing to do with either of us because of the way she treated him. It has to be perfectly planned. Or a total surprise visit.

"I was thinking . . . would you want to go see him together?" she says.

"In Chicago?" I say, wondering if she's kidding.

"Yes," she says. "I mean . . . only if you want to. You could meet my parents, too. . . . But maybe you want to go alone?"

"No. I want you there," I say, thinking of the photo of the two of them, how much time has passed. My entire lifetime and exactly half of theirs. I feel a chill pass through me as I say, "When can we go?"

The next evening, right after dinner, my parents suggest that we go to Ted Drewes for frozen custard, the one family tradition I would never buck—the ice cream is that good. Charlotte asks if she can bring Noah. My mother hesitates, then looks at me, as if it's my call. I shrug and say sure, but my father overrules the decision.

"Char—do you mind if we make it just the four of us this time?" he says.

My sister looks disappointed but agrees without pouting, pulling out her phone to text Noah. I try to remember the last time she caused any sort of trouble in our family but can't think of a single instance. It's abnormal. She stands to help me clear the dishes, but my mother, in her version of spontaneity says, "You know what? The messy kitchen can wait! Let's go now!"

Moments later, we are all in the car, my parents chattering away, my sister still texting Noah, but trying to be sly about it, her eyes downward, her thumbs moving a mile a minute whenever my mother turns to look out the front window. At one point, I catch a glimpse of her screen, littered with smiley faces, exclamation points, and one red heart.

247

As we pull into the parking lot off Chippewa, there is already a long line that reaches back to the street. And it's not even summer. We spill out into the muggy spring evening, squinting up at the menu as if we haven't memorized it long ago and don't already have our tried-and-true favorite concrete—the name given the custard mixed with toppings. Sure enough, we all go with our usuals and wander around the building, leaning on the black metal railing for a few minutes, before migrating back across the lot to our car. We are mostly silent, all of us rapidly working our red plastic spoons. My mother finishes her mini Frisco first and reaches for my dad's.

He pulls his Grasshopper out of her reach and says, "Honey! I told you not to get a mini!"

"But I'm on a diet," she says. "I have to lose ten pounds before Kirby's graduation!"

"And calories from my cup don't count?" my dad asks, laughing.

"C'mon! One taste!" she says.

I tune out their banter, wondering how to broach the subject of Chicago, until I finally just clear my throat and come out with it. "So I talked to Marian last night," I say.

Charlotte interrupts, all grins. "How's my birth aunt doing?"

The question does not go over big with my mother, who looks instantly downcast. As smart and pure-hearted as Charlotte is, she can be pretty clueless about stuff. In fact, it might be the one thing that I'm better at than her—although it doesn't really get me very far.

"She's fine," I say. "Good."

"Wonderful!" my dad says, a little more loudly than his usual loud voice. He stirs his ice cream, takes a bite, and

248

then says, "I think it's just *wonderful* that you are talking to her."

"Did you tell her we invited her here?" my mom says.

"And that she's welcome to stay with us?" my dad adds.

"Art, I'm sure she'd be more comfortable at a hotel. It might not be *the* Plaza, but the *Chase Park* Plaza is nothing to sneeze at."

"Well. We were actually talking about taking a trip . . . together," I say.

"When?" my mom asks.

"Next weekend."

"But that's prom!" she and Charlotte say in unison, both looking aghast.

I shrug and say I changed my mind. The dress can be returned.

"Did you and Philip get in a fight?" Charlotte asks.

I shake my head and say everything is fine with him.

"Is this because we said we had to meet him first?" my dad guesses.

"No," I say. "And believe it or not—you'd actually approve of him. He's clean-cut. And smart. Maybe his parents wouldn't approve of me—but you guys would be fine with him."

My parents don't know what to make of this comment, exchanging a glance.

"Well, where are you planning on going?" my mom says.

"Chicago."

"Why Chicago?" my dad asks, as if it isn't obvious. As if they hadn't signed adoption papers there.

"Um. Because that's where my biological father lives," I say, resisting the urge to add a well-placed "duh" at the end of my sentence.

"Omigod! How awesome! He's a musician," Charlotte eagerly informs my parents.

"Oh?" my dad says. "Is that right?"

"He *was* a musician," I say. "We don't really know what he's doing now."

"We?" my dad asks.

"Me and Marian. She hasn't spoken to him in a pretty long time."

Approximately eighteen years.

"That's pretty typical of high school romances," my mother says with a knowing look to Charlotte. She might as well just say, *Don't go getting yourself knocked up by this Noah character or else you, too, might have a teenager at your door someday.* She turns back to me and says, "They were in high school, right?"

"Yeah. They had just graduated," I say, thinking that Charlotte must have fed her this information; I've been careful not to give her any details.

"And where did he go to college?" my mom asks, trying to sound casual, despite the controversial subject.

I feel a smug rush as I take my last bite. "Actually, I don't think he went to college."

"Really?" my dad says.

I can't resist my next sarcastic dig. "Yeah. And somehow Marian loved him anyway."

Once again, Charlotte misses the point. "Why wouldn't she love him for that? You might not go to college and we love you!"

"Right," I say. "Thanks, Charlotte."

"Of course we love Kirby no matter what she decides," my mother says. "But *because* we love her, we want her to go."

"But it's up to you, Kirby," my dad says. "We're not going to push."

"Although the deposit deadline is right around the corner," my mother says. "Just as a little reminder."

"Because the big sign on the fridge isn't reminder enough?"

"We're just saying, honey . . . you're running out of time," my dad says. "And no decision *is* a decision."

"Maybe your biological father will be able to shed some light on the subject," my mom says. "Give you some good advice."

"Yeah. Maybe," I say. "Marian said he's really smart."

"Well, that's great. Just great," my dad says with the same trace of worry that's been in my mother's voice all along. "I bet he's very excited to meet you."

I consider telling my dad the truth—that Conrad has no idea that I exist, but instead I simply say, "Yeah. It should be a fun time."

Then I say a silent prayer that the whole plan isn't a total disaster. That Conrad is an example of a successful—or at least happy—person who didn't go to college. That he doesn't resent me for what Marian did. And that, in Mr. Tully's words, it isn't too late for either of us.

22

Marian

The following evening and with Kirby's permission (after her usual balking that it isn't their business and that she's eighteen and can do what she wants), I call her parents. As the phone rings, I feel more nervous than I thought I would, especially after Kirby's dad answers, his full-bodied and exuberant "Hello, Art speaking!" doing nothing to put me at ease.

"Hello," I say, staring out my office window. "This is Marian Caldwell. Is this Kirby's father?"

"Yes! Of course! Hi! I'm Arthur Rose," he says. "But you can call me Art. Everyone does."

"Thanks, Art," I say. "So . . . I guess you're . . . aware of all . . . the activity in recent weeks." I close my eyes and shake my head, thinking that for someone who writes scripts for a living, I'm pretty pitiful at my own opening.

"Yep, yep! We sure are," he says. "It's really something. My wife and I are real happy for you and Kirby. To have found each other and . . . all that good stuff." He laughs as I suddenly sense that he is overcompensating—and is probably as uncomfortable as I am.

"Yes. It's been wonderful," I say. "And I guess Kirby told you about our idea for this weekend? A trip to Chicago?"

"Yes. Yes, she certainly did," Art booms. "To meet your folks, I assume?"

"Yes," I say.

"And . . . what should we call the fella? I'm sorry, I just never gave him much thought until . . . lately."

"I know, Art. The terminology can be . . . troublesome. I don't really know what to call him, either. Her biological father? Her birth dad? Perhaps we should just stick to names. That might be easier on everyone."

"Good idea," he says. "I like it . . . What's his name, anyway?"

"Conrad Knight," I say, feeling my stomach drop, the reality of what I'm about to do coming into sharp focus. "So the plan is to try to see him."

"Well, my wife and I are a little concerned about all of this . . . but we just want what's best for Kirby, and we really want to support her. And we're so glad Kirby *told us* about this trip rather than just running off like she did to New York." He chuckles, as I hear Kirby say something terse and sharp-tongued in the background. She then shoots me a text that says, *Sorry. He's a rambler.*

"But yes, we're over that one," Art says. "We understand why she did it—and we *always* supported her finding you if that's what she wanted. We're so happy for her. And for you. Both of you."

"Thank you," I say.

"And goodness gracious! My wife and I feel lucky that you turned out to be such a sharp lady. Wow." He whistles, a long one that rises and falls. "A producer. Wow!"

"Well, thank you, Art," I say. For some reason, talking to him feels more surreal than the moment I met Kirby, perhaps because my connection to him, while significant, is utterly random. I got pregnant and had a baby; they wanted one; an agency made a match; and here we are.

"Really. What an amazing accomplishment," he says. I

can tell he means it—and that he's a really nice man, but I still wish he would change the subject. But no such luck.

"Kirby's so proud of you," he says. "As she should be. That's really a neat thing—producing a show and living in New York City. The Big Apple. Man. My wife and I went once." He unleashes another whistle. "That place is overwhelming. We had a blast but I don't know how you do it . . . Wait. Hold on one sec . . . would you, Marian? I'm sorry . . ."

I say yes, straining to hear a whispered exchange, likely a corrective interview from Kirby. When Art returns, he has mellowed one drop.

"So anyway. Here. Let me put my wife on. She's dying to talk to you."

I take a deep breath, bracing myself, thinking that Art is one thing, but Kirby's mother is another. My heart pounds in anticipation of her voice, the woman who raised my baby.

"Hello?" she says as I realize that I am already scrutinizing her, both wanting to like her and find fault with her.

"Hi," I say, sure that whatever confusing mix of emotions I'm experiencing must be double for her. "I'm Marian."

"I'm Lynn."

"Nice to meet you," I say, swallowing. "Over the phone."

"Yes," she says. "It's nice to meet you, too."

Our conversation comes to an abrupt standstill as I search for the right thing to say, something to put her at ease, assure her that I'm a responsible adult, but that I'm not trying to take her place.

"I really appreciate you and Art letting Kirby come to Chicago," I finally say.

"Well, she's eighteen. We don't have to *let* her do any-thing," she says with a hint of snippiness that surprises me;

I wonder why I expected her to be a doormat. "But you're welcome. We support her. And we support you."

They are nice words, but stiff ones, and I can tell she only wishes she means them. The feeling I have seems suddenly familiar and I struggle to place it, realizing that it comes during my occasional exchanges with Peter's ex-wife. She wants her son to like me—but not too much. And of course, I must always be aware of my role, the boundary. Even if I marry his father, I'll never be his mother. Just as I will never be Kirby's.

"Thank you," I say, walking that careful line. "It's been wonderful getting to know your daughter."

Your daughter, I repeat in my head, and I have the feeling Lynn is repeating the words, too, because I feel her soften a bit as she says, "You've been very nice to her. Thank you."

"Of course," I say.

"So this weekend?" she says. "Art and I are excited for Kirby. We just wish she weren't missing prom."

Another text comes in from Kirby that says, *Jesus. See what I deal with?*

"Prom can be overrated," I reply, knowing instantly that it was the wrong thing to say.

Sure enough, there is a beat of chilly silence and then— "It just makes no sense to Art and me. Why she'd want to miss such a special, special night when she already made plans and has a dress and everything."

Thinking of Belinda's dress, I take a deep breath, searching for a way to change the subject.

Lynn continues, "But that's Kirby. She marches to her own drums. Literally."

Just like Conrad, I think, my heart fluttering again.

"So Art and I are going to leave this up to her. Whether she misses prom. That's up to her. She knows how we feel. And now you do, too."

"Right," I say, choosing my words as carefully as possible. "And whatever she decides . . . I just want you to know that you can count on me to be a responsible chaperone. I'm not her parent . . . I'm not a parent at all," I say with a release of anxious laughter. "But I will do my very best for Kirby. For *your* daughter."

Peter calls and invites me to lunch the following morning. I accept because he is, after all, my boss, and my show is, after all, in peril. He suggests Aquavit, and I veto it because I'm not in the mood for an upscale restaurant, especially one with herring and gravlax and venison tartes on the menu.

"Okay. You pick," he says.

"Burger Heaven," I say, intentionally choosing a fluorescently lit spot that caters to tourists and midtown worker bees—two things Peter is decidedly *not*.

"Burger Heaven? Really?" he says predictably. I can see him making a face over the phone.

"Yes," I say.

"Isn't that a *chain*?" he says as if it's a bad word.

"Yes," I say. "With the best tuna fish sandwiches in the city. Let's go to the one on Fifty-fourth and Madison. One-thirty."

A few hours later we are seated across from each other in a blue plastic booth the likes of which Peter hasn't seen in years.

"Burger Heaven, huh?" he says, sitting down at our two-top, tossing his tie over his shoulder and unfolding his paper napkin. "You really are pissed at me."

256

"Get your nose out of the air," I say.

"Oh—and you're not a food snob? Right. Nice try," he says.

"I'm not," I say, thinking of Kirby and her parents and feeling determined to distance myself from the relentlessly haughty opinion Manhattan has of itself. "I'm not a snob at all."

Peter leans toward me and says, "One tuna fish sandwich doesn't save you on that front." He winks at me, looking infuriatingly gorgeous, just as our waitress arrives, flips open her pad, and asks if we're ready.

"The lady would like a tuna sandwich," Peter says, now more amused than ever. "With all the fixings."

"Plain," I interject. "I'd like it plain. On white toast."

"Oh. You simple creature, you," he whispers to me, then looks back up at our sullen waitress. "And I will have one of your heavenly burgers."

"With cheese?"

"Indeed. Cheddar. And bacon."

"Fries?"

"Why not."

"Anything to drink?"

"Just water," we say at once.

"Tap for me. Bottled for him," I say, and give him a triumphant smirk when he doesn't protest.

"Sparkling, please," he says. "Do you have Perrier?"

She nods, asks if that's all, then turns on her heels to go.

"Okay. What's this venue all about?" he says, glancing around the restaurant.

I shrug. Because the truth is, I really don't know what I'm trying to prove other than to point out that he is sanctimonious and judgmental—about everything. From

257

burger joints to secret adoptions. "So. You tell me. What's the status of my show? I assume that's why we're here."

"Yes," he says, smiling. "We released Angela from her contract, but I saved your show. You're still in the eight but you get to keep Thursday and your budget was only cut by ten percent."

I nod and give him the smallest smile in return, acknowledging that it could have been much worse.

"You're welcome," he says.

"Thank you," I say, wondering why I'm not happier.

"It was a very close call—without Angela. You're really going to have to knock it out of the park—at least with those first few episodes."

"We will," I say.

"You have a story lined up?"

"Yes. We're going to McLean her," I say, referring to McLean Stevenson and the death of his character after he left *M*A*S*H*.

Peter smiles, getting the reference, as I quote Radar from one of my first favorite shows: " 'Henry Blake's plane was shot down over the Sea of Japan . . . It spun in . . . There were no survivors.' "

"And that's one of the many reasons I love you," he says, laughing. "I should warn you, though, the advertisers might not like the tone of her violent death."

"Tell them I'm great at endings," I say.

He shakes his head as if charmed by my innuendo. "I miss you, Champ. I'm ready for us to be *us* again."

"Which *us* might that be?" I say. "The power couple *us* in perpetual limbo at fine restaurants all over Manhattan?"

"Don't forget Brooklyn," he says. "You know how I love Peter Luger."

I stare at him, refusing to smile.

He glances around, accustomed to nearby patrons knowing exactly who he is, then gives me a seductive look.

"What?" I say.

He shakes his head, then leans across the table and grabs both of my wrists, holding them tightly in his hands. "The *us* in bed. Mine. Yours. Fine hotels or Super Eights. Take your pick."

I feel a surge of attraction that I try to resist. I pull away, but he holds on to me harder—which only makes the attraction stronger. I hate how much I love it.

"Stop," I say, pretending to mean it.

He waits a beat before letting go, our eyes still locked.

"Come home with me now," he says. "I need to make love to you."

"To prove that you do?" I say.

"You know I do."

I shake my head. "I have a character to kill off," I say. "And a trip to pack for."

He raises his brows and says, "Where're you going?"

"To Chicago. I'm leaving Friday."

"A visit home?" he says. "Wasn't your mom just here?"

"I'm going to see Conrad," I say. "With Kirby."

Peter gives me a smile that would make me melt if I were any less scared, his whole face lit up with surprise and approval. "Good for you," he says with only the slightest trace of condescension. So little that I can't really hold it against him—unless I'm prepared to hold *everything* against him—his career, his intelligence, his impossibly good looks. "Do you want to talk about it?"

"No."

"How about *us*? Can we talk about *us*?"

"We can talk about *us* when I get back," I say, knowing that I can't possibly think about our relationship before Chicago.

"So we'll talk. And *then* make love?" Peter asks, pushing a piece of my hair out of my face, behind my ear.

"We'll see," I say, hoping he can't see my goose bumps, and knowing there's about as much chance of me turning down Peter as there is Conrad being okay with what I did to him.

23

Kirby

It's Friday evening, the week before prom, and I've yet to tell Philip we're not going. We've exchanged texts and voice mails and even a series of quips on his Facebook wall, but we haven't had the chance to really talk since I made my decision. So when I finally reach him on the phone, I'm relieved and excited to hear his voice live.

"What're you doing?" I ask, sitting up and hugging my knees.

He informs me in a low voice that he's browsing at Left Bank Books.

"Do you always go to bookstores on Friday nights?" I say, meaning the question sincerely, but worried that I sound like Belinda, mocking anything that involves voluntary enlightenment.

"I thought there was a book signing here tonight. An author I like," he says. "But I screwed up the dates. It's *next* Friday . . . So I'm just kinda hanging out, reading some stuff. Wanna come join me?"

"Yes," I say, without hesitation. "I'd love to join you. Are you in the Central West End?"

"Yep," he says. "On Euclid. Hurry."

"Why?" I ask, wondering if the store is closing soon or if he just has somewhere else to be tonight.

"Why? I don't know . . . Because I kinda miss you?"

"Oh," I say, grinning. "Well, I kinda miss you, too."

Giddily replaying our exchange, I hang up and run out the door, managing to avoid my parents, along with a fresh peppering of questions about how I could possibly choose to miss prom. *Oh, I don't know, guys, maybe because meeting three blood relatives is just a teensy bit more meaningful than watching a bunch of idiots, including one in a stolen dress, gyrate to Kesha.*

The Central West End is only six miles from my neighborhood in St. Louis Hills, a quick drive now that rush hour traffic is pretty much over, yet it feels like a different world, and I feel cooler simply approaching the little corridor of hip boutiques and restaurants. I find an open meter right outside of the bookstore, and neatly parallel park the beat-up Honda Accord I share with Charlotte, instantly spotting Philip through the open door. He is sitting cross-legged on the floor, petting a gray long-haired cat, a stack of books beside him.

As I get out of the car, he looks up at me with a big grin. "Hey!" he says. "Long time, no see."

"Hi," I say, walking into the shop and plopping down on the floor next to him, the cat too satisfied to even glance my way.

"Kirby, meet Spike, the world's most literary feline. Spike, this is Kirby," Philip says. "The world's . . ." He looks at me, searching for words.

"Well, Spike, let's just say I'm far from the world's most literary girl," I confess.

"Yeah, but she's way smarter than she lets on," Philip whispers in the vicinity of Spike's free ear, the one not getting a thorough scratching. "And she's an audiophile to boot. Best taste in music I've ever seen. And that's a fact."

I smile, loving this compliment, as I notice he's wearing a royal blue T-shirt that reads, in block letters: WILLIE, EMMYLOU, MERLE & LACY J.

"I like your shirt," I say.

"You like country music?" he says.

I laugh and say, "Um, that'd be a big no, but I do appreciate its crossover influence. And I gotta give it up to Merle."

"Oh, yeah. Spike agrees. He can rock out to 'Okie from Muskogee' like the best of them, but his overall taste is eclectic. Like yours." Spike purrs, falling farther onto his back, his hind legs splayed.

I smile and murmur my general approval of Spike. Something along the lines of him being a nice cat.

"Yeah. He's a good one . . . Did you ever meet Captain Nemo or Jamaica? Spike's predecessors?"

I shake my head, wondering how virtually everything out of his mouth can be so charming.

"They were cool, too. Captain Nemo was the first. He was rescued after a near drowning incident . . . Hence the name. And Jamaica was named after Jamaica Kincaid. The two Jamaicas actually met when she was here for a signing . . ."

I nod, deducing that Jamaica Kincaid is a writer, wondering whether she's a famous one I should have heard of, and making a mental note to look her up later as I did with Edith Wharton after my trip to New York. I also tell myself that college or not, I really have to start reading more, especially if I'm going to be hanging with such smart people.

"Yeah, Neems and Jamaica were cool, but I'm partial to Spike here. He's a bold, persistent one. He knows what he wants and isn't afraid to tell you," Philip says just as Spike revs up with a very long, garbled, multisyllable meow.

"See what I mean?" Philip says, smiling.

I laugh and say, "Yeah. I see what you mean."

Philip and I make fleeting but meaningful eye contact, my skin feeling prickly and warm.

"Spike did get in trouble once, though," Philip says. "Didn't you, Spikey boy?"

"What did he do?" I say, grinning.

Philip lowers his voice. "He tried to steal a furry children's book. Swiped it right off the shelves and hid it in the back room. Got in a little hot water with the owner."

My smile fades a bit, thinking of Belinda, wondering if Philip knows what happened. Is it possible that Belinda confessed to Jake? Could he know the story and think that I'm being as uptight as Belinda does? No chance, I think. His joke about Spike notwithstanding, I just can't see him taking shoplifting lightly. I consider confiding the whole incident, my loyalty feeling stretched, but decide against it, just as I did with Charlotte.

Philip must read the look on my face because he sits up, brushes his hands on his jeans, cat hair floating into the air, and says, "What's up?" before sneezing three times.

I ignore the question and say, "Bless you. Are you allergic?"

He nods. "Yep. But he's worth it."

I smile, thinking of Belinda again. Wondering if she's worth it.

"So I wanted to talk to you about something," I say, trying to convince myself that Marian is right. Aside from the waste of money on his tux (which I'm hoping he can still cancel), no guy is going to care that much about missing prom. "Can we go somewhere? To talk?"

"Sure," he says. "You hungry? Wanna grab a pizza at Pi?"

I shake my head and say, "I'm not really hungry. Could we just walk for a while? It's such a nice night. I mean, unless you're hungry?"

"No. I'm fine. I'd love to walk," he says, giving me a knowing look before waving good-bye to the clerk at the cash register, saluting Spike, and leading me back through the open door onto Euclid Avenue.

It is just before dark, and we are both silent, wandering up the quiet, tree-lined block, until I finally say, "So about prom . . . I'm going to have to bail . . ."

"For real?" He stops and looks at me, disappointed.

I nod. "I'm sorry. I wanted to go but I . . . can't."

"It's okay," he says. "Just please tell me I'm not getting dissed for some DuBourg cool boy?"

"No!" I say, thinking of another SAT word. "That's an oxymoron anyway."

He smiles as we start to walk again.

"It's not that I don't want to go. It's just that . . . Belinda and I are in a pretty major fight. And I think it would be awkward to go before it's . . . resolved."

"Well, maybe it will be by then?" he says.

"I don't think so."

"Okay," he says. "Well, are you sure you don't want to just go alone? The two of us without Jake and Belinda?"

I shake my head and say, "See, the thing is . . . she's really my only good friend at school." I watch his reaction closely, trying to determine if I've lost points in his eyes, but he seems not to mind this confession in the slightest. "I'm sort of a loner."

He nods, unfazed.

"So I think I'd rather just skip the whole thing," I say. "I was never really the prom type to begin with."

"I can see that," he says, smiling.

"Yeah. Belinda sort of talked me into it. And I agreed because . . . well, I liked the idea of going somewhere all dressed up with you."

"Aww. Really?" he says. "Don't make me blush."

"You? Blush?" I say.

"What, you think Asians can't blush?" he says with a laugh.

"I didn't mean that," I say, as I feel my own skin turn pink. "You just don't seem like the type to get embarrassed."

"I bet you could make me blush," he says, as if challenging me.

"Okay," I say, our flirting making me sweat and breathe funny. "I like your eyes."

"Thanks."

"What color are they, anyway?"

"Light brown."

"I think of them as topaz."

He gives me a shy smile, then looks back down at the ground.

"And I like your smile," I say as it grows. "And I think it would have been really nice to go to prom with you."

"Okay. I think I'm blushing now. You can stop."

I look at him, and sure enough, there is the slightest pink cast to his smooth, golden cheeks.

"But I can't go. Because of Belinda. And I have to go to Chicago anyway. I'm going to meet Marian's parents. And my dad. Not my real dad, of course—but . . . the other one," I say, swallowing nervously. "It all came up sort of suddenly. And Marian's free this weekend—"

"Look. I get it, Kirby. I completely understand," he says as our arms swing in tandem. They graze, seemingly by his

266

design, and seconds later, my hand is tucked in his, a neat fit. "I'm really excited for you—and I can't wait to hear all about it when you get back."

"Yeah. It's *really* exciting," I say, although the only thing that I can focus on at that moment is that I'm officially holding hands with the only boy in the world I have ever liked.

Then, as if I weren't already *dying*, Philip abruptly stops walking, right in front of the fountain on Maryland Plaza, turns to face me, and takes my right hand in his left. He pulls me toward him, so that our bodies are just inches apart, close enough for me to tell that he is as wildly nervous as I am. And then it finally happens. He leans in, as our faces collide. He smiles, changes angles and tries again. This time it works. The kiss is sweet and slow and it does something to my insides that makes me think of Charlotte and I melting fudge squares from Merb's in the microwave, how the outside stays firm, the center becoming molten.

Seconds later, we separate, nervously glance around to see if anyone saw us, then continue walking, as if something earth-shattering hasn't just happened.

"So tell me about these drums of yours?" he says.

"What?" I say, because I've been careful not to discuss drumming. I'd be shocked if he were one of those fools that think all girl drummers are sort of weird, but just in case, I haven't said anything yet.

"I saw a picture of drums on your Facebook page. Are those yours?"

"Yeah," I say.

"That's cool," he says, and I can tell he means it.

I smile and start talking about drumming, feeling

happier by the second. He asks a lot of questions, like he's really interested in the subject—and *me*.

"Seriously," he says. "That's, like, the coolest thing I've ever heard about any girl. *Ever*."

"Thank you," I say. And I can feel myself beaming as we keep talking, turning right, then left, then right again, winding our way through the Central West End.

24

Marian

It is the night before my trip, and Claudia and Jess are over, helping me pack and generally offering me moral support—or, as Jess likes to call it, "immoral" support. She is in one of her particularly irreverent, wildly cheerful moods, fueled by the Ketel One and Red Bull she's drinking, and an earlier visit to her dermatologist. As Claudia says, Botox and fillers always seem to enhance her personality, too.

"This is adorable! When did you get it?" Jess asks, pulling a cable knit Chanel sweater dress from my closet. She spontaneously undresses, peeling off her jeans and white T-shirt, before trying it on. I cringe—as it is both woefully too short *and* baggy on her long, impossibly narrow frame.

"Take that off at once," I say. "I'd prefer that you just *call* me short and fat—rather than illustrate the point."

Jess shakes her head as if I'm being ridiculous, but I see her cinching in the waist of the dress and sneaking a glance in the mirror as if to determine what it might look like a size or two smaller.

"Focus," Claudia tells her, snapping her fingers twice. It is a casual reprimand, but I can tell she's slightly annoyed with Jess, wanting to get down to the emotional core of what's about to unfold in my life.

"I *am* focused," Jess says, now wearing only her jeans and a leopard-print bra. She leans down, scrutinizing the contents of my suitcase, then says, as if I'm not in the room,

269

"And I really think she should pack some nicer underwear, don't you?"

Claudia glances down at my short stack of perfectly decent, white cotton panties and says, "Jess. Her underwear's fine."

"I think she should shoot for something north of *fine*." Jess tries to make a face but her frozen forehead won't allow it.

"And why's that?" I say, even though I know what she's getting at.

"In case you and Conrad . . . hit it off . . . again."

"Jess!" Claudia says, looking as appalled as I am.

"What?" Jess asks. "It's *possible* that they'll, you know, rekindle that old spark."

"The spark that unraveled my life?" I ask.

"The spark that created one," Jess says, suddenly the sage one.

I nod, as if to give her this point, silently acknowledging that I can never really regret what happened, especially now, after knowing Kirby.

Jess continues, "Besides, didn't your mother always tell you never to be caught in anything less than your best underwear?"

"Yes," I say. "In case of a *fire*."

"Exactly," Jess says, pointing at me.

"Oh, God," I say. "Do you seriously see this weekend as one with romantic potential?"

"Yes," Jess says. "I see *every* weekend as one with romantic potential."

I tell her she's warped as Claudia reminds her that I already have a boyfriend.

"They're on a break," Jess says.

"Famous last words. Remember Ross and Chloe from the copy room?" I say, always enjoying when I can reference any television show.

"Pfft," Jess says. "Only Ross, a spineless, noodge *fictional* character, would be dumb enough to admit to a fling that occurred while *on a break*."

Claudia gives her a look, obviously thinking of her own, brief affair during her breakup with Ben. "Or your best friend here? Might I remind you of Richard?"

Jess laughs. "Good point. You and Ross. That makes *two* fools."

"Okay, look," I say, adding a pair of my most cozy pajama bottoms and an ancient Michigan T-shirt to my suitcase before zipping it shut. "I'm not going to be kissing anyone this weekend. Break with Peter or otherwise."

Jess looks disappointed, then clears her throat and says, "Okay. So what do you think it will be like? When you see him again? What are you going to say to him?"

"No clue," I say.

"Do you think you should call him first—give him some warning before you just knock on his door?" Claudia asks.

"Do you think I should?" I say, as if the rather obvious question has never once crossed my mind.

"I don't know—you tell me. Do you wish Kirby had called before she showed up?" Claudia says.

Trying to justify my decision, I tell her I'm not sure that it would have made a difference; it might just have made me nervous.

"I think you're just *hoping* he won't be home," Jess says. "Classic conflict avoidance. Could buy you another decade. Or two."

As soon as she says the words, I realize that she's just nailed it. I've been talking a big game for Kirby's sake, but pretty much the last thing I want to do in the *world*, including discussing the layers of domestic deceit with my father, is see Conrad Knight again. The thought of it makes me so sick to my stomach, in fact, that I ask my friends if they think it's really necessary for me to join Kirby when she knocks on her second door.

"Are you *fucking* kidding?" Jess says, dropping her jaw dramatically as if to compensate for her inability to make any other expression.

Even Claudia agrees, firmly shaking her head. "Marian, no. You can't do that to Kirby. And you certainly can't do it to Conrad."

"It was just a suggestion."

"A really shitty one," Jess says as Claudia nods her agreement.

"Yeah. You gotta suck it up, girl. Put on those cotton, big-girl panties," Jess says. "It's time."

"High time," Claudia chimes.

"Okay. Okay. I got it!" I say, unaccustomed to being in the hot seat, Jess's usual role in our threesome. I take a deep breath, wondering how I will get through the next seventy-two hours—and knowing only one thing for sure: It won't be the same way I got through the last eighteen years.

Twelve hours and a painfully early morning flight later, I'm standing in the baggage claim of O'Hare, waiting for my suitcase and father, in no particular order, something I've probably done fifty times since I went away to college. But, of course, this time feels completely different, and as I stare at the metal carousel overflowing with luggage, I start to wish I had either rented a car or asked my mother to get me. But she insisted that this was for the best—that my father and I needed some time alone before Kirby showed up to, in her words, "confront the past." My dad and I have yet to speak since everything came to light, and as I spot my bag descending from the chute, it occurs to me that in some ways, this will be our first *truly* honest moment in eighteen years—our entire adult relationship. As nervous as I am, I am also excited for our fresh start, and hope that he feels the same.

Seconds after I collect my bag, I turn toward the exit and see him coming toward me. He is always thin, but looks thinner than usual, tired too, with an expression of focus and determination that he gets during the sleeplessness and angst of a big trial.

"Hi, Dad," I say when he is just one step in front of me.

"Hi, sweetheart," he says, then peppers me with his usual questions. *How was the flight? Only one bag? Are you hungry?*

Fine, yes, no, I answer on the way to his car, then initiate some small talk of my own. *How's work? Any summer trips planned? It sure is hot out—summer is coming, even in Chicago.*

The more minutes that pass, the more the tension between us grows, only it isn't a typical, anxious tension, but rather an almost comforting suspense. It's as if we both know the whole point of the visit and what we will soon discuss, but neither of us is in a hurry to get there. We've waited this long; what's another few miles, one more car ride home. So he continues to drive, the songs on the radio changing the mood of the car on the margins.

When we finally exit on Green Bay Road, close to home, he clears his throat, and I think for sure it's finally coming. Something about that summer. Something about my choice.

273

Something about our visitor from St. Louis, arriving in only a couple hours. But instead he says, "Your mother is in a bit of cooking frenzy right now. Going a little overboard, as usual. What do you say we give her a little more time? . . . We could play the direction game? It's been a while . . ."

I glance at him, confused for a second, then remember the ancient game we made up together when I was no older than five or six. We'd get in the car and I'd close my eyes and whenever he got to an intersection, he'd say "Left, right, straight?" and I'd pick one of the three, sometimes alternating, sometimes sticking with one direction for the entire duration of the game.

Left, right, left, straight, I'd demand, to which he'd joke that we were going to end up in Guatemala or Saskatchewan— and every time, I'd picture such a destination as a distinct possibility. Or, even more terrifying and simultaneously thrilling, that we'd wind up completely lost. In the middle of nowhere, stranded without food or water, in extreme temperatures. Of course, I knew that such a thing couldn't really happen, that we'd never get any farther than Naperville or some other western suburb; yet whenever we reached our dead end, and my father instructed me to open my eyes, I still felt a surge of wonderment by whatever ordinary spot we had arrived at together, be it a car dealership, an optometrist, a stranger's driveway. It was always hilarious in its randomness, especially when we continued our charade and actually went inside to shop for the cherry-red Audi convertible, or peruse reading glasses, or even, once, knocking on someone's door, pretending we'd lost our puppy.

As I got a little older, and actually knew my way around town, I'd peek while my dad would pretend not to know I

274

was peeking, and lo and behold, we'd end up at Cold Stone Creamery or the mall or one of our favorite parks, both of us exclaiming at what a lucky day it was. It occurs to me now that those moments weren't unlike what is happening in the car today—both of us pretending, yet well aware that the other knows.

So I say, "I'd love to play," then promptly press my forehead against my window. "Ready when you are."

"Your eyes shut?"

"Yes," I lie.

"All right. Go," he says when we reach our next stop. "Left, right, or straight?"

"Right," I say, trying to read his mind, determine where it is he'd like to go, then deciding that Gillson Park will be our final destination. "*Definitely* right."

I proceed to direct him from Green Bay east to Sheridan, the familiar stretch of road that connects the North Shore's string of suburbs, winding along the lake with views of gorgeous homes, harbors, and glens, the classic scenery of John Hughes's films.

"Straight," I continue to instruct, as we drive southward, past preppy Winnetka and sleepy Kenilworth until we reach the intersection of Lake and Sheridan.

"Left," I say, and then direct him to a quick right on Michigan Avenue, then through the south entrance gates of the park.

"Okay! Dead end!" my father announces with glee. "And you'll never believe where we are!"

I turn from the window, feigning shock. "Ohhh! Gillson Park! I can't believe it!"

He shakes his head and laughs, making his way to the parking lot near the softball fields.

"Nice work," he says as we get out of the car.

"Whatever do you mean?" I say as we exchange a sideways glance. "I couldn't see a thing. We could have ended up anywhere."

"Even Saskatchewan," he says.

"Even Saskatchewan," I say as we meander along the path toward the small-boat harbor. It is a sunny day, warm but gusty, and I keep holding my hair back in my hand so it doesn't blow in my face.

At one point, he reaches in his pocket for a rubber band and hands it to me.

I shake my head and say, "You just happen to have one of them on you?"

"I have a paper clip, too, if you need one," he says, grinning.

"How about a safety pin?" I ask.

"In the car."

"Good to know."

We reach a bench near the water and sit, both of us toward the middle. I tell him I remember when my feet used to dangle. He says he can top that; he can remember pushing me in a stroller when I was a baby.

And there it is. *Baby.* The subject no longer avoidable.

I break down first and say, "So Dad . . . Mom says you wanted me to keep her?"

Without missing a beat, he says, "I'm just glad you had her."

I nod, realizing how much alike we are—to have the restraint to avoid a topic for this long, then launch right into the meat of it. I also realize that he didn't answer the question. "But you wanted me to keep her. Right?"

"That's a difficult question . . . I didn't want to lose her forever," he says. He is wearing dark aviators, yet he still

276

squints out over the water, lines appearing around his eyes, extending down toward his mouth. "But look. As it turns out, we didn't."

"Dad?" I say, turning to face him, my eyes hidden behind my own glasses.

"Yes, honey?"

"I'm sorry I didn't tell you . . . I wish I had."

"It's okay, honey."

"I was just so . . . embarrassed," I say, my voice cracking. The word isn't strong enough for what I felt. "I was mortified, ashamed. And I didn't want to let you down. I'm thirty-six years old and I can see now that the situation . . . was not the end of the world. But at eighteen, I couldn't see that . . . I just couldn't."

"Sweetie. I understand. I *always* did. I never thought any less of you . . . I just wish I could have been there for you."

"It wasn't just that, though," I say. "I didn't want to upset you. You work so hard—and have always given me everything. And there I was about to go out into the world, making the biggest mistake a girl could make, and I just—"

"But honey—that's just it. It was a *mistake*. You didn't *try* to hurt anyone. You might have let yourself down, but you didn't let me down."

"That can't be true," I say. "You might say that now, but then . . ."

"Marian. Look at me," he says, as he removes his glasses. "Your mother and I have always been proud of you. Always."

I nod, then whisper thank you.

A long moment of silence follows, until I sigh, then say, "This is really Mom's fault." I smile but his expression doesn't change.

"She did the best she could, too," he says, and I can't help feeling touched by his defense of her.

"I was just kidding," I say.

"I know . . . But for a long time, I *did* blame her. Longer than I even realized . . . Every time we saw a baby. Or a friend had a grandchild . . . I wanted her," he says. Then he reaches into his wallet and pulls out a photo of her. The same one I have. The *only* one I have.

"She has your face," he says. "She looks exactly like your newborn pictures."

I nod.

"Does she still?" he asks, blinking. "Look like you?"

"Yes. She definitely has my ears," I say, pressing them against my head. "And yours. Thank you very little."

He tries to laugh, but it comes out as a choking sound, as if narrowly converting a sob into something else.

"You'll see," I say. "I can't wait for you to meet her."

"I know," he says. "I just can't believe that she grew up . . . She is a young woman now."

I nod. "It makes me feel so old."

"You have no idea," he says, running his hands through his silver hair. I have a sudden pang, thinking about him getting older, worried about him being gone. So grateful that nothing happened to him before this day.

"You know, I was shaving this morning, thinking about this baby picture," he says, staring down at it again. "How I look at it every so often when I'm alone . . . Counting the years . . . trying to imagine her, at whatever age she is. And I thought to myself, that although I'm meeting her today, finally, that that baby, that little girl, is gone forever."

I nod, knowing by the pattern of his speech that he is not only musing, but making a larger, more organized point.

"And then. It struck me . . . that that happens no matter what. That happened with you. My baby is gone. My little girl is gone."

278

"Dad! I'm not *gone*," I say.

"I know, I know. But in many ways you *are*," he says. "Sure, we see you. We talk to you. We know what you're doing and we watch your friendships and relationships and career and life unfold. But for all intents and purposes, you aren't *ours* anymore."

He looks up, the way he does in a courtroom, as if searching for words that I know he will find. "It's like this," he says. "Kirby is eighteen, right?"

"Yes," I say, realizing that it is the first time he's said her name.

"And she'll be leaving home soon. Going off into the world to do whatever it is she's going to do. God willing, productive and worthwhile work. And although we would have had all those years with her. *You* would have had those years with her . . . She'd *still* be leaving you now . . . So I guess what I'm trying to say is that life is fast. And it keeps speeding up. Sometimes I lose track of the season—or even the year. And we just have to make the best of it all. Our choices. Our fleeting moments together." He takes a gulp of air, then slowly exhales. "We missed out on a lot of days and years and memories with her. But we can know her now. And we can embrace her now. And we will."

His chin quivers, making him look old again, but he manages not to cry. "Son of a gun," he says, shaking his head.

"What?"

"I have a rubber band and paper clip but no handkerchief."

I laugh and he leans over and hugs me harder and longer than I can ever remember being hugged.

"Let's go home," he says. "I want to meet my granddaughter."

We take the most direct route home, and find my mother in the kitchen whipping up an elaborate spread. Although she often cooks from her own memorized recipes, today she has consulted at least two cookbooks, both open on the counter.

"Hello, my dears," she says, with a curious look. Her gaze moves from my dad to me, back to my dad. Naturally she wants a report, but my father and I give her absolutely nothing, both of us commenting on her appetizers instead.

"Everything looks delicious," Dad says.

"And beautiful," I say.

She thanks us with great impatience, then says, "Well? How did it go?"

"How did what go?" I say.

"Did you talk?" she says.

"Yes," I say.

"Yes," my dad echoes. "We sure did."

"And?"

"We sorted through eighteen years of lies," I deadpan.

"There weren't *plural* lies," she says, covering a plate of deviled eggs with Saran Wrap and putting it in the refrigerator.

"Lie number one," I say, then quote her. " 'I will not tell your father.' "

"Lie number two," my father says, ticking it off on his fingers. " 'We can't tell Marian you know.' "

My mother pretends not to hear us as she puts the finishing touches on her bruschetta. Then she unties her apron, hangs it on a big iron hook inside the butler's pantry, and spins merrily toward us, revealing a persimmon-colored silk dress with gold anchor buttons. Paired with three-inch heels, she looks beautiful but overdressed—perhaps not for the occasion, but for what I know of Kirby. Still, I think it is important that we all be utterly ourselves today—the true, honest version of who we are, as individuals and as a family. And this includes my mother overdressing and overcooking.

"So," my mom says briskly. "You've decided to make me the fall guy."

"Yep. Pretty much," I say.

"That's an excellent summation," my dad quips, before going to her and putting one arm around her waist. He clears his throat, his expression changing to a serious one.

"Marian and I had a very nice talk," he continues in a low voice, as if intended only for her, although we all know that I can hear him, too.

"It feels good, doesn't it?" my mom says. "We're finally all on the same page."

For one second, I am filled with a feeling of warmth and well-being—but then I think of Conrad. A worried look must cross my face because my father says, "What's wrong, honey?"

Deciding that there is no room for deceit of any kind today, I sit at the kitchen table, feeling unsteady, then force myself to reply, "I was thinking about Conrad."

"Who?" my dad says.

I look at him, puzzled, then even more stupefied as it computes that we never once touched on Conrad in Gillson Park; nor did my mother really discuss him in New York.

"Kirby's biological father," I say. "Remember him?"

"Not so much," my mom says with a shrug. "Vaguely. We only met him once."

"Yes. Right here in the kitchen," I say, remembering the day I took the pregnancy test.

As my head starts to spin, I catch my father glancing at my mother with a purposeful look.

"What?" I say. "What was that for?"

My mom shakes her head.

"No more secrets," I say.

"Fine," she says. "We saw him one other time."

"When?" I say, nauseated. "Where?"

"Oh, it was nothing. We just ran into him . . . somewhere. I think it was that little organic market in Winnetka," my mom says, glancing at my dad. "By the tomato stand."

Before my father can confirm that he remembers Conrad or the stand of tomatoes, I demand to know when all of this occurred.

"Kirby would've been about six," my dad says.

"More like eight," my mom says.

"Did you speak to him?"

"Briefly," my mom says, stiffening. "We said hello."

"So you recognized him?"

"Not at first," she says. "He had filled out a bit. And his hair was . . . different."

"Different how?" I ask, my heart palpitating.

"Just . . . different," my mom says. "Maybe shorter? I don't know . . . That was ten years ago."

"Did he speak to you?" I say.

"He actually said hello first, I believe. Then we said hello back," my dad says. "That was it. It wasn't like we had a conversation. We were civil, but we weren't too keen on him after how he handled the whole . . . situation."

"What?" I say, shifting my gaze to my mom and giving her an accusatory look.

My mother frowns, guilty as charged.

"Mom? C'mon? Lie number three?" I say. Then I turn to my dad and say, "Conrad never knew I was pregnant."

"He didn't?" My father looks confused.

"No," I say. "I never told him. I never even *saw* him again after I took the pregnancy test. And that was *my* choice."

"Right," my mom says. "That was *your* choice, Marian. So don't go blaming me."

"So wait. He *never* knew?" my dad says, clearly as shocked as Peter and my friends.

"No. And Mom's right—that was my fault. He did *nothing* wrong," I say.

My mom sighs and says, "Okay, fine. But can't we all agree that that's water under the bridge?"

I shake my head, resolute. "No. We *can't* agree to that. And we certainly will say no such thing to Kirby. Conrad is just as much part of her as I am."

My mom makes a face. "I wouldn't go that far."

"You wouldn't?" I say. "So I belong to you more than Dad?"

"Oh, for heaven's sake," my mom says, with the sudden audacity to be indignant. "The point is, *you* carried her for nine months and made the responsible choice to give her away—when that boy probably—"

"Conrad," I say. "His name is Conrad."

Deep down, I know that my self-righteousness doesn't make any sense when I set the whole chain of lies in motion. But still. Kirby is in the picture now. And we are going to find Conrad. And at the very least, I think we all need to acknowledge that he has a name and a place in this story.

"Furthermore, we have no idea what he would have done," I say, remembering my conversation with Peter, realizing that I am now taking his side in the debate. "I never gave him that chance."

"Well, what are you going to do, Marian? Go tell him now?" she asks, throwing her hands up.

"Yes," I say. "Tomorrow with Kirby."

My mother stares at me, her eyes wide. "Isn't it a little too late for that?"

"Was it too late for her to find me? Is it too late for you to meet her?" I ask.

My father shakes his head, although I'm not sure whether he's answering my question or simply digesting the whole situation.

"So what else did he say? When you saw him that day? Besides hello?" I say, wondering if he asked about me.

"Nothing else," my mom says.

My father winces as if concentrating, then says, "I believe he also said, 'Those are some nice-looking tomatoes.'"

Coming from anyone else, I would have heard sarcasm, but my father is simply being as accurate as possible about the details, one of the many reasons he is such an amazing trial lawyer.

"And that was it?" I ask.

"That was it," he says quietly.

I nod, then tell my parents I'm going to my room for a few minutes before Kirby arrives. As I turn toward the stairwell, I picture Conrad at the tomato stand, remembering his hands, the way they looked and felt, warm on my skin, wondering if there was a ring on his left one that day my parents saw him. Wondering whether he'll be wearing one tomorrow.

25

Kirby

I have another forty or so miles to go on I-55 and about ninety minutes left in my five-hour trip which, so far, has been a breeze. I've only stopped once to fill up my gas tank and use the restroom. I also remember to call my parents, reassuring them that I am completely fine, and that it's a clear, sunny day with very little traffic. My father reminds me to stay in the right lane, no passing, avoid big trucks, and stay off my phone.

"Oh. And your mother says don't forget the pecan pie. It'll melt if you leave it in the car," my dad adds, referring to the pie she made as my hostess gift, along with four linen cocktail napkins hand-embroidered with the letter *C*. She screwed up the first time on both projects, overbrowning the crust on the pie and choosing a mauve satin stitch for the napkins that just "didn't thrill her." So late last night, I found her in the kitchen, still baking, still sewing. She was deep in concentration, with the look she gets when she's praying hard for something, and I couldn't help feeling sorry for her as I poured myself a glass of chocolate milk.

"Do you need any help, Mom?" I asked, standing over her. She had switched to a peacock blue thread for the napkins, and according to the pattern book on the table, a Celtic knot.

She looked up at me over her reading glasses, shaking her head with a wistful smile, and said, "Kirby, honey. You know you can't sew. Or bake." She sighed. "One of my many failings as a mother."

"You don't have failings as a mother," I said, mostly believing this to be true.

"Of course I do," she said. "Every parent does. It is inevitable. You'll see."

I nodded—how can you argue with such a thing?—then asked if she wanted company.

She looked at me, surprised. "You should get some sleep." But she didn't protest when I sat down at the table.

"Are you excited?" she asked.

"A little," I said, through a monstrous yawn.

"It's okay to be excited," she said.

"I know."

"I'm excited for you."

"Thank you."

"I can't wait to hear all about your . . . second family."

I could tell it was a test, and an annoying one at that, but I still said what she wanted to hear. "They're not my second family. I only have one family."

"It's okay to think of them that way."

"But I don't," I said. "They're strangers."

"Marian's not a stranger."

"Okay, well, not her. But she's more like a friend."

"She doesn't feel like a mother—"

"Mom, don't. Okay?" I said, cutting her off.

She stifled a yawn of her own, as I told her I was going back to bed.

"Yes. Go to bed. Tomorrow is a big day."

I finished my milk, put the glass in the sink, and walked back past her on my way to the stairs.

"Mom?" I said, awkwardly pausing beside her.

"Yes, honey?"

286

"Thanks."

"For what?" she asked with her wide-eyed, martyrlike stare, as if it is perfectly normal to bake and sew at all hours of the night.

"For doing all of this," I said. "I'm sure the Caldwells are going to love the napkins."

"Yes. I think they will," she said. "I'm so glad I changed to blue. Everyone loves blue, don't you think?"

"Yes. And who doesn't love a pecan pie?" I added, both humoring and appreciating her at once.

She nodded, then said, "God willing they don't have any nut allergies. That thought just occurred to me."

"Yes," I said on my way to the stairs. "God willing."

And here I am on I-55, catching myself praying. An actual, specific request to God to have the weekend go well. To have everyone like me and approve of me and be okay with the fact that I am their blood relative.

My phone rings in the passenger seat, interrupting my conversation with God. Although I can hear my father telling me not to pick it up while I'm driving, I see Philip's name and grab it, pressing it to my ear. As much as I'm thinking about the weekend ahead, at least half the miles logged have been spent on Philip. Since Friday night, we've talked every day for at least an hour and kissed two more times. Last night, I even let him go up my shirt.

I also find myself thinking about Conrad and Marian, and wonder if their relationship felt anything like ours. I know that Philip and I won't last forever, that he will go off to Alaska and then Colorado, and the best that I can really hope for is that we stay in touch. But I can't imagine losing him as a friend, any more than I can imagine what it must be like for Marian to be finding Conrad, after all these years gone by.

A good hour of Ray LaMontagne tunes later, my MapQuest directions end at Maple Hill Road, a beautiful street with houses that are all quadruple the size of anything in my neighborhood. Marian's parents' house turns out to be the most elegant in a whole line of pretty ones with a perfect, crew-cut lawn and jewel-toned flower bed. As I pull up the driveway, I realize that it bears a striking resemblance to the house in *Father of the Bride*—and then wonder if it is *that* house. I park behind a Land Rover and a Mercedes convertible, both waxed to a high shine.

Stalling before I get out of the car, I check my reflection in the rearview mirror, send my parents a text that says, *Made it here safe,* then another, slightly wordier version of the same text to Philip. I then take a deep breath, reach back into the backseat for my purse, the pecan pie, adorned with a sticker that says "From the kitchen of Lynn Rose," and the linen napkins, nestled in a gold gift bag. Then I open the door, climb out, and close it with a hard hip bump.

I am nervous, my breathing shallow, on the way to the door, but I also have a feeling of crazy curiosity to meet Marian's parents, see where she grew up. I imagine Conrad standing on her front porch, waiting to pick up his girlfriend. Then I ring the doorbell, its chime a grand six-note melody.

I hear heels coming toward me before the door bursts open and there stands Marian's mother, even more glamorous than Marian, in an orange dress, her arms open to greet me.

"Hello, Kirby!" she exclaims as I inhale amazing food smells.

"Hi, Mrs. Caldwell," I say as Marian appears just behind her in the foyer.

"Call me 'Pamela,'" she says as she starts to hug me, then decides against it.

I nod, then hand her the pie and the napkins and say, "My mother made you these."

"Well, wasn't that sweet of her," she says, patting them before placing them on a table in the hall. She then takes the pie, proclaiming it a beauty, as Marian pushes past her mother to hug me hello. Our embrace feels both formal and comfortable at once, and I wonder if both are possible, and if not, which one is in my head.

"So good to see you," Marian says.

"You too," I say.

"Come in, dear, come in," Pamela says, then leads me back down a wide hallway to a large kitchen filled with food. "What can I get you to drink? We have freshly squeezed grapefruit juice, orange juice, prune juice, water—both flat and sparkling."

Prune juice? I think, comforted by the realization that everyone is a little weird.

"Mom, give her a second," Marian mumbles, but Pamela does no such thing, opening the refrigerator then glancing back at me expectantly.

"I'll take some water, please," I say.

She nods, removes a large bottle of Evian from the door and pours it into a tall, mottled blue glass that my mom's napkins will match perfectly.

"Sit, sit," she says, pointing to the counter as Kirby's father enters the room, filling it with an immediate, strong presence. I like him instantly.

"Kirby," he says, walking over to me and covering my hand with his. "At long last. Welcome."

"Thank you," I say, overcome with a warm feeling.

He returns his hand to his pocket, staring at me with a smile. He finally nods, as if satisfied with what he sees, and says, "I'm glad you're here. It's just . . . so *good* to meet you."

"Thank you, Mr. Caldwell," I say, knowing that he will correct me, too.

He does, of course, telling me to call him "Jim." Although Marian's mother is nice enough, I get a completely different vibe from her dad, and the only way I can describe it is that I feel related to him. Or perhaps, more significantly, he seems to feel related to *me*.

Sure enough, he says, "Are you looking at my big ears? I understand an apology may be in order?"

I laugh a real genuine laugh and say, "Yeah. I don't care for them."

"You don't care for them on me," he says, turning to Marian. "Or her?"

"On any of us," I say, loosening up.

"At least you girls have your hair to cover them up," he says.

"Yeah. Thin hair," Marian says.

He runs his hand through his own full head of thick gray hair, only slightly receding at the temple, and says, "Whoah. Whoah! You can't blame me for that one."

Marian turns to look at her mother, who doesn't appreciate the accusation. "We don't have thin hair. We have *fine* hair. There is a difference."

"And what is that, exactly?" Marian asks.

"The hairs are fine, but we have a lot of them," Pamela says, turning toward the gift bag.

I think of my mother and her thick, curly hair that my

sister inherited, and realize how nice it is to finally know where I got mine. Then I think of how my mom has always told me she loves every hair on my head—and I feel an unexpected pang for her.

"Oh, these are *soo* lovely," Pamela says, exclaiming over the napkins.

"My mother made them," I say.

"Well, they are beautiful. Just *beautiful*," Pamela says, going a little too overboard.

I tell her I'm glad she likes them, as she continues to gush. I watch her while tuning her out, recognizing her type. Then I realize that, ironically, she reminds me of a richer, more polished version of my dad. They are both chatty, friendly, and outgoing, yet there is something about her that makes me feel that I'd never really get to know her, that she'd always keep me at arm's length in the same way my dad uses sports. No matter how close a friend he has, they never really seem to progress beyond the Cardinals and Rams. I can imagine that it is this way with Pamela, only with a different, narrow focus.

"So what would you like to do today?" she says. "Go to the city? Have you been to Chicago?"

"She was born here," Marian says under her breath.

I glance at her then look back at Pamela. "Not for a long time," I say.

"Well, there is so much to do. Museums, art galleries, shopping. Do you like to shop, Kirby?"

"Sure. Sometimes," I say, thinking the apple doesn't fall far from the tree.

"Honey. I don't think this is a day to shop," Jim says. "Wouldn't you all just rather talk? Get to know one another?"

291

Pamela holds up her hand as if to say my bad, then says, "Well, are we allowed to eat? Because I've prepared a feast!"

"Yes," Marian says. "We're allowed to eat, Mom."

"Good," she says. "Then let's eat!"

I smile, thinking that this is at least one thing my family has in common with this one, and maybe families everywhere. When in doubt, go ahead and eat.

26

Marian

The next morning, after Kirby and I successfully dodge my mother's attempt to make us breakfast, we hop into my dad's Land Rover, unshowered, and commence driving aimlessly around my hometown per her request to see where I grew up. She even has a list of all the places she wants to see, my high school, our church (although I told her we almost never went), Conrad's childhood home, and Janie's house.

"So how's Philip?" I ask her as we back out of my driveway. I don't tell her that I heard her across the hall, talking and laughing until nearly midnight.

"He's good," she says.

"So things are going well?"

"Yeah," she says, smiling. "I think we're kind of dating . . ."

I wait for more details, but I can tell she is finished talking about her personal life, so I decide not to press.

A few minutes later, we turn the corner, nearing my old stomping ground. "There's New Trier High School," I say, pointing to the familiar brick building. "Home of the proud and mighty Trevians."

She nods, as I reach for my travel mug, take a sip of black coffee, and take a one-handed turn onto the mostly empty school grounds. I pull around the school, then into a parking spot, staring down at the track, deluged with memories.

"What are you thinking? About your cheerleading days?" she asks with a hint of sarcasm.

"Ha," I say, although I pretty much was. "I heard they got rid of the squad here. Not enough interest. It's a good thing. I think girls should come up with something better to do than cheer for their male classmates."

She smirks. "You didn't like being a cheerleader?"

"It was okay. But I wish I had stuck with soccer. I loved the game but quit to cheer. For Todd. Ugh," I say, rolling my eyes. "He was our quarterback."

"Of *course* he was," Kirby says.

"Hey! I'm telling you I regretted it. Doesn't that redeem me?" I ask, although secretly I don't *altogether* regret being on the squad. Janie and I had a blast—and that short, pleated skirt and those pom-poms really did make me feel pretty cool during a time when feeling cool seemed to matter so much.

Kirby glances at me, then faces the track again, as we both watch a boy sprinting up and down the bleacher steps with Olympian determination. "Yeah, that redeems you . . . But Conrad redeems you more."

I nod, his name a Pavlovian bolt of electricity that I try to hide now by singing the cheer I can still say in my sleep: *We say New Trier; you say Trevians! New Trier!* I look at her, cueing her with my right hand.

Kirby plays along and give me a less than rousing, "Trevians."

I smile and continue with the next stanza: *We say green and you say blue. Green!*

"Blue," she says with a lackluster fist pump.

We drive to the front of the school as I point out a big red and white NO PARKING sign in an area reserved for buses. "You see that sign?" I ask.

"Yeah?"

"I ran up onto the curb and plowed it down just days after I got my driver's license, right into a six-feet drift of snow."

"On purpose?" she asks, as if the story is part of my riveting, rebellious lore rather than a small mishap, albeit traumatic in that moment.

"No," I say. "It was an accident. I had a bag of McDonald's on the dash. When I made the turn, it fell off the dash. I leaned down to grab it, and didn't let go of the steering wheel to adjust after the turn. I rolled right up onto the curb. I was with Todd—who started yelling for me to brake, but I accidentally slammed down on the gas pedal. The whole thing unfolded right in front of the math team and the wrestling team, both loading up on buses. And of course, Todd promptly abandoned me to get on one himself."

"Lemme guess. He got on the math bus?"

"Funny," I say. "Wrestling of course. Second in state in the one-hundred-sixty-pound weight class."

"Only second?"

"Yeah," I say, then imitate his meathead voice. "But it was the worst call, dude! Highway robbery!"

Kirby laughs and says, "So did you get in trouble? For hitting the sign?"

"Yeah. The dean came out guns a-blazin' until he saw it was me—I had a good reputation, so he mellowed a bit. But he gave me an extra two hours of driving practice with the driver's ed teacher, who had the worst halitosis. That sucked."

"Was that the only time you ever got in trouble?" she asks, giving me another pointed look, as if she is thinking, *Before you got knocked up.*

"Yes. That was it, pretty much. I didn't even ditch on senior-ditch day," I say, as I turn back onto Winnetka Avenue. "Pretty Goody Two-shoes vanilla."

Sure enough, she comes out with it. "Does a Goody Two-shoes really get herself pregnant?"

"This one did," I say. "Where to next?"

"Conrad's house," she says.

I can feel my hands growing tight and clammy on the steering wheel, my heart rate quickening as we drive toward the area of town known as the Presidents because all the streets are named after presidents. I take the long way, but we still get to Conrad's old house in less than five minutes.

"That's it," I say, slowing to a crawl and pointing at the ranch house, now painted a dusty blue with a brick-red front door. "It used to be white with green shutters," I tell her.

"Does it . . . bring back memories?" she says.

"Yes," I say, "that's for sure. Good and bad. Mostly good."

I stare at the house, remembering the nights spent inside, listening to him strum the guitar, the two of us talking and laughing, watching movies, making love. "That was his room," I say, pointing to the right corner window. Then I tell her we pretty much broke up in his family room. "Right after I lied to him about my pregnancy test."

She nods, then swallows hard.

"My only big regret," I say.

"Your *only* big one?" she says. "Really? What about . . . you know? . . . Getting pregnant in the first place?"

"How can I regret that?" I say, looking at her.

"Okay. Maybe not now. But then. It had to be a regret then."

I nod, making the difficult admission. "Of course. I wouldn't wish that on any teenager . . . I wouldn't want that for you. I think you should wait to have sex, if not until marriage, then at least for a long, long time. So that if you did get pregnant—you'd be ready to deal with it better than I was," I say, hoping she's still a virgin.

"You mean able to keep the baby?" she asks.

"Yes," I say. "That's what I mean."

I turn to look at her and choose my words carefully. "I wish I could have kept you. I wish that had been the right decision for you."

"I wish that, too," she says. "I love my parents and my sister—but I wish that, too."

My heart feels torn as I say her name, and then, "I'm not going to say things happen for a reason—because I really don't believe that. I think much of life is random . . . But I will say this. I'm glad everything happened the way it did. I'm glad I got pregnant with you. I'm glad I had you. I'm glad you have a family who loves you. And most of all, I'm glad you're here now."

She gives me a small smile as I continue, not letting myself off the hook.

"But God . . . I shouldn't have lied to him." I shake my head and mumble, "That was *so wrong*."

"But you're going to fix it," she says. "Today. Right?"

"I'm going to try," I say, as my stomach drops, thinking that if driving by his old house is this hard, how will I ever make it to his actual doorstep?

She says we can go whenever I'm ready, and I take a deep breath and pull away, headed back across the train tracks to Janie's house, the last stop on her list. When we arrive, I spot Janie's mother in the front yard, gardening in khaki

297

Bermuda shorts and a straw hat. She flags down my car and hustles over to the window, too quickly for me to share with Kirby that I never liked her much. She is the type of person who says "I'm the type of person who" and then fills in the blank with a virtue that is either blandly universal or is downright self-congratulatory ("I'm the type of person who likes to help others"). She annoyed me when I was a kid—and more so the older I got, although I probably haven't seen her in a good six or seven years.

"Marian! I thought that was you! Your mother told me you were coming to town this weekend! How are you, dear?"

"I'm well, thanks," I say, noticing that she gives Kirby only a cursory glance, evidence that my mother did not divulge the true purpose of my visit. I wonder how long it will take for the barriers of our secret to completely crumble. Like the Berlin Wall—just a few openings here and there until the sledgehammers came out and the dancing began. Somehow, I can't imagine my mother ever initiating an open conversation about Kirby, and I wonder why this is. To hide the underlying truth—or the fact that we lied in the first place? And is it really possible to separate the two after so many years?

"How's Janie?" I say, knowing that I will have to endure a twenty-minute monologue on Janie's life in Cincinnati that will inevitably repeat all of the bullet points in the letter I received from Janie herself, stuffed into her holiday card adorned with a snapshot of the family donning summer whites on the shore of Lake Michigan. The letters are the same, year in and year out, exhaustively covering her three sons' extracurriculars ("Cub Scouts! Chess club!!") and athletic feats ("Brandon's first homer!"), her myriad of volunteer do-gooding ("five hundred Easter baskets for underprivileged youth—a record!"), and of course, details of her husband Keith's latest promotion and triathlon adventures ("I don't know how he does it all!"). I tune in to Mrs. Wattenberg now, wrapping up her coverage of Janie's life, with a general touting of the Midwest—including family values and a slower pace.

"So how's life in the big city?" she finally asks.

Before I can answer, she shakes her head, says how proud she is of me, how much she loves my show. And even though it isn't her husband's cup of tea, he watches it, too, and that they've told all their friends to at least record the show, because it is good for my ratings. They're doing their part!

I thank her as she takes a deep breath, exhausted, then shifts gears. "So when have you and Janie last talked?"

"It's been a while, unfortunately," I say, thinking that it had to have been around the ten-year reunion, which I told her I had to miss because of work when it actually had more to do with Conrad. I knew he wouldn't come, but I didn't want to hear his name. I didn't want to be around anyone who knew him. I didn't want to think about him at all.

"But there are no hard feelings, right? You girls didn't have a falling-out, did you?"

"Oh, no, Mrs. Wattenberg, it was nothing like that. We just . . . grew apart. It happens."

"Well, you have such different lives—that is true," she says, glancing at my left hand, as I notice that I'm still gripping the steering wheel.

"Any wedding news? Getting closer to a ring?" she asks. "Your mother just loves that boyfriend of yours. I saw a photo. He looks like a young Richard Gere, who has always been my favorite. Ever since *Pretty Woman*. And who would think you could love a man who'd hire a hooker?"

I smile and say, "Yeah. That's a feat, all right."

"So?"

I shake my head, hold up my naked left hand, and chirp, "No ring yet!"

"Well, hang in there! It'll come! And babies to follow. You still have time. And who knows? You could have twins. Do you know that your chance of twins increases with age? Older women are more likely to drop two eggs. Maybe you'd even have triplets! You could catch up to Janie in one fell swoop."

I have a fleeting fantasy of telling her that procreation isn't a contest, any more than SAT scores and making the cheerleading squad and getting into a good college and all the other things, both big and small, that she turned into a contest when Janie and I were young, going all the way back to whose baby teeth came in first, according to my mother. I could never understand why she was so keen on keeping score between Janie and me when Janie herself refused to bite; if anything her mother's efforts caused a reverse effect.

But looking back, I can see that I *was* participating in the contest. Maybe that was why I was so acutely aware of Mrs. Wattenberg's little remarks. And maybe that was part of the reason I didn't want Janie or anyone else to know the truth—because I believed that she, and others like her, might have relished the drama. The girl voted most likely to succeed, going to Michigan on an academic scholarship, from a great family with a high-powered attorney for a father. Pregnant at eighteen, with Conrad Knight's baby, no less. The ultimate shock and fall from grace.

300

I can also see now how self-centered I was to think that my news would have made that much of a difference in anybody's life. People would have talked about me for a few weeks, or perhaps just one night at the dinner table, before moving on to something else. And who cares, anyway, what they would have said? I realize now, years too late, how little it mattered. How much I sacrificed because of a mistake, including my friendship with Janie. Although too much time has gone by to miss her, I feel regret that I didn't maintain our friendship. Even if we no longer have much in common, we would have always had the past, which, in some ways, is just as important as the present or future. It is where we come from, what makes us who we are.

I glance over at Kirby, and catch her staring at Mrs. Wattenberg with faint disdain. I consider making a quick getaway, for both of our sakes, but I know what I must do. So I clear my throat and take the plunge. "Oh, I'm sorry I haven't introduced you . . . Mrs. W, this is Kirby Rose."

"Hi," she says, without the slightest flash of curiosity. Yet this time, I decide I'm going to *make* her be interested.

"Kirby is my daughter," I say.

Mrs. Wattenberg freezes, literally, the way we used to look like statues playing freeze tag. "Pardon? Your daughter?" she says with a nervous laugh. "You don't have a daughter! Wait." She peers around the car as if there might be a camera crew hiding in the hedges. "Is this a big-sister program type thing? A reality show?"

"No. It's not a show," I say. "It's real life."

"But . . . what do you mean?" she asks.

"Kirby's my *daughter*," I say again. "Right, Kirby?"

Kirby nods, smirking, seeming to follow right along with every emotional nuance. "Right, *Mom*."

"But . . . ?" Mrs. Wattenberg says. "Is she a step—"

"No," I say, shaking my head. "She's my *biological* daughter."

"But how? How old are you?" she asks, staring at Kirby with newfound fascination.

"Eighteen," Kirby says.

"Yes, Mrs. Wattenberg. I got pregnant with her the summer after we graduated. That's the real reason I deferred college a year. Then I had her—and made the difficult decision to give her up for adoption. I thought it was the right thing to do at the time. Fortunately, she came back and found me. We're all getting to know each other." I flatly deliver the news—because it isn't really about the news. It's about the act of telling it, finally. I feel strangely freed, basking in the feeling of utter openness and honesty. *This is who I am. Take it or leave it.*

"Well. My stars. I had no idea," Mrs. Wattenberg says. She looks not only flabbergasted but flustered, clearly not equipped to receive gossip this easily; usually it's fought for, scrap by scrap.

"Yeah. Don't worry about it, Mrs. W. Nobody did. We kept it a secret . . . But we shouldn't have. Please tell Janie—and tell her I'm sorry I lied to her. In fact, feel free to tell whomever you'd like," I say as if, without my permission, she still wouldn't have hit the pavement with the juiciest Maple Hill Road nugget since two neighbors switched spouses, the wives staying put, the husbands moving across the street, a seamless shift, the running joke that one husband got an uncomfortable couch but big, fake boobs in the trade. I start to tell her who the father is—as I know she's dying to ask—but decide I should tell Conrad first.

302

"Well, that is quite stunning news!" she says with a look that tells me she can't quite decide whether I should be embarrassed or very proud. One liberating second later, I decide that it doesn't much matter. Because I *am* proud.

As we pull away, I smile to myself, shaking my head, thinking if she only knew where the story all began. Right upstairs in her very own four-poster bed.

"What's so funny?" Kirby asks.

The girl misses nothing.

"Oh, I don't know . . . That just felt good."

"Rocking her world like that?"

"Yeah," I say. "And just . . . telling her you're my daughter. Telling her the *truth*."

"Consider it your practice run," Kirby says.

"I guess so," I say.

"Should we just go for it now?" she asks. "Drive to his place and get it over with?"

"It's not even noon," I say.

"Yeah. You should wait until afternoon to deliver bad news," Kirby says.

"This is *good* news," I say.

"Yeah," she says, flashing an exaggerated, pageant-girl smile. "Surely I'm the daughter he's always wanted."

She is joking, but I give her a serious look and nod, as if to tell her that's *exactly* how I feel.

27

Kirby

An hour later we are both showered, dressed in virtually identical outfits of jeans and sleeveless navy tops (mine an inexpensive version of her designer one). Meeting in the hall, we look at each other and laugh, then proceed to put on makeup in her room, side by side. At one point, I notice that Marian's hands are shaking as she paints black liquid liner along her upper lid. She frowns, displeased with the result, then removes it and begins again, biting her lip as she goes more slowly the second time. It looks no different, maybe even better the first time, but I watch her surrender with a long sigh and move on to her blush.

When we're ready, we head downstairs, where she leaves a brief note for her parents on the counter, checks the contents of her purse at least four times, opens a bottle of water from the refrigerator, takes one sip, then asks if I want anything, not paying the slightest bit of attention to the answer—which is no.

"Marian," I finally say.

"Hmm?"

"Let's go, okay?"

She nods, smiles, then moves absentmindedly toward the front door as if this weren't a mission about eighteen years overdue.

Then, finally, we are on the way to the city, the Lincoln Park address entered into the navigational system, the loud voice of a smug British woman telling us where to turn. She irritates Marian who finally imitates her in an English accent.

"Oh, *do* shut up," she shouts, but can't figure out how to turn the volume down even after fiddling with the system for several minutes.

"Do you think he's married?" I blurt out at one point.

She stares straight ahead and says, "I'm guessing no. But I don't know why. Maybe just a serious girlfriend. Maybe he's divorced." She lets out a tight laugh. "I really have no idea. I can't picture him. I mean—I remember him exactly as he was, and I can even imagine what he might look like, you know, almost twenty years later, but I can't imagine his *life* now. What he's doing . . . I guess we'll find out soon enough."

I nod, and twenty quick minutes later, our British friend informs us that we've reached our final destination at 1130 Armitage, a gray brownstone flanked by two red-brick buildings.

"Well. We're here," she says, looking paler than usual as she parallel parks into an open spot in front of it.

"You sure you want to do this?" I ask. "I mean—we can just go. Or I can do it alone."

She looks tempted by this idea, but then shakes her head. She turns the ignition off, then grips the steering wheel as if steadying herself. "Nope. I'm ready."

We get out of the car, cross the sidewalk, then march up the front steps, like we're on our way to a funeral. She reaches out, her hand shaking as she rings the buzzer of "2C Knight." We wait. Nothing. Her hand hovers over the button as she takes a deep breath and tries again. A few seconds pass. Still nothing.

"He could be out of town," I say, partly relieved, at least for her.

"Or maybe he's just out . . . running errands," she says, looking like she might faint. "We could try again in an hour or so. Maybe grab lunch and come back?"

"Okay," I say, reluctantly turning to follow her back down the stairs. She hesitates at the bottom then turns right, then changes her mind and does a one-eighty, squarely into a man's path. They almost bump into one another, but don't, and I suddenly recognize him, even before it seems to register with either of them. But as they both back up a pace, I see them process it, and I get goose bumps as I watch them together. My parents. Here the three of us are, I think. For the first time. Here is what could have been.

My next thought is totally embarrassing—and that is: My father is hot. Way better looking than any other father I know. Rugged in an artsy way, with dark wavy hair and amazing eyes. He is wearing faded blue jeans, brown leather boots of a construction worker–cowboy hybrid, an untucked white linen shirt, and a long, patterned cotton scarf, twisted and looped haphazardly around his neck. I imagine that it smells like incense or pot or some combination of the two, until I realize that he actually *does* carry with him that aroma—at least the incense part. In one arm is a bag of groceries, a baguette poking out of the top of a cloth sack. Everything about him looks urban cool.

They both continue to stare at each other, expressionless, motionless, in the weirdest standoff I've ever seen, almost as if they're calling the other's bluff. It is the way you'd look at a perfect stranger, although if they were actually strangers someone would break down and exchange a pleasantry after such prolonged eye contact. I start to wonder if maybe I shouldn't reintroduce my own parents.

He finally speaks, saying her name as statement of fact, a slight nod with his chin. And then, "What are you doing here?" His voice isn't entirely rude, but it is remote and icy. He shifts his bag to the other arm and I look at his free hand. No wedding ring.

Marian opens her mouth to speak, then shoots me a desperate glance. I already knew she was nervous but had no idea that she'd be this rattled. "I'm . . . we're . . . I wanted to talk to you," she stammers.

Smooth, I think. *Real smooth.*

"Talk?" he says, cocking his head to the side.

"Yes."

"About what?" he says, all cool and calm and chilly.

She glances at me again, and I wonder if she's contemplating divulging everything right here on the street. I shake my head, signaling that this isn't the best plan of action, but she's already turned back to him. "Can we go somewhere . . . to talk?" she says. "Maybe get some coffee?"

"I don't drink coffee."

"You used to."

"I don't anymore."

I realize I am holding my breath as I continue to watch them. It is as riveting as any scene on television. I make myself exhale.

"How about tea?" she says. "Or can we just go sit somewhere? Anywhere?"

He shrugs and then looks at me for the first time, no glimmer of recognition, only indifference with a trace of annoyance. He glances at his watch and mumbles that he doesn't have long.

"It won't take long," she says.

He nods. "Okay. Let me put these away. I'll be back."

As he turns to go, taking the stairs two at a time, I notice that Marian's chest is literally rising and falling through her top. It is the the first time I've seen her look anything less than perfectly composed, including when I knocked on her door, and for some reason, it makes me not only feel closer to her, but it also makes me *like* her more. Before I can change my mind, I reach out and touch her arm and say, "Well, that's a good start."

"He hates me," she says, as we sit beside each other on his bottom step.

"It's better than not caring at all," I say, although in truth, cold indifference is more of what I just observed than hate.

"Is it?" She gives me a funny look, as if she hopes this is true.

I nod, then shoot a quick text to Philip, telling him that I've just seen my father.

One minute later, the front door opens, and Conrad reappears. We leap up and stand at military attention, all eye level again. I notice that his scarf is gone, the boots replaced with flip-flops, as if their brief exchange had overheated him. I take this as a good sign—but then wonder what exactly I want him to feel. What do I want to come from this other than his acceptance of my birth, of me? And can't he accept me while still hating her?

He holds my gaze, as if seeing me for the first time. "I'm Conrad," he says without offering his hand.

I stare at him, overwhelmed, thinking that he might as well have just said, "I'm George Clooney," for how surreal the moment feels, how almost famous he seems to me.

"And you are?" he says.

"Kirby," I say, feeling foolish for forgetting to speak.

"Oh. Kirby. I see," he says, with a hint of annoyance. My paranoid translation: *Thanks for your name but who the hell are you and what are you doing here with her?*

Marian clears her throat and says, "Where can we go?"

He shrugs and says, "There's an Argo Tea a few blocks up. At the corner of Sheffield."

"Okay," she says. "That'd be great."

He looks at her blankly, indicating there is nothing "great" currently in the works. At best, whatever is happening is bizarre and uncomfortable. At worst, it is downright hostile. But he descends the final few stairs, then turns left, walking swiftly up the street. Marian and I fall in line behind him, the three of us walking single file in silence.

As we enter Argo, the buzz inside is a relief, as is the warm lighting and smell of baked goods. Conrad starts to get in line, then turns to us and says, "Grab a table. I'll order. What do you want?"

"I'll have . . . green tea, please," Marian says, then looks at me.

"I'll have the same," I say, although I actually don't like tea at all.

Marian opens her purse, then wallet, rifling through to find a few bills, but Conrad looks at her with scorn and says, "I got this."

"Thanks," she says, putting her money away.

"Thanks," I echo, then follow her to one of the only open tables in the center of the dining area.

After we sit, I look at her and say, "You need to tell him.

As soon as he gets back to the table, you need to tell him who I am."

"You already did," she says.

I roll my eyes, feeling a stab of impatience at her epic lameness. "Tell him I'm his daughter," I say, leaning toward her. "Or I will."

28

Marian

By the time he returns to the table with our tea, I am a complete nervous wreck. As I take my cup, I notice (and so, probably, do they) that my hands are shaking. I feel light-headed, sweaty, queasy, and can't seem to get my breathing regulated.

"How have you been?" I start, hating myself for choosing such an absurdly casual opener. Out of the corner of my eye, I see Kirby shoot me a look of disgust.

"Um. Fine," Conrad says. "And you?"

"Fine," I say. "Good. Well."

"Great." He peels back the plastic lid on his cup, checking the progress of the bag without letting too much steam escape. "I see you've made it big," he says, without looking at me. "I haven't seen your show, but I'm sure it's great. Congratulations."

I assumed there was a chance he'd know about my career, but am still surprised that he'd mention it. "Thanks," I say, staring down at my hands, resting on the table. "What have you been up to?"

"This and that."

"Oh." I nod a little too eagerly given that he shared no information.

"Do you mean what do I do for a living?" he asks, still managing to avoid eye contact.

"I guess. Yeah," I say.

"You can ask that then."

"Okay," I say, my leg now bouncing under the table. "What do you do?"

"I work at a bar," he says.

I nod some more, this time smiling.

"About what you expected?"

"What do you mean?" I say, although I know exactly what he means.

"Look, Marian. What is this about?" he says, staring directly into my eyes. My palms start to tingle. *Everything* is tingling—my whole body and mind suffering from sensory and emotional overload. For one bizarre second, it's like we're eighteen again, but then I remember we're not—*she* is. And beyond anything that happened in the past, that is the hardest part of all of this. The fact that she is watching me, waiting for me to try to fix something that really can't be fixed. Not entirely. Maybe not ever. And certainly not at this table, over tea.

When I can't manage a reply, he says, "It's nice to see you, I guess. But really . . . why are you here?"

I look at him, bracing myself, wondering how he hasn't put it together. Her age. Her mere presence at the table. Her *eyes*. I glance at her now and see that she is pissed, likely thinking that she's waited eighteen years for *this*? I lick my lips, my throat tight and dry, then take a sip of tea that burns the roof of my mouth.

He shakes his head. "They make it hot here. Should've warned you."

"It's fine," I say, my voice cracking.

And then, two labored breaths later, I hear myself start to spew disjointed apologies and explanations while both of them stare at me, one nonplussed, the other aghast with the train wreck that is her mother.

That day at your house . . . The last day I saw you . . . I lied . . . I was scared . . . I did the wrong thing . . . I'm sorry I never told you . . . I was pregnant . . . And then I had her . . . But I gave her away . . . I thought it was the right thing . . . But I still should have told you . . . I'm so sorry.

When I abruptly stop talking, he says, "Wait. What do you mean you were pregnant?"

"I was pregnant," I repeat dumbly. "I told you I wasn't . . . that day at your house . . . but I . . . was."

"You found out later?" he says, squinting in confusion.

"I found out that day," I say. "In the bathroom. At your house. The test was positive. But I told you . . . it was negative. I . . . lied to you."

"Why would you do that?" he shoots back.

"I don't know."

"You don't *know*?"

"I was scared."

He nods, but clearly doesn't accept this as any sort of decent explanation. "So you *had* the baby?"

"Yes," I say. "But then I gave her up for adoption. I thought it was for the best . . . since we were so young . . ."

"We?" he says. "*We* didn't know *you* were pregnant." His face is tight, his words cutting.

"I know," I say. "I'm sorry."

"Yeah. You mentioned that."

"Right. Sorry." I shake my head, close my eyes, open them.

"So who adopted her? Where is she?"

I hold my breath, realizing, with horror, that he *still* hasn't put it together. And then, as his gaze shifts to her, I see it happening, everything hitting him at once.

Sure enough, he whispers, "Shit. You're . . . ?"

313

"Yes," Kirby says with perfect, regal composure. "I'm her."

"My kid?" he says, staring into her eyes. *His* eyes.

"Pretty much. Yeah," she replies.

Still holding her gaze, he shakes his head as if in shock, and I say again, to both of them, how very sorry I am.

29

Kirby

W hat did you say your name was again?" Conrad asks me after Marian does the world's worst job of telling someone: *Surprise, it's a girl! Oh, and PS you're the father.* And then babbles a long-winded explanation and apology which he has yet to accept. By all indications, he has no plans to. And I can't blame him.

"Kirby," I say, thinking that I should probably add some other bit of autobiographical information. *Kirby, from St. Louis . . . Kirby, fellow musician . . . Kirby, I'm not trying to hit you up for child support.*

"Well, Kirby," he says. "I should probably say something really profound . . . but . . ." He holds his hands up, empty.

I nod, feeling suddenly desperate to please him—or at least not piss him off more than he already is. "I don't need profound," I say.

"Well, yeah. That's good. Because I got nothing."

"It's okay," I whisper.

"And I have to get to work anyway." He pulls an iPhone out of his pocket and says, "You wanna give me your number? Maybe we can talk sometime. Catch up on the last . . . how old are you, again?"

"Eighteen."

"Yeah. The last *eighteen* years." He shakes his head, then mumbles something under his breath that sounds like "this is unreal."

I swallow, then give him my number, slowly reciting the digits, watching him enter them in his phone, wondering if he will ever call.

"And what's your last name?" he says, looking at me again.

"Rose," I say, rattled.

He types in the four letters as he nods and says, "Nice name."

"Thanks."

"I hope they are, too?"

"Who?"

"The Roses? Your family?"

"Oh. Right. Yeah. They're nice. Normal. You know . . ."

"Yeah. Well, good. I'm really glad to hear that," he says, his voice angry but controlled as he shoots a pointed look at Marian. Then he stands with his tea and says, "Well, look, I gotta get going. But thanks for coming. Both of you. I appreciate it."

Marian nods, her eyes glued to the table, as he looks at me and says, "Nice to meet you, Kirby."

"You, too," I say, on the verge of tears. I know this is her fault, but I'm still hurt that he doesn't want to stay and talk to me longer. The whole thing feels like a disaster. I watch as he stands, walks away from the table, then out the door, disappearing around the corner. Gone.

I am filled with crushing disappointment but tell myself it isn't personal; he doesn't even know me. And besides, rejection is just part of the adoption territory. What did I expect? I was lucky not to have *two* doors slammed in my face.

"Well," I say as I sip green tea that tastes as bitter as I feel. "That went really well."

*

We return home to find Marian's parents in the kitchen with another gourmet spread. Apparently aware of our mission, they ask a few tentative questions, but quickly determine that the meeting was far from a rousing success.

Marian's mom looks annoyingly pleased by this, uttering some version of "I told you so" and "It's for the best" while Marian's dad seems to understand that it actually *isn't* for the best. At least not for me. As he crosses the kitchen to the icemaker, he pauses to put his hand on my shoulder, gently squeezing.

"Give him a chance to catch his breath," he says to me. "It's a lot to take in at once. He'll come around."

Marian looks as skeptical as I feel, but neither of us says what I'm thinking: No *chance* he comes around. He hates her, and by extension, me. It's not his fault, I keep telling myself. I mean, it's one thing to warm up to a kid you never met but, at the very least, knew *existed*. It's another to meet me the way he did. An emotional ambush.

Although I haven't lost sight of the fact that all of this is Marian's fault, I can't help feeling sorry for her. She's clearly suffering. Besides, I have to give her some credit for manning up and going with me. She could have written him a letter (which, with hindsight, might have been the better plan). She could have dropped me off and hidden around the corner (also probably a better idea). She could have delivered the news with arrogance or indifference. I mean, in a way, all her stammering and hemming and hawing showed me how much she cares—and that she knows she screwed up bad.

Thirty minutes of small talk later, none of which I can focus on, my phone vibrates with an incoming text. I look

317

down at my lap, hoping to see a message from Philip. Instead it is a 312 number I don't recognize. Before I can speculate, I click on the text and read: *Kirby. Was caught off guard today. I know this isn't your fault. Conrad.*

I stare down at the words, realizing Marian's dad was right—*exactly* right—and I feel awash with relief and hope as the phone buzzes again and a second text comes in. *Would like to talk more. Call or come by if you can. Zelda's on Rush. Live music, decent food. Will be here all night.*

My face must give me away because Marian stares at me and says, "What?"

"It's from him," I say. "Conrad."

"What . . . did he say?" Marian asks.

Marian's mom purses her lips and gets up from the table.

I hand Marian the phone and she reads, expressionless, then looks at me and says, "Do you want to go?"

"Go where?" Marian's mom says from the sink. "We have dinner plans tonight."

Marian gives her mother a stern look, signaling her to stay out of this one, then returns her gaze to me. "Don't worry about dinner. Do exactly what you want to do."

I nod.

"Do you want to go?" she says.

I lower my eyes and whisper, "Yes."

Because I do. More than anything.

"Okay," Marian says. "I'll take you."

I look at her, wondering what she means by this. Will she be my chauffeur or escort?

"Thanks," I say, choosing my words carefully. "But could you just . . . drop me off? I think maybe I should try it alone this time."

"Yes, of course," she says, nodding as if she understands

318

completely. But there is an unmistakable flicker of disappointment in her eyes, which she overcompensates for by saying a little too loudly and happily that this is an excellent idea. "You two should be alone. Definitely. Now that he knows about you, Conrad and I have nothing left to talk about."

"Nothing at all," her mother echoes.

At dusk, Marian drops me off at the nondescript, red-brick building on Rush Street, easy to miss but for a small, orange neon sign that says ZELDA'S—LIVE MUSIC 365 DAYS A YEAR.

"I'll be back at eleven," she says as I'm halfway out of the car. She looks skittish, and I wonder if it has more to do with the thought of Conrad on the other side of the door, or because I'm headed into a bar and she knows my parents would kill her for it. "Unless you want me to come sooner. Just call if you do."

I nod, thinking there is no chance I'll want to leave before eleven, if only because of the thrilling sound of live music pulsing its way onto the street. "Eleven is good."

"And you have money for dinner?"

"Yes," I say. "I'm good. All set."

"And you're not . . . going to drink . . . alcohol?"

"No, Marian," I say, rolling my eyes.

When she doesn't drive away, I give her a purposeful wave and turn away from her car, stepping onto the curb, crossing the crumbling sidewalk, then walking down a short flight of steps to the garden-level entrance. I pull open the heavy metal door and walk into a long narrow room, instantly falling in love with the warm, intimate atmosphere made even cozier by the low ceilings and the sheer mass of bodies crammed into the room. Stubby candles dripping with knotted wax fill the room with a flickering light, and white Christmas lights are strung behind an old, oak bar.

There is hardly a free seat anywhere, many people standing at the bar, others clustered on risers running along the side of the room, still others sitting at round tables surrounding the small stage in the back of the room. Some young guy just finished a pretty cool rendition of Stevie Ray Vaughan's "Tin Pan Alley" and now the stage is empty except for an ebony baby grand piano and a glittering white drum set. Clusters of guitar cases, amplifiers, and other equipment fill one darkened corner adjacent to the stage. The crowd is eclectic, multiracial, and multigenerational, but mostly older, bohemian, and very chill, with zero cheese factor. I have the feeling that most are regulars, here for the music rather than the pickup potential so prevalent in the few bars Belinda and I have sneaked into in St. Louis.

I scan the room, looking for Conrad, and when I don't find him, I make my way to the bar as he instructed in his final text, our meeting place. A lady bartender with a Bettie Page hairdo, muscular arms tattooed with Japanese characters, and an absurdly flat stomach exposed between a cropped tank and low-riding jeans, asks me what I'd like to drink. I consider ordering a vodka tonic or at least a beer, having the feeling she won't card me, but decide not to try my luck. Instead I ask for a Coke and hand her a five-dollar bill.

She refuses it, saying it's on the house, filling it from a tap at the bar. "You're here to see the boss, right?" she asks, handing me my Coke.

"Um, I'm here to see Conrad?" I say.

"Yeah. He's the owner."

"Oh," I say, wondering why he hadn't told Marian that he *owned* the bar.

An old black guy sitting two stools down from me signals her with a nod, and she acknowledges him with one of her own. "Ready for another?"

He nods, and she mixes a bourbon with water, sliding it toward him. Then she walks back to me and points toward the stage. "Conrad's back there somewhere. Sometimes open mic night starts out a little slow so he's gotta encourage them a bit . . . Otherwise, he knows he's gonna wind up on stage all night."

"Does he still sing?" I ask, now even more excited.

"Does he still sing?" she says with a friendly chuckle. "Hell, *yeah,* he still sings. And he still plays the bass and the guitar and the horn and the piano. You ever heard him?"

I shake my head, bursting to tell her he's my father, that we just met today, especially as I see him approaching us, fielding hellos every few steps, looking rock-and-roll cool in the same jeans he was wearing earlier, only now in a black T-shirt and a green John Deere baseball cap, the brim frayed and curved. My heart is pounding as he settles onto the bar stool beside me, looks at me, and says, "I'm glad you came." His expression is relaxed, with no trace of the tension I saw earlier.

"Thank you for inviting me," I say as a woman in a purple dress and black patent heels takes a seat at the piano and starts singing a hauntingly beautiful version of Joni Mitchell's "Both Sides Now."

Conrad watches her for a moment, nodding his approval, then raises his voice one drop, although the din is just low enough that nobody needs to yell to be heard. The same

321

girl bartender hands him a Coors Light as he thanks her and then says to me, "You met Steph?"

"Yes," I say, looking at her. "I'm Kirby."

She nods and says, "Yeah. I was telling her open mic night's hit or miss . . ."

Conrad shakes his head. "There's seldom a miss. Even our amateurs are good. And that includes our bartenders." He smiles at her.

"Hey. Who you callin' amateur? I got paid fifty bucks for my last gig."

"Oh, yeah? And where was that?"

"My niece's graduation party. So technically, I've turned pro."

Conrad barely smiles, then says, "We're all about the love of live music here. No karaoke bullshit. Just the real deal, whether it's rock, soul, funk, jazz, or the blues."

I nod and try to think of some way to show him that I know music—*good* music—and that he's not dealing with, say, a Charlotte or Belinda. "Yeah, I can see that. You go from Stevie Ray Vaughan to Joni Mitchell on open mic night? Not bad."

He raises his eyebrows, smiles, and says, "You know your stuff."

I nod.

"Do you play?"

"Yeah. I sing some—and play a little guitar. But mostly, I drum." It is more than I've ever come out and admitted to anyone, at least right out of the gate. I think of Philip and how he had to see my drums on Facebook before the subject came up. I'm making progress.

"You're a drummer?" he says, looking less surprised and more respectful than most.

"Yeah," I say, feeling like I have to pinch myself. I can't believe I'm having this conversation in a place like this with my *father*.

"That's impressive."

"Why? Because I'm a girl?" I ask, only pretending to be offended, secretly relishing his attention and obvious approval.

"Because drummers always impress me. And yeah, partly because you're a girl." He gives me a teasing look. "An itty-bitty girl. What are you? A buck five soaking wet?"

"Maybe. But I can play," I say. "I'm no light hitter."

He flashes me a huge smile. "What do you listen to?" he asks.

"A little bit of everything. Rock, folk, R & B, even rap," I say. "Everything but country. My family is big into country. They think Alan Jackson did the original 'Summertime Blues.'"

He throws his head back and laughs a deep belly laugh. Then he gives me a serious look and says, "Top five bands?"

"Wow. That's hard," I say. "Maybe Wilco, Radiohead, Van Morrison, R.E.M., and the Velvets," I say, counting them off on my fingers. "Maureen Tucker is my hero. Bar none. Though Yael comes close."

"Damn. You really *are* my daughter."

"Yeah," I say, getting goose bumps. "I am." I take a long drink of my Coke, ditching the straw on the bar, then say, "What about you? Marian told me that you used to play in a grunge band?"

He visibly bristles at the mention of her and says, "That was a long time ago. But yeah, I used to live in flannel shirts and loved that sludgy guitar sound with all the fuzz and feedback. I played all that stuff."

"Like what?" I say.

"Nirvana. Pearl Jam. Alice in Chains. Mudhoney." He looks fleetingly wistful, then shakes his head and says, "That was a long time ago. I've diversified since then."

"Diversified to what?" I say, still trying hard to be cool, still mystified over how handsome my *father* is. It is a little unsettling actually.

"A little bit of everything. Like you. From Mike & the Mechanics to Bo Diddley to the Violent Femmes. I love classic rock. The Stones, the Beatles, Bob Dylan. Hell, I even listen to country. You get a little older and you might appreciate the simplicity of those lyrics. It's authentic. No pretense. I mean—Waylon Jennings? Hank Williams? You gotta like those guys."

I think of Philip's T-shirt and say, "Yeah. But they're not really country."

"The hell!" He laughs. "How do you figure?"

"They're from the Golden Age."

"The Golden Age, huh?" he says. "How old are you again?"

"Eighteen," I say, and his face changes again, as I wonder whether he's thinking about her. *Eighteen years ago.* That's when I blurt out, "So how pissed are you at her?"

I expect him to look surprised, or play it off, but instead he shakes his head, the answer clear even before he replies, "Pretty damn pissed."

I nod, looking down at my cardboard coaster.

"Let's be clear here, though. I'm pissed at *her*. Not you," he says, which might seem like it should be a given by now, but still fills me with joy to hear him confirm it. "What she did was really . . ." He starts to say "fucked up," but changes it to "messed up."

"I know it was," I say, looking into his eyes. "She knows it, too."

"Yeah. Well." He shrugs then cracks his knuckles.

"She was scared," I say. "Too scared to keep me."

"She didn't have to keep you to tell me."

"I don't think she wanted *you* to keep me, either."

"That's pretty obvious."

"Yeah," I say.

"But you know," he says, "that really wasn't up to her."

I say, "If you kept me, everyone would have known. She didn't want that."

"Again," he says, folding a napkin in half, then quarters. "That wasn't up to her. Even if she ultimately made the right decision for you—and it sounds like she did—she still had no right not to tell me about my own kid."

"I know."

We are both quiet for a second until he finally speaks.

"Well. She got her ivory-tower life. So that's all good. For her."

I know what he's getting at—that neither of us was part of her grand plan for her grand life on Fifth Avenue. And although I know I should resent her, too, I can't help feeling sorry for her, especially because I think she would change things if she could.

"Her life's not perfect," I say, a sudden revelation to me. "I don't even know if she's that happy. With all her success and money. I mean . . . she has this ridiculous apartment in New York—and a rich boyfriend who is probably going to propose any day now, and owns, like, the whole network . . ."

Conrad holds up his hand and says, "Yeah. It's cool. But I don't really need to know the details."

"Right," I say. "Sorry."

"It's cool," he says again. "Look. It's no big deal . . . It's just . . . Marian and I are different. Very different. We always were."

"Are you married?" I ask.

He shakes his head. "Nah . . . But I was. For about three years."

"Did you have kids?" I ask, nervously awaiting his answer, although I'm not sure what I want it to be. It would be pretty neat to have a half sibling with him as our father—and I have the feeling that any kid of his would be okay with me, and probably a whole lot more like me than Charlotte. Then again, it'd be pretty awesome to have him all to myself, too.

"No kids," he says. "She didn't want them."

"But you did?"

"Very much so." He smiles at me, and I feel a chill run up my spine, thrilled to hear him say this, so much more unequivocally than Marian ever has.

"Is that why you split up with her?" I ask, thinking it'd be ironic if having a baby factored into his one breakup and not having one factored into the other.

He laughs, exchanging a look with the bartender who seems to be eavesdropping on our conversation, or at least keeping very diligent tabs on our drinks. "Not exactly."

"Sorry," I say. "I know that's really none of my business."

"No. That's okay," he says. "But you might as well ask her." He points at Stephanie and says, "She's the ex. Hell of a bartender. Shitty wife."

Stephanie throws a lime wedge at him that he bats back over the bar. "Hey! Check yourself. I wasn't *that* bad."

"Yeah. If you hadn't been pretending to be straight, you would have been the perfect wife."

They both laugh, clearly no hard feelings between them. "I'm *bi*. Get *that* straight. And you weren't exactly easy to live with, babe . . ." Stephanie laughs some more, then migrates to the other end of the bar to make a margarita. As I watch her grinding the top of the glass into a dish of salt, I say, "Does she know who I am?"

Conrad shakes his head. "Nope. I haven't told anyone yet." He looks at me, starts to say something, then thinks better of it.

"What?" I say.

He glances back over his shoulder toward the stage and says, "I was just going to tell you that she *does* know who your mother is."

"How?" I ask, wondering if she went to school with them.

"Because," he says, shrugging.

I don't let him off the hook, but keep staring at him until he says, "Because Marian was the love of my life. For a long time. And that's the kind of information you share when you're young and stupid and hoping that you're in something that is going to be even bigger and better than what you once lost. It's the kind of shit you waste your time thinking about. Lemme tell you—it does no good. Remember that, okay? Things are what they are and there's no point dwelling in the past or wondering what could have been."

I stare at him, and he stares right back at me. "I know, I know. The love of my life doesn't even tell me when she has my kid. Isn't that some pathetic shit?" He shakes his head with a little laugh.

"It's not pathetic," I say.

"Yeah. Well, it has to say something—"

"I don't think it says *anything* about you. Or me," I say, the truth crystallizing in my head. "I think it says something about *her*. The person she once was."

"And still is," he says. "People don't change."

I tell him I'm not so sure about that, realizing how foolish I probably sound imparting wisdom to someone twice my age. My own *father*.

Sure enough, he gives me a skeptical look. "Oh, really?"

"Okay. You might be right," I say. "But at least she *tried* to fix it. She's the one who found you, ya know? And she showed up today."

"Sort of eighteen years too late, don't you think?"

"I guess so," I say. "But at least we're here now."

He smiles, takes a long swallow of beer, and says, "Yeah. That's a good point, drummer girl. A good way to look at life. Try to keep that up if you can."

I smile, thinking that it doesn't sound like me; it sounds like my parents. Like Charlotte. *Look on the bright side. Be grateful for what you have. Count your blessings. Optimism is the foundation of courage.* I feel a sudden wave of homesickness, but not the kind that makes you sad. The kind that reminds you of who you are and where you come from.

"So what are your parents like?" I ask him, sure that they are nothing like Marian's folks.

"My dad is a bit of a nomad. Pie-in-the-sky drifter. He's been married three times and has never really held a steady job because, you know, all of his bosses are idiots. So don't count on him for shit . . . But he's likable. Never had an enemy."

"What about your mom?" I say.

Conrad looks at me, his eyes changing suddenly. "My mom died in a car accident when I was eleven."

328

My heart sinks. "Oh . . . I'm sorry," I say, wondering why Marian hadn't told me such an important fact about him.

"Yeah. It sucked. She was an awesome mother . . . And I'm not just saying that because she died. She really *was* special. She had this way of making everything fun—even when we were dirt poor. And man, could she sing. Gorgeous mezzo-soprano."

I feel myself grinning as he says, "Is that what you are?" I nod.

"That's really cool," he says, smiling back at me. "So what do you think? You wanna play tonight? Sing a little?"

"On stage?" I say.

He laughs and says, "Yeah. On stage. Drum kit right up there."

I shake my head and tell him I don't think so.

"Why not?"

I shrug.

"You ever played live? In front of an audience?"

I shake my head.

"Well, then, it's about time, don't you think?"

I shake my head again, this time smiling.

"C'mon. We can do it together," he says, sliding off the stool and leading me to the back of the room toward the stage. "You pick the song. I'm cool with anything."

"Anything?" I say, the music getting louder as we approach the main speakers.

"Just about," he says.

We sit at a small table just to the left of the stage, marked with a little folded reserved sign, as he orders us burgers and fries and another Coke for me. Meanwhile, a steady stream of people come up to him, say hello, ask when he's going to sing, some even making requests.

"We're debating that now," he says, pointing to me, introducing me as "Kirby, a drummer and my partner tonight."

Two hours pass quickly, with lots of good conversation and music. The crowd isn't at all judgmental, seeming to appreciate every effort, but that doesn't lessen the terror I feel that Conrad might actually make me get up on stage. Every few minutes he suggests a song, which I dismiss for one reason or another—the meaning, the lack of a distinct drum break, the fact that I simply don't like it. Mostly I'm stalling, though, vetoing some of my favorites that I know I can sing and play such as Creedence Clearwater Revival's "Have You Ever Seen the Rain?" and Neil Young's "Good to See You."

Around quarter to eleven, when he says, "C'mon, Kirby, what do you got to lose?" I finally bite the bullet and agree to Pearl Jam's "Small Town," his suggestion.

"You mean 'Elderly Woman Behind the Counter in a Small Town'?" I say, recalling Eddie Vedder saying in an interview that the unabridged title was a reaction to the band's mostly one-word song titles.

"That's the one," he says. "You know it?"

I nod, going over the lyrics in my head.

He crosses his arms, shakes his head, and says he hasn't played it since the summer of 1995.

"Then it sounds appropriate, huh?" I say.

"Well, I guess so," he says, grinning, bending down the brim of his cap in such a way that it hides his eyes. "Let's do it."

My heart pounding, we make our way on stage, as I take my seat on a stool behind a DW drum set in a titanium sparkle finish, a real beauty. I feel my way around it, working the pedals, gripping the sticks, even testing them out. I decide I will skip the cymbals, the way the great Moe always did.

I watch Conrad take the mic, the crowd treating him like a huge star, everyone sitting up straighter, smiling more broadly, clapping or whistling in anticipation. He is not only the owner, but clearly a crowd favorite.

"Good evening, everyone," he begins, his voice even deeper over the speakers. He spins his cap around, the brim now in the back.

A few dozen people bellow out his name; others wish him a "good evening" back.

"Tonight I'd like to introduce you to the great Kirby Rose. A talented drummer visiting us from St. Louis. I haven't known her for very long," he says, turning back to look in my eyes. "But she's a solid girl. I really like her. And I know you will, too. So let's give her a warm, Zelda-style welcome."

The crowd begins to wildly applaud as I feel like I might faint, sweat pouring out of every pore, the bright lights burning my eyes. Gripped with fear, I watch Conrad walk to the edge of the stage, remove his guitar from a case covered with bumper stickers, then throw the strap over his head, strumming a few chords. Just as I'm about to pass out, he turns, walks a few paces over to me, and says, "Just relax. Take a few deep breaths. And follow my lead. You can do this, kid."

I nod, hearing the rhythm of the song in my head, the way I always do right before I begin to play.

And then the bar falls silent, everyone watching, waiting, as Conrad begins to strum his guitar, then sing the words, his tenor smooth and rich, reminding me of Eddie but with his own distinct, scratchy sound.

331

I have chills, despite the heat of the stage, as the beat of the song comes to me, as naturally as all the notes do for him. At one point, he walks over and tells me to sing. I shake my head. And he says, "C'mon, Kirby. I wanna hear you. Sing, girl."

So I do, finding an impromptu harmony, singing tentatively at first, then as strong as I'm drumming.

That's when I look up and see her, standing in the back of the room, next to the bar, watching us.

"She's here," I tell him, the next time he comes near me.

He reads my lips, gives me a slight nod. Maybe he's already spotted her, but I can hear him, see him, *feel* him suddenly playing with even more passion. He closes his eyes, strumming as I drum, both of us singing together.

30

Marian

I knew Kirby could play the drums from her little rap in the writers' room. But I am still moved and mesmerized when I walk into the bar and see her playing real drums, under lights on a stage, before a live audience, with her *father*. It is overwhelming and surreal, and I am filled with pride and pain.

And yet, here they are, found, together, singing the song I remember so well him playing. It was one of my favorites in his repertoire—one that I always requested as we whiled away the hours on the futon in his bedroom. One that he played in the woods that day when we took our only photograph. His voice is even better now, more mature, although I never saw him in this element, in a real performance. His guitar playing is polished and confident, and *God,* so sexy that I can hardly stand it. I am watching the boy I fell in love with, feeling like the girl I once was, the memories rushing back so hard and fast that it hurts my head and heart.

After the last beautiful chord, there is a standing ovation, wild cheering, and whistling. People call out his name; some know hers. A man in a black felt fedora cups his hands around his mouth and shouts for an encore—at which point Conrad turns and consults with her. His back is to me, but I can see her nodding, smiling, then leaning in to whisper something back to him. They are a team tonight, their first together.

Conrad paces back to the front of the stage, lowers his head, and coolly mutters into the microphone, "Yo. Did I mention she's my daughter?"

With this announcement, the applause escalates, as do the calls for an encore. But Kirby stands up, takes a quick bow, and then deadpans into the microphone that she has a curfew but thank you very much. People laugh. They like her. They *love* her. *I* love her.

She sees me and gives me a quick wave and a generous smile, then whispers something to Conrad as they step off the stage and work their way over to me, amid backslaps and praise. As they get closer, I can see they are both sweaty and breathless. Then they are right beside me. Conrad's smile from on stage has faded, but so has his animosity from earlier today.

"Wow," I say. "You guys were incredible."

"Thanks," Kirby says, her cheeks bright pink, her eyes sparkling. There is pure joy on her face that makes me want to cover it with kisses.

I want to kiss Conrad, too—the urge is overwhelming, *scary*—and against my better judgment, I look into his eyes and say, "That brought back memories."

He nods, accepting this statement without exactly agreeing, as he drapes his arm over Kirby's shoulder. "She's a natural," he says, deflecting the remark.

"It's clear where she gets it," I say.

"Yeah," he says, then turns away from me, converting the conversation into a private moment with Kirby. "Thanks for coming out," I overhear. "I had a blast."

"Me, too," she says, flushed with pride and adrenaline and obvious affection for him.

"Come back soon," he says, wiping sweat off his brow with the back of his hand.

"Maybe this summer?" she says. "After I graduate?"

"Anytime," he says. "Absolutely anytime."

I think back to the end of our visit when she first came to New York, how different that sentiment sounded from my lips. How different our first night together was on those stools in my kitchen—careful and restrained. How different he is from me. He is real and raw—the two things I loved about him. The two things I've never really been able to be, at least not in my real life, only in the worlds I create on paper. At least not since that summer.

Kirby steps away, exchanging a few words with the bartender, the two appearing to be friends, as Conrad looks at me. *Really* looks at me.

"I hate what you did," he says. "But I'm trying not to hate *you*."

"Thank you," I say, overcome with a fresh wave of emotion.

"Thank you for coming back," he says, then reaches up to lower his cap, hiding his eyes. "Well, I better get back to work."

"Right. Sure," I say.

"See ya, Marian," he says, then turns once again, to have a final private moment with Kirby, giving her a sweaty hug good-bye.

In the car ride home, she is quiet, as if digesting everything that happened, *basking* in it, a small smile of triumph on her face. I want to respect her privacy, the emotional integrity of her experience, yet I'm dying to know what she and Conrad talked about, and what he may have told her about his life. Finally, I can't stand it another second and come right out and ask whether he's married.

She shakes her head.

"Kids?" I ask hesitantly.

"Only me," she says, staring out the side window as we drive away from the city back north to the suburbs.

"Well, it's good to see he's still playing music," I say, searching for an opening—anything to get her to talk about the night, Conrad, her feelings.

"Yeah. But he's also a businessman," she says. "Zelda's is his bar. His creation."

"Oh?" I say, surprised, pleased. "That's great."

"Yeah. It started out as a jazz club, like, fifteen years ago—and he brought in all these great musicians from the city, friends and other people he knew. And then word of mouth just spread and now the bar is like a legend in Chicago—and musicians come from all over the country to play all types of music." It is the most excited she has ever sounded about anything.

"Well, I'm not surprised," I say, even though a small part of me is *very* surprised, and I think she sees right through it, the way she always seems to cut through any bullshit.

"He never went to college," she says. "But look at him. He's *really* happy in that bar. He called it his home. His family. His ex-wife even works there—and they're still friends."

I file this fact, wondering what their relationship was like and why they broke up, then say, "You two were amazing together."

"Thanks," she says. "It was really fun."

We fall silent as we approach Glencoe, then drive onto Maple Hill. The houses are mostly dark, except for an occasional porch light. When we pull into our driveway, she turns to me and says, "You broke his heart, you know."

I freeze, then turn to look at her, her face in a shadow. "He told you that?"

"Not in so many words—but yeah. He really loved you."

I can tell she is on his side, and I don't blame her. *I'm* on his side.

"And I think . . ." she says, her voice trailing off.

"What?" I say, turning off the ignition and facing her.

"Never mind," she says, shaking her head.

"You can tell me," I say, bracing myself for something hurtful he said, something truthful that I know I will deserve.

But instead she says, "I don't know. I kinda get the feeling he still does."

Before I can reply, she is out of the car, slamming her door, walking toward the front walk. I get out and follow her, wishing I could go back in time. Wishing I had been a little more like her when I was eighteen.

The next morning, Kirby knocks on my bedroom door just before nine. She is dressed, with her suitcase at her feet, and says she has to get going, she has finals to study for. I quickly rally and throw on sweats, and a few minutes later, we are standing in the foyer, my parents coming in from the kitchen to meet us.

"Are you sure you can't stay for breakfast?" my mother says.

"I really have to get back to study for exams," Kirby says. "If I want to pass precalc and graduate."

My father nods and says, "We certainly understand that."

"Well," Kirby says, her voice sounding bolder than it did when she arrived, as if she grew up on stage last night. "Thanks so much for having me. It was really nice getting to know you guys."

337

"Oh, you, too, Kirby," my dad says, stepping forward to give her a big hug and kiss on the cheek. "It's nice to finally meet our granddaughter. We know you have a family who loves you very much, but we hope we can add to that. We really hope this is just the beginning." He looks at my mother and she nods her unconvincing agreement, nervously twisting her pearl necklace.

Kirby smiles, then shocks me by saying, "Thanks, Grandpa."

He grins, the happiest I've seen him look in a long time.

After a few seconds of awkward silence, in which it becomes clear my mother is not going to hug her good-bye, I announce that I'm going to walk her out. My parents nod, getting the message that I want to be alone with her, as I grab her suitcase and head outside. By the time we get to her car, she has become quiet and serious again, but I tell myself it has more to do with the nature of good-byes, especially in fragile, new relationships. It will take time to establish trust and a real bond, whether a friendship or something more maternal, and I am willing to work for it.

"So, I'm graduating in a couple of weeks," she says.

"Yes?" I say, hopeful.

"My parents wanted me to invite you. So. You're invited . . . But I know how busy you are with your show and everything so it's cool if you can't—"

"I will be there," I say. "Definitely."

She nods and says, "Cool. I'll text you the details. Or call or whatever."

"That would be great," I say.

"Well. Thank you," she says, even though we both know that the invite is her gift to me—and not the other way around.

*

338

Back inside, my mother refreshes her cup of coffee and then pours one for my father and me. She then begins to crack eggs in a bowl, preparing to make omelets. I remind her that I have an early flight and not much time before I have to go pack.

"Final exams and television scripts," my dad says, still looking reflective. "It never stops."

"Or big trials," I say, smiling.

"So how did it go last night?" my mother asks, her voice breezy. As if Kirby merely went to the movies.

I look at her, wondering why she can't acknowledge the full weight of what's happening—or accept the idea of Kirby in our lives. Maybe she feels guilt over the decision she helped me make and wants to justify to herself that it was the right one. Maybe she stills sees a stigma in what happened and is worried about what people will think. Maybe she simply fears Conrad, worries that he will derail me once again.

"Conrad and Kirby really hit it off," I say, telling them briefly about the scene when I walked into the bar, but unable to do it—or them—justice. "It was emotional . . . very touching. I'm happy for them."

My dad puts down his mug and holds my gaze. "That is really something," he says.

"I should have told him so much sooner," I say.

My mother shakes her head, steadfastly refusing to see it this way.

I ignore her and turn to my dad. "It seems pretty clear that he'll never forgive me for what I did to him."

"You can't go back," he says. "Just look forward. You're doing the right thing *now*."

"I'm trying," I say.

"That's all you can do," my dad says, hugging me just like he hugged Kirby in the foyer.

I sleep on the whole flight home, but am still groggy when I walk into my apartment, late in the afternoon. My housekeeper came on Friday, and the place is even more pristine than usual, everything in its place. I open the refrigerator, but as usual, there is nothing to eat—not that I'm hungry anyway. I wander over to my desk and glance at a stack of scripts that I meant to pack and read on the plane, but feel completely uninspired to deal with now. I contemplate a run in the park, but am not in the mood for that, either. I turn on my stereo, but music—*any* music—reminds me of Conrad and that look on his face when he realized who she was. I will never get over that look. So I finally pick up the phone and call Peter, ask him to come over. He says yes, of course, he will be there as soon as he can, his voice comforting.

He arrives around five, straight from the office. He says he's been there all weekend, putting out fires. I wonder if one of them has anything to do with my show, but don't ask. At the moment, I'm too drained to really care. We sit on my sofa and I tell him about the weekend—the conversation with my father in the park, Conrad's hostility, his touching performance with Kirby. I tell him everything except for the way I'm feeling now—because I don't even know how to describe it to myself.

"That's great progress," he says when I'm finished. He has that satisfied look he gets in meetings after he's found a solution to a problem, and I realize he deserves a lot of the credit for what happened this weekend. For making me see that I had to confront the past and tell the truth. That as

340

much as I owed that to Kirby and Conrad and my father, I also owed it to myself. "Are you glad you went?"

"Yeah," I say. "It was tough . . . But yeah."

"Anything worthwhile is tough," he says, taking my hand and squeezing it.

"Yeah. Well, you were right."

Peter shakes his head as if to say it's not about being right. "I'm sorry I was so hard on you. I just had a difficult time accepting . . . all the secrets."

"I know," I say. "I understand."

"But we can move on," he says. "Right?"

I nod, every part of me trying to do just that.

"I've missed you, Champ," he says.

I tell him I've missed him, too, and after we look at each other, *really* look at each other, he pulls me over to him and kisses me. I murmur apologies, and he whispers back his understanding and forgiveness.

"I want you," he says, his hands running over, then under, my blouse.

"Let's go," I say, leading him back to my bedroom where we silently undress, each of us helping the other with buttons and snaps and belts. Our eyes stay locked the whole time, a silent conversation taking place, until we are both naked, kissing again. He tells me I'm beautiful, running his hands along my hips and back before lowering me to the bed. He is smooth and sure in each movement, every word. I think of all that has happened since we were last together like this, a few nights before Kirby knocked on my door. It feels like a lifetime ago.

"Are you ready?" he says.

I tell him yes. I tell him how much I want him and need him and love him.

His body still covering mine, he pushes up on his hands, one on either side of my face, and shakes his head, as if to tell me I misunderstood. "That's not what I meant by 'ready,' Champ . . . Are you ready to take the next step? Together?"

I stare at him, in disbelief. This was the last thing I expected. The last thing I've been thinking about over the past few days and weeks.

"What do you mean?" I say, just to be sure.

He collapses his full weight back on me, kissing me again. "I'm ready, Champ," he whispers in my ear. "I'm ready to get you the ring of your dreams. Get married. Have a baby. All of the above. In any order you want."

I feel myself trembling as I imagine a small ceremony with our families. Aidan and Kirby at our sides. The life I've always wanted. We kiss in a way we haven't kissed in a long time, and certainly not since she found me. Then we slowly make love, his breath in my ear, his arms wrapped tightly around me. We last a long, long time, until we can't take it another second and both release, together. I can feel him explode inside me, softly moaning my name, telling me he's going to make me his wife. I tell myself I'm the luckiest woman in the world. I tell him I couldn't be happier. And as I fall asleep with my head on his chest, I almost, very nearly, believe it.

31

Kirby

My parents, sister, and Noah are just finishing lunch when I walk into the house after my five-hour drive. They all light up when they see me, even my mother. I force myself to sit and join them, despite my strong urge to be alone.

"Well?" Charlotte says, as my mother stands to fix me a plate. "How was it?"

"It was awesome," I say, wishing there was some way to describe just *how* awesome. "How was prom?"

She and Noah look at each other and grin as she says it was the *best* time ever. She then informs me that Mr. Tully had to kick five people out for dirty dancing—and eight others for drinking.

"Did you see Belinda?" I can't help asking.

"Just for a minute right when we got there," she says. "Her dress looked *sick*. So good. She ended up getting that turquoise one she tried on."

I nod, pretending to be surprised, feeling not only disappointed that she didn't change her mind about wearing it but strangely sorry for her, too. It can't have made her feel good—no matter how good she looked.

Charlotte pushes away her plate of half-eaten tuna salad and says, "So? Did you meet him? Your birth dad?"

"Yeah," I say, as my mother hands me a plate of tuna salad and a bowl of tomato soup.

"What's he like?" she asks, everyone staring at me in anticipation.

"He's still a musician. He owns this bar called Zelda's and it has live music three hundred sixty-five days a year." I avoid eye contact with my parents as I stand and grab a can of Coke from the fridge, then sit again, cracking it open and taking a long drink.

"You went to a bar?" my mother says. She just can't help herself.

"Yeah," I say. "But I didn't drink. It's no different than half the restaurants in St. Louis. Anything on the Hill," I say, referring to the Italian restaurant district where my dad always grabs a mixed drink at the bar before he joins us. "It was all kosher, Mom. Trust me."

She nods and says she *does* trust me. Completely.

Seeming eager to get off the subject of Conrad, my father says, "What about Marian's parents? Were they nice?"

"Yeah," I say. "I liked her dad more than her mom. Her mom was kind of a snob. But nice enough."

My mother looks intrigued with this, perhaps relieved that I still have my snob radar working. "What do they do for a living?"

"She doesn't work. He's a lawyer for, like, Oprah. They're rich."

My parents nod, as if they assumed this already.

"What's he look like?" Charlotte says. "Your dad."

"My dad's right there," I say, pointing to my father who grins back at me.

Charlotte goes, "Right! You know what I mean—your *birth* dad."

"I can't lie—he's good-lookin'. He looks like a . . . rocker," I say, laughing. I glance at my mom, who looks all worried again. "Not a long-haired, druggy, eighties rocker, Mom.

344

Just, you know, an artist. He's really cool. Really, really nice." I start to tell them how we sang together on stage but decide I want to keep that to myself for a while. Besides, I don't want to upset my dad. I know how I feel about him having more in common with Charlotte; there's no point in making him feel the same way. Then, just to throw my mother a bone, I say, "Oh—and Mrs. Caldwell really liked the napkins."

"She did?" my mother says, perking up.

"Yeah. She thought they were really pretty. And she appreciated the pie, too."

"Did you eat it?" she asks.

"No," I say. "But probably just because she wanted to save it. They're not allergic to nuts or anything."

My mother beams as Charlotte and Noah stand to go, announcing that they're headed to a pool party. "You wanna come?" Charlotte asks me, clearly a gratuitous invite, her hundredth of the year, but still nice.

I tell her no, thanks, I'm pretty beat after the drive, and have a lot of studying to do. Then, as I watch the two leave hand in hand, I think of Philip, excited to call him, see him, kiss him again.

I tell my parents I'm going to go unpack, but they stop me, say they have something else to talk to me about.

I brace myself, expecting one last lecture about college, but instead they say it's about Belinda.

"What about her?" I say. My mind races, trying to determine what they know and if I'm going to be somehow implicated.

"We know about the dress she stole from Robin's," my dad says. Then, before I can debate whether to play dumb, he says, "You knew about it, right?"

345

I stare at him, thinking this is typical and so *unbelievable* that I'm about to get in trouble, but I know it will be worse if I lie, so I say, "Yeah, I knew about it. How do *you* know about it?"

"The manager of the store called me," my mother says. "On Sunday morning. She remembered that Belinda had tried on that dress and suspected her when she realized it was missing from their inventory late last week. She was waiting to see if she wore it to prom."

"Why'd she call you?" I say.

"She thought Belinda was my daughter."

"What did you tell her?"

"I said she actually wasn't my daughter, but a close family friend. And that I would find out and get back to her."

"And?"

"I asked Charlotte what dress Belinda wore. I didn't tell her why I wanted to know. But she confirmed that yes, she wore that dress."

"Is she going to get arrested?" I ask, panicked.

My mother looks at my dad, who says, "No. The manager *was* going to call the police. Until your mother and I paid for it."

"You did *what*?" I ask, floored. It is pretty much the last thing I could ever picture my parents doing. Covering for a criminal.

"They were going to press charges," he says. "I told her I'd pay for it and handle the matter. Then I called Belinda."

"And what happened?"

He says, "We asked her to come over and we sat down and just . . . talked to her."

"Belinda is very confused right now," my mother says. "It's been hard for her since her dad left. And they're having

346

a lot of money problems. Not that that excuses what she did. But we don't want her future ruined. We think she's a good kid, deep down, but she's just a little lost right now."

"What did she say?" I ask.

"She was really upset. And not just because she was caught. She seemed genuinely sorry. She promised to pay us back and begged us not to tell her mother."

"Are you going to?"

"We have to," my father says. "We'd want to know if you did something like this."

"I wouldn't," I say.

"We know. She told us about your fight. And that's why you didn't go to prom."

I nod, waiting for them to tell me I should have come to them. I should have done something more. Instead my mother says, "That must have been a really tough spot for you, Kirby."

My father nods and says, "Yes. And most kids wouldn't have been strong enough to take a stand like that."

I look down, embarrassed, although I'm not sure why. I guess it's because I'm not used to this sort of attention. It's been a long time since they said they were proud of me. "I wanted to go to Chicago, too," I mumble, my head bowed, wondering why I'm trying to give back some of the credit.

"Why don't you call Belinda?" my dad says. "She's waiting for you."

A few minutes later, I arrive at Belinda's front door, knocking this time. She answers right away and leads me upstairs to her room. We sit on her bed, in silence. Her skin looks terrible, like she's either been crying or binge drinking or both. I look away, over at her wall, which is covered with writing—mostly lyrics of dumb pop songs such as, *Where would we be if we couldn't dream?* A decent enough quote if she hadn't lifted it from a Jonas Brothers' song.

"My parents told me what happened," I say, the words barely out of my mouth before she starts crying. I lean over and hug her.

"I'm sorry," she says. "I was such a bitch to you . . ."

"Yeah, ya were," I say, pulling back and smiling at her.

"I'm sorry," she says again. "I don't know what's wrong with me . . . I'm just so depressed all the time . . . and sick of being poor and never having anything cute to wear."

"I know, Bel," I say.

She shakes her head and says, "It's different for you. You don't have a deadbeat dad—you have *two* dads and *two* moms and one's really rich. And Charlotte told me you were going to meet your birth dad . . . Was he a total rock star?"

I shrug, trying to downplay it, but say, "He was really cool. . . . But we can talk about that later . . ."

She blows her nose and says, "I guess I've been a little jealous, too. About all the exciting stuff happening for you. And even Philip. He *really* likes you."

"Jake likes *you*," I say.

"No he doesn't. He's just like all the rest. He just wants sex—that's it . . ."

"They all want sex," I say, smiling, even though I know Belinda is right—it *is* way different with me and Philip.

"And your parents. God. I know you think your parents suck, Kirb, but they are so awesome," she says.

I scoff. "Okay. I'm gonna have to beg to differ with you there."

348

"No. Seriously. I woulda been dragged off in handcuffs if it weren't for your dad. God. I owe him. More than the four hundred dollars, I *really* owe him. You are *soo* lucky to have them as parents. I've always wished they were mine . . ."

I look at her, surprised that she feels this way. In all the years of listening to me rag on them, she never once said anything like this.

"They're strict, but at least they care," she says, tearing up again.

"Your mom cares, too," I say.

"I know, but it's not the same. She's never around . . . Not that it's her fault—she has to work . . . But I don't know. It just sucks, Kirb . . . I mean, I know it's my fault—and that there's no excuse for what I did. But I'm just . . . so sick of . . . *everything.*"

I hug her again, wondering how I didn't know that my best friend in the world felt this bad. It occurs to me that maybe everyone does. Except for Charlotte, that is. And God, maybe *even* Charlotte.

"Do you forgive me, Kirb? For how I treated you?"

"Yes. Of course I do. You're my best friend. You always will be."

Then I look into her eyes and tell her that everything is going to be all right. Really all right. Like with our lives and our future and everything. I say it again, and for the first time in a long time, I actually believe it.

On Monday morning, I find Mr. Tully in his office and ask for a guidance pass to get out of PE. "Unless you think I need badminton skills in life?"

He smiles, points to my usual chair, and says, "How's studying for precalc coming along?"

349

"Perfectly shitty," I say. "Or is it 'shittily'?"

He ignores my language, and my grammar question, and says, "I see you need a seventy-two to graduate. Think you can pull it off?"

"Yeah," I say, waving the question off. "It's in the bag."

"Well," he says. "That's a refreshing bit of confidence!"

"I'm a changed girl."

"Oh? Does this have anything to do with your trip to Chicago? Or your new boyfriend?"

I look at him, surprised and a little embarrassed. "How do you know about Philip?"

"Facebook espionage," he says, as I think of the increasingly sweet messages that we've been exchanging on our walls.

I smile. "Yeah. Philip's good, but this is all about my birth dad."

"Do tell," Mr. Tully says, cracking his knuckles and leaning toward me.

I start to grin, then divulge the whole story, how much we hit it off, how thrilled I am to be related to someone so talented, even sharing the emotions I felt onstage.

Mr. Tully seems to hang on every word, even more than he usually does, and tells me he wishes he had been there to see it. "One day," he says. "When you're the next American Idol."

I roll my eyes.

"And I can say I knew you back when . . ."

I smile. "Yeah. Maybe I'll even get you backstage passes."

He laughs and says, "You better not big-time me!"

I laugh and promise him I won't. We chat for a few more minutes until he says, "So? You know we have something else to cover, don't you? One final housekeeping matter . . ."

350

I give him a look. "Please tell me this isn't about Mizzou."

"Kirby."

"Ugh! C'mon, Mr. T!"

He ignores my groan, continuing, "Kirby, I really think you should go. Give it *one* semester. You can always quit or transfer . . ."

"Did my parents put you up to this?" I say. "The deadline passed, you know."

"And you know they paid your deposit?" he says.

I didn't *know* for sure, but sort of assumed they had when they stopped mentioning it shortly after the deadline.

"Look, Kirby. This is my honest, bottom-of-my-heart opinion. I think you should go to college. It doesn't mean you can't pursue music, even as a profession. But college is an experience—and at least something you should try. Get a solid education and you can still have your plan B."

"Why can't college be my plan B?" I say. "And music my plan A?"

"The two aren't mutually exclusive. Look at R.E.M. and Radiohead."

I roll my eyes again.

"You could get into the School of Music at Missouri, Kirb." He turns and plucks a printout from his desk, my name written at the top. He hands it to me and I scan it: *Instrumentalists should prepare one or two pieces. Material demonstrating tone quality and technical proficiency is appropriate. Percussionists should be prepared to play at least two of the following: a solo/etude on keyboard percussion (marimba/xylo/vibes), snare drum, timpani, styles on drum set (swing, rock, funk, Latin, etc.).*

I stop reading and look up at him.

"You could do this, Kirb."

"You've never even heard me play," I say.

"I *know* you're good," he says. "I just know it."

I don't answer.

"Think of what you could learn with real professors."

"Think of all the other crap I'd have to learn."

"Knowledge isn't crap."

I cross my arms, pretending to be more annoyed than I actually am.

"Just give it some thought?"

I tell him that I already have.

"Just a *little* more thought?" he says. "Please? For me?"

I sigh my weariest sigh and say, "Fine. A tiny bit more."

It seems the least I can do for the only person who has consistently believed in me, from the very beginning.

That evening after dinner, Conrad texts me. *Hey drummer girl. What's goin on?*

Grinning, I type back: *Not much. Just studying for exams. You?*

He writes back immediately: *Listening to a little Sly and the Family Stone . . . There's a Riot Going On is a sweet album if you don't know it. Think you'd love it.*

I know a few songs of theirs, like "I Want to Take You Higher," but am not really familiar with that album, so I instantly download it from iTunes and after listening to a few songs, text him back with my report: *Amazing. Love "Poet" and "Family Affair." Thanks for the tip.*

A second later, the phone rings. It's him. I grab it, excited.

"Hey," he says. "Good stuff, huh?"

"It's great," I say.

"Thought you'd appreciate it."

"Most definitely."

352

"So . . . how is the studying coming?"

I tell him I'm just trying to pass precalc so I can graduate. He says he was in the same boat, with the same class.

"And?"

"I passed," he says. "Barely. I didn't go to college, but at least I wasn't a high school dropout."

I inhale, then ask him the million-dollar question. "Do you wish you had gone?"

"Nope," he says. "That's probably the wrong answer. But it's the truth. . . . Although I got lucky."

"I'm just trying to figure out what to do with my life. Or at least my next few years," I say.

"Are you asking for advice?"

"Not really. I got plenty of that already."

"Yeah. I figured . . . I'm sure Marian gave you an earful."

"Yep. She thinks I should go. But she didn't get all preachy," I say, wondering if he's just trying to find an excuse to bring her up like she's always doing with him.

Sure enough, he says, "So did you enjoy the rest of your time together?"

"I left the next morning. But yeah, it was good. We had a nice time . . . She's coming to my graduation so I'm gonna see her soon."

"Oh," he says. "That's great. Good for you. Good for both of you."

"Yeah," I say. "I know you have to run Zelda's and . . . it might be weird to be with her . . ." I hold my breath then say, "But you're invited, too . . ."

"Thank you, Kirby. That's really nice of you . . ."

"It would probably be too weird, though, right?" I press, giving him an out.

"Yeah. It probably would be pretty awkward . . . but

lemme know when it is . . . Steph can always hold down the fort. Maybe I could pop in and out . . ."

"Sure," I say as casually as I can, trying to control my excitement, telling myself that it probably won't work out, but at least he's thinking about it. "That'd be really cool. But whatever. It's no big deal either way."

"Right," he says. "I gotcha."

"Well, I better go study," I say.

"Okay," Conrad says. "Just remember—the second derivative measures acceleration. Think: fast cars."

I laugh. "Yep. The second derivative measures how the rate of change of a quantity is itself changing. So yeah, acceleration. How do you remember that, anyway?"

"I remember a whole *lot* of useless shit," he says.

"So it *is* useless?" I say.

"One hundred percent."

"I knew it," I say, grinning.

32

Marian

When I get to work on Monday, Alexandre finds me in my office and hands me a fresh script that Jeanelle wrote and he polished. "Enjoy the *Gilmore Girls* meets *Cheers*," he says.

I sigh and say, "Seriously? Will I hate it?"

"You won't love it. I addressed all the network notes. And then sprinkled in a few 'golly gee, Beavers' to make our point."

"At least we're still on the air, right? And I haven't even married the boss yet . . ."

I try to hide a smile behind the papers, but he must see it because he says, "Oh, shit, Caldwell. Are you engaged?"

"Yeah. I think so," I say, still digesting the news. "Don't tell anyone. It's not official. Although we both know Standish doesn't really change his mind."

Alexandre shakes his head, amused. "You'll be the next Julie Chen and Leslie Moonves. Maybe he'll give us back our nine o'clock slot."

"Yeah," I say, laughing but feeling uneasy. "It's the least he can do for us, right?"

That night, I meet Jess for dinner in the Village and give her the update on the weekend as well as the news about Peter.

"So no sparks with Conrad?" she asks, seemingly ignoring the fact that I'm about to get engaged.

I glance down at my menu and shake my head. "Nope."

"You wanna look me in the eye and say that again?" she says.

I stare her down and say, "If by sparks you mean that he hates my guts and I think he's more beautiful than ever, then yes, there were sparks. Otherwise, no."

"Just how beautiful are we talking?" she says.

"Drop-dead. Gorgeous," I say.

"Compare him to someone we know."

"I can't."

"Famous?"

I quickly reply, "Cross between James Franco and Bradley Cooper. And that doesn't do him justice."

"You've given this some thought."

"Maybe. A little . . . *Anyway*," I say. "Can we talk about Peter? Please?"

"Right. Yes. Congratulations," she says, as if I just told her I won a year's worth of free paper towels. "That's great news."

"Yeah. He wants to go ring shopping this week."

"Exciting."

I narrow my eyes and say, "Jess! Why don't you like him?"

"I do like him. I just don't think you love him."

"I do, too!" I say. "What's not to love?"

" 'What's not to love' is hardly a reason *to* love," she says. "And the *catch* of your life is not the same thing as the *love* of your life. Be careful of that subtle but rather crucial distinction."

I shake my head, wishing that Claudia could have made it out, and thinking that Jess is the last person who should be doling out relationship advice.

"I'm well aware of the difference," I say. "And Peter is both."

"If you say so," she says. "But I've never seen you light up when you talk about him the way you just did with Conrad."

"Conrad was a childhood fantasy. Nothing more."

She wags her finger at me. "He could be more, though. And you already have a kid with him."

I tell her she's way off base, then close my menu with authority.

"You know what you want?" she says.

"Yes," I say. "I do."

"What do you think?" Peter asks as we sit in a small office in the diamond district, meeting with his longtime jeweler, Ari Zwacker. I've decided not to let it bother me that Ari designed Robin's ring—and most of the jewelry she owns— and instead try to focus on the lineup of gorgeous stones displayed on his desk. Underneath each is a description of the color, carat, and clarity, and I notice that there is nothing less than a VS1, three-carat, G-color rock. I don't know much about diamonds, but I am pretty sure that any one of these stones costs more than what I made my first five years in television.

"They're all gorgeous," I say, part of me wishing I'd just let Peter surprise me. I once offhandedly mentioned that I wanted to pick out my own ring, something I have to look at every day, but there is something decidedly unromantic and a little bit depressing about having a symbol of love reduced to such scientific classifications—especially classifications focusing on imperfections.

"Which one is your favorite?" Peter says, gazing at me expectantly.

I pretend to deliberate in case there is a big price differential, but there is a clear winner in the group—a four-carat, F-color, VVS1 emerald-cut stunner. I finally point to it. "That one is gorgeous . . . But they all are," I say. "Which one do you like?"

Ari nods and says to Peter, "As you predicted." He then carefully picks it up with a pair of tweezers and drops it into the setting of a ring, then slides the whole ensemble onto my finger. I stare at it in disbelief. It is, quite simply, the most beautiful diamond I have ever seen, including the ones in magazines on the hands of celebrities.

"Do you love it?" Peter says.

I look at him, still speechless, as he grins then gives Ari a wink. "I'll call you."

Ari nods as we say our good-byes, then head back onto Forty-seventh Street, past a throng of Hasidic Jews and several window-shopping couples.

"Are you happy?" Peter asks, as we turn onto Fifth Avenue.

"Ecstatic," I say, flashing him a big smile to prove it.

He leans in and gives me the kind of kiss that you don't often see on crowded sidewalks. A kiss that goes with a four-carat, near-flawless diamond. A kiss I would have done absolutely *anything* in the world for on the night I first brought up the subject of marriage. The night I met Kirby and my whole life began to change.

The following evening, Peter and I attend a lavish Doctor Zhivago–themed, black-tie birthday party for an old friend of his (and Robin's) at the Peninsula. We have already made our first round of hellos, and sampled the many varieties of vodka, smoked salmon, and beluga caviar being served, but neither of us is really in the mood for a scene, and the feeling is only amplified when Robin and her sculptor boyfriend corner us.

"So when are you two getting married?" Robin blurts out after we've covered our usual topics.

Peter slips his arm around my waist and shocks her by saying, "Soon."

As if on cue, a waiter hands us two glasses of champagne from a silver tray. Robin raises hers, demanding we do the same. "Well, cheers to that! I'm really happy for you. You're the perfect couple. It makes me sort of sick you're so perfect."

"Thanks, I guess," I mumble, raising my glass and taking a sip.

"Here's to a big, blended, crrr-azzzy family," Robin says, then turns to fill her boyfriend in on just how unusual our situation is, including the story of Kirby's return. Then, before anyone can get a word in, she asks if she can come to the wedding. "Please, please, Petey?"

Peter smiles, but shakes his head and says absolutely not.

"Marian will let me," she says. "Right, Marian?"

"Oh, sure. Of course," I say, then deflect with a joke about inviting her to the honeymoon, as well. A few seconds later, she stumbles off with her boyfriend, and Peter and I migrate to the outside terrace. We lean on a high railing, looking out over the lights of Fifth Avenue. It is a clear, beautiful night, the kind that should make you euphoric, thrilled to be a New Yorker, happy to be *alive*, but as we sip our champagne and admire the view, my mind starts to race as it has since I returned home from Chicago. At one point he asks me a question, but I haven't heard a word.

"Hmm?" I say.

"What's on your mind, Champ?" he says. "You seem a million miles away."

I apologize and say I was thinking about my show—a script rewrite I was working on earlier.

He gives me a quizzical look, then says, "Is there something else you're trying to rewrite?"

I glance at him nervously and say, "Well, I guess I was also thinking about the ring . . ."

"What about it?" he asks.

"Um . . . I don't think you should buy that one . . . yet," I say as I catch a young model type giving Peter a not so subtle once-over. I feel a territorial pang, then try to refocus on our conversation.

"Why not?" Peter says, draining the rest of his champagne and putting the glass on a table behind him.

"I don't know," I say. "It might be *too* big."

"It's not too big."

"Well, I'm not sure about the cut . . . I'm just not sure it's . . . the *one*."

He crosses his arms, then says, "You're not sure *it's* the one—or you're not sure *I'm* the one?"

I swallow, trying to get my breath and courage to continue, wondering if I'm doing the right thing or if this will be another choice I regret for years to come.

"Peter," I say. "I don't think we should get married."

"And why's that?" he says, the lights of the city reflected in his eyes.

"Because . . . I'm not sure we're really in love. The way we should be to get married," I say, thinking of my conversation with Jess, finally admitting to myself that she is right.

"*I'm* sure," he says as I think how certain he is about everything. It's what makes him a great CEO. He never second-guesses himself.

I shake my head, on the verge of tears, too upset to tell him that I think he's only in love with the *idea* of me. Just as I am with him. All the boxes are checked, especially now that we've rectified the complications around Kirby.

"It just doesn't feel right . . . anymore," I say. "Maybe it never was . . ."

I wait for him to show passion, anger, *any* strong emotion. But instead he only says, "Is there anything I can say or do to convince you otherwise?"

I shake my head, wishing he'd at least try. But when he doesn't, I say, "It's hard to explain. I just feel *changed*."

"Does this have anything to do with last weekend?" he asks.

"Not exactly," I say, but deep down, I know that it does. That it has *everything* to do with last weekend, Conrad, and coming to terms with my past. Recognizing what I once had and what I threw away. I desperately want to feel that way again. To be in a relationship that I'm not trying to script or water down. It's about wanting something real—even if it's messy and complicated. It's what Kirby has taught me.

"I think I should go home," I say, putting down my glass of champagne.

Peter looks at me, as handsome and composed as ever, and asks if he can escort me home. Or at least to the valet. His eyes are sad and confused, but he remains the perfect, poised gentleman.

I look into his eyes and say, "I think I'd better go alone."

He nods, then walks me to the elevator, kisses me softly on the cheek, and whispers good-bye.

33

Kirby

I end up with an eighty on my precalc exam—a friggin' miracle. Not only is it eight points more than I need to pass the class, but it's a *B*. I have never gotten a B on a math test in my entire life. After I tell Mr. Tully the good news, he gives me a high five and then removes a card from his desk. He tells me to go ahead and open it now, so I do. There are puffy blue clouds on the outside and the inside reads, *The sky's the limit!* Underneath, in small, neat script, he has written, *I got this BEFORE your exam. I knew you could do it. Onward and upward!!! Your friend, Mr. T.* Then there is a PS that says, *Music majors are often good in math and vice versa. If you get my drift.*

I laugh and tell him not to hold his breath, although I'm beginning to think I might actually just go for it. What the hell. What's the worst that could happen? I think back to that first knock on Marian's door. The downside was huge—and yet what if that had stopped me? Why should it now?

"I'm going to miss you next year," Mr. Tully says.

"I'll come visit."

"You better."

I smile, but feel surprisingly sad given that all I've wanted to do for four years is escape this joint.

"And don't forget your promise," he says as the bell rings, and I stand to head back to the auditorium for our last assembly of the year—a painful two-hour presentation of all the awards for seniors who actually accomplished something this year.

"What promise?" I say, thinking he's going to give me one last plug for Mizzou.

But instead he says, "Back. Stage. Passes."

"You got it," I say, laughing. Because I can almost picture such a thing.

The night before graduation, my parents take me to LoRusso's, my favorite restaurant on the Hill, for our official celebration with Charlotte, Belinda and her mother, and Philip. It is the first time my parents have met Philip, so it's sort of awkward, but he is one of those rare kids who is great with adults without being a kiss ass. Belinda, too, is back to her old self, even though her mother grounded her indefinitely—or at least until she pays off my parents for the dress. She's already turned over about five graduation checks, and I chipped in fifty bucks from my last paycheck, partly to be nice, but also selfishly, because I get totally bored when Belinda is grounded. We only have about seventy dollars to go before she's free.

Meanwhile, my mother's the only one acting all strange. She has been cleaning like a fiend, getting ready for Marian, even though she's staying at a hotel—the Chase Park Plaza, just as my mother once predicted. I assured my mom that it wasn't because Marian doubted our accommodations, only that she didn't want to intrude. I happen to believe this is the truth, and have told myself that I'm not allowed to be ashamed of my neighborhood, my house, my family, or anything else that is a part of me.

363

"I'd like to propose a toast," my father says now as we all raise glasses of Coke. "To Kirby, for passing precalculus! And to Kirby, Belinda, and Philip . . . Congratulations on your upcoming graduation and best of luck with all your future endeavors—whatever they entail!"

He looks me right in the eyes and smiles, his way of throwing in the towel about college, telling me it's okay—that *I'm* okay—no matter what I decide.

The next day is a whirlwind of activity. You'd think someone was getting married for all the primping and ironing and cooking—to say nothing of the jangling nerves and raw emotion. Even Charlotte looks rattled and misty-eyed when she finds me in my bedroom. I look up from my drums, acknowledging her, but still playing softly. She sits on my still unmade bed, and says, "I'm going to really miss you next year."

"Who says I'm going anywhere?" I say.

"Mom thinks you're going to move to New York," she says. "Or Chicago."

"Oh, does she, now?" I say, doing a little three-beat Paul Shaffer maneuver that punctuates all of Letterman's jokes.

"Are you?" she asks, pulling her wet hair up in a ponytail.

I put down my sticks, shrug, and say who knows.

"*You* do," she says. "I know you have a plan."

"Okay," I say, going to sit next to her on the bed. "I'll let you in on a little secret."

She leans in and whispers, "What?"

"I think I'm going to Mizzou."

She starts grinning and asks who I've told.

"You're the first," I say. "And it's not definite. So keep it under wraps."

"Mum's the word," she says. "I promise. So long as you promise me you'll call and talk to me all the time, wherever you are next year."

"But I don't talk to you all the time now," I say, smiling at her.

She cracks up, acknowledging that I'm not much of a conversationalist, then says, "Promise?"

"Promise," I say, thinking that shockingly enough, I might miss her a little bit, too.

Just before we have to leave for the ceremony, Marian calls me and wishes me good luck, then confirms our plans for afterward.

"I'll look for you. What color are you wearing?" I ask, as my mother pretends not to listen.

"Red," she says proudly, as I remember that I told her that was our school color.

I glance at my mother, who is also wearing red, and say, "Okay. That'll be easy." Then I ask her again if she has directions to the house.

"Yes," she says. "Don't worry about me. Just savor this. And I'll see you afterward."

"Okay," I say, thinking of Conrad, who told me late last night that he'd be coming after all. I nearly tell her, but decide that he probably wouldn't want me to, and that he'll probably do his best to avoid her. So I just thank her and say good-bye.

Without missing a beat, my mother says, "So what color is she wearing?"

"Um, red," I say. "What a coincidence, huh?"

My mother frowns and says, "I knew it . . . Maybe I should change?"

I think of how long and hard she searched for the right dress, and something compels me to go to her, put my arm around her, and say, "No, Mom. You should wear this dress. It looks awesome on you." I look at her and hope she knows what I'm thinking. That it doesn't matter what she wears; I only have one *real* mother. And she's it.

A few hours later, after my parents and Charlotte have dropped me off and gone to park the car, I'm standing among my classmates, gathered in the entrance of the Cathedral Basilica. I look around at the nearly one-hundred-year-old narthex walls covered with a mosaic depicting our city's namesake—King Louis IX of France. In fact, according to my mother's nervous chatter on the way over, it comprises the largest church mosaic in the world. It is clear she not only wants our family to show well to Marian—but also the city and my school, and I can't say I don't feel the same way.

At some point, the chaos of hundreds of kids becomes organized, and we line up in twos, the girls in white caps and gowns, the boys in red. Most of the faculty is with us, too, also in caps and gowns, including Mr. Tully who looks unusually somber and handsome. A taped version of "Land of Hope and Glory" begins to play, our cue to begin the processional. Everyone quiets down completely, including the rowdier kids, and I feel a strange, collective swell of emotion, a communal reverence crossing clique lines—something I never thought possible. I guess endings will do that to people.

I take a deep breath and enter the cool, dark sanctuary. Flashbulbs go off everywhere—which feels sort of weird in church—and there is a buzz of quiet activity from all the people packed in the pews. I look up at the breathtaking ceiling, hearing my mother's words: "forty-one million glass pieces in more than seven thousand colors." As we begin to walk again, I search the crowd and pick out Marian, then my family. They are on opposite sides of the aisle, but in pretty much the same row, so there is no way to make eye contact with everyone when I pass. I decide to play it safe and simply stare straight ahead, my hands folded as we've been instructed to do. I do not see Conrad, and tell myself not to be disappointed if he decided not to come.

As the music stops, I take my seat at the end of a long pew, all of us in assigned alphabetical order, and flip through the program, highlighted with names of all my star classmates—*best* this and *brightest* that. I close the program and my eyes and begin my own private meditation, tuning everything out, although I'm sure Father O'Malley's homily and Gena Rych's valedictorian speech are inspiring to many.

I think about my birth and my adoption and my first eighteen years. I think about the last few months and my trip to New York and finding Marian. I think about this day, what it means to my family, sitting behind me. I think of everything that had to happen to bring me to this moment. I think about where I am going and who I want to be.

And then our names are called, one at a time. There are cheers for everyone, some louder and more boisterous than others—pretty much directly correlating to popularity— and as we approach the *R*s, my heart starts to race almost as much as it did when I got on the stage with Conrad, though for very different reasons this time. Aside from my brief precalc scare, graduating from high school has always been something of a given, so it's not that I'm surprised to find myself here. But I am still proud, and surprisingly grateful, too. I'm grateful to Marian for having me—and then giving me to a family who wanted a baby. I'm grateful to Conrad, whether he's here or not, for accepting me right away, no questions asked. I am grateful to my little sister for never trying to make me feel like an outsider, even though she easily could have, even when I was doing it myself. And most of all, I am grateful to my parents for loving me and making me their own.

I hear my name—*Kirby Katherine Rose*—and stand and walk up the stairs to the altar where I shake hands with the president of our school and receive my diploma. As I turn to descend the stairs and just before I take my seat again, I catch my first glimpse of Conrad, who gives me a little salute with an invisible hat. I give him a big smile, then tip my cap in return.

We've been home for thirty minutes—just enough time for me to change into a T-shirt and jeans and my mom to get really nervous—and for that matter, really get on my nerves.

"Are you sure you don't want to put on a dress?" she asks me.

"Yeah, Mom. I'm sure," I say, trying to be patient with her. "Can we all just try to chill and be normal?"

"I agree with Kirby!" my dad calls up the stairs and I cringe, knowing that will mean he will talk Marian's ear off.

The doorbell rings just moments after my parents and I are awkwardly assembled in the living room—where we never sit. I stand and bite my lip, wondering how many more dramatic knocks at the door can possibly exist in my life. When I open the door, there Marian is

368

with a big bouquet of pink flowers, already in a vase. It is my least favorite color, but I have to admit they are pretty.

"Congratulations," she says, handing them to me, along with a card. "That was a beautiful ceremony . . ."

"Thanks," I say.

"I love your house."

"Thanks," I say again, my anxiety building. I turn and lead her into the living room, putting the flowers on an end table, out of the way. Then I stand in the middle of the room and, with as much composure as I can muster, introduce my parents to my birth mother.

"Mom, Dad, this is Marian Caldwell," I say, having practiced the precise wording earlier this morning. "Marian—this is my mom and dad. Lynn and Art Rose."

They shake hands, first my dad and Marian and then my mom and Marian, all of them smiling and nodding, murmuring hellos, as if they speak different languages and are waiting for an interpreter to bridge the gap.

Charlotte pokes her head in the room and gives me a little wave. "Oh, yeah. And that's Charlotte. My sister," I say, pointing at her.

"Hi!" Charlotte says, waving again.

"It's so nice to meet you all," Marian says.

My dad clears his throat and starts throwing out all kinds of rambling niceties. "Welcome to St. Louis! Glad you could make it! That was very kind of you to come all this way. Very kind. I know Kirby appreciates it. So do we. Thank you."

"Thank you for including me," Marian says to my father. Then she looks at my mother and says, "It was very gracious of all of you."

369

I stare at her, thinking that everything about her, from her hair to her clothes to the words from her lips, is smooth and elegant. I notice she is wearing sleek, nude peep-toe heels, in contrast to my mother's clunky black leather pumps. I don't know fashion, but feel sure that Marian made the better choice to go with red. It occurs to me that I'd know these things if I were Marian's daughter—but then I think that I don't really have any desire to know them. It would probably just have been a whole lot of pressure to be perfect. My parents only want me to try *my* best, a considerably lower bar.

"Marian, what could we get you to drink?" my dad says. "Wine? Beer? A soft drink? Lemonade? Water?"

She hesitates, then says she'd love a glass of wine.

"Great!" my dad says, turning to go, as my mother stops him with a hand on his arm.

"Um, Art. Does she want red or white?" she asks, with a big frozen smile, continuing her streak of not speaking directly to Marian.

"Oh. Whatever you have open," Marian says. "I like both."

My dad gives her a befuddled look, unsure what to choose for her, so she says, "White would be wonderful. Thank you."

My dad nods then looks at my mother. "Honey? For you?"

She tells him she'll take a white wine, too, then turns stiffly back to Marian, points to the couch, and says, "Won't you please have a seat?"

"Thank you," Marian says, as the two sit side by side in their red dresses, a sight that sort of freaks me out. I turn and give Charlotte a look that says *help* as she takes the last chair in the room and begins her usual babble—which has never been more appreciated. She talks about the ceremony, how cute Mr. Tully looked in his cap and gown, how proud she was when I got my diploma. "Did you hear me yell your name?" she asks.

"*Everyone* heard you," I say, smiling.

Meanwhile, my dad appears, handing out our drinks, then realizing there is nowhere left to sit.

"Here, honey," my mom says, sliding down toward Marian and patting the sofa next to her. Now the three are in a row, even freakier, as more awkward small talk ensues.

At one point, I glance down at my phone and see a text from Conrad, who I was not able to find in the mayhem following the ceremony.

Great job, drummer girl. Glad I was there to see it.

I frantically text him back: *Where are you?*

He fires back: *Some pub in town, having a bite to eat.*

My mother clears her throat and says, "Kirby, could you put your phone down, please?"

"It's kind of important, Mom," I say.

Then I type back, as fast as I can: *Would love to see you. Stop by if you can. No worries either way.* Then I type my address. In my haste, I massacre the spelling of Eichelberger Street, but figure he's smart enough to track me down. If he really wants to, that is.

"Sorry," I say, putting the phone down and exchanging a look with Marian. She raises her eyebrows as if she knows or suspects or hopes and I nod back, to give her a little warning. Just in case.

A minute later, at my mother's suggestion, we head to the kitchen for lunch, passing by my cake, displayed in all of its glory on the dining room table.

Marian stops to admire it. "What a beautiful cake!" she exclaims, as I wonder if she can tell my mother made it from scratch.

Charlotte says, "Wait till you taste Mom's frosting! *Sooo* yummy."

My dad snaps like he forgot something and then says, "We don't have any candles!"

"We don't need candles for a graduation cake," I say as my dad begs to differ, belting out a line of "Happy graduation to you!"

"Ugh. Please. No," I say.

"Yes. Please, Art," my mom says, smiling. She turns to Marian and says, "Kirby didn't get her singing voice from us—that's for sure!"

It is the first mention of the obvious, and everyone laughs as Marian says, "She didn't get it from me, either."

The ice isn't broken, but it definitely feels a little thawed as we head into the kitchen, sitting around the table, already set for lunch with our best dishes. After a long-winded blessing, my father looks up and says, "I don't want to get all mushy . . ."

"Then don't, Dad," I mumble.

He looks at me, holds up his hand and says, "Just one thing—I promise."

I roll my eyes and brace myself as he turns to Marian. "Lynn and I just want to thank you for giving us the greatest gift one person can give another. We prayed to God for someone like you. And He brought you—and Kirby—to us." He starts to get choked up while I pray he won't actually start bawling. "She and Charlotte are our greatest blessings."

"Okay, Dad," I say gently. "Let's just eat, okay?"

"Yes! That's all! That's all!" he says.

Marian takes a deep breath, as if composing an eloquent reply, but then stops and simply says, "You're welcome. It was the most difficult thing I've ever done, but after meeting you . . . I know I made the right decision." She gives me a fleeting glance, but one filled with sadness. "For Kirby's sake. You have a wonderful family."

I analyze her words, and know that I will for a long time. *For Kirby's sake.* So maybe she regrets it for her *own* sake? Or maybe it is just the best possible way of saying she's glad she gave me away. Either way, I realize that I can't deny I feel the same way. I would not change my childhood if I could.

A moment later the doorbell rings, and everyone looks toward the door.

"Is Belinda coming?" my dad asks.

I shake my head, knowing she is with her grandparents, as he guesses again. "Philip? What a great kid he is!"

I shake my head again and round the corner toward the foyer, too nervous to answer my dad. Right away, I see a quadrant of Conrad's face through a stained-glass pane in the front door and feel myself start to relax. I throw open the door and say hello, so happy to see him.

"Hi, you," he says, stepping forward to give me a warm, easy hug, handing me a small wrapped present that feels like a book. "Congrats."

"Thanks," I say. "You didn't have to get me anything."

"It's nothing," he says. "Just some sheet music. I wrote you a little song . . . it's got a great beat and drum solo . . . so I fully expect you to play it with me this summer."

"Cool," I say, smiling so hard my face hurts.

We stare at each other for a second and then I remember to invite him the whole way in. "We're having lunch . . . Marian's here."

373

"I figured," he says. "I won't stay long. But I did want to meet your folks."

Feeling more giddy than tense, I lead him to the kitchen, where everyone gets really quiet—except for Charlotte who gasps, "Omi*gah*, is it *him*?" Like he's an actual rock star. Which he sort of is to me.

I smile at her and nod, then say, "Everyone, this is Conrad." Then point out my mom, dad, and sister for him.

They all shake hands as I say, "And of course you know Marian."

Since you two had sex and accidentally made me.

"Hi, Marian," he says. He's not at all chummy with her, but all traces of anger are gone.

"Hi, Conrad," she says, gripping her glass of wine, with that deer in the headlights look she always gets around him, as my father goes to retrieve a chair from the dining room, squeezing it in between me and Charlotte.

"Are you hungry?" my mother asks Conrad, standing. "Let me get you a plate."

"No, thank you," he says. "I just ate—and can't stay long."

Charlotte says, "We were just talking about Kirby's singing voice a few minutes ago. She must get it from you. Aren't you a musician?"

Conrad nods modestly, then says, "Your sister's got a lot of talent. I wish I could take credit . . ."

"You *can* take credit," Marian chimes in. Then she turns to my mother and says, "You should have seen them together on stage."

Of course, I haven't told anyone in my family about this, so a long discussion begins of our performance in the bar, Marian leading the charge, telling everyone how brilliant we were together. Her intentions are good, but I wish she

374

hadn't brought that up as my mother looks sad again, probably because I hadn't told her myself.

"I was going to tell you," I say to her. "But the Belinda stuff . . . things just got hectic."

My mom nods, like she understands, as my dad heads to the refrigerator, bringing back a cold Budweiser for Conrad. "I don't know if you like these. But you sorta have to in St. Louis!"

I look at Conrad, holding my breath, hoping he'll stay, and sure enough, he takes it and says, "I'm always in the mood for a Bud. Thanks, man."

I exhale, relieved and happy, then start laughing—I don't know why. I try to stop but can't.

"What's so funny?" Charlotte says, looking for the literal joke, as she always does.

I shake my head then say, "Nothing . . . Just raise your hand if you think this is really, *really* bizarre?"

Everyone raises their hand and the ice is officially broken.

Sometime after we eat my mom's cake (and my dad makes everyone sing and pose for photos), we all head to the family room, including Conrad who is on his second beer and has stopped looking at his watch. When my dad turns on the Cards game, the two start talking baseball (Conrad is a White Sox fan) and really seem to hit it off—which is great except that it highlights the fact that my mom and Marian have nothing to say to each other. They've exhausted all the surface topics and it is clear that they have nothing much in common. And that's when Charlotte busts out with the family photo albums.

"Wanna see some pictures of Kirby when she was little?" Charlotte asks Marian, handing her three huge albums.

"Charlotte!" I protest. "Those are so boring!"

But I'm secretly pleased when Marian lights up and tells my sister it is an excellent idea, she'd love to see some photos. She opens the first album and freezes, staring down at my earliest baby pictures, including ones taken on the very day she gave me away. I see my mom watching Marian with a tense, almost pissed-off, look on her face, and I start wishing she would hurry up, turn the page, and get to my toddler days. But she doesn't. She just keeps lingering there at the beginning, looking sort of sad, until she finally says, "Conrad. C'mere. Baby pictures of Kirby."

He nods, gets up from his chair and walks over to her, looking down over her shoulder, then sitting on the couch next to her. "That's one good-looking baby," he says to no one in particular.

I can't help feeling proud, because *he* looks proud, but I still say, "Okay. Guys. Move it along. You have eighteen years to cover."

Marian finally turns the page as my mom works her way over to the couch and begins to narrate over Conrad's shoulder. That was the day I first smiled, rolled over, ate solid foods, pulled myself up in my crib. As the pages keep turning, my mom finally sits on the other side of Marian, loosening up, telling stories about me—and Charlotte— some of them funny, but most of them pretty dull. Conrad and Marian look far from bored, though, and ask my mom lots of questions. She answers, and my dad and Charlotte fill in with occasional color commentary.

When they get to my first drum kit, and my mom starts telling the story about how I slept with it next to my bed, I get this funny feeling inside and then realize what it is. It's the feeling of belonging. Right here where I am. In this house.

With my parents and Charlotte. The people who know all my stories, from the beginning. The people who know *me.*

"And that's when Art and I got our first earplugs," my mom says, with a laugh. "Not that Kirby wasn't talented from the start. Just very, *very* loud and talented."

She looks over at me and smiles. And I smile back at her because I can tell she knows what I'm thinking and feeling. Even better, I can tell she's feeling the same way.

Sometime after seven, when we all start to yawn, Conrad says he's going to hit the road. My dad says he is welcome to stay for the night, but he politely declines, insisting that he loves night driving.

Marian says she should go, too, then asks my dad if he wouldn't mind calling her a cab.

"I can take you," Conrad quietly offers.

"Are you sure?" Marian says, looking surprised.

"Yeah. No problem," he says with a shrug.

Everyone says their good-byes as Marian gathers her purse and my father writes down directions back to the hotel. I walk to the foyer, waiting for them, hoping nobody else follows. Nobody does, and a moment later, I'm outside with them, standing next to Conrad's car. It is not yet dark, but it looks like a storm might be coming, thunder rumbling in the far distance.

"Well," Marian says after a few quiet seconds pass. "Thank you for having us."

"Yeah. Thank you, Kirby," Conrad says.

"It was a really nice ceremony. And day," she says.

I nod, feeling a lump in my throat. There are so many things I want to say, yet my mind goes blank and all I can do is *feel.*

"I'm glad you were both here," I finally manage, thinking how strange it is to be standing with the two people who *made* you, something most kids take for granted every day of their lives, but something I never really believed would happen. And certainly not like this—on such a big, important day.

"We're proud of you," Marian says.

Conrad nods his agreement, accepting her "we," and even adds, "We wish we could take credit."

I smile, then take a deep breath and give them both a hug, first Marian, then Conrad—which sort of turns into a fleeting, awkward three-way hug. I fight back tears that seem to come from nowhere, and then say a quick, final good-bye. Only this time, I know it's not really final.

Once safely back in the shadows of my porch, I turn and watch them get in the car and back up, waving when Conrad honks twice, one beep for each of them. Then I take a deep breath and go back inside to join my family.

34

Marian

It is impossible not to think of the past as Conrad drives me back to my hotel. We've just spent several hours with Kirby and her family, and I haven't begun to process those emotions—from her moving graduation ceremony to the first strained moment I walked into her house and met her parents, to Conrad's surreal arrival, to the end of the evening when Kirby's sister got out all the old family albums and her mother began telling the stories only she could tell. I think of how difficult it must have been for Lynn and Art to share such an important, special day with strangers, even if we are her blood relatives. *Especially* because we are. I am happy for Kirby and excited for her future, but it is so hard to see, up close and in vivid color, all that I missed and will never be able to get back, no matter how many stories I'm told or photographs I'm shown. I meant what I said—that I made the best decision for *her*—but I cannot deny a sense of profound loss for what I gave up. For what could have been.

In this moment, though, I am thinking about Conrad and Conrad only. I have kept the memories at bay all day, even when he stood so near me that I could inhale his still familiar scent, but now they are rushing back, fast and strong and unfiltered. I have to fight the sudden urge to reach over and rest my hand on his leg like I used to whenever we drove around in his black Mustang.

"Merge onto I-44," I say, following the directions Art scratched out for us on a napkin. I am trying to make every mile, every second, count, wishing Conrad would slow down or at least turn down the radio and talk to me.

He nods. "Got it."

I covertly study his profile, but he glances my way, catching me staring.

"What?" he says. There is no hostility, but no warmth, either. Just blankness. For a second, I almost miss the anger.

"Nothing," I say, looking straight out at the highway again. The view is urban but generic. We could be anywhere.

He sighs, turns the station once, twice, then obviously dissatisfied, turns the radio off altogether. We drive another few minutes in silence until I point out our exit on Vandeventer Avenue.

He veers to the right, then finally speaks. "She's a great kid."

"I know," I say. "She's awesome."

"So's her family," he says. "I really like them. Art's a character."

"Yeah," I say. "She really got lucky."

"*You* got lucky, too," he says, shooting me a pointed glance. "If she had ended up in a bad situation . . ."

He shakes his head, as I finish his sentence for him. "You would never have forgiven me."

"No," he says.

I point out our final turn onto South Kingshighway. "So you have?" I say. "Forgiven me?"

He takes a deep breath and shrugs, as if I've just asked an impossible, philosophical question rather than a relatively straightforward one. "I don't know, Marian."

I bite my lip and say nothing, having no choice but

to accept this, along with his obvious reluctance to talk. About a mile later, I point to my hotel. "That's it. Up on the right," I say.

He nods, then pulls into the drive as a valet appears.

"There's a bar in the lobby," I say, feeling frantic. "Will you come in for one drink?"

He shakes his head. "I have a five-hour drive ahead of me."

"Just one drink?" I say. "Ten minutes?"

He takes a deep breath, exhales, and says, "Okay. One drink."

I open the door, and tell the valet I've already checked in but my friend will be staying for a few minutes. Then we both get out of the car, and walk through the mostly empty lobby to the Eau Bistro, finding two seats at the end of the bar. A beat later, the bartender finds us. I order a Chardonnay, he asks for a Stella. He stares straight ahead until our drinks arrive and he takes his first long sip. Then he turns to look at me, squarely in the eyes, and says, "Why didn't you tell me?"

I tell him that I don't know.

"That's bullshit. You *do* know."

"I . . . don't . . . I just don't think I was mature enough . . . I wasn't ready to handle adult truths . . . and complicated choices. Keeping a secret made it all seem easier."

"It wasn't a secret. It was a lie," he says.

I nod, realizing that Peter was right—there really is little difference between the two.

"Did you think I'd try to talk you into an abortion?" he asks.

"No," I say, putting my glass down without taking a drink. "It wasn't that. It was more . . . that I was afraid you'd talk me *out* of an abortion . . . Then, once I talked *myself* out of it, I was afraid you'd talk me into keeping her."

"I wouldn't have tried to talk you into *anything*," he says. His voice is more confused and hurt than angry. "I would have let *you* choose. That's what I told you before you took the test."

"Okay. Well, maybe I was afraid that if I told you . . . I would talk *myself* into keeping her," I say.

He gives me a look of utter exasperation, then literally throws his hands up.

"I loved you," I say—as if this explains it all. And in a strange way, it sort of does.

"I loved you, too," he says, staring me down again.

I hold his gaze, feeling light-headed, and in that instant, I know for sure it's not just nostalgia making me feel so funny inside. It is Conrad himself, here in the present.

"I could have helped you," he says, lowering his voice. "At the very least, you could have let me say good-bye."

"I know. I should have," I say, remembering that day. "I'm glad you got to see the photos."

He shakes his head. "I was talking about saying good-bye to *you*."

I catch my breath and then say, "Oh."

"I always knew we wouldn't stay together, Marian. That we were probably too young. And that you were definitely too good for me . . . But I thought I was good enough for a *good-bye*."

I shake my head. "I wasn't too good for you."

"Yeah. Right." He takes a sip of his beer and rolls his eyes. "Ms. Highfalutin producer about to marry some . . . damn . . . Hollywood bigwig."

I give him a look of surprise.

"Kirby told me."

"Well, did she tell you we broke up?" I say, realizing that I never told *her* that news.

Conrad shrugs, as if it makes no difference either way. And I'm sure it doesn't.

"I'm not highfalutin," I say, my voice quiet.

"You're big-time," he says. "Big fish. Big pond. Big-*time*."

I look at him, thinking that I'd give it all away to go back and tell him the truth that day. But I know he wouldn't believe that, so instead I say, "Yeah. Okay. I'm big-time. But you have the better, truer life. I saw you up there on stage. You're doing what you love."

"So are you," he says.

I shake my head, realizing that although television and writing have always been my passions, I've often let my goals supersede the journey—and the love of what I'm doing. A constant battle to stay in control, get to the next level, ensure that my life stays perfectly, carefully scripted.

"It's not the same. You seem so . . . *happy*," I say.

"I've had some setbacks here and there. A divorce. Few too many drugs. But overall . . . I can't complain. So far." He knocks on the bar.

"Do you want kids?" I blurt out.

"I have one," he says.

"You know what I mean," I say. "Do you want more? A family?"

"Sure. Yeah. I always have . . . What about you?"

I nod and say, "Yes. If it's right."

Like where we just came from, I think, picturing Kirby and her family, their home filled with love. "But if it doesn't happen, it doesn't happen," I say.

"You'll always have Kirby," he says.

"Yeah," I say. "So will you."

He gives me a sideways smile and says, "Hard to believe that she is the result of one stupid summer night, huh?"

I shake my head and say, "It wasn't a *stupid* night."

"You know what I mean. We were just a couple of dumb kids. Fools."

"Yeah. I guess so. But in some ways I think I was smarter then," I say, thinking of how I followed my gut that night when I said yes to him. For years, I regretted it. Regretted him. Even regretted her. But now I can see that there is redemption and beauty in an accident emanating from love. Now I can see that she is the best thing I ever did.

He takes a long drink of his beer, then smiles to himself.

"What?" I say, expecting something profound.

He gives me a look that I remember well, the same one he gave me in Janie's backyard. "You might have been smarter then, but you're better lookin' now." He shakes his head. "*Damn.*"

I smile, taken aback—a compliment was the last thing I expected tonight. "You are, too," I say, my insides fluttering.

He raises his eyebrows, signals the bartender for our check, and says he better go. "I remember what happens when I drink with you."

"You were drinking Dr Pepper that night," I say, smiling.

"Was I?" he says.

I nod.

"Well, then, I remember what happens when *you* drink. You took advantage of me."

I can tell he is kidding, but my heart still pounds wildly. "Don't go yet," I whisper.

"I have to," he says. "But maybe I'll see you again. At Kirby's college graduation."

"I don't think she's going to college," I say.

"Oh, she's *going*," he says with a wink, as if he has the inside scoop. And I bet he does. "So see you in four years?"

I nod, but say I really hope we can talk before then. He says I know where to find him; Zelda's is open three hundred sixty-five days a year.

I look at him, hopeful. It almost sounds like an invite. "Why's it called Zelda's, anyway?" I ask, trying to remember his mother's name, wishing we could talk about her tonight. Wishing we could talk about so many things.

"*The Great Gatsby*'s my favorite book," he says. "F. Scott Fitzgerald dedicated it to Zelda."

"His wife?" I say.

"Yeah. His crazy-ass wife who he had no business loving that much," he says, giving me a loaded look. "You know what their joint epitaph says? It's a quote from the book . . . Their kid picked it for them."

I shake my head. "What's it say?"

His eyes close halfway as he recites, " 'So we beat on, boats against the current, borne back ceaselessly into the past.' "

I stare at him and he stares right back with those intense blue-gray eyes.

"Now," he says, sliding two bills onto the bar. "I really gotta go."

"Okay," I say. "But just remember—"

"What's that?" he says, getting up from his stool, standing so near me that our legs touch and I feel his warm breath on my cheek.

I inhale deeply, then say, "You can run. But you can't hide."

"So I've heard," he says with a small smile, and I can tell he remembers his words on that unforgettable night. I can tell he remembers *everything*.

He stands, zips up his jacket, and gives me a nod good-bye. Then he walks out of the bar while I replay our conversation, the entire day, and the night we made our perfect mistake, under the ceiling fan in Janie's parents' room. I order one more glass of wine, feeling a wave of intense loneliness. I miss Peter for a moment—and then realize it's not Peter I miss, but the idea of what I once thought we shared. I think about my career and what I want to write when this show eventually dies, whether because it's canceled or because I decide to move on.

I know I have another story to tell. I can even make out the main characters—a talented musician and his spirited daughter—and the start of their journey together. I don't know where they will end up, or exactly where they're headed, but that's okay. There will be plenty of time to sort that out later. Time to see where the current takes me. For now, I will sit alone in this hotel bar in St. Louis and finish my wine. It is not what I planned—this day, this moment, these unlikely relationships, both old and new. Yet I feel overcome with peace and certainty that, for once, I am exactly where I should be.